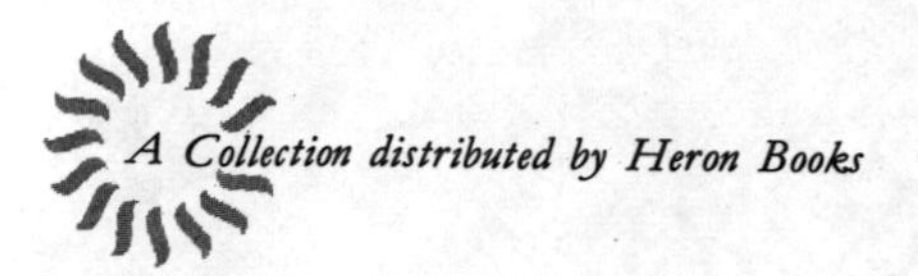
A Collection distributed by Heron Books

THE GREATEST MASTERPIECES OF RUSSIAN LITERATURE

LEO N. TOLSTOY

ANNA KARENINA

I

Translated by Rochelle S. Townsend

Introduction by Nikolay Andreyev

Original Illustrations and Frontispiece
by Roland Topor

Distributed by
HERON BOOKS

Published by arrangement with
J.M. Dent & Sons Ltd.

13 005 05 R3

INTRODUCTION

FATE gave Leo Tolstoy everything for which an ordinary man could wish: longevity, magnificent physical health, a lusty appreciation of everyday life, an original and ruthless mind, a capacity to feel deeply and passionately, and a profound intuitive understanding of nature and human psychology. His wealth and social position gave him freedom to indulge his every interest. He married for love and had a large family. During his lifetime he achieved literary fame and an almost unique moral influence throughout the world.

But Tolstoy's life was not that of a detached, wise observer, but the tragic experience, fraught with disappointment, struggle, and failure, of one who sought a final answer to all the problems of existence. In an early work, the *Sevastopol Tales*, he writes: 'My only hero, whom I have always loved with all my soul, whom I have tried to portray in all his beauty, and who always was, is, and shall be most beautiful—is Truth,' and these words might serve as a suitable epigraph for his life and work. In pursuit of truth, both temporal and eternal, he had no hesitation in revolutionizing not only the social, moral, and religious canons of his day, but his own life as well. It is this which gives to Tolstoy's realism the unique quality which distinguishes him from the other great realists of his day.

Tolstoy was born on 28th August (Old Style) 1828 on the picturesque estate of Yasnaya Polyana in central Russia, which he inherited from his mother's side of the family nineteen years later, and which was always to remain his home. The fourth son of an old and famous Russian aristocratic family, surrounded by foreign tutors, Tolstoy spent, as he himself remembered, a 'vivid, tender, poetic, loving, mysterious childhood.' One of the child Tolstoy's favourite games was the search for the 'little green wand' inscribed with the secret of universal happiness. His closeness to nature, the forest, and the Russian village imbued him from his earliest years with a deep understanding and 'an almost fraternal love of the peasant.' As a youth, he was dreamy and ambitious, according a passionate admiration to the 'ideal' of the aristocratic dandy, 'l'homme comme il faut.' At the university of Kazan he broke off his study of oriental languages in favour of law, which, subsequently, he also gave up. At the same time, he read voraciously and Jean-Jacques Rousseau became his hero. He read all twenty volumes of his work and even wore Rousseau's portrait in a locket round his neck 'instead of a cross.' Tolstoy continued to day-dream, although his dreams now were of self-education, self-perfectionment, and work for the benefit of the peasants like the future hero of his *Morning of a Landed Proprietor*, but, at the same time, he made frequent journeys to Moscow, where he abandoned himself to the dissipations of social life. Tolstoy himself later called this period, 1848–51, 'aimlessly squandered years.' In 1851 he entered the artillery as an officer cadet and served first in the Caucasus and later, when promoted officer, in the Crimean War, where he proved himself a courageous and intelligent soldier. It was at this time that he began to write.

Tolstoy first won literary recognition with his semi-autobiographical *Childhood*, which was published in September 1852, and his name was finally established by his *Sevastopol Tales*, which evoked with unprecedented clarity both the near-animal excitement and the painful absurdity of war. Success did not lead Tolstoy to alter his way of life or to consort with his literary contemporaries, whose democratic ideas and manners were equally uncongenial to him. He continued his existence as a grand seigneur and, retiring from the army in 1856 with the rank of lieutenant, he set off in the following year on a tour of western Europe, an experience which he repeated in 1861 when he stayed six weeks in London. His tutors having seen to it that he spoke perfect English, as well as French and German, he was able to take an intense interest in everything from parliamentary procedure to cock-fighting, boxing, and London tailoring. On the whole, however, western civilization produced an unfavourable impression on this disciple of Jean-Jacques Rousseau.

On his return to Russia, Tolstoy devoted himself with typical enthusiasm to educational work among the peasant children, founded a school on his estate in 1859 and, in 1862, began to edit a journal for primary school-teachers. He also took an active interest in the preparations for the liberation of the serfs, and after it was achieved in 1861 he was elected an Arbiter of the Peace, in which capacity it was his duty to settle disputes between landlords and peasants. In 1862 Tolstoy married Sophie Behrs, the daughter of a well-known Moscow doctor. An entry in his diary for 1863 reads: 'The happiness of family life absorbs me completely.'

In 1863 *The Cossacks* appeared in print. This story had been drafted ten years earlier and deals with the unsuccessful attempt of a 'civilized man' to return to the 'natural life. The conclusion is typical: 'Happiness is just this: happiness is in living for other people.' Between 1864 and 1869 Tolstoy was engaged in writing *War and Peace*, 'the *Iliad* and *Odyssey* of Russian literature,' which was to earn him world fame. Seven times his wife copied out the ever-changing versions of this immense work, in which Tolstoy's own state of domestic happiness found its expression in the affirmation of the ideal of family life. Having completed *War and Peace*, Tolstoy returned to his educational work, composing an ABC and four elementary readers along the lines of an American series which had pleased him by its liveliness and simplicity.

Towards the beginning of the seventies the theme of another novel came to him—the future *Anna Karenina*—on which he began work in 1873 after an unsuccessful attempt to write an historical novel about Peter the Great. *Anna Karenina*, completed in 1877, was Tolstoy's last great work of fiction before his so-called 'spiritual crisis,' of which he writes fully in his *A Confession*, 1879–81. This crisis did not come suddenly. As early as the forties Tolstoy had been profoundly disturbed by the gap between the ways of life and thought of the 'gentry and the people.' The motif of a return to the simple life as a condition of happiness haunted his thoughts throughout the fifties. In *War and Peace* the theme was taken up again in the portrayal of the peasant Platon Karatayev as the embodiment of instinctive popular wisdom and in *Anna Karenina* it found a new expression in the description of Levin's relations with his peasants. At the same time, Tolstoy re-examined the moral foundations of his own life and of society's. In a series of tracts—*What I believe*, *What is Art?* and many others—he denounced town life, political parties, the state, the established church, and even his own art. He called for a thorough-going revision of religious tradition with the emphasis on morality, Christian love for one's neighbour, and the principle of non-resistance to evil by force.

Tolstoy was attacked from all sides—by the State, by the Orthodox Church, which excommunicated him in 1901, by the socialists, and by the liberals. He also acquired enthusiastic disciples who attempted to put his theories into practice. He continued to write fiction, which, however, became increasingly didactic and hortatory. In spite of this, he continued to produce works of profound interest, such as *The Death of Ivan Ilych*, *The Powers of Darkness*, and *Master and Man*. The folk-tales which he wrote during this period are masterpieces of style and clarity. During 1898–9 he wrote a long and powerful but consciously tendentious novel, *Resurrection*, and between 1896 and 1904, *Hadji Murat*, one of his most brilliant works of art, which bears witness to the stubborn vitality of Tolstoy's almost pagan veneration for sheer physical strength and the forces of nature.

The extraordinarily intense and passionate evolution of Tolstoy's convictions had tragic results for the man himself. He was tormented by the compromise inherent in his own life. His wife, defending the interests of her children, opposed his desire to renounce his author's rights: afraid for his health, she did all in her power to discourage his attempts to lead an ascetic life. The family drama ended on a dark autumn night in 1910 when Tolstoy secretly left his home accompanied by his Slovak friend Doctor Makovitskiy. Tolstoy was then 82. He was taken ill in the train and died at the railway station at Astapovo in the station-master's flat on 7th November (O.S.) 1910.

Tolstoy was consistent only as a seeker. His character as a whole was one of conflicting extremes. He combined rationalism and emotionalism, for instance, in a truly fantastic manner. He taught equality but had an aristocrat's impatient contempt for all classes except his own and the peasantry. His library contained over 20,000 volumes in twenty different languages, almost all of which are studded with his comments. He enjoyed skilled trades, such as cobbling, and all sports. He was an excellent shot, a dog-fancier, an expert in the use of the scythe, a connoisseur of music and a lover of lyrical poetry. He would fearlessly follow any line of thought through to its logical conclusion and was, at the same time, oppressed by an immense, paralysing fear of death. Possessed of a dour genius for seeing through the vanities of the human spirit, he was yet most gentle of heart.

INTRODUCTION

Bernard Shaw once called Tolstoy a 'Don Quixote in a peasant's smock,' thereby coining one of the happiest epigrams on his personality. Tolstoy opposed everyone and everything under the banner of non-resistance to evil.

However interesting or controversial Tolstoy's ideas and his perfectionist pronouncements as a moralist, his greatness is nevertheless founded on his genius as an author. On this all are agreed—the last Russian Emperor Nicholas II and Lenin, Flaubert and Galsworthy, Turgenev and Somerset Maugham, Maxim Gorky and the high police functionary who kindly explained to Tolstoy why he had never been arrested: 'Your fame is too great to be contained by any prison.'

Anna Karenina is a work in which all the characteristic features of Tolstoy's artistry are in evidence. To start with, the main characters are illuminated as it were from within: a detailed and gradual explanation of their psychology and their actions is provided. Then, a feature at a time, they are described. Anna herself only emerges after several chapters, when we find out that she has 'grey eyes,' 'thick eyebrows,' 'rosy lips,' 'black hair with a profusion of little natural curls that strayed down the back of her neck and over her temples,' 'her plump shoulders and breast were as if carved out of old ivory and her arms were gently rounded with delicate wrists.' 'She was very beautiful but there was something terrifying and cruel about her charm.' Although the basic problem was always the same—to portray 'the type of a society woman who has lost her reputation'—Tolstoy sought long for the final form of his book, at which he worked stubbornly for four years. Some chapters of the novel were rewritten no fewer than twelve times, which, however, failed to prevent an occasional slip on the part of the author, such as the inaccurate description of the Orthodox wedding ceremony, the unaccountable movement of the stars in the wrong direction, or Kitty's eleven-month pregnancy. It is an interesting fact that in the first draft Anna herself, the heroine of the novel, appeared to Tolstoy as a fat woman with neither beauty nor charm whose whole fascination lay in her luxuriant sexuality, whereas her husband Karenin was not merely technically the injured party but was a kindly and profoundly touching figure. Tolstoy eventually found the prototype for the outward characterization of the enchanting beauty Anna Karenina in Mariya Hartung, the eldest daughter of the poet Pushkin. In its final form the novel immortalizes the way of life of Tolstoy's own class, and the problems which beset them at the time he was writing, in a series of extraordinarily vivid pictures of St Petersburg, Moscow, and provincial society, although the chief interest must always lie in the fate of the characters themselves, who, as the story unfolds, seem to acquire an almost independent existence.

Anna Karenina is perhaps the most artistically irreproachable of Tolstoy's novels, and the freest from literary influences and the didactic element which obtrudes itself on the reader in other novels. In *War and Peace*, for instance, something of the manner of Stendhal is still apparent, particularly in the battle scenes, and the pages devoted to the explanation of Tolstoy's opinions on the meaning of history read as though Tolstoy were doubtful of his readers' ability to draw their own conclusions from the story as it stands. Tolstoy's later works —*Resurrection* or the *Kreutzer Sonata*, for instance—are often built around some moral thesis. One of the most remarkable qualities of *Anna Karenina* is the architectural balance of the novel as a whole. Tolstoy himself wrote in 1878: 'The arches [of the novel] are so constructed that you cannot even see the keystone. And this above all is what I was trying to achieve. The architrave of the construction rests neither on the plot nor on the relationships between the characters, but on its inner co-ordination. This is very true. Some critics have reproached Tolstoy with the final eighth part of the novel, which, on a superficial reading, appears to be a rather clumsy gathering up of loose ends after the death of the main character, but, bearing in mind Tolstoy's own emphasis on 'inner co-ordination,' this criticism appears ill founded. What exactly is the basic conception which gives Tolstoy's novel its inner unity?

Broadly speaking, there are four main interpretations of this work. Some say it is a family novel. Tolstoy, who saw the family as the foundation of any society, depicts a world in which 'all happy families are alike and each unhappy family is unhappy in its own way.' In their opinion Tolstoy here returns to the problem which he had already examined in *Family Happiness* and in *War and Peace* to show the emptiness of selfish passion and romantic sentiment: the breaking up of a marriage, according to this interpretation, is a sin which brings down on the adulteress the wrath of God.

Others consider that Tolstoy, the exposer of hypocrisy,

wished to criticize the social order which destroys Anna, who has had the courage to challenge the shibboleths of St Petersburg society. This theory would account for the obviously satiric characterization of such figures as Princess Betsy Tverskaya and Countess Lydia Ivanovna.

A third school sees the core of the plot in the contrast between the idle life of the town and healthier principle of life close to nature in the country. Whereas a fourth considers that the problem is conceived on rather a different plane—that of the author's ethico-religious persuasions. The novel was written on the threshold of Tolstoy's 'spiritual crisis.' It is indisputable that the troubles of Levin are a direct reflection of Tolstoy's own spiritual experience and even the transparent pseudonym of his hero indicates this (Levin is derived from Lev, Tolstoy's Christian name). Still free from conscious tendentiousness, Tolstoy already approached his characters from a moral standpoint. According to this point of view the moral of the novel is inherent in the fate of its dramatis personae. Who best surmounts the crises depicted in the novel? First and foremost, Dolly, the wife of Stiva Oblonsky. For the sake of her children she forgives her husband his irresponsible infidelity and finds, in this immolation of her natural pride, the strength to carry on their life together. It is not fortuitous that Tolstoy conceived Dolly as a deeply religious woman. After Dolly—Levin, who finds after long searching not only happiness, for this alone could not satisfy him, but the justification of happiness. He, like Tolstoy himself, was a seeker after truth. From this point of view Tolstoy attempts, as it were, to classify his characters according to moral type. There are those like Stiva Oblonsky, epicurean hedonists, who have absolutely no sense of 'sin.' For Oblonsky the discovery of his infidelity is regrettable only because it upsets the hitherto comfortable pattern of his existence. Anna's tragedy is conditioned by her lack of religion. Even in moments of crisis she can never find in herself that 'seed of faith' which could help her to find a way out from her trials. Another such soul is Nikolay Levin, who dies unreconciled and without hope. In the light of this conception the last part of the novel acquires a particular significance, when Vronsky, who belongs to the category of people who have no faith, leaves for the war in the Balkans as a volunteer in search of danger and perhaps of death—at least of some way to stifle his sense of guilt towards Anna. From this point of view it is understandable also why Tolstoy felt so little sympathy for characters like Karenin, who see every problem in a dryly conventional spirit or in the light of a face-saving exercise.

What did Tolstoy himself think was the basic conception of his novel? In a letter of 26th April 1876 he wrote: '. . . if short-sighted critics think that I wanted to describe only the things which give me pleasure, like Oblonsky's dinners or Anna Karenina's shoulders, then they are mistaken. In everything, in almost everything that I have written, I was guided by the exigencies of a collection of thoughts, which could attain their full expression when seen in conjunction; but each thought, expressed in words on its own, loses its significance, and loses terribly in value when taken alone outside the relationship in which it stands to the others. This interrelationship is not worked out by thought (I think), but by something else, and it is impossible to express its foundation directly in words, but only indirectly, in words describing images, actions, situations. . . .' Tolstoy emphasizes: 'It is senseless to look for separate thoughts in a work of art.'

Tolstoy's comment is exceptionally discerning. His novel cannot be stretched or lopped to fit the Procrustean bed of a single idea. His heroes are not representatives of distinct, carefully worked out characteristics which decide their fate: they are people whose actions occasionally happen 'quite unexpectedly' for the author because they are 'organically inevitable' for those particular personalities. Tolstoy was later to instance Vronsky's attempted suicide as an example of a character acting of its own volition.

Dostoevsky said that *Anna Karenina* as a novel was 'perfection.' He saw the theme of the novel as Tolstoy's 'insight into human guilt and sinfulness.' This theme 'is expressed after intense psychological study of the human soul, with immense depths and power and with unique realism.' This evaluation of the work of one great author by another is not necessarily a contradiction of Tolstoy's own statement that his work had no central idea. Tolstoy is chiefly concerned with eternal values. The social and historical conditions under which the action of the novel takes place and the psychological atmosphere which brought about the tragedy of Anna Karenina are no more. But the novel retains its power to stimulate the reader's thought and rouse his emotions, because it is written by a man with a profound understanding of the human heart, with an extraordinary talent for bringing to life that which he describes, and because the problems are delineated with that uncompromisingly honest aspiration towards the naked truth which was so characteristic of Tolstoy both as a man and a writer.

NIKOLAY ANDREYEV.

1958.

PART I

I

All happy families are more or less like one another; every unhappy family is unhappy in its own particular way. The Oblonsky household was in a complete state of confusion. The wife had discovered that their former French governess was her husband's mistress and had declared that she could no longer live in the same house with him. This state of tension had continued for three days, tormenting alike to husband and wife, to every member of the family, and to all the Oblonsky domestics. They all felt that there was no sense or meaning in their living together and that any company of people accidentally thrown together in a wayside inn had more interests in common than they. The wife did not leave her own rooms and it was now the third day that the husband had not been at home. The children ran all over the house not knowing what to do with themselves, the English governess had quarrelled with the housekeeper and had written to a friend asking her to find her another place. The cook had gone off the evening before just at dinner-time, the under-cook and the coachman demanded their wages.

On the third day after the quarrel, Prince Stepan Arkadyevitch Oblonsky—Stiva, as he was called amongst his friends—awoke at the usual hour, at eight o'clock in the morning, not in his wife's room, but in his own study, on a leather-covered couch. He turned over on the springs, embraced the pillow in both arms, pressing his cheek against it as though to doze off again, when suddenly he sat up and opened his eyes.

"Let me see, how was it?" he thought, trying to recall a dream. "How was it? Oh, yes! Alabin gave a dinner at Darmstadt; no, not at Darmstadt, it was something American. I see! Darmstadt seemed to be in America. Alabin gave a dinner on glass tables and the tables sang *Il mio tesoro.* No, it wasn't *Il mio tesora,* but something nicer. Then there were some sweet little decanters—they were women," he recollected.

Stepan Arkadyevitch's eyes sparkled as he continued his thoughts smiling. " How jolly! how awfully jolly! It was all so distinguished; you can hardly put it in words, hardly think about it clearly." Then noticing a ray of light penetrating at the side of one of the heavy curtains, he gaily thrust his feet down, found his gold embroidered slippers — they had been presented to him by his wife on his last birthday—and according to the old custom which he had observed for nine years he stretched out his hand to the place where his dressing-gown usually hung in his wife's bedroom. Then he suddenly remembered everything; how and why he had slept there and not in his wife's room. The smile vanished from his face and he frowned.

" Oh, dear! oh, dear! " he exclaimed, recalling everything that had taken place. And he went over all the details of the quarrel with his wife, all the hopelessness of the situation, and, worst of all, his own fault.

" No, she will never forgive me! she cannot forgive me! And it's all my fault; yes, my fault. But I'm not to blame. The whole tragedy lies in that," he thought. " Dear me! dear me! " he moaned in despair, as he recalled all the unpleasant memories of the quarrel.

The most unpleasant moment of all was when he had returned from the theatre contented and happy with a large pear in his hand intended for his wife, and not finding her in the drawing-room, nor, to his surprise, in the study, he had at last discovered her in her room with the unfortunate letter disclosing everything in her hand.

She, the ever worried, busy, foolish Dolly, as he considered her, was sitting there motionless, gazing at him with an expression full of horror and wrath.

" What is this? This? " she had demanded, pointing to the letter.

As the scene came back to him Stepan Arkadyevitch was more tortured by the thought of the manner in which he had replied to his wife's words than by the event itself. He felt at that moment as all people feel who have been suddenly discovered in some mean act. His face could not assume an expression adapted to the situation. Instead of getting offended, denying it, justifying himself, begging forgiveness, or being indifferent (anything would have been better than what he had really done)—in spite of himself (by a reflex action of the brain, as Stepan Arkadyevitch put it, for he had a leaning towards physiology), absolutely in spite of himself, he suddenly smiled with his habitual good-humoured, stupid smile.

He could not forgive himself for that stupid smile. When Dolly saw that smile she trembled as with physical pain, flew into a passion, natural to her hasty temper, poured forth a torrent of bitter words, and fled from the room. Since then she had refused to see her husband.

" If it were not for that stupid smile! " Stepan Arkadyevitch thought.

" But what can I do? What can I do? " he asked himself in despair, but found no answer.

II

STEPAN ARKADYEVITCH was a man perfectly sincere with himself. He could not deceive himself and pretend that he repented of what he had done. He could not feel sorry that he, a handsome, susceptible man of thirty-four, was no longer in love with his wife who was only one year younger than himself and the mother of his seven children, five of whom were living. He only regretted that he had not been able to hide things from her better. But he felt the whole weight of his position, pitied his wife and children and himself. He might possibly have hidden things from her better had he suspected the effect that the knowledge would have upon her. He had never clearly thought the matter out, but had a vague feeling that his wife had known all along that he was unfaithful to her and that she took no notice of the fact. It had seemed to him that being what she was, no longer young or attractive, in no way distinguished, merely a good simple mother to his children, that she would through an innate sense of justice treat the thing with a certain amount of indulgence. But it turned out quite otherwise.

" How awful! how awful! " Stepan Arkadyevitch reiterated, but he could think of no way out of it. " And how well we got along before this happened! She was perfectly contented and happy with the children. I never interfered with her in anything. I let her have her own way with the house and the children. True, it wasn't nice that *she* should have been our own governess. Not at all nice! There is something so trivial and vulgar in making love to one's own governess! But what a governess!" He recalled Mlle Roland's mischievous black eyes and smile. "But still, so long as she lived in our house I didn't allow myself any liberties. And the worst of it is that she's now. . . . Everything happens just to spite me! Oh, dear! oh, dear! What shall I do? What shall I do?"

But there was no answer to this question, except the common answer that life gives to all complicated and insoluble questions—live according to the circumstances of the day, that is, forget. But as you cannot forget in sleep, at any rate until night comes, and as you cannot return to that music which the decanter-women sang, so you must forget in the dream of life.

"We shall see later on," Stepan Arkadyevitch said to himself, and rising he put on his grey dressing-gown lined with silk, tied the girdle into a knot, and drew a deep breath. Then with his usual firm step he walked over to the window, pulled back the curtains, and gave a loud ring at the bell. It was answered by his old friend and valet Matvey bringing his clothes, boots, and a telegram. Behind Matvey came the barber with the shaving things.

"Are there any papers from the office?" Stepan Arkadyevitch asked, taking the telegram and sitting down before the looking-glass.

"They are on the table," Matvey replied, giving his master a searching glance full of sympathy, and after a pause he added with a cunning smile, "Some one has just been from the livery stables."

Stepan Arkadyevitch made no reply, but he looked at Matvey in the mirror, and as their glances met you could see how perfectly they understood one another. Stepan Arkadyevitch seemed to say, "Why do you say that? Don't you know the circumstances?"

Matvey put his hands into his coat pockets and stood with his legs apart gazing down silently at his master with a scarcely perceptible smile on his good-natured face.

"I told him to come again on Sunday and meanwhile not to trouble you uselessly," he said—an obviously prepared answer.

Stepan Arkadyevitch could see that Matvey wanted to jest a little and attract attention to himself. He tore open the telegram, read it rapidly, guessing at the words that were omitted. His face brightened.

"Matvey! my sister Anna Arkadyevna is coming to-morrow,"

he said, staying for a moment the plump, shiny hand of the barber as he was making a rosy parting between his long, curly whiskers.

"Thank God!" Matvey exclaimed, clearly showing that he understood the full importance of this visit every bit as much as his master. It meant that Anna Arkadyevna, Stepan Arkadyevitch's favourite sister, might effect a reconciliation between husband and wife.

"Is she coming alone or with her husband?" Matvey inquired.

Stepan Arkadyevitch could not reply as the barber was at that moment occupied with his upper lip, so he held up one finger. Matvey nodded.

"Alone! Shall I have her room prepared?"

"Tell Darya Alexandrovna; she'll tell you what to do."

"Darya Alexandrovna?" Matvey repeated in surprise.

"Yes; tell her. Take the telegram and let me know what she says."

"You want to try her," Matvey thought, but he only answered, "Yes, sir."

Stepan Arkadyevitch had finished washing and arranging his hair and was just about to dress himself when Matvey with creaking boots came slowly into the room holding the telegram. The barber was no longer there.

"Darya Alexandrovna asked me to say that she is going away and that you are to do what you like about it," he said with a smile in his eye, and putting his hands into his pockets and his head on one side he stood staring at his master.

Stepan Arkadyevitch was silent. In a little while a good-humoured rather pitiful smile lighted up his handsome face.

"Well, Matvey?" he asked, shaking his head.

"It's nothing, sir. She'll come round."

"Come round?"

"I think so."

"Really? Who's that?" Stepan Arkadyevitch asked as he heard the rustle of a woman's dress outside the door.

"It is I," said a powerful, pleasant woman's voice, and the severe pock-marked face of Matriona Filimonovna the nurse appeared in the doorway.

"Well, what is it, Matriosha?" Stepan Arkadyevitch asked, advancing to meet her.

In spite of the fact that Stepan Arkadyevitch was entirely in the wrong as regards his wife, as he himself admitted, every one in the house, even the nurse, his wife's best friend, was on his side.

"Well?" he asked despondently.

"You go to her, sir, and ask her forgiveness. God will do the rest. She is tormenting herself frightfully; it's pitiful to see her. And everything in the house is upside down. Besides, you must take pity on the children. Ask her to forgive you, sir. What else can you do?"

"But she won't see me."

"Never mind that, sir; go just the same. God is merciful, sir. Pray to God, sir."

"All right. You can go now," Stepan Arkadyevitch said, blushing suddenly. "Let me have my things," he added, turning to Matvey and resolutely throwing off his dressing-gown.

Matvey took up a stiff shirt, blew off some invisible specks of dust, and with evident satisfaction proceeded to invest his master's luxurious form.

III

HAVING finished dressing, Stepan Arkadyevitch sprinkled some scent over himself, arranged his shirt cuffs, thrust his pocket-book, cigarettes, matches, and watch with its double chain and various charms into his pocket, according to his wont, and shaking out his pocket-handkerchief he issued from the room feeling sound in body and mind, despite his trouble. He went into the dining-room where coffee was awaiting him together with his letters and papers from the office.

He proceeded to read his letters. There was one very disagreeable one from a merchant with whom he was in negotiation about the sale of a wood on his wife's estate. It was absolutely essential that this wood should be sold, but unless a reconciliation could be effected with his wife it would be impossible to mention the matter. It was most unpleasant for him to think that monetary interests should play any part in their reconciliation. The idea that any self-interested motive should lead him to seek a reconciliation was most humiliating to him.

Having disposed of his letters he took up the documents from the office, glanced through them rapidly, made several notes with a large pencil, then, laying them aside, he turned his attention to the coffee. As he was drinking it he unfolded a morning paper on which the ink was scarcely dry and began reading.

Stepan Arkadyevitch always read a Liberal paper. It was not extreme in its views, but advocated those principles held by the majority of people. In spite of the fact that he was not really interested in science, or art, or politics, he strongly adhered to the same views on all such subjects as the majority and this paper in particular advocated, and changed them only when the majority changed. Or, rather, it might be said, he did not change them at all — they changed of themselves imperceptibly.

Stepan Arkadyevitch never chose his opinions any more than he chose the style of his hat or coat. He always wore those which happened to be in fashion. And for one who moved in society where some form of mental activity was sometimes necessary it was just as essential to have opinions as to have a hat. And if there was any reason why he preferred the Liberal mode of thought rather than the Conservative, to which many of his circle adhered, it was not because he found it more rational, but merely because it corresponded better with his character. The Liberal party declared that Russia was in a very bad state, and the fact was that Stepan Arkadyevitch had a great many debts and not enough money to meet them with. The Liberal party said that marriage was a moribund institution and that it was necessary to reform it, and really family life afforded Stepan Arkadyevitch but little pleasure; he had to be always pretending and lying, a thing quite contrary to his nature. The Liberal party maintained, or rather took it for granted, that religion was merely a curb on the more barbarous portions of humanity and Stepan Arkadyevitch could not bear even the shortest service and failed to understand the sense of all the awful, high-flown words about the next world when it was really so pleasant to live in this. And then Stepan Arkadyevitch was very fond of a joke and sometimes enjoyed shocking a quiet man by saying that any one who was proud of his origin ought not to stop at Rurik and deny his earliest ancestor the monkey. And so a Liberal mode of thought became a habit with him; he enjoyed his newspaper just as much as a cigar after dinner, because of the mistiness with which it enveloped his mind. He began to read the leading article, which spoke of the hue and cry that had been raised about Radicalism having swallowed up all the Conservative elements, to the extent that it was necessary for the government to step in and protect itself against the hydra of revolution. This was quite an error it said. "In our opinion the danger does not lie so much in the revolutionary hydra as in the rooted traditions that hinder progress." He went on to read another article on finance, mentioning Bentham and Mill and ending up with some smart hits at the ministry. With his ready wit he comprehended each point, guessed from whom it proceeded and whom it was aimed at, and this, as usual, afforded him great satisfaction. This morning, however, the pleasure he derived from it was rather marred by the recollection of Matriona Filimonovna and the advice she had given him; also by the fact that things were far from smooth in the house. He went on to read that Count von Beust was reported to have gone to Wiesbaden and that there was to be no more grey hair; that a light carriage was for sale and that some young woman wanted a place. He did not, however, derive his usual, quiet, ironical pleasure from these items of interest.

Having finished his paper, a second cup of coffee, and a roll and butter, he stood up, brushed a few crumbs from his waistcoat, expanded his chest, and smiled joyfully. Not that he felt so light of heart; the smile merely signified a good digestion.

But this very smile brought everything back to his mind and he became thoughtful.

The voices of two children, whom Stepan Arkadyevitch recognised as belonging to Grisha the youngest boy and Tania the eldest girl, reached him from the other side of the door. They were dragging something which had upset.

"I told you you couldn't put passengers on the top," cried the little girl in English. "Pick them up!"

"There is no order in the house," Stepan Arkadyevitch thought. "The children are running wild." And going to the door he called to them. They dropped the box that served them as a train and ran to their father.

The little girl, her father's favourite, ran in boldly, hugged him and clung around his neck, laughing with delight. As usual she enjoyed the odour which exhaled from his whiskers. Then kissing his face that was reddened by his stooping position and beaming with tenderness, the little girl disengaged her arms and was about to run off again when her father stopped her.

"What is mamma doing?" he asked, stroking her smooth, tender neck. "How are you?" he added, turning to the little boy who had just greeted him.

He felt conscious that he was not so fond of the boy and

always tried to be fair to him. The boy, however, felt the difference and did not respond to his father's cold smile.

"Mamma? She is up now," the little girl replied.

Stepan Arkadyevitch sighed. "That means another sleepless night," he thought.

"Does she seem cheerful?"

The little girl was aware that something was wrong between her father and mother and that her father knew that she could not be cheerful under the circumstances and that he was dissembling when he questioned her so lightly. She blushed for her father. He instantly perceived it and also blushed.

"I don't know," she replied. "She said we were not to have any lessons to-day, but were to go to grandmother's with Miss Hull."

"Well, run along, little one. But stop a moment," he added, still detaining her and stroking her tiny hand.

He took a box of sweets out of his pocket and gave her two, choosing those she liked best.

"For Grisha?" she asked, pointing to one of them.

"That's right," and still stroking her shoulder, he kissed her on the nape of the neck and let her go.

"The carriage is ready," Matvey announced. "And then there is some woman who wants you to do something for her," he added.

"Has she been here long?" Stepan Arkadyevitch asked.

"About half an hour."

"How many times have I told you not to keep people waiting?"

"You must have time at least to eat your breakfast," Matvey replied in his kind, rough voice at which no one could ever take offence.

"Well, ask her up, instantly," Stepan Arkadyevitch said, frowning.

The woman, wife of a certain Captain Kalenin, had come to ask some perfectly impossible, senseless favour, but Stepan Arkadyevitch according to his habit asked her kindly to be seated, listened most attentively to everything she had to say, gave her most detailed advice as to how and whom to apply, and even wrote her a note in his large sprawling clear handwriting to a some one who might be of use to her. Disposing of the lady, Stepan Arkadyevitch took up his hat and paused, trying to think if he had forgotten anything. He had forgotten nothing excepting the one thing he wanted to forget—his wife.

"Oh, dear!" He hung his head and an expression of intense anguish passed over his handsome face. "Shall I go, or shall I not go?" he asked himself, and an inner voice told him that it was useless to go; that nothing but falsehood could come of it; that to alter their relations was impossible; because it was impossible to make her attractive or lovable again, or to make him an old man incapable of love. Nothing but falsehood and lying could come of it, and falsehood and lying were against his nature.

"But I shall have to go some time or other! you can't leave things as they are," he said, trying to gain courage. He straightened his shoulders, lighted a cigarette, inhaled the smoke once or twice, threw it into a mother-of-pearl ash-tray, and with a firm step walked quickly through the drawing-room and opened the door leading into his wife's bedroom.

IV

Darya Alexandrovna in a dressing-jacket was standing in the middle of the room before an open chest of drawers, out of which she was emptying the contents. Her hair, at one time luxuriant, was now fastened in two thin little plaits at the nape of her neck. Her face was wan and pale, and her great, large eyes had a hunted expression. The room was in great disorder. When she heard her husband's step she turned to the door trying to assume a hard, forbidding expression. She was afraid of him and dreaded the coming interview. For the tenth time during the last three days had she attempted to gather together her own and the children's things in order to depart for her mother's house, but she could not bring herself to do it. She kept on telling herself that things could not remain as they were, that she must do something, punish, shame him, if only to pay him back a little of the pain he had caused her. She kept on assuring herself that it was her duty to leave him, but felt that it was impossible. She could not cure herself of the thought that he was her husband and she loved him. Besides, she felt that if it had been difficult in her own home to look after her five children, it would be still worse at her mother's. Then the youngest child had been ill for the last few days because he had been given some badly cooked soup, and the others had gone to bed the night before with scarcely any dinner. She knew that to go away was impossible, but kept on packing her things and trying to deceive herself into thinking that she was going.

When she caught sight of her husband she thrust her hand into the drawer as if searching for something and did not look up until he was close to her. Instead of the hard, forbidding expression she had tried to assume her face was full of pain and indecision.

" Dolly! " he said in a quiet, timid voice. He hung his head, wishing to appear sorry and submissive, but he looked radiant. She raised her head and looked him up and down. " Yes, he is contented and happy—and I? " she thought. " And this good nature of his that others find so pleasant, how I hate it! " She pressed her lips tightly together and the muscles of her pale face twitched nervously.

" What do you want? " she asked in a quick unnatural voice.

" Dolly! " he repeated, his voice trembling, " Anna is coming to-day."

" What is that to me? I cannot receive her! "

" But don't you see, Dolly, we must . . ."

" Go away! go away! go away! " she cried without looking at him, as though the words were torn from her by physical pain.

Stepan Arkadyevitch could be calm when he only thought of his wife; could go on hoping that everything would come right as Matvey had said; and that he might still be left to drink his coffee and read his paper in peace, but confronted by his wife's agonised face and piteous cry a lump rose in his throat and his eyes filled with tears.

" My God! what have I done! Dolly! In Heaven's name! I . . ." He could not utter another word for the sobs that choked him.

She shut the drawer with a bang and turned to him.

" Dolly! What can I say? Forgive me. . . . Just think; cannot nine years of life together pay for one single moment . . . moment . . . "

She dropped her eyes and stood listening to what he had to say as though hoping that he might convince her that the whole thing was not true.

" One moment of temptation . . ." he got out at last. At this word Dolly pressed her lips together again as if in physical pain and again the muscles of her face contracted nervously.

" Go away! go away from here! " she shrieked. " Don't speak to me about your temptations and your meanness! "

She turned to go out, but almost fell over and had to lean

against a chair for support. Stepan Arkadyevitch's eyes filled with tears.

"Dolly!" he repeated, sobbing. "For God's sake think of the children. They are not to blame. If I have sinned, punish me alone. Tell me what I'm to do. I'll do everything you want of me. I'm sorry! I can't tell you how sorry I am! Forgive me, Dolly!"

She sank into a chair. He could hear her heavy breathing and his heart ached for her. She attempted to speak once or twice, but could not. He stood waiting.

"You only think of the children because you like to play with them. But I think of them too, and I know that they are ruined now." She repeated one of the phrases that had been in her mind for the last three days.

She had spoken kindly to him. He felt touched and wanted to take her hand, but she tore it away in disgust.

"I am always thinking of the children and would do everything in the world to save them, but I am not sure whether I would do better to remove them from their father or to leave them with a father who is a libertine. . . . Yes, a libertine. . . . Do you think . . . we could go on living together after what has happened? Is it possible? Tell me, is it possible? My husband, the father of my children . . . carrying on with their governess. . . ."

"But what can I do? What can I do?" he asked in a pitiful voice, hanging his head.

"You are hateful to me!" she cried, working herself up more and more. "Your tears are no more than water! You never loved me! You have no heart, no honour! You are abominable, revolting. Henceforth you are a perfect stranger to me! Yes, a perfect stranger!" She repeated the terrible words that sounded so strange to her own ears.

He gazed at her. Her spiteful expression bewildered him. He could not perceive that his pity exasperated her. She could feel that he pitied her, but did not love her.

"She hates me," he thought. "She will never forgive me."

"This is terrible! terrible!" he exclaimed.

At this moment one of the children began to cry in the next room, and Darya Alexandrovna's face softened.

She tried to collect herself as if not knowing where she was or what she wanted to do and walked quickly towards the door.

"At any rate she loves my child," he thought, observing

how the child's cry had affected her, "*my* child; then how can she hate me?"

"Dolly, one word more," he said, following her.

"If you come near me I shall call the servants, the children! Let them all know how infamous you are! I am going away to-day and you can stop here with your mistress!"

She fled from the room, banging the door behind her.

Stepan Arkadyevitch sighed, wiped his brow, and left the room quietly. "Matvey talks of her coming round," he said to himself, "but how? It seems impossible. How terrible! And how she shrieked," he went on, recalling the words "infamous" and "mistress." "The servants might have heard her! It's awful! awful!"

It was Friday, and the German clock-maker was winding the clock in the dining-room. Stepan Arkadyevitch recollected a joke he had once made about this bald little German, that he was himself wound up for life so that he might wind clocks, and the recollection caused him to smile. Stepan Arkadyevitch was fond of a good joke. "Perhaps she will come round after all! What a nice expression, *to come round;* I must repeat it to some one."

"Matvey!" he called, "tell Marya to get one of the rooms ready for Anna Arkadyevna."

"Yes, sir," Matvey replied as he came in.

Stepan Arkadyevitch put on his coat and went out.

"Shall you dine at home?" Matvey asked as he escorted him outside the door.

"I'm not sure. Here, take this if you need any money," he added, giving him a ten-rouble note. "Is it enough?"

"I suppose it will have to be enough," Matvey replied as he shut the carriage door and went back to the house.

Meanwhile Darya Alexandrovna, having pacified the child, and knowing by the sound of the carriage that her husband was gone, came back to her own room. It was her only refuge from the many domestic troubles that enveloped her the moment she left it. Even now, for the short time she had been in the nursery, the English governess and Matriona Filimonovna had plied her with all sorts of questions that she alone could answer. How were the children to be dressed for their walk? should they be given milk? ought they to send for another cook?

"For heaven's sake leave me alone!" she cried, and escaped to her room, where she sat down on the very spot where she had spoken to her husband. Then clasping her thin hands on whose fingers the rings would scarcely stay, she began reviewing their conversation. " He has gone. But has he broken with *her?* " she thought. " Does he still see her? Why didn't I ask him? No, no, we can never come together again. Even if we continue living in the same house, we must be perfect strangers to one another. Strangers forever! " Again she repeated the terrible word. " And how I loved him! O God, how I loved him! how I loved him! And do I not love him still, even now? The most awful thing of all. . . ." She was cut short by Matriona Filimonovna, who appeared at the door.

" Shall I send for my brother? " she asked. " He can cook some sort of a dinner. Otherwise it will be like yesterday. The children didn't get anything to eat till six o'clock."

" Very well. I'll come and see about it. Have they sent for some fresh milk? "

And Darya Alexandrovna lost herself in her daily tasks and for the time being forgot her sorrow.

V

STEPAN ARKADYEVITCH had done well at school, thanks to his natural ability, but he was very idle and had consequently come out at the bottom of his class. In spite of his youth and the gay life he had led, he was fortunate enough to occupy the important position of president in a government department in Moscow, for which he received a very liberal salary. He had stepped into the place through the influence of his sister's husband, Alexei Alexandrovitch Karenin, a great personage in the ministry to which this department belonged. Had Karenin not secured him this place there were a hundred other people, brothers, sisters, cousins, uncles, and aunts, who would have found it for him or another quite as good, together with six thousand roubles a year, for Stepan Arkadyevitch, despite his wife's large estates, had need of money.

Half the people in Moscow and St. Petersburg were either relatives or friends of Stepan Arkadyevitch. He was born amidst the rich and powerful of the land. One-third of the most influential government officials had been his father's friends and had known him from his babyhood; the second third were all friends of his, and the others old acquaintances.

So that all the powerful people who could bestow earthly happiness in the shape of good places, concessions, etc., were his friends, who could not afford to overlook one of their own circle. Oblonsky took no trouble to obtain this place. He had merely to avoid petty jealousies and quarrels, a thing not difficult with his peculiarly good nature. He would have thought it ridiculous had he been told that he could not have any place that he wanted with the necessary salary, particularly as his demands were not out of the way. He only asked for what his friends were obtaining, and felt that he was quite as competent as any of them of doing the work.

Stepan Arkadyevitch was liked by all those who knew him, not only on account of his amiable disposition and unimpeachable honesty, but also for his brilliant personality. There was something about his sparkling eyes, black eyebrows, hair, his very complexion, that was pleasant to behold, and acted like a tonic on all who looked on him. "Why, here's Stiva Oblonsky!" people would say with a smile of pleasure on meeting him. And if they sometimes found his conversation rather disappointing, they were nevertheless just as pleased to see him the next day and the next.

During the three years he had been president of his department Stepan Arkadyevitch had won the love and admiration of all his colleagues and subordinates, and of every one with whom he had come in contact. The principal quality that gained Stepan Arkadyevitch this general esteem was the extreme indulgence with which he treated other people, a quality no doubt founded on the consciousness of his own shortcomings. Then he was so extremely liberal to every one, no matter who it was, not with the Liberalism of his newspaper, but with that which flowed freely in his own veins. And, above all, he was so absolutely indifferent to the business which he transacted that he never lost his temper or made any mistakes.

On reaching the office Stepan Arkadyevitch went into his private room, accompanied by a porter who carried his portfolio. He put on his uniform and issued forth into the general office. The clerks rose and greeted him with a respectful smile. Stepan Arkadyevitch hastened to his place as usual, and after shaking hands with the other members of the council, he sat down. He made a few jocular and friendly remarks, not any more than the occasion demanded, and proceeded with his work. No one knew better than Stepan Arkadyevitch the exact amount of freedom and natural simplicity that could be permitted in official relations without in any way upsetting the equilibrium of things.

His secretary came up and with a familiar, yet respectful air, common to all who surrounded Stepan Arkadyevitch, handed him some documents. He spoke in the free and easy tone that Stepan Arkadyevitch had introduced.

" At last we have those reports from the government of Pensa. Do you wish to . . . "

" Got them at last? " Stepan Arkadyevitch interrupted him, pushing the papers away with his finger. " Well, gentlemen." . . . And the council began.

" If only they knew," he thought, putting his head on one side with an important air as he listened to the report, " if only they knew what a naughty schoolboy their president looked only half-an-hour ago! " His eyes sparkled mischievously. The council general lasted until two o'clock without interruption, and then followed an interval for luncheon.

Just before two o'clock the great glass doors of the hall were thrown open and some one came in. Every one was glad of the diversion and turned to look round, but the porter instantly ejected the intruder and shut the door upon him.

When they had finished reading the report Stepan Arkadyevitch rose, stretched himself, and paying a tribute to the Liberalism of the times, he took out a cigarette in the council chamber and proceeded to his private room. He was followed by his two chums, Nikitin and Chamberlain Grinevitch.

" We can finish the thing after luncheon," Stepan Arkadyevitch said.

" Of course we can," Nikitin agreed with him.

" What a scoundrel that Fomin must be! " Grinevitch remarked, referring to one of the men mixed up in the case they had been investigating that morning.

Stepan Arkadyevitch frowned at Grinevitch's words, as though he wished him to understand that it was not the thing to prejudge any one in that way, but he did not say anything.

" Who has just come in? " he asked of the porter.

" Some person, your excellency, has come in without permission when my back was turned. I asked him to wait until you had finished. . . . He wishes to see you."

" Where is he? "

" In the corridor most likely. He kept walking about here. Ah, here he is! " the porter exclaimed, pointing to a well-built, broad-shouldered young man with a curly beard and a sheep-skin cap on his head, who was running up the well-washed steps of the stone staircase. One of the clerks on his way down with a portfolio under his arm looked indignantly at the man thus running up and turned to Oblonsky with a look of inquiry. The latter was standing at the top of the stairs, and his beaming, good-natured face, set off by the embroidered collar of his uniform, became even more radiant when he recognised the visitor.

" Why, Levin! " he exclaimed, with a friendly, half ironical smile, gazing at the newcomer. " And you have actually ventured to find me in this awful place! " he added, and not satisfied with pressing his friend's hand, he kissed him affectionately. " When did you arrive? "

" I've only just arrived and wanted to see you," Levin replied timidly as he gazed around uneasily.

" Come into my office," Stepan Arkadyevitch said, being aware of his visitor's peculiar egotistical self-consciousness, and taking his arm he led him away as though to avoid any possible danger.

Stepan Arkadyevitch was extremely familiar in manner with nearly all his acquaintances, familiar alike with old men of sixty, young men of twenty, actors and ministers, merchants and generals; and as he numbered among them the two extremes of the social scale, some of his friends would have been extremely astonished to know of the others. He was on terms of intimacy with any person he had ever drunk champagne with, and he drank champagne with all. If, however, in the presence of his subordinates, he sometimes came in contact with his disreputable acquaintances as he called them in jest, he had the good sense to save them from any unpleasantness. Levin was not one of his disreputable acquaintances, but Oblonsky, with his usual tact, felt he might find it unpleasant to make a parade of their intimacy, and therefore hastened him away to his private room.

Levin was about the same age as Oblonsky and their intimacy was not of the champagne kind. Levin was a friend of his boyhood. They were attached to one another in spite of the differences in their tastes and dispositions, as only people can be attached who have known each other from childhood. But as often happens among men of different interests and activities each honestly tried to approve of and justify the other, but in their heart of hearts they could not help despising one another. Each felt that his own mode of life was the only rational one and the other's nothing but an illusion. At the sight of Levin Oblonsky could not repress an ironical smile. How many times had he seen him arrive in Moscow just from the country, where he was supposed to be doing something, but what exactly it was Stepan Arkadyevitch did not know, and was not sufficiently interested to find out. Levin always appeared in Moscow in a state of excitement, always in a hurry, always self-conscious, and always annoyed at his own self-consciousness, and always with some perfectly new ideas upon life and things in general. Stepan Arkadyevitch was amused at his friend, but liked him all the same. Just as Levin at bottom despised Oblonsky's worldly life and laughed at his occupation, which he considered utterly valueless. But whereas Oblonsky, who lived as other people live, laughed at his friend good-naturedly, as one who felt certain of being in the right, Levin, who did not feel so sure of himself, sometimes got angry.

"We have been expecting you for some time," Stepan Arkadyevitch said, as they entered his office. He let go his friend's arm to show that the danger was past.

"I am so glad to see you!" he continued. "Well, how are you? When did you come?"

Levin was silent, and stood looking at the unknown faces of Oblonsky's two colleagues. He was so absorbed in the elegant Grinevitch, with his long white hands, long yellow nails that turned over at the tips, and large glittering shirt-studs, as to be robbed of the power of speech.

Oblonsky noticed it with a smile.

"Ah, yes, allow me to introduce you," he said, "my colleagues, Philip Ivanitch Nikitin, Michail Stanislevitch Grinevitch." Then turning to Levin, "And this is my friend, Konstantin Dmitrievitch Levin, a landed proprietor, a rising man in his *zemstvo*, a splendid athlete, who can lift two hundredweights in one hand, a capital huntsman, and brother to the famous Sergei Ivanitch Kosnishev."

"Charmed to make your acquaintance," Nikitin observed.

"I have the honour of knowing your brother," Grinevitch remarked, extending his thin hand with the long nails.

Levin frowned, shook hands coldly, and immediately turned to Oblonsky. Although he had the greatest admiration for his brother, famous throughout Russia for his literary works, he nevertheless found it very unpleasant to be addressed not as Konstantin Levin, but as the brother of the famous Kosnishev.

"I am no longer on the *zemstvo*. I've quarrelled with

every one all round and never go to the meetings now," he said.

"Really!" Oblonsky exclaimed with a smile. "But how? Why?"

"Oh, it's a long story. I'll tell you some other time," Levin replied. "To make a long story short," he nevertheless went on, "I don't think you can ever do anything with the *zemstvo*. It's just like playing at parliament, and I am not young enough or old enough to be amused by toys. Besides," he said with a pause, "it's merely used by a certain set to get what they can out of it. Whereas before there used to be guardians and judges and bribe-taking, now we have a host of officials living on unearned salaries." He concluded fiercely, as though expecting that some one would contradict him.

"That's quite a new phase for you! You're becoming quite a Conservative," Stepan Arkadyevitch remarked. "We must talk it over later on."

"I wanted to see you most particularly," Levin said, gazing at Grinevitch's hand with disgust.

Stepan Arkadyevitch gave a scarcely perceptible smile.

"Why, didn't you say that you would never again put on European clothes?" he asked, examining Levin's new suit that had obviously been made by a French tailor. "This is really a new phase!" Levin suddenly blushed, not as grown men blush, without perceiving it, but as self-conscious schoolboys blush. It gave his intelligent, manly face such a childish appearance that Oblonsky turned away.

"But where can I see you? I must have a talk with you," Levin said.

Oblonsky thought a moment.

"Let us go and have luncheon at Gurin's. I shall be free until three o'clock."

"I am sorry, I can't come now," Levin said hesitatingly.

"Very well, let's have dinner together."

"Dinner? I have nothing very particular to say. I only want to ask you two words, but we can have a chat afterwards."

"Come, ask me your two words and leave the rest till dinner-time."

"It's like this you see . . . however, it's not really very important." His face assumed a hard expression, due to his efforts to overcome his timidity.

"What are the Shcherbatskys doing? the same as usual?" he asked.

Stepan Arkadyevitch had known for some time that Levin was in love with his sister-in-law, Kitty. His eyes twinkled, and he gave a scarcely perceptible smile.

"I can't answer you as quickly as that," he said, "because . . . Excuse me a moment."

His secretary had just come in, and with a familiar yet respectful bearing common to all secretaries who assume that they know more about business than their superiors, approached Oblonsky with some document and under the form of a question proceeded to explain some difficulty. Stepan Arkadyevitch, without waiting for the end, laid his hand kindly on the secretary's arm.

"No, you must do it the way I asked you to," he said, trying to soften his remark with an amiable smile. He gave a brief explanation of the matter and pushed the papers away. "Do it like that, please, Zahar Nikititch," he added.

The secretary retired in confusion. Levin meanwhile had collected himself, and leaning against the back of a chair stood listening scornfully.

"I can't understand, I simply can't understand!" he said.

"What can't you understand?" Oblonsky asked gaily, taking out a cigarette. He was expecting some fresh outbreak from him.

"I can't make out what you're doing," Levin went on with a shrug of the shoulders. "How can you treat it so seriously?"

"But why not?"

"Why, because, because . . . it's not work at all."

"You think so? And yet we're head over ears in work."

"Work on paper! However, you've got a gift for that sort of thing," Levin added.

"That's as much as saying there's something that I lack."

"Perhaps there is," Levin remarked. "However, I can't help admiring you and feeling awfully proud to have such an important person for my friend. But you haven't replied to my question yet," he added, making a tremendous effort to look Oblonsky straight in the face.

"Very well, very well, you'll get to it in time. It's a good thing for you that you've got a few thousand acres of land at Karasinsk, such muscles, and a complexion of a school-girl of twelve, but you'll come to us in the end. By the by, as for the thing you asked me about, there are no changes exactly, but it's a great pity you haven't been here for so long."

"Why?" Levin asked in alarm.

"Oh, nothing particular, we'll talk it over presently," Oblonsky replied. "What has brought you up?"

"Oh, we can talk about that too later on," Levin replied, blushing to his very ears.

"All right. I understand," Stepan Arkadyevitch remarked. "I should have asked you to come home, but my wife is not very well. Should you want to see them, they are most certain to be at the Zoological Gardens between four and five. Kitty has taken to skating. You had better go there, and I'll meet you just before dinner."

"Very well. Good-bye."

"But mind you don't forget and go off into the country or something," Stepan Arkadyevitch called after him laughing.

"I'll be there."

Levin went out and only remembered when he had passed the door that he had not taken leave of Oblonsky's two colleagues.

"A very energetic man I should think," Grinevitch remarked as soon as Levin was gone.

"Yes," Stepan Arkadyevitch agreed, shaking his head. "He's a lucky beggar! All that land down at Karasinsk and his future before him. We can't beat that."

"But what have you to complain of, Stepan Arkadyevitch?"

"Oh, things aren't very grand with me," Stepan Arkadyevitch replied with a deep sigh.

VI

When Oblonsky had asked Levin what had brought him to Moscow, Levin had blushed and felt angry with himself for doing so, but how could he have told him that he had come up on purpose to propose to his sister-in-law, Kitty? Yet he had come for no other reason than that.

The Levins and Shcherbatskys, two ancient Moscow families, had always been on close, friendly relations with one another. While Levin was at the university the intimacy had grown closer on account of his friendship with young Prince Shcherbatsky, the brother of Dolly and Kitty. At that time Levin was a frequent visitor at the Shcherbatskys' house and was in love with the whole family, especially with the feminine portion of it. Levin's mother had died when he was too young to remember her, and as his only sister was much older than himself, he first discovered in the Shcherbatskys' house that cultured, charming life, common to the nobility, that the death of his father and mother had deprived him of. Every member of the family, particularly the ladies, seemed to him to be surrounded by some mysterious, poetical halo, and not only could he find no fault in them, but he imbued them with the most lofty sentiments and the most ideal perfections. Why the three young ladies had to speak English and French alternately every other day; why they had to practise on the piano for hours at a time, the sounds of which travelled up to their brother's room, where the young students were at work; why professors of French literature, of music, dancing, and drawing came to give them lessons; why they had to take a drive out at a given hour with Mlle Linon, get out at the Tverskoi Boulevard and walk up and down in their satin coats, Dolly in a long one, Natalie in a shorter one, and Kitty in quite a short one, showing her shapely legs in bright red stockings; why a footman in livery with a gold cockade in his hat was obliged to accompany them in their walk—all this and much else was utterly incomprehensible to him; but he felt that everything that they did in their mysterious world was perfect, and he loved the very mystery of it.

When he was still a student he almost fell in love with Dolly, but she was soon married to Oblonsky. He then turned his attentions to the second one, feeling it a necessity to fall in love with one of the three, but as soon as Natalie came out she was married to a diplomat. Kitty was still a child when Levin left the university. Young Shcherbatsky went into the navy and was drowned in the Baltic, so that the relations between Levin and the Shcherbatsky family became more and more distant in spite of his friendship with Oblonsky. When, how ever, at the beginning of the year, Levin had come to Moscow after a year's absence in the country and had been to see the Shcherbatskys, he learned for the first time which of the three sisters he was destined to love.

It would have seemed that there was nothing easier than for a young man of thirty-two, of good family and ample fortune, to propose for the hand of the Princess Shcherbatsky, especially as he would have been looked upon as a desirable suitor. But Levin was in love, and Kitty seemed to him a being so perfect from every point of view, so infinitely superior to anything else in the world, that it could not be possible for either her or any one else to consider him worthy of her.

But after having spent a couple of months in Moscow in a perfect fever of excitement, meeting Kitty in society every day, he suddenly decided that the union was impossible and departed for the country without delay. It seemed to him that her relatives did not consider him a sufficiently good match for the charming Kitty, and that she herself did not love him. To Kitty's family he seemed to have no definite occupation suitable to one in his position. Whereas all his contemporaries were either colonels, aides-de-camp, professors, directors of banks and railway companies, or presidents of government departments, like Oblonsky, he was only (he knew very well how others regarded him) an ordinary country squire, who spent his time rearing cattle, building barns, shooting, and doing all those uninteresting things that according to the opinion in society no man would do who was not an utter failure. And then, how could the divine Kitty possibly love such an uninteresting, commonplace man as he considered himself to be? Besides which his former relations with her during his intimacy with her brother had been those of a grown man to a child: an additional obstacle towards love.

A simple, plain man like himself, he thought, could not inspire a woman with the sort of love he felt for Kitty; she might love him as a friend. He had heard of women falling in love with ugly, uninteresting men, but he could not believe it; it would have been impossible for him to fall in love with any woman who was not beautiful, poetic, and distinguished.

After having spent two months alone in the country he became convinced that his passion was not like those he had experienced in his youth. He could not get a single moment of peace; he could not live until he knew for certain whether she would marry him or not. After all there was no absolute certainty that she would refuse him. So he returned to Moscow, resolved to marry if Kitty would accept him, and if not . . . He could not bear to think what would happen to him if she refused.

VII

LEVIN had come to Moscow by the morning train and had gone straight to the house of his half-brother, Kosnishev. He washed, changed his clothes, and proceeded to his brother's study, intending to tell him everything and ask his advice, but he was not alone. He was engaged in talking to a famous professor of philosophy who had come up from Kharkov with the express purpose of clearing up some misunderstanding over a philosophical point that had arisen between them. The professor was writing a series of articles against materialism, and Sergei Kosnishev, who followed them with interest, had written to him disapproving of his last one and upbraiding him with letting the materialists down too gently. This had brought the professor up at once to explain what he meant. They were discussing the question whether there was a dividing line between the psychological and physiological phenomena in human action.

Sergei Ivanovitch greeted his brother with his usual affable, though somewhat cold smile, introduced him to the professor, and continued the discussion. The professor a little man in spectacles, with a narrow forehead, paused for a moment to shake hands, and then went on talking without paying any further heed to him. Levin, who was on pins and needles for the professor to be gone, became absorbed in the discussion in spite of himself. He had come across the articles in question and was interested in them in a general way, as a man who has studied science at the university is likely to be in any new developments, but he had never been able to see any connection between scientific hypotheses about the origin of man, of biology or sociology, and the more profound questions of the meaning of life and death that had engaged his attention of late years.

He noticed, however, that his brother and the professor did not separate scientific questions from spiritual ones, and once or twice they almost touched upon this very point, but they immediately drew away from it and took refuge in the domain of abstract distinctions, quotations, etc., making it very difficult for him to follow them.

" I cannot admit," Sergei Ivanovitch said, in his clear, elegant manner of speech, " I cannot possibly admit that Keis is right when he says that all knowledge of the outer world comes through the senses. The fundamental consciousness of *being* does not come through the senses; there is no special organ through which it reaches us."

" Yes, but Wurst, Knaus, and Pripasov will tell you that your consciousness of being comes from the union of all the senses; is, in fact, the sum total of sensation. Wurst even goes so far as to say that without sensation there could be no consciousness of being."

" On the other hand, I think . . . " Sergei Ivanovitch began.

But here it seemed to Levin that they were again diverging from the main issue, and he determined to ask the professor a question.

" But what would happen," he began, " if all my senses disappeared, if my body were dead, would that be an end to all existence? "

The professor, annoyed at the interruption, fixed his eyes on his interlocutor, who seemed to him more like a clown than a philosopher, then turned to Sergei Ivanovitch as if asking him what he thought of it. But the latter, who was not so narrow-minded as the professor, and was able to see the direct rational point of the question, said with a smile—

" I don't think we have yet gained the right of answering the question."

" We have not sufficient knowledge," the professor agreed, and continued his arguments. " No," he said, " I maintain that if Pripasov says plainly that sensation is based upon impression, then we must carefully examine the two different propositions. . . ."

Levin did not listen any longer and only waited for the professor to take his departure.

VIII

As soon as the professor had gone Sergei Ivanovitch turned to his brother. " I'm so glad you've come. Shall you stay long? How are things on the estate? "

Levin knew that his brother took little interest in the estate and had only asked out of sheer politeness, so he merely said something about the sale of his wheat and the price he had received for it.

It had been Levin's intention to tell his brother that he wished to marry and ask his advice about it, but after the conversation with the professor and the patronising tone in which he had asked about the affairs of the estate (Levin managed his own as well as his brother's portion of the estate that had come to them through their mother), he felt that he could not broach the subject. It seemed to him that his brother would not look upon the matter as he should wish him to.

" Well, how is your *zemstvo* getting on? " Sergei Ivanovitch asked. He took a great interest in the zemstvos, to which he attached great importance.

" I really don't know. . . ."

" What! Aren't you a member of the council? "

" Not now. I've resigned. I no longer attend the meetings."

" What a pity! " Sergei Ivanovitch exclaimed with a frown.

In order to defend himself Levin began to explain the sort of thing that took place at the meetings of his district assembly.

" But it's always the way! " Sergei Ivanovitch interrupted him. " We Russians are always like that! It may be a good thing to see your own defects, but we exaggerate them too much. We're always ready to sneer at everything. Any other European nation, the Germans or the English, for instance, would have worked wonders with our county councils, they would have derived liberty from them, and we can do nothing but sneer at him."

" But what can we do? " Levin asked shamefacedly. " It was my last attempt. I really did try to do something. It was impossible. I'm not clever enough."

" Not clever enough! You don't look at the matter in the right spirit," Sergei Ivanovitch said.

" Perhaps not," Levin replied dejectedly.

" Were you aware that our brother Nikolai has turned up again? " Sergei Ivanovitch asked.

Nikolai was Levin's elder brother and half brother to Sergei Ivanovitch. He was a ruined man, had run through the greater part of his fortune, and was mixed up with all sorts of disreputable people, on account of which he had quarrelled with his brothers.

" What did you say? " Levin asked in alarm. " How did you get to know? "

" Prokofy met him in the street."

" Here, in Moscow? Where's he staying? Do you know? " Levin jumped up from his chair as if ready to go to him that moment.

" I'm sorry I told you," Sergei Ivanovitch remarked with a shake of the head, observing how the news had affected his brother. " I sent to find out where he lived, and forwarded his draft in favour of Trubin, the amount of which I had paid. But this is what he writes me." Sergei Ivanovitch handed his brother a note which he drew out from under a paper-weight.

Levin glanced at the note written in the strange hand that he knew so well. " Please leave me alone. That is all I want of my affectionate brothers.—Nikolai Levin." Konstantin Levin, without lifting his head, stood motionless before his brother with the note in his hand. An impulse arose within him to forget all about his unfortunate brother, but felt that it would be wrong.

" He evidently wished to insult me," Sergei Ivanovitch continued, " but he can't do that. I should have liked to help him with all my heart if I could have seen a way of doing it."

" Yes, yes," Levin put in, " I quite understand and fully appreciate your feelings towards him, but I'm going to see him."

" If you want to, go by all means; only I should not have advised it," Sergei Ivanovitch remarked. " I'm not in the least afraid that he'll prejudice you against me. It was only for your own sake that I did not wish you to go. You can't do any good. However, you must please yourself."

" It may be of no use, but I can't help feeling, particularly at this moment . . . but that's another matter. I should feel uneasy if I didn't go."

" I simply can't understand that," Sergei Ivanovitch observed. " I only know it's been a lesson in humility to me. I can look much kindlier on that sort of thing since Nikolai has become what he is. Do you know what he has done? "

" It's terrible! terrible! " Levin exclaimed.

Levin asked his brother's servant for Nikolai's address, with the intention of starting off to see him at once, but after a moment's consideration decided to postpone his visit until the evening. In order to gain peace of mind he must first decide the question that had brought him to Moscow. So he went direct to Oblonsky's office, got news of the Shcherbatskys, and proceeded to the Zoological Gardens, where he expected to find Kitty.

IX

At about four o'clock in the afternoon Levin left his driver at the gates of the gardens, and with a beating heart wound his way along the path that led to the skating rink. He knew that Kitty would be there, as he had seen the Shcherbatskys' carriage outside.

It was a clear, frosty day. Lines of cabs, carriages, and sledges stood waiting at the entrance. Crowds of gaily-dressed people were walking to and fro in the brilliant sunlight along the bright, clean foot-paths between the little wooden houses. The old birch trees, their branches laden with snow, looked as if they were arranged for some triumphant festival.

As Levin walked along the path he kept saying to himself, " Do be calm! Why are you so agitated? What is the matter with me? Be quiet, you fool! " Thus he addressed his heart. But the more he tried to calm himself, the more agitated he grew. An acquaintance called to him as he passed, but he did not even notice who it was. He drew near to the ice hills on which people were tobogganing; the sounds of happy voices mingled with the clanging of chains drawing up the little sledges. A few steps further on he got a view of the whole rink, and there, amidst the many skaters, he immediately recognised *her*. He knew that she was there from the joy and terror that seized his heart. She was on the opposite side of the rink engaged in conversation with a lady. There was nothing particularly striking about her garments or her pose, but for Levin she seemed to stand out from the rest as a rose among nettles. Her presence brightened all about her. She was like a smile shedding radiance all around. " Can I really walk across the ice? go up to her? " he thought. The place where she was seemed to him like a sanctuary which he dared not approach. For a moment such terror seized him that he almost turned to go away, but mastering himself by a great effort, he assured himself that he had every bit as much right to be near her as all those other people.

He walked across the rink, his eyes averted from her as though she were the sun too dazzling to behold, but he saw her all the same, though he did not look at her.

This was a day when the rink was much frequented by a certain set all known to one another. There were masters in the art of skating who had come to show off, there were others who were merely learning by the aid of chairs, which they kept pushing before them; there were young boys and old men who had come for the good of their health, and one and all seemed to Levin to be especially favoured by fortune, because they were near Kitty. And they all seemed so indifferent to her presence. They came close to her, glided past her, even addressed her, but did not seem to depend on her for their happiness; they were merely enjoying the splendid condition of the ice and fine weather.

Nikolai Shcherbatsky, Kitty's cousin, in a short jacket and tight trousers, was sitting on a seat with his skates on, when he caught sight of Levin.

"I say!" he called to him. "Have you been here long? Get your skates on, quick! the ice is splendid. Why, you're the best skater in Russia."

"I have not my skates with me," Levin replied, amazed that any one should dare to speak so freely in Kitty's presence. He did not lose sight of her for a moment, although he was not looking in her direction. He felt the sun's rays upon him. Kitty was coming round the corner, evidently not quite at her ease. A youth in a Russian costume, waving his arms about wildly, rushed past her. She drew her hands out of her muff, attached round her neck by a cord, and held them in readiness to clutch at anything that came in her way. She smiled when she caught sight of Levin, and endeavouring to keep up till she got to her cousin, she caught hold of his arm. To Levin she seemed far more beautiful than his imagination had pictured her.

Whenever he thought of her, a vivid mental picture of her lovely golden head, set so gracefully on her stately shoulders, her kind, simple, child-like expression, so full of charm, would arise before his mind. But what always struck him afresh was her wonderful eyes and her still more wonderful smile, which seemed to transport him to some enchanted world, such as he remembered in the rare, happy days of his early childhood.

"Have you been here long?" Kitty asked, extending her hand. "Thanks," she added, as Levin picked up her pocket-handkerchief which had dropped out of her muff.

"I? I only came yesterday . . . that is, to-day," he replied, too agitated to know what he was saying. "I wanted to call on you," he added, but remembering suddenly with what purpose he had wished to see her, he became confused and blushed deeply. "I did not know that you skated, and so well too."

She looked at him closely, trying to divine the reason of his embarrassment.

"It's awfully good of you to say so, particularly as I hear you're a champion skater yourself," she said, brushing the hoar-frost from her muff with her daintily-gloved hand.

"Yes, I was passionately fond of skating at one time. It was my ambition to be a master in the art."

"You do everything passionately, it seems," she said with a smile. "I should like to see you skate. Do put on your skates and let us try together."

"Skate together!" he thought, "is it really possible?"

"In a moment," he said, hastening away to find some skates.

"It's a long time since we've seen you here, sir," the attendant remarked, fixing on Levin's skates. "No one can skate like you nowadays. Is that right?" he asked, tightening the strap.

"Quite right, quite right, only make haste," Levin replied, unable to restrain a smile of joy that illuminated his face. "This is life!" he thought. "This is happiness! *Together,* she said. *Let us try together.* Should I tell her now? Not now. I feel so happy, happy with hope. And after . . . But I must tell her! I must! I must! I won't be weak!"

Levin arose, took off his coat, and making one or two circles over the rough, uneven ice round the little house, he glided out into the smooth rink without any effort and made his way straight towards Kitty. Her smile reassured him.

"I should learn very quickly with you," she said. "I somehow feel confidence in you."

"I am confident in myself when you lean on me," he rejoined, and becoming abashed at what he had said he blushed deeply. In fact, the words had scarcely passed his lips when suddenly, as the sun disappears behind a cloud, her face lost all its kindliness and a frown spread over her smooth forehead.

"Has anything disagreeable happened to you? But I've no right to ask," he added quickly.

"Why not? Nothing disagreeable has happened to me," she replied coldly. "Have you seen Mlle Linon?" she asked, to change the subject.

"Not yet."

"Do go to her; she's so fond of you."

"What's the matter? I must have offended her. Heaven help me!" Levin thought as he made his way to the old, grey-haired French governess who was sitting on a seat close by. She gave a broad smile, exposing all her false teeth, and greeted him like an old friend.

"You see how we've grown up," she said, glancing towards Kitty. "And we're getting old too. The tiny bear has grown large," the old governess continued with a smile, recalling how Levin had once named the three young ladies after the three bears in the English fairy story. "Do you remember what you used to call them?"

Levin had entirely forgotten it, but the little old lady had laughed at the joke for the last ten years.

"You can run along and skate now. Doesn't our Kitty do it beautifully!"

When Levin joined Kitty her face had lost its severe expres-

TOPOR

sion; she looked at him again frankly and kindly, but there was something unnatural in her very kindliness which troubled him. After a few remarks about her eccentric old governess, she began to talk about his own life.

"Don't you get tired of the country in the winter?" she asked.

"No, I'm much too busy," he replied, crushed by her calm, indifferent tone, just as he had been at the beginning of the winter.

"Are you going to stay long?" Kitty asked.

"I don't know," he replied, scarcely conscious of what he was saying. The thought that he might once more fall into that friendly tone with her and go away without speaking became unbearable to him.

"How is it you don't know?"

"I really can't say. It depends on you," he said, becoming terrified at his own words.

She either did not hear him or pretended not to hear. She seemed to stumble once or twice and hastened away from him straight to Mlle Linon. After a word or two with the old governess she went towards the lodge to have her skates removed.

"My God! what have I done? Heaven help me! show me what to do!" Levin prayed within him, and feeling the need of some violent exercise he began executing a series of intricate curves on the ice.

Just then a young man, the best skater among the newer generation, came out of the little *café* with a cigarette in his mouth and slid down the stairs with his skates on, bumping all the way as he went. Without even changing the free and easy position of his arms, he glided out upon the ice.

"That's a new trick!" Levin exclaimed, and walked up the steps to see if he could do it.

"Take care you don't kill yourself! You've got to get used to it," Nikolai Shcherbatsky called after him.

When Levin reached the top he got as far away from the stairs as he could to get a good start and rushed down, balancing himself with his arms. At the last step his foot caught against something and he nearly went over, but regaining his equilibrium by a great effort he sailed on, laughing, upon the ice.

"How charming! What a dear he is!" Kitty thought. She was just in time to see him as she came out of the little lodge with Mlle Linon and gave him an affectionate smile as she would to a favourite brother. " Is it my fault? Have I done anything very bad. People say that I'm a flirt. I know I don't love him, but I like to be with him all the same. He's so nice. Only what possessed him to say that? " Thus her thoughts ran.

Seeing Kitty about to depart with her mother, who had just come for her, Levin, flushed with the violent exercise, after a moment's hesitation, took off his skates and hastened after them.

" I am glad to see you," the princess said. " We receive on Thursdays as usual."

" May I call to-day? "

" We shall be pleased to see you," the princess replied coldly.

Her mother's coldness wounded Kitty and she was seized with a desire to make amends for it. " Good-bye! " she said, turning to him with a sweet smile.

At this moment, Stepan Arkadyevitch, his hat on one side, brimming over with joy, came into the garden. On seeing his mother-in-law his face assumed a melancholy, penitent expression. He answered all her questions about Dolly's health quietly and took Levin by the arm.

" Well? Shall we go? " he asked. " I'm awfully glad you've come," he added, looking him significantly in the eyes.

" All right, come along," Levin said, beside himself with joy, as he thought of the word " *good-bye* " and the smile that had accompanied it.

" To the Hôtel d'Angleterre or to the Hermitage? "

" I don't mind which."

" Then we'll go to the Hôtel d'Angleterre," Stepan Arkadyevitch said. He had chosen the former because he owed more there than at the Hermitage and therefore considered it his duty to patronise it. " Have you got a cab? So much the better, for I've sent off my carriage."

They did not speak all the way. Levin kept thinking of Kitty and wondering at the change in her manner. First he assured himself that there was hope, the next moment he was in the depths of despair. Nevertheless, he felt that he was another man since he had seen Kitty's smile.

Stepan Arkadyevitch was busy all the time making out the menu for dinner.

" Do you like turbot? " he asked as they were entering the restaurant.

" What? " Levin exclaimed. " Turbot? Yes, I'm awfully fond of turbot."

X

As they entered the restaurant Levin could not help noticing how Stepan Arkadyevitch's face and whole person seemed to shine with suppressed joy. Oblonsky removed his coat and, with his hat on one side, proceeded to the dining-room, where a Tartar, in a frock coat and napkin under his arm, immediately came towards him for orders. He bowed to right and left to his many acquaintances, who were as usual delighted to see him, and walking up to the bar he called for a glass of vodka. He made a few jocular remarks to the French girl sitting at the desk, who burst into a peal of merry laughter. Levin did not join him. The sight of the girl, painted, befrizzled, smothered in lace and ribbons, disgusted him. His heart was filled with longing for Kitty, and his eyes shone with triumph and happiness.

"This way, your excellency, come this way and you will not be disturbed," the old, grey-haired Tartar said to him; the tails of his coat kept flapping about at every movement he made. "This way, your excellency," he said to Levin, feeling it his duty to look after him as Stepan Arkadyevitch's guest. In a twinkling he spread a clean cloth on the table, which, already covered, was standing under the bronze chandelier, and drawing up two upholstered chairs, he placed himself behind Stepan Arkadyevitch with a napkin and card, awaiting orders.

"If your excellency would like a private room, one will be at your service in a few moments. Prince Galitsin is dining with a lady. We have fresh oysters to-day."

"Ah, oysters!" Stepan Arkadyevitch thought a moment.

"Supposing we change our plan, Levin," he said solemnly, with his finger on the bill of fare. "Are the oysters good?"

"They are from Flensburg, your excellency; there are none from Ostend."

"I don't mind where they came from, but are they fresh?"

"We received them only yesterday."

"Then we'll begin with oysters. But how about the rest of the plan, eh? Shall we make a complete change?"

"It makes no difference to me. I should be perfectly content with *slichi* and *kasha*,[1] but I don't suppose they have any here."

[1] *Slichi* is cabbage soup. *Kasha* is some sort of porridge prepared from buck-wheat.

"Would you like *Kasha à la Russe?*" the Tartar asked, bending over Levin as a nurse over a child.

"However, I'll have what you like. Skating has given me an appetite. Don't imagine," he added, "that I won't be pleased with your choice. I shall enjoy a good dinner."

"Of course you will! Say what you like, but eating is one of the nicest pleasures in life. Well," he said, turning to the Tartar, "bring us two or three dozen oysters, vegetable soup . . ."

"*Printanier,*" the Tartar suggested, but Stepan Arkadyevitch did not allow him the pleasure of enumerating the dishes in French. "Vegetable soup, you know the kind," he continued. "Then some turbot with thick sauce, some roast beef, but see that it's well done, some capon, and preserves."

The Tartar, recollecting that Stepan Arkadyevitch did not like to call the dishes by their French names, waited till he had finished, then gave himself the pleasure of repeating the order according to the bill of fare. "*Potage printanier, turbot, sauce Beaumarchais, poularde à l'estragon, macédoine de fruits.*" Then with a quick movement he removed the bill of fare and put the wine list before Stepan Arkadyevitch.

"What shall we drink?"

"Whatever you like, only let us have a little champagne."

"What? At the beginning? But after all, why not? Do you like the white seal?"

"*Cachet blanc,*" the Tartar put in.

"All right. That will go with the oysters."

"Yes, sir, and what other wine shall I bring you?"

"Oh, some *nuit,* but wait a moment, let us have some classic *chablis.*"

"Yes, sir. And cheese, will you have the usual kind?"

"Yes, some *parmesan.* Or do you prefer some other kind?"

"It's all the same to me," Levin replied, scarcely able to contain a smile.

The Tartar dashed away, his coat tails flying out behind him, and returned shortly after with a dish of oysters and a bottle of wine.

Stepan Arkadyevitch unfolded his napkin, tucked it into his waistcoat, and proceeded to attack the oysters. "They're not bad," he remarked as he disposed of them one by one with the aid of a silver fork. "Not at all bad," he repeated, as he glanced from Levin to the Tartar, his eyes gleaming with satisfaction.

Levin ate his oysters, though he would have preferred bread and cheese. He looked at Oblonsky with admiration. Even the Tartar, as he uncorked the bottle and poured the sparkling wine into the thin glasses, gazed at Stepan Arkadyevitch with a smile of pleasure.

"You don't care for oysters? Or are you preoccupied?" Stepan Arkadyevitch asked as he emptied his glass. He was anxious to get Levin into good spirits. The latter, who was not exactly depressed, felt ill at ease. His heart was so full that he felt out of place in that room, amidst the confusion of people coming and going, surrounded by private rooms, where men and women were dining together. Everything was hateful to him, the gas, the bronzes, the mirrors, even the Tartar. He felt that they defiled the love that filled his soul.

"I? Yes, I am rather preoccupied, but apart from that, you can't think how all this annoys me. It seems so barbaric compared to my life in the country, as barbaric as the nails of the man I met in your office. . . ."

"Yes, I noticed how interested you were in poor Grinevitch's nails," Stepan Arkadyevitch said with a laugh.

"I couldn't help it," Levin rejoined. "Try and put yourself in my place, and look at it from the point of view of a person living in the country. There our one object is to get our hands so that we can work with them. For that purpose we cut our nails short and are not afraid to turn up our sleeves. Here you let your nails grow as long as possible, and fasten your cuffs with studs as large as saucers so that you can't do anything with your hands."

Stepan Arkadyevitch laughed gaily.

"It shows that rough toil is not necessary for us; we work with the brain."

"Perhaps, but all the same there is something barbaric about it, just as there is something barbaric about our dinner. In the country we eat merely to satisfy our hunger, in order to make us more fit for work; here you try and prolong your appetite as much as possible, so you eat oysters. . . ."

"Quite so," Stepan Arkadyevitch put in; "to make a pleasure of everything we do seems to me the whole aim and object of civilisation."

"If that's the sole aim of civilisation, then I'd sooner be a savage."

"But you are a savage as it is. All you Levins are savages."

Levin sighed. With a pang he suddenly recollected his

brother Nikolai and frowned. At the next moment, however, Oblonsky spoke of something that made him forget again.

" Well, are you going to our people this evening? I mean the Shcherbatskys," Stepan Arkadyevitch asked, pushing away the dish of empty oyster-shells and taking possession of the cheese.

" Yes, I shall certainly go," Levin replied, " although I was not very pleased with the princess's reception."

" Nonsense! It's only her manner. Let us have the soup," he said, turning to the Tartar. " It's only her manner, *grande dame*," he added. " I shall look in too, but I have to be at the Countess Vinina's this evening. But, really, you are a savage! What on earth made you disappear from Moscow? The Shcherbatskys kept on asking me about you just as if I must know. And all I know is that you always do something that no one else ever does."

" Yes, you're quite right. I am a savage," Levin said quietly. " Not because I went away, but because I've come back. I've come back to . . . "

" Happy man! " Stepan Arkadyevitch exclaimed, looking him straight in the eyes.

" Why? "

" By the steps of your steed you can tell his fine breed and a young man in love by his eyes," Stepan Arkadyevitch said. " You have your future before you."

" And you, have you nothing but the past? "

" No, not only the past. There is the present which is not always very rosy."

" But what is the matter? "

" Oh, nothing much. But I won't talk of myself, particularly as I can't explain the circumstances," Stepan Arkadyevitch added. " Now tell me why you've come back to Moscow. . . . Here, take these things away! " he called to the Tartar.

" Can't you guess? " Levin asked, not taking his eyes off Stepan Arkadyevitch.

" I think I can guess, only I can't bring myself to talk about it first. It may be a sure sign that I've guessed aright," Stepan Arkadyevitch observed with a smile, returning Levin's gaze.

" Well, what have you to say to me? " Levin asked in a tremulous voice, conscious that every muscle of his face was twitching nervously. " What is your opinion? "

Stepan Arkadyevitch finished his wine slowly. " I? " he asked. " Nothing would please me better. It's the best thing that could happen."

" But you're not mistaken? You know what you're talking about? " Levin asked, with a searching look at Oblonsky. " Do you think it possible? "

" Of course it's possible! Why should it not be? "

" But, really, do you mean to say it's possible? Tell me frankly. Supposing I should be refused. I am almost certain . . . "

" What makes you think so? " Stepan Arkadyevitch asked, smiling at his friend's agitation.

" I don't know, I sometimes think so. It would be terrible both for me and for her."

" In any case there would be nothing terrible for her. Every girl likes to be proposed to."

" Yes, every girl, but not Kitty."

Stepan Arkadyevitch smiled. He knew Levin's feeling so well. For him all women were divided into two kinds. The first contained all the women besides her, quite ordinary women, possessed of every human weakness; the second contained only her, who had not a single human fault and was more exalted than any human being.

" I say, you must have some sauce," he said, staying Levin's hand as he was pushing away the dish.

Levin helped himself to some sauce obediently, but would not allow Stepan Arkadyevitch to go on eating.

" Just wait a moment," he said. " You must understand that it's a question of life and death with me. I have never spoken about it to any one, and couldn't speak about it to any one as I can to you. We are almost strangers to one another; we have different tastes, different ideas, but I know you understand and are fond of me; that is why I am so fond of you. So for heaven's sake tell me the truth."

" I tell you exactly what I think," Stepan Arkadyevitch said with a smile. " I'll tell you something more. My wife . . . wonderful woman . . . " Stepan Arkadyevitch sighed, remembering the strained relations between himself and his wife, and continued after a pause. " She has a wonderful intuition, can see through and through people. But that's nothing; she always knows what's going to happen, especially if it has anything to do with weddings. For instance, she always maintained that the Shahovsky girl would marry Brenteln. Everybody pooh-poohed the idea, but it's come off just the same. And she's on your side."

" What do you mean? "

" She says that Kitty is not only in love with you, but that she will be your wife."

A smile of joy lighted up Levin's face at these words. His eyes almost filled with tears.

" Does she say that? " he exclaimed. " I always said that your wife was a dear! However, we mustn't talk about it any more," he added, rising from his chair.

" All right, sit down."

But Levin could not. He walked up and down the room once or twice with a firm step, blinked his eyes very hard to hold back the tears, and only then resumed his seat at the table. " You must understand me," he began; " this is not love. I have been in love, but it was not like this. It is more than a sentiment; it is an inward power that controls me. I left Moscow because I had made up my mind that such happiness was impossible for me, that it was too good for this earth. I've struggled with myself in vain, and have come to the conclusion that without it life is not worth living. It must be decided once and for all. . . . "

" But why did you go away? "

" Oh, stop! How many times have I thought of it? Listen! You can't think what courage your words have given me. I am so happy that I am becoming quite selfish and forgetting everything. Do you know . . . my brother Nikolai is here. . . . I was told this morning . . . and I've forgotten all about him. It seems to me that he must be happy too. But this is like a fit of madness. Still one thing seems terrible to me. You are married and probably know the feeling. It seems terrible to me that we, already getting old, with our past sins . . . should be suddenly brought in close contact with a pure, innocent girl. It's revolting. I feel unworthy of her."

" You have not many sins to reproach yourself with."

" Yes, but all the same," Levin continued, " all the same, as I look at my past life, I am filled with disgust."

" But what can we do? The world is made like that," Stepan Arkadyevitch observed.

" There is only one consolation, and that is in the prayer that I've always loved. ' Pardon me not according to my deserts, but according to Thy mercy.' Thus only can she forgive me."

XI

Levin finished his glass and for a few minutes the two friends were silent.

" There is one thing I ought to tell you," Stepan Arkadyevitch began. " Do you know Vronsky? "

" No; why do you ask? "

" Let us have another bottle," Stepan Arkadyevitch said to the Tartar, who was filling their glasses and fussing generally round the table, particularly when he was not wanted.

" Because Vronsky is a rival of yours."

" But who is this Vronsky? " Levin asked, and his face, which a moment ago had astonished Stepan Arkadyevitch by its youthful enthusiasm, suddenly grew dark.

" He is a son of Count Kirill Ivanovitch Vronsky, and one of the most dashing young men in St. Petersburg society. I came across him at Tver when I was on duty there. He had come with the recruiting service. He is immensely rich, handsome, has influential connections, is an aide-de-camp, has charming manners, and on top of that is a jolly good fellow. And he's more than that too. I've seen a good deal of him here and find him an extremely clever, cultured young man. He'll make a name for himself one of these days."

Levin knit his brows, but did not say anything.

" He appeared in Moscow soon after you left and has fallen head over ears in love with Kitty. Of course, you'll understand, her mother . . . "

" Pardon me, I understand nothing," Levin said with a frown. He suddenly recollected his brother Nikolai, and hated himself for having forgotten him.

" One moment, one moment," Stepan Arkadyevitch went on with a smile, gently putting his hand on Levin's arm. " I've told you everything I know, and I repeat, as far as one can judge of these delicate, intricate matters, the chances are all on your side."

Levin leaned back in his chair. His face was deadly white.

" But I should advise you to settle the matter as soon as possible," Oblonsky continued, filling Levin's glass.

" No, thanks. I won't take any more," the latter said, pushing away his glass; " otherwise I should be drunk. Well, how are you getting on? " he asked, evidently anxious to change the subject.

"Just one more word. Whatever happens I advise to you decide quickly. Don't speak to-night," Stepan Arkadyevitch continued, "but go to-morrow and make a formal proposal. And here's my blessing . . ."

"Do you still want to come to my place for the shooting? Why not come in the spring?" Levin asked. He repented from the bottom of his heart that he had ever opened this conversation. And above all he was most hurt at Stepan Arkadyevitch's advice and insinuations about his pretentious rival.

Stepan Arkadyevitch smiled. He guessed what was passing in Levin's mind.

"I'll run down some time. Well, my dear fellow, take my word for it, woman is the shaft on which the world goes round. My own affairs are bad, very bad. And all because of women. Tell me what you think," he continued, taking out a cigar with one hand and holding his wine-glass in the other, "give me your valuable advice."

"But what about?"

"It's like this. Supposing you were married, and whilst loving your wife, you were attracted to another woman . . ."

"Pardon me, I can't understand that. It seems as if . . . it would be the same as if we left here after a good dinner and stole a loaf of bread from a baker's shop."

Stepan Arkadyevitch's eyes sparkled more than usual.

"Why not? Bread smells so sweet sometimes that you can't resist the temptation.

"'Himmlisch ist's, wenn ich bezwungen
Meine irdische Begier;
Aber doch wenn's nicht gelungen
Hatt' ich auch recht hübsch Plaisir!'"

As he repeated these lines Oblonsky smiled. Levin also could not help smiling.

"But jesting aside, imagine a woman, a poor, dear, affectionate creature, who has given up everything for you. And now that it's all over is one to cast her off? I'll allow that it's necessary to break with her to preserve peace in the family, but can one not feel pity for her, make the parting less painful, arrange for her future?"

"Excuse me. You know that for me women divide themselves into two classes . . . that is . . . to speak more correctly . . . there are women and there are . . . I have never seen, nor ever shall see, a fallen woman that was charming.

They are all like the little painted French girl with the false curls sitting at the desk, and one and all are hateful to me."

"But what about Magdalen in the New Testament?"

"Oh, stop, please! Christ would never have said those words had he known to what use they would be put. People remember them more than they do any others in the whole gospel. However, I am saying not what I think, but what I feel about the matter. Women like those are revolting to me. They give me the sort of creepy feeling that spiders do you. You have probably never studied the habits of spiders, any more than I have studied the habits of these creatures."

"That's all very well. You're just like that person in Dickens who always threw all difficult questions over the right shoulder with the left hand. But to deny a fact is not to answer it. What is one to do? That's what I want to know. Now look at me. My wife is getting old and I can't love her, much as I respect her. Now I'm still a young man, full of life. I meet some one else and it means nothing but ruin. Nothing but ruin!" Stepan Arkadyevitch repeated in despair.

Levin gave a sarcastic smile.

"But what am I to do?" Oblonsky asked.

"Don't steal a new loaf."

Stepan Arkadyevitch burst out laughing. "O moralist! Now here are two women; the one insists on her rights, that is your love, which you can't give her; the other gives you everything and asks for nothing in return. Now what are you to do? How are you to act? It's a tragedy."

"There is no tragedy at all if you want to know my opinion. According to Plato there are two kinds of love, both serving as a touch-stone to men. Some people can feel only the one and some the other. Those who do not understand Platonic love have no right to speak of tragedy. Such love is too superficial for tragedy. Platonic love, on the other hand, can also never end in tragedy, because it is too pure and serene, because . . ."

At this moment Levin recollected all his own shortcomings and the inward struggle that he had undergone.

"But, however, perhaps you're right," he added suddenly. "It is quite possible that I know nothing, absolutely nothing, about it."

"I know you're a man with a purpose in life. It's your one great virtue and fault at the same time. You want all the facts of life to conform to that purpose, but that never happens. You despise the service of the state because it seems to you useless and purposeless. You want every man to work with some purpose, some aim in view. You admit of no compromise even in love and family life. But that's impossible. All the beauty in life consists in subtle differences of light and shade."

Levin sighed, but made no reply. He was buried in his own thoughts and did not listen to Oblonsky. And suddenly they both became conscious that this dinner, which ought to have brought them closer together, had widened the differences between, in spite of their great friendship; that each was absorbed in his own interests; in fact, that there was nothing in common between them. Oblonsky, who had had occasion to experience this sort of thing before, knew exactly what to do under the circumstances.

"My account," he called to the Tartar, and proceeded to the next room where he met an acquaintance with whom he entered into conversation about an actress and her lovers. It was a pleasant change after his talk with Levin, which had proved too great a mental effort for him.

When the Tartar had brought the account, which amounted to twenty-eight roubles and some odd coppers, Levin, who at another time would have been shocked at spending so much on a dinner, paid his share of fourteen roubles without noticing it, and went home to change his clothes for the Shcherbatskys' reception, where his fate was to be decided.

XII

The Princess Kitty Shcherbatsky had reached her eighteenth year. She had come out that winter, and had proved a greater success than either of her two sisters, surpassing all her mother's anticipations. Apart from the fact that nearly all the young men who frequented balls and parties were raving about her, there were two serious aspirants for her hand—Levin and, shortly after his departure, Vronsky.

Levin's appearance at the beginning of the winter, his frequent visits, and his unconcealed love for Kitty, had been the cause of a serious consultation between the prince and princess concerning their daughter's future. The prince was on Levin's side and declared that he could not desire a better match. The princess, on the other hand, with the usual way that women have of avoiding the main issue of a question, insisted that

Kitty was still too young, that Levin did not seem so very serious in his attentions, that Kitty did not seem to care for him, and so on, not wishing to admit that she was far more ambitious for her daughter; that she did not like Levin, whom she could not understand. She was therefore delighted at his sudden departure, and felt that she had gained a point over her husband. When Vronsky appeared on the scene she was still more pleased, and became more than ever convinced that Kitty was destined to make a brilliant match.

For the princess there could be no comparison between Vronsky and Levin. She could never stand the latter's strange views, his awkwardness in society, which she said was merely due to his pride. And then, according to her ideas, he lived like a savage in the country, amongst his cattle and peasants. But what annoyed her most of all was the fact that he had come constantly to their house for the space of six weeks without having spoken, just as if he had considered it too much of an honour. She was relieved when he went away, and congratulated herself that he was not sufficiently attractive for Kitty to have fallen in love with.

Vronsky, on the other hand, satisfied all her requirements. He was rich, clever, distinguished, with a brilliant career before him, a most fascinating man. Nothing better could be desired. Vronsky paid marked attentions to Kitty at balls, danced with her a good deal, came often to their house; there could be no doubt of the seriousness of his attentions. For all that the poor mother had passed a winter full of doubts and anxieties.

The princess herself had been married thirty years ago to a man chosen for her. The hero, about whom everything was known beforehand, had come to inspect her and she had inspected him. Their mutual impressions, which were favourable, were made known to them by a professional match-maker, and on a given day her parents received a formal proposal. It was all so simple and easy; at any rate, that is how it seemed to the princess. In the case of her own daughters, however, it did not seem quite so easy. What fears, perplexities, quarrels with her husband, terrific expenditure she had gone through before she had disposed of her two elder daughters, Dolly and Natalia! Now she had to go through it over again with the younger. And this time her husband was still more difficult to deal with. The old prince, like all fathers, was excessively punctilious about everything that concerned the honour and purity of his daughters. He was absurdly jealous of them, especially of Kitty, who was his favourite, and constantly accused his wife of compromising her. The princess had become accustomed to these differences in the days of her elder daughters, and felt that perhaps this time there was more reason for her husband's strictness. The times had changed and a mother's duties were growing daily more and more difficult. Kitty's contemporaries nearly all belonged to some sort of society, attended lectures, conversed freely with men, walked about the streets unaccompanied, and, what was worst of all, declared that to choose a husband was their own affair and did not concern their parents. "Marriages are no longer made as they used to be," these young girls would say, and find sympathy among some of the older people. "But how are marriages made?" the princess would ask, and no one could give her an answer. The French custom, which allows the parents full liberty to decide the lot of their children, was no longer accepted. The English custom, which allows girls absolute freedom, was impossible in Russian society. The old Russian custom, which arranged marriages through a professional match-maker, was considered obsolete and ridiculed even by the princess herself. But how the thing ought to be done no one knew. "It's high time we put an end to such barbarism," every one would say when the princess chanced to mention the subject. "It's the young people who are to marry and not the parents; let them arrange their own affairs."

It was all very well to talk like that when you had no daughters of your own, but the princess knew that in allowing Kitty full freedom she ran the risk of seeing her daughter full in love with some one who did not wish to marry her, or with some one who was quite unfitted to be her husband. According to her you might just as well allow a five-year-old child to play with a loaded pistol as young people to marry whom they chose. So that Kitty had given her mother a great deal more anxiety than she had had with either of her other daughters.

Just at present her one fear was that Vronsky might not be serious in his intentions. She could see that Kitty was in love with him, and consoled herself by thinking that Vronsky was a man of honour. At the same time she knew that with the present day freedom permitted in society it would be easy for a man to turn a girl's head, and that generally men were none too scrupulous about such things. The week before Kitty had told her mother of a conversation that she had had with Vronsky whilst they were dancing a mazurka, and this conversation partly reassured the princess, though it did not altogether allay her fears. Vronsky told Kitty that he and his brother had got so used to allowing their mother decide things for them, that they never undertook anything serious without first consulting her. " And now," he added, " I am simply longing for my mother's arrival from St. Petersburg."

Kitty had attached no importance to these words, but her mother thought them very significant. She knew that the old lady was expected from day to day, and felt certain that she would approve her son's choice. It seemed strange to her, however, that Vronsky did not propose before his mother's arrival, as though he feared to offend her. She was so keen on the marriage herself that she was ready to believe anything favourable. Bitterly as she felt the unhappiness of her eldest daughter Dolly, who was preparing to leave her husband, she was nevertheless completely absorbed in her youngest daughter's fate. Her meeting with Levin that day was an additional anxiety. She was afraid that Kitty might refuse Vronsky out of respect to the sentiment that she had once felt for Levin, and that generally his appearance on the scene would put difficulties in the way of the thing she most desired.

" When did he arrive? " the princess asked, referring to Levin, as soon as they reached home.

" This morning, *maman*."

" I have just one thing to say to you . . . " the princess began, and by the serious expression of her face Kitty guessed what was coming.

" Mamma! " Kitty burst out, turning towards her, " please, please don't talk about it. I know, I know what you want to say."

She desired what her mother desired, but her mother's motives were repugnant to her.

" I merely wished to say that as you have held out hopes to one . . . "

" Mother, darling, for heaven's sake don't talk about it! It's so terrible."

" Very well," the princess said as she saw the tears gathering in her daughter's eyes. " But, my dear, I want you to promise that you'll never have any secrets from me. Will you? "

" Never, mother. I'll never keep anything secret from you," Kitty replied with a blush, looking her mother straight in the face. " But I've nothing to tell you now. I . . . I . . . even if I wanted . . . I don't know what to say . . . I don't know . . . "

"No, with those eyes she could never speak a falsehood," the mother thought, smiling at her daughter's emotion, happiness, and inexperience.

XIII

KITTY's feelings from dinner until the arrival of the guests might be compared to the feelings of a young soldier just before his first battle. Her heart beat violently and she could not concentrate her thoughts.

She felt that when those two met for the first time her fate would be decided. She pictured them in her imagination, sometimes together, sometimes separately. A sense of pleasure and tenderness filled her heart when she thought of her past relations with Levin. Recollections of her early childhood, of Levin's friendship for her dead brother, invested him with a sort of poetic charm. His love, of which she felt certain, flattered and pleased her. She could think of Levin lightly. On the other hand, she felt uneasy when she thought of Vronsky. There was something false in their relationship for which she blamed herself more than him—he was always natural and charming in his manner. With Levin she was quite herself. But whereas a future with Vronsky seemed to open out a vista of brilliant happiness, with Levin the future seemed enveloped in a mist.

When she went up to her own room to dress she glanced at herself in the mirror and saw that she was looking her best that day. She was perfectly calm and serene, mistress of all her faculties, and quite equal to anything that the evening might have in store for her.

At about half-past seven, as soon as she entered the drawing-room, a footman announced Levin. The princess was still in her room, the prince had not yet come down. "At last!" Kitty thought, and all the blood rushed to her heart. She grew frightened at her own pallor as she glanced at herself in the mirror.

She felt certain that he had come early on purpose to propose to her. And suddenly the situation appeared to her in a strange, new light. It no longer concerned herself alone. It was no longer a question as to which would make her more happy or whom she loved the most. She was about to wound another person who was dear to her, and she would wound him cruelly. But why? Merely because he was so nice and loved her. But there was nothing else to be done.

"Heavens! must I tell him myself?" she thought. "Must I tell him that I don't love him? That wouldn't be true. What shall I say? Should I tell him that I love another? No, that's impossible. I must run away."

She was already at the door when she heard his step. "No, that wouldn't be honourable. There is nothing to be afraid of. I've done nothing wrong. Come what may, I'll speak the truth. I shall not be ill at ease with him. Here he is!" She got a glimpse of his strong figure with his bright eyes fixed timidly upon her. She looked him full in the face as if begging for mercy and extended her hand.

"I've come much too early," he remarked, glancing round the empty room. Now that the moment had come and there was nothing to prevent him from speaking, his face assumed a severe, solemn expression.

"Not at all," Kitty said, sitting down by a little table.

"I did so on purpose, because I wanted to find you alone," he began without sitting down or looking at her, lest he should lose courage.

"Mamma will be down in a moment. She tired herself out yesterday. Yesterday . . ." She did not know what she was saying, and did not remove her imploring, caressing gaze from his face. He looked at her; she blushed and ceased speaking.

"I told you this afternoon that I did not know if I should stay long . . . that it depended on you . . ."

She lowered her head, not knowing what reply she would make to what he was about to say to her.

"It depends on you," he continued. "I wished to tell you . . . to tell you . . . I've come up on purpose . . . because . . . I want you to be my wife!" he got out at last, hardly conscious of what he was saying. Then feeling that the worst was over, he stopped and looked at her.

She was breathing heavily and looking away from him. She felt in the seventh heaven of delight. Her heart was overflowing with happiness. She had never dreamed that he would make such a strong impression on her. She raised her bright, innocent eyes, and seeing the look of agony on his face said hastily—

"I'm sorry . . . it can't be."

How dear and near she had seemed to him a moment ago! And how strange and far away she seemed to him now!

"I knew it couldn't be otherwise," he murmured, without looking at her. He bowed and turned to go out.

XIV

At this moment the princess entered. A look of terror came over her face when she saw that they were alone. Levin bowed, but did not speak. Kitty too was silent and did not raise her eyes. "Thank Heaven she has refused him," the mother thought, glancing at them more closely, and the smile with which she invariably met her guests on Thursdays reappeared on her lips. She sat down and began questioning Levin about his life in the country. He too sat down, hoping to make his escape unobserved when the other guests arrived.

In a short while in came the Countess Nordston, one of Kitty's friends, who had been married the winter before. She was a dried-up, highly-strung little woman, with large, black eyes and a bad complexion. Kitty was very fond of her, and she in her turn adored Kitty, whom she wished to see happily married, according to her own ideas. She had fixed on Vronsky as the man. Levin, whom she had met a good deal at the Shcherbatskys' house during the early part of the winter, she did not like, and always made fun of him on every possible occasion.

"I simply love him to look down on me from his majestic height, or to cut short his lofty conversation because I am too silly to understand him. Or better still, I simply love him to patronise me, condescend . . . I am delighted that he can't stand me," she would say of him.

And she was right. Levin could not endure her, and despised her for the very qualities that she regarded as a merit — her highly-strung temperament, her snobbish contempt and indifference for anything coarse or material.

The relationship between Levin and the Countess Nordston was such as is often met with in society, where two people, friends in all outward appearances, despise each other to such an extent as to admit of no serious intercourse. They could not even get offended with one another.

The Countess Nordston instantly pounced upon Levin as soon as she entered.

"Why, Konstantin Dmitritch! back again to our corrupt Babylon?" she exclaimed, extending her tiny, yellow hand. When she had last seen him Levin had compared Moscow to Babylon. "Well, do you find Babylon better or worse?" she asked, with a mocking smile in Kitty's direction.

"I am greatly flattered, countess, that you keep such an accurate account of my words," Levin replied. He had managed to collect himself, and immediately entered into the facetious, hostile tone that characterised his relations with the Countess Nordston. "They seem to have made a strong impression on you."

"Of course! I make a note of everything you say! Well, Kitty, have you been skating again to-day?" And she began talking to Kitty.

However awkward and unpleasant it would have been for Levin to take his departure now, he would have preferred to do so rather than endure the torture of being near Kitty the whole evening. She glanced at him from time to time, but refused to meet his gaze. He was about to rise when the princess, having noticed his silence, turned to him.

"Do you intend to stay long in Moscow?" she asked. "I hear you are a justice of the peace, and suppose you can't be away for any length of time."

"No, princess, I am no longer a justice of the peace," he replied. "I've only come up for a few days."

"I wonder what's the matter with him," the Countess Nordston thought, as she looked at Levin's stern and serious face. "He doesn't seem to take on, but I'll soon draw him out. It's such fun making him look a fool before Kitty."

"Konstantin Dmitritch," she began, "do tell me what is the matter with our peasants. You're so clever that you know everything. In one of our villages they have drunk up everything they own and won't pay us anything. What is one to do, pray? And you always speak highly of the peasants."

At this moment a lady arrived and Levin stood up.

"Excuse me, countess, I really can't say. I know nothing about it," he replied, taking stock of an officer who came in behind the lady.

"That must be Vronsky," he thought as he looked at Kitty. Kitty in her turn glanced from one to the other. Her eyes lighted up at sight of Vronsky, and in that one glance Levin could see that she loved the man, better than if she had told him in so many words. "I wonder what he's like?" Levin thought, and resolved to stay and find out what sort of a man it was that Kitty loved.

There are some men who fail to see any good qualities in a fortunate rival; whilst others see nothing but the merits that have won him success and go over all his good points with an aching heart. Levin belonged to the latter class. It was not difficult for him to discover what amiable and attractive qualities Vronsky possessed; they were apparent at a glance.

Vronsky was a dark, handsome, well-built man, of middle height, with a wonderfully firm, serene countenance. Everything about him, from his black, closely-cropped hair, his clean shaven chin, to his new, well-fitting uniform, was perfectly simple and elegant. He made way for the lady with whom he had come in, then greeted the princess and approached Kitty. As he drew near to her, his beautiful eyes lighted up tenderly, and with a scarcely perceptible smile, modest, yet triumphant (so it seemed to Levin), he bowed and extended his small, broad hand. Having greeted every one, he sat down without once looking at Levin, who did not take his eyes off him.

" Allow me to introduce you," the princess said, " Konstantin Dmitritch Levin, Count Alexei Kirillitch Vronsky."

Vronsky rose and with a friendly look into Levin's eyes extended his hand.

" I was to have had the honour of dining with you some time ago," he said with his frank and amiable smile, " but you departed for the country."

" Konstantin Dmitritch despises and hates the town and all us Philistines," the Countess Nordston put in.

" I see my words make a strong impression on you, countess," Levin remarked, and recollecting that he had said something like that before he blushed deeply.

Vronsky glanced from one to the other with a smile.

" Do you always live in the country? " he asked. " I think it dull in the winter."

" Not at all when you have an occupation. Besides it's not dull to be by yourself," Levin replied curtly.

" I am very fond of the country," Vronsky observed, noticing Levin's peculiar tone and pretending not to do so.

" I hope, my dear count, that you are not proposing to bury yourself in the country," the Countess Nordston remarked.

" I don't know. I've never stayed in the country for long at a time. But I've got far more bored during a winter in Nice than I've ever been in a Russian village among our peasants.

Nice is a most boring place, and Naples and Sorrento are only pleasant for a short time. You soon get to long for Russia, especially for the country. They are so . . ."

He said just what came into his head, turning from Kitty to Levin with his friendly, caressing glance. Noticing that the Countess Nordston wished to say something, he stopped and listened to her attentively.

The conversation did not lag for a single instant. The princess had no need of bringing forward her two stock subjects of conversation reverted to at difficult moments, about classic and realist education or the general condition of military service, and the countess did not get a single opportunity of teasing Levin. The latter wanted to join in the conversation, but could not. He kept telling himself that he must go, yet stayed on as though expecting something.

After a time they began to talk about spiritualism and table-rapping, and the Countess Nordston, who was a spiritualist, told them of some wonderful apparition that she had seen.

"My dear countess, do take me with you the next time you go!" Vronsky exclaimed with a smile. "I have never been able to see anything, though I've tried ever so many times."

"All right, you can come next Saturday. Do you believe in spiritualism, Konstantin Dmitritch?" she asked, turning to Levin.

"My dear countess, why do you ask? You know exactly what I shall say."

"But I want to hear your opinion."

"Then I think, countess, that all this table-rapping merely shows that our cultured classes are no better than our peasants. They believe in the evil eye, in witchcraft, magic, and we . . ."

"Then you don't believe?"

"I can't believe, countess."

"But I have seen things with my own eyes . . ."

"Peasant women declare that they see hob-goblins."

"So you think I am not speaking the truth?" she asked, laughing gaily.

"No, Masha, Konstantin Dmitritch merely said that he can't believe in spiritualism," Kitty remonstrated with a blush. Levin saw the blush and knew that she was interceding for him. It angered him the more, and he was just about to make some reply when Vronsky, with his habitual smile, seeing that the conversation had taken a dangerous turn, came to their aid.

"But don't you think there might be something in it?" he

asked. " For instance, we admit the existence of electricity, though we know nothing about it. Might there not be another new force as yet unknown to us, which . . . "

" When electricity was discovered," Levin interrupted him, " we knew only its phenomena and did not know what produced or where it came from. Centuries passed before people dreamt of making any practical use of it. On the other hand, your spiritualists began by making tables write and spirits come out of them, and only afterwards thought of explaining it by reference to some unknown force."

Vronsky listened attentively, evidently interested in what Levin was saying.

" Spiritualists merely say that they don't know what the force is, but that there is a force, which acts under certain conditions. You must get your learned men to find out what it is. I really cannot see why there should not be a new force, if it . . . "

" Because," Levin interrupted him again, " in electricity, when you rub a piece of resin against anything woollen you invariably produce a certain electrical action, and in spiritualism your results do not always come off. Consequently you cannot regard it as a natural phenomenon."

Perceiving that the conversation had taken too serious a turn for the occasion, Vronsky made no reply. He attempted to change the subject, and turned to the ladies with a smile.

" Supposing we try now, countess," he began, but Levin, who was anxious to explain himself, went on.

" I think it a great mistake," he said, " for you spiritualists to attribute your wonders to some new force. You talk of a spiritual force, and yet you submit it to a material test." He felt that they were all waiting for him to finish.

" I think you would make a most excellent medium," the Countess Nordston remarked. " There is something so enthusiastic about you."

Levin was about to make some reply, but blushed and held his peace.

" May we experiment with your tables, princess? " Vronsky asked, and stood up searching around for one.

Kitty was standing near a little table, and on passing Levin her eyes met his. She pitied him from the bottom of her heart and blamed herself for his unhappiness. " Forgive me," her eyes seemed to say, " I feel so happy."

" I hate myself and you and everybody," his glance seemed

to answer as he looked around for his hat. But he was not yet destined to make his escape.

As they were arranging the tables the old prince came in, and after greeting the ladies he turned to Levin.

"What a surprise!" he exclaimed. "Delighted to see you. I did not know you were here. How long since you came?"

He embraced Levin and continued talking to him, paying no heed to Vronsky. The latter stood waiting quietly until the prince should turn to him.

Kitty felt that her father's friendliness must seem hard to Levin after what had happened. She noticed too that her father greeted Vronsky very coldly and that Vronsky wondered at his coldness, and she blushed.

"Prince, do return Konstantin Dmitritch to us," the Countess Nordston implored. "We want to make some experiments."

"What experiments? You are not going to turn tables upside down? Really, you must excuse me, ladies and gentlemen, but I think playing at forfeits is much more amusing," he said with a glance at Vronsky, as though he felt him responsible for the arrangement. "There is some sense in forfeits."

Vronsky turned to the prince with a look of amazement, and with a scarcely perceptible smile he began talking to the Countess Nordston about some ball that was to take place the following week.

"Shall you be there?" he asked, turning to Kitty.

As soon as the old prince turned away from him, Levin slipped out unobserved. The last impression of the evening that he carried away with him was Kitty's happy, smiling face as she was replying to Vronsky's question about the ball.

XV

WHEN the guests had all departed, Kitty told her mother about the conversation with Levin. Notwithstanding the fact that she pitied him, the idea that he had proposed to marry her flattered her vanity. She felt that she had nothing to reproach herself with, yet it was long before she could get to sleep that night. She was haunted by Levin's sad face, as he stood talking to her father and casting a look at her and Vronsky every now and again with those kind, friendly eyes of his. To get rid of the impression she tried to think of Vronsky. She pictured him with his strong, manly face and calm dignity, that every one liked so about him, and tried to think how he loved her and how she loved him. Gladness filled her soul. She sank back on the pillow with a sigh of satisfaction. " But how sad! how sad! " she exclaimed when she thought of Levin. " What could I do? It was not my fault." Thus she tried to console herself, but an inner voice gave her no peace. She did not know whether she should reproach herself for having been attracted to Levin or for having refused him.

Her happiness was marred by doubts. " Heaven have mercy on me! Heaven have mercy on me! " she kept on repeating to herself until she fell asleep.

Meanwhile one of those scenes was taking place below in the prince's little study that frequently occurred between the parents over their favourite daughter.

" What? " the prince shouted, as he wrapped himself in his squirrel dressing-gown. " You want to know why? You have no sense of pride or dignity. You bring your daughter to shame by the vulgar way in which you go about hunting for a husband for her! "

" For Heaven's sake tell me what I've done," the princess implored, almost in tears.

She had just left her daughter, and feeling happy and contented had gone in to say good-night to her husband as usual, with the fixed intention of not mentioning Kitty's refusal of Levin. She could not, however, resist throwing out one or two hints that she considered her engagement to Vronsky almost as settled, and that everything would come right when his mother arrived. At these words the prince suddenly flared up and began showering abuse upon her.

" What have you done? In the first place, you have been enticing a young man to the house and all Moscow will be talking about it. And with reason too. If you want to give 'at homes' then invite everybody. Let them all come, all these young fops. Get some one to play and let them dance, but don't throw your daughter at them. It's revolting to me to see how you've turned the poor girl's head. Levin is worth a thousand of them. As for this St. Petersburg fop who looks as if he were turned out of a machine, he's no good I tell you. Even if he were a prince of the blood there is no reason why my daughter should run after him."

" But what have I done? "

" You have . . . " the prince began again angrily.

"If I listened to you," the princess interrupted him, "we should never get Kitty married at all, and in that case we might just as well go into the country."

"It would be far better if we went."

"Now is it my fault? Have I done anything? A nice young man falls in love with our daughter, and she seems . . ."

"Yes, seems! What if she were to fall in love with him in real earnest and he not have any more intention of marrying than I have? That we should have come to this! 'Ah, spiritualism! ah, Nice! ah, the ball!'" Here the prince, attempting to imitate his wife, made a courtesy at every word. "And when we have made our Kitty unhappy, when we have completely turned her head . . ."

"But what makes you think so?"

"I don't think, I know. I've got eyes to see with if you haven't. I see one man who has serious intentions—that's Levin—and then I see this conceited peacock who only wants to amuse himself."

"What ideas you get into your head."

"You'll see when it's too late, just as with Dolly . . ."

"Very well, don't let us talk about it any more," the princess interrupted him hastily, recollecting her unfortunate daughter Dolly.

"That's right. Good-night."

The husband and wife kissed and made the sign of the cross over each other and separated, but each was firmly convinced that the other was wrong, and held fast to their own opinion.

Although the princess was convinced that there could be no doubt of the seriousness of Vronsky's intentions, yet her husband's words had alarmed her. When she got to her own room she was seized with terror at what the future might have in store for her, and prayed from the bottom of her heart as Kitty had done. "Lord have mercy, Lord have mercy," she repeated again and again.

XVI

VRONSKY had never been accustomed to an orderly family life. His mother, who had been a brilliant, handsome woman in her youth, was famous in society for her many romances, and his father had died when he was too young to remember him.

When, as a brilliant young officer, he left the corps of pages, where he had been educated, he soon fell into the same rut followed by all other rich St. Petersburg army men. Though he occasionally went into society, yet all his love interests were outside of it.

After several years of a luxurious, dissipated life in St. Petersburg, it was in Moscow where he was for the first time brought in contact with a charming, innocent girl of his own class, who, judging by all appearances, was in love with him. It never entered his head that there was anything wrong in his relationship with Kitty. At balls he preferred to dance with her; he frequently called upon her; he talked the usual society nonsense to her, but instinctively gave a significant meaning to every word he said. Although he said nothing that might not have been heard by all, it yet established a sort of bond between them, which grew closer day by day. He did not dream that there was anything dishonourable in his relations with Kitty, nor that such conduct as his, common to men of his kind, was very much condemned in society. He merely imagined that he had discovered a new pleasure, and gave himself up to the enjoyment of it.

Could he have heard the quarrel between her parents that evening, or been told that Kitty would be very unhappy if he did not marry her, he would have been extremely surprised. He could not have believed that a relationship so pleasant to both of them could possibly be bad, or that it involved any obligation to marry.

Marriage had no attractions for him. He did not like family life. According to the opinion current in the bachelor circle in which he moved, there was something extremely prosaic and ridiculous about it, especially about the husband.

But although Vronsky had no idea of the conversation between the parents when he left the Shcherbatskys' house that evening, he nevertheless felt that the mysterious bond between himself and Kitty had grown stronger than ever, and that he really must do something. But exactly what it was he had not the remotest idea.

" What is so charming," he thought, as he left the Shcherbatskys' house, carrying away with him, as he always did, a feeling of freshness and purity, due to the fact perhaps that he had not smoked the whole evening, and also to a new sensation of tenderness caused by her love for him, " what is so charming about it all is the fact that neither of us have said anything, and yet we understand each other so perfectly. By her look and tone I can tell that she loves me, better than if she had told me so. What a dear, trusting little thing she is! It makes me feel a better man. What lovely, caressing eyes she has! How sweet she looked when she spoke. . . . What is to come of it? Why nothing. It is pleasant for me and pleasant for her." And he tried to think how he could best finish up the evening.

"What about the club for a game of bezique and a bottle of champagne with Ignatov?" he thought. "No, not there. There's the *Château des Fleurs* where I could find Oblonsky. There's sure to be dancing and singing. No, I'm sick of them. That's just why I love the Shcherbatskys'. I feel better when I've been there. I think I'll go home."

He went straight to his rooms at Dusseaux's, ordered supper, after which he undressed, and had scarcely laid his head on the pillow when he was sound asleep.

XVII

At about eleven o'clock on the following morning when Vronsky went down to the station to meet his mother the first person he met was Oblonsky, who had come to meet his sister by the very same train.

"Ah! your excellency!" Oblonsky exclaimed. "What are you doing here?"

"I've come to meet my mother," Vronsky replied with a smile, shaking hands. "She is expected from St. Petersburg to-day." They ascended the stairs together.

"I waited for you until two o'clock last night. What did you do after you left the Shcherbatskys'?"

"I went home," Vronsky replied. "To tell you the truth, it was so nice at the Shcherbatskys' that I didn't feel like going anywhere else afterwards."

"By the step of your steed you can tell its fine breed, and a young man in love by his eyes," Stepan Arkadyevitch said, just as he had done to Levin.

Vronsky smiled, as much as to say that he did not deny it, but hastened to change the subject.

"And whom are you meeting?" he asked.

"A very pretty woman!" Oblonsky replied.

"I say!"

"*Honi soit qui mal y pense!* My sister Anna."

"Madame Karenina?" Vronsky asked.

"Do you know her?"

"I think I do. But no . . . I really don't know," Vronsky said absent-mindedly. The name Karenina suggested some tiresome, affected person.

"You know my distinguished brother-in-law, Alexei Alexandrovitch, no doubt? The whole world knows him."

"I know him by sight and have heard of him. People say he's very clever, learned, and rather pious. But you know that's not . . . not in my line," Vronsky concluded in English.

"Yes, he's a most remarkable man. Rather conservative, but a very good sort," Stepan Arkadyevitch remarked. "A really good sort."

"So much the better for him," Vronsky observed with a smile. "Are you here?" he asked, catching sight of his mother's old footman standing by the door. "Come here."

Vronsky had of late become even more attached to Oblonsky than he had been before. Besides the pleasure that most people felt in his society, there was the additional pleasure that he was connected with Kitty.

"What do you say to giving the prodigy a supper on Sunday night?" he asked with a smile, taking his arm.

"By all means. I'll collect the subscriptions. By the way, did you meet my friend Levin last night?" Stepan Arkadyevitch asked.

"Yes, but he went away early."

"He's a fine fellow," Oblonsky continued, "isn't he?"

"I can't make out," Vronsky began, "why you Moscovites—of course, present company excepted," he added with a smile—"are all so bitter. You're always on the war path, as if you want to make one understand . . ."

"That is true enough," Stepan Arkadyevitch said with a laugh.

"Is the train due yet?" Vronsky asked of a porter.

"In a few minutes," the porter replied.

The station was soon in an uproar. Porters and policemen were running to and fro, jostling against people who had come to meet their friends. Workmen in short coats and soft felt boots were passing backwards and forwards over the rails. A shrill whistle announced the approaching train, and the sound of a terrific rumbling could be heard in the distance.

"No," Stepan Arkadyevitch continued, who was anxious to

inform Vronsky of Levin's intentions in regard to Kitty, " no, I don't think you quite appreciate my friend Levin. He is a very excitable man and says unpleasant things sometimes, but is really very nice. He has a staunch, upright nature, and a heart of gold. Last night there was a special reason why he should have been either very happy or very unhappy," he added with a significant smile, quite forgetting his former sympathy to Levin in his present sympathy to Vronsky.

" Do you mean that he proposed to your *belle sœur ?* " Vronsky asked, stopping short.

" He might have done," Stepan Arkadyevitch replied. " But if you say that he left early and was out of sorts, then . . . He's been in love with her for so long that I feel quite sorry for him."

" Really! I should have thought that she could have made a better match," Vronsky remarked, and drawing himself up he began walking up and down again. " But, however, I don't know him," he added. " Yes, it's a difficult position I admit. That's why the majority of us prefer our Claras. Their only care is if we have money enough, and the others weigh our merits in the balance as well. But here comes the train."

A shrill whistle could be heard, and the train came puffing along, driving the steam before it, condensed by the frosty air. Slowly and rhythmically the connecting rod of the big wheel rose and fell as the engine drew near the platform. First came the luggage-van, out of which the barking of a dog could be heard; then came the carriages with the passengers, and with one big jolt the train drew to a standstill.

A smart conductor blew a whistle and leapt on to the platform. Soon after him the passengers came pouring out one by one, an officer of the guard who held himself erect and looked around severely, a smiling merchant carrying a bag, a peasant with a sack over his shoulder. . . .

Vronsky, who was standing beside Oblonsky, gazed at the carriages and passengers vacantly, completely forgetting about his mother. What he had just heard about Kitty had pleased and excited him. He drew himself up involuntarily, his eyes sparkled, he felt like a conqueror.

" The Countess Vronsky is in that carriage," the smart conductor said, approaching him.

He started, recollecting what he had come for. In the bottom of his heart he did not respect his mother, and, without confessing as much to himself, did not love her. But he would not have permitted himself to treat her with any but the greatest respect and consideration, a thing that both his education and custom demanded of him. It did not, however, alter his feelings towards her.

XVIII

VRONSKY followed the conductor to his mother's carriage. As he was about to enter a lady came out, so he stood aside to let her pass.

A single glance at the lady made him feel by the instinct of a man of the world that she belonged to the best society. He begged her pardon and was about to enter when he was seized by an unconquerable desire to look at her again, not because of her beauty, her grace, her elegance, but because of a certain caressing, tender expression in her lovely face.

She also turned her head as he looked at her. With her bright, grey eyes, that seemed dark under her thick, long lashes, she gave him a searching, friendly look, as though recognising him, then turned, casting about for some one in the crowd. In that short glance Vronsky was struck by the peculiarly restrained, vivacious expression of her face, her sparkling eyes, and the scarcely perceptible smile that played about her rosy lips. She seemed overflowing with radiance, which against her will shone out in her glance, her smile. The light in her eyes that she tried to hide gleamed out in the splendour of that smile.

Vronsky entered the carriage. His mother, a little dried-up old lady, with dark eyes and grey curls, greeted him with a smile on her thin lips. She stood up, and handing her maid a small bag, she extended her shrivelled hand for her son to kiss, then taking his head in both her hands she kissed him on the cheek.

"Did you get my telegram? Are you quite well? Thank God."

"What sort of a journey did you have?" Vronsky asked, sitting down beside her, yet listening to the sound of a woman's voice that reached him from outside. He felt certain it was the voice of the lady he had met at the door.

"I don't agree with you," the voice was saying.

"That's your St. Petersburg taste, madame."

"Not at all, simply a woman's taste," she replied.

"Never mind; allow me to kiss your hand."

"Good-bye, Ivan Petrovitch. If you should happen to see

my brother, please send him to me," the lady said as she entered the door of the carriage.

Vronsky guessed that she must be Madame Karenina.

" Your brother is on the platform, madame," he said, rising. " Pardon me, I did not recognise you. Our acquaintance has been such a short one though," he added, bowing low, " that I fear you will not remember me."

" Oh, yes I do. Your mother and I have been talking about you all the way," she said, smiling sweetly. " I wonder where my brother is? "

" Go and find him, Alyosha," the old countess said.

" Oblonsky! here! " Vronsky called, as he stepped on to the platform.

Madame Karenina suddenly caught sight of her brother and rushed out to meet him. As soon as he approached her, with a quick movement, which struck Vronsky by its boldness and grace, she threw her arms around her brother's neck, and drawing him towards her, kissed him on the lips. Vronsky, who did not take his eyes off her, smiled involuntarily, but recollecting that his mother awaited him, he went back to the carriage.

" Isn't she charming? " the countess remarked, referring to Madame Karenina. " I was delighted when her husband put her in my carriage. We've been chatting all the way. Well, and how are you? I've heard . . . *vous filez le parfait amour. Tant mieux, mon cher, tant mieux.*"

" I don't know what you're referring to, *maman*," Vronsky remarked coldly. " Come, let us go."

Madame Karenina came in again to say good-bye to the countess.

" Well, countess, at last you've got your son and I've got my brother," she began gaily. " I had come to the end of all my stories. Had the journey lasted much longer I should have had nothing more to tell you."

" My dear," the countess said, taking her hand, " I could travel round the world with you without a dull moment. You are one of those rare women with whom it is pleasant to talk or be silent. Now don't be worrying about your boy; it's impossible to be always with him."

Madame Karenina was standing erect with a smile lurking in her wonderful eyes.

" Anna Arkadyevna has a boy eight years old," the countess explained, turning to her son. " This is the first time she has ever been parted from him, and it worries her."

"We kept talking about our respective sons all the way, I of mine and the countess of hers," Madame Karenina remarked, and again a smile spread over her face, a caressing smile, meant in some way for him.

"It must have been awfully boring for you," he said, seizing upon the coquettish tone that she had introduced.

"Thank you so much," she said, turning to the countess, evidently not wishing to continue in that strain. "The time flew so quickly yesterday. Good-bye, countess."

"Good-bye, my dear," the countess said. "You must let me kiss that pretty face of yours. I've simply fallen in love with you, if you don't mind an old woman saying so."

Whether the countess meant what she said or not, Madame Karenina was touched. She blushed, bent down slightly, and brought her face within reach of the countess' lips; then she raised herself, and with the same smile playing about her eyes and lips, she extended her hand to Vronsky. He took the tiny little hand held out to him, and was delighted to feel its firm, frank pressure in response to his own. She walked out with a light, rapid step.

"Isn't she charming!" the countess exclaimed as soon as she had gone.

Her son was of the same opinion. He stood watching her until her graceful figure was hidden from view, and a smile spread over his handsome face. He could see how she approached her brother and, taking his arm, entered into some lively conversation with him. It vexed Vronsky to think that he had no connection with it.

"Well, and how are you, *maman?*" he asked a second time, turning towards her.

"Very well, thanks. Alexander is such a dear and Marie is improving lately. She is getting so interesting."

And she proceeded to tell him of her grandson's christening, an occasion that had taken her to St. Petersburg, and how well her eldest son had been received at court.

"Here comes Lavrenty," Vronsky observed, "let us go now if you're ready."

An old footman came to announce that everything was ready, and the countess got up to go.

"Come along, *maman*, there are not many people about now," Vronsky said.

Her maid took possession of her little pet dog and a small bag, the footman and a porter of the rest of the luggage. Vronsky

took his mother's arm and led her out, but they had scarcely taken a few steps up the platform when several people rushed past them in a state of alarm. The station master in his strange coloured cap also came rushing up. Evidently some accident had happened. All the passengers who were still about hastened back to see what it was.

"What's the matter? What's the matter? Where? Did he throw himself under? Was he run over?" people were asking excitedly.

Stepan Arkadyevitch, arm in arm with his sister, also came back and stood at the door of the carriage to avoid the crowd. They both looked terrified.

Vronsky put the two ladies into the carriage and went with Stepan Arkadyevitch to find out what had happened.

The guard, either because he was drunk, or because his ears were so muffled up from the intense cold that he could not hear the train shunting back, had been run over.

The ladies had learnt all the details from the footman before Vronsky and Oblonsky came back. Oblonsky was very much upset and almost on the verge of tears. They had both seen the mangled form.

"Oh, it's terrible! You should have seen it, Anna! It's terrible!" he kept on repeating.

Vronsky was silent. There was a solemn expression on his calm, handsome face.

"You should have seen it, countess," Stepan Arkadyevitch repeated, turning to her. "His wife was there. . . . It was terrible to look at her. . . . She threw herself on the body. They say he had a large family dependent on him. How terrible!"

"Can't something be done for her?" Madame Karenina whispered in an agitated voice.

Vronsky glanced at her and immediately left the carriage.

"I shan't be long, *maman*," he said at the door.

When he got back a few moments later Stepan Arkadyevitch and the countess were discussing some new singer, while the countess kept looking impatiently towards the door for her son to appear.

"We can go now," Vronsky said as he entered.

They all went out together, Vronsky and his mother walking in front, Stepan Arkadyevitch and his sister behind them. At the door the station master overtook them.

"You have given my assistant two hundred roubles," he said,

turning to Vronsky. " Will you kindly tell us how we are to dispose of them? "

" I meant them for the widow, of course," Vronsky replied, shrugging his shoulders. " There was hardly any necessity to ask."

" Did you give as much as that? " Oblonsky asked. " How nice of him! " he said, pressing his sister's arm. " Isn't he splendid? Good-bye, countess."

He waited while his sister was looking for her maid, and when they at last left the station the Vronskys' carriage had already departed. Everybody leaving the station was talking about the accident.

" What an awful death! " one man was heard to say. " They say he was cut in half."

" Not really so bad when you think of it. It was so instantaneous," another remarked.

" I wonder they're not more cautious," said a third.

Madame Karenina took her seat in the carriage while her brother observed with astonishment that her lips were trembling and the tears were gathering in her eyes.

" What is the matter, Anna dear? " Stepan Arkadyevitch asked as the carriage started.

" It's a bad omen," she replied.

" What nonsense! " he exclaimed. " You've arrived safely, that's the main thing. You can't imagine how I've been looking forward to your coming. I have such hopes in you."

" Have you known Vronsky long? " she asked.

" For some time. Do you know? We think he's going to marry Kitty."

" Really? " she asked softly. " Well, now let us talk about yourself," she added, shaking her head as if trying to rid herself of some oppressive sensation. " Now tell me about your affairs. I got your letter and here I am."

" You are my only hope," Stepan Arkadyevitch observed.

" Well, tell me everything."

Stepan Arkadyevitch began telling her the whole story.

When they reached home, he helped her out of the carriage, took leave of her with a sigh, and departed for his office.

XIX

When Anna entered, Dolly was sitting in the smaller drawing-room listening to a fair, chubby boy, the very image of his father, who was learning a lesson out of a French reading-book. The boy was reading aloud and fingering a button on his coat that was hanging loose on a thread. The mother stopped him several times, but each time the chubby little hand again found its way back to the button. At last she cut it off and put it in her pocket.

"Keep your hands still, Grisha," she said, taking up a bed-cover that she was making. It was an old piece of work that she was in the habit of attacking at difficult moments. Her fingers moved nervously as she counted the stitches. Though she had told her husband that his sister's coming in no way concerned her, she had still made every preparation for her arrival and now sat waiting for her impatiently.

Dolly was completely overcome by her grief, but she could not help remembering that Anna was the wife of a highly influential St. Petersburg personage—a St. Petersburg *grande dame*. "Besides, it's not Anna's fault," she thought. "I know nothing but good of her, and she's always been very nice to me." It is true she had not been favourably impressed with the Karenins when she had stayed with them in St. Petersburg. She did not like their house, and there seemed something unnatural about their family life. "But why should I not receive her? I only hope she doesn't take it into her head to console me!" Dolly thought. "I know what all these Christian consolations and exhortations mean. I've gone over them again and again, but they are utterly futile."

The last few days Dolly had spent alone with the children. She did not wish to talk of her sorrow to any one, and could not bring herself to talk of indifferent things while that was eating away at her heart. She knew that sooner or later she would tell Anna everything. She felt glad that at last she would be able to unburden herself to some one, but hated the idea of having to speak of her humiliations to his sister. She dreaded to hear the conventional phrases of sympathy that Anna might have prepared for her.

She sat there watching the clock, expecting her sister-in-law every moment, but as often happens in such cases, she became so absorbed in her thoughts that she did not hear the door-bell ring.

The light rustle of a dress coming from the other side of the door made her start, and an expression of surprise instead of pleasure appeared on her wan, haggard face.

" Have you come already? " she asked, embracing her sister-in-law.

" Dolly! I am so glad to see you! "

" And I am glad to see you," Dolly replied with a faint smile. She tried to guess by Anna's expression whether she had been told or not. " I think she knows," Dolly thought, observing the look of compassion on Anna's face. " Come along, I'll take you to your room," she added, anxious to put off the moment for explanations.

" Is this Grisha? How he's grown! " she exclaimed, kissing him without taking her eyes off Dolly, who blushed a deep red. " Let us stay here, if you don't mind."

She took off her hat and scarf and began arranging her thick, black hair.

" How well you look! " Dolly exclaimed, with a touch of envy in her voice.

" Do I? " Anna asked. " Heavens! is that Tania? " she exclaimed, turning to a little girl who had just run in. " She must be the same age as my Serioja." She took the little girl by the hand and kissed her. " What a sweet child! Do let me see the rest."

She could remember all their names, respective ages, all their characteristics, and even all their little ailments. Dolly could not help being touched.

" Come into the nursery," she said. " It's a pity that Vassia is asleep."

After they had seen the children they came back to the drawing-room, where coffee was awaiting them. Anna drew the tray towards her, then pushed it away again.

" Dolly! " she said, " he told me everything."

Dolly gazed at her coldly, expecting some expression of feigned sympathy, but Anna said nothing of the kind.

" Dolly, dear! " she continued, " I don't want to intercede for him, or try to console you; I know it's impossible. I just feel so sorry for you, you poor darling, sorry from the bottom of my heart."

The tears could be seen glistening under her long, thick lashes. She drew nearer to her sister-in-law, and taking her hand, pressed it firmly in her own. Dolly made no resistance, but the cold, severe expression did not leave her face.

" It's impossible for me to be consoled after what has happened," she said; " everything is now over, lost! "

As she said these words her face softened. Anna raised her shrivelled, cold hand to her lips.

" But, Dolly, what is to be done? What is to be done? " she repeated. " How can you get out of this frightful position? We must think it over."

" All is over; there is nothing to be done," Dolly said. " The worst of it is that I can't leave him because of the children. I'm simply tied hand and foot. And I can't live with him; it's torture for me to see him."

" Dolly, darling, tell me all about it," Anna implored. " He told me, but I want to hear everything from you."

Dolly gave her a searching glance. Anna's face was full of love and sympathy.

" Very well," she said, " but I must begin from the beginning. You know how I was married. With the education *maman* had given me I was not only ignorant; I was a perfect fool. I knew absolutely nothing. People say that husbands always tell their wives about their past, but Stiva . . . Stepan Arkadyevitch," she corrected herself, " told me nothing. You may not believe me, but until this happened I thought I was the only woman he had ever loved. That's how I lived with him for eight years. It would never have entered my head to suspect that he was unfaithful; I thought it impossible. You can imagine my feelings when I suddenly discovered all the horror, the disgust. . . . Put yourself in my place. To take your happiness for granted and suddenly . . . " Dolly continued, trying to hold back her sobs, " and suddenly this letter from his mistress, my own governess. It's too awful! " She hastily drew out her pocket-handkerchief and covered her face. " I could have forgiven a moment of temptation," she continued after a pause, " but to go on deceiving me, lying to me . . . and for whom? To continue living with me and her at the same time . . . it's frightful! You can't understand . . . "

" Oh, yes I do. I quite understand, Dolly, dear," Anna said, stroking her hand.

" And do you think he appreciates the horror of my position? " Dolly continued. " Not a bit; he is perfectly happy and contented."

" Oh, no! " Anna interrupted her warmly, " he is full of grief and remorse. . . . "

" Do you think he can feel remorse? " Dolly asked, with a searching look into Anna's face.

" Yes; I know him well. I could not help feeling sorry for him. You know him too. He so kind, but he's very proud, and now he feels humiliated. What touched me most " (Anna knew that this would touch Dolly too) " was the fact that he was so concerned about the children and you . . . because while loving you . . . yes, yes, he loves you more than any one in the world," she added vehemently to prevent Dolly from interrupting her, " he has made you suffer, has almost killed you. He thinks you will never forgive him."

Dolly sat looking pensively before her, listening to Anna's words.

" Yes, I admit his position must be dreadful. In a way, it is worse for the guilty than the innocent," she said, " that is, if he admits his guilt. But how can I possibly forgive him? How can I live with him again as his wife after her? It would be torture for me. My former love for him is still dear to me." Her sobs prevented her from speaking.

As soon as she felt herself softening towards him, as if on purpose she began talking of the thing that hurt her most.

" She is young and pretty, you see," she continued. " And I? But for whom have I sacrificed my youth and beauty? For him and his children. I have served my day; I have given him all that I had, and now he has cast me off for some one younger and fresher. They have probably discussed me between them, or worse still, were silent. . . . " A look of hatred came into her eyes. " And after this he will tell me . . . How shall I ever believe him again? I couldn't. It is all over, gone. Everything that gave me recompense for my suffering and pain. I've just been giving Grisha a lesson, and, would you believe it? it used to be such a joy to me before, but I couldn't bear it now. What is the use of working? Why have I children? It's terrible to think that my love for him should have turned to hate. Yes, hate. I could kill him, I . . . "

" Dolly, dear, don't torment yourself. You feel so insulted and outraged that you don't see things clearly."

Dolly grew calmer, and for a few moments the two were silent.

" But what am I to do, Anna? Help me. I've thought of everything, and cannot see a way out."

Anna could think of nothing, but her heart went out to her sister-in-law.

" I may say one thing," Anna began. " I am his sister and know him so well. His capacity for forgetting everything " (she touched her forehead) " sometimes leads him to give way to temptation, but he is always filled with remorse afterwards. He can't believe or understand now how he could ever have done what he did."

" Oh, yes he can! " Dolly interrupted her. " But I . . . you quite forget me . . . is it easier for me? "

" One moment. When he first told me I must confess I did not realise all the horror of your position. I felt sorry for him and my first thoughts were of the family, but now that I've spoken to you, as a woman, I see things differently. I can see how you suffer, and I can't tell you how sorry I feel for you! But, Dolly, dear, there is one thing I don't understand about you. I don't know . . . I don't know . . . if you still love him. You only know if you love him enough to forgive him. If you do, forgive him, Dolly."

" Never! " Dolly exclaimed. Anna kissed her hand and would not allow her to go on.

" I know the world better than you do," she said. " I know how men like Stiva look at these things. You were afraid he discussed you with her, but, believe me, he did no such thing. These men may be unfaithful, but their homes and their wives are always sacred to them. They despise these women and draw a line of demarcation between them and their families that is never crossed. I cannot understand how it is, but it is so."

" Yes, but he has kissed her . . . "

" Listen, Dolly, dear. I saw Stiva when he was in love with you. I remember the time when he used to come to me and talk about you with tears in his eyes. You were a being of a higher world to him, and I know the longer he lived with you the more he admired you. We used to laugh at the way he raved about you. You were like some goddess in his eyes. I know he loves you yet, and this temptation has in no way touched his heart. . . . "

" But supposing it should occur again? "

" I don't think it will."

" That's all very well, but could you have forgiven him? "

" I don't know, I can't tell. . . . Yes, I can though," she added after a moment's consideration. " I should have forgiven him. I could not have been the same again afterwards, but I should have forgiven him in such a way as to show that the past was forgotten, wiped out."

"Of course," Dolly interrupted her, as though Anna had given expression to her own thoughts; "otherwise it would not be forgiveness. If you forgive, it must be absolutely, absolutely. Now let me take you to your room," she said, rising and embracing her. "My dear, how glad I am that you came! I feel as if a load had been taken off my heart."

XX

ANNA spent the rest of the day at home, that is to say, at the Oblonskys', and refused all visitors who, having learnt of her arrival, had called to see her. She devoted the whole morning to Dolly and the children, merely dropping a note to her brother asking him to be sure and dine at home. "Come, God is merciful," she had said.

Oblonsky accordingly dined at home. The conversation was of a general character, but Dolly addressed her husband as "thou," a thing she had not done since their quarrel. Although her manner towards him was still unfriendly, yet there was no further talk of a separation and Stepan Arkadyevitch began to feel hopeful about a complete reconciliation with her.

Soon after dinner Kitty arrived. She knew Anna Arkadyevna only very slightly and had gone to her sister's not without certain misgivings as to how this worldly St. Petersburg dame, whom every one praised so much, would receive her. She soon saw, however, that Anna was favourably impressed by her. Madame Karenina was completely captured by her youth and beauty, and Kitty in her turn fell head over ears in love with Anna, as young girls often do with married women older than themselves. Anna had nothing of the worldly dame about her, nor did she look like the mother of a boy of eight years old. By her graceful, lithesome movements, the vivacious expression of her face, her eyes that changed from grave to gay so rapidly, you would have taken her for a girl of twenty. Her manner was natural and simple, yet Kitty felt that there was something about her that suggested an inaccessible world of interests, complex and poetical, that were foreign to her.

After dinner Dolly went to her own room and Anna walked hastily over to her brother who was smoking a cigar.

"Stiva," she said to him with a merry wink in the direction of the door, "go to her, and God help you," and she made the sign of the cross over him. He threw away his cigar and instantly left the room.

As soon as he was gone she went back to the couch where she had been sitting surrounded by the children. Either because they saw that their mother loved this aunt, or because they themselves were drawn towards her, the two eldest and after them the youngest, had taken complete possession of her even before dinner. They kept vying with one another as to who should sit next to her, kiss her tiny hand, play with her rings, examine the frills on her dress.

"Let us sit as we were before," Anna said, returning to her place. And Grisha, proud and happy, thrust his head under her hand and pressed it against her garments.

"When did you say the ball was?" she asked, turning to Kitty.

"Next week. It will be a lovely ball! One of those where you always enjoy yourself."

"And are there balls where you always enjoy yourself?" Anna asked with a playful smile.

"Why, of course there are. It's always jolly at the Bobreshchevs' and at the Nikitins', but it's deadly dull at the Mieshkovs'. Have you never noticed it?"

"My dear, no balls are jolly to me," Anna said, and again Kitty saw in her eyes that mysterious world unknown to her. "There are some that are less boring and trying than others, that is all. . . ."

"But how can *you* be bored at a ball?"

"Why not?" Anna asked.

Kitty felt that Anna knew the sort of reply she would make.

"Because you are always the loveliest of all."

Anna blushed.

"In the first place, that is not true," she observed, "and even if it were, what does it matter to me?"

"You will come to this ball, won't you?" Kitty asked.

"I can't very well get out of it. Take this one, dear," she said to Tania, who was amusing herself by drawing off her rings from her white, delicate fingers.

"I do so want you to come. I should like to see what you look like at a ball."

"Well, if I have to go, I shall at any rate console myself with the thought that it will afford you some pleasure. Grisha, dear, don't pull my hair; it's untidy enough as it is," she said, rearranging it.

"I can imagine you at a ball in a violet dress."

"Why particularly violet?" Anna asked with a smile. "Run along, children, run along. There's Miss Hull calling you for tea," she said, leading them towards the dining-room door.

"I know why you want me to go to this ball. You are expecting something wonderful to happen there and you want us all to have a part in it."

"How did you know?"

"I know what you are passing through just now," Anna continued. "Who does not know that purple haze more wonderful than that which hangs over the Swiss mountains? That glorious time when childhood ends and everything seems gay and happy and beautiful. We have all gone through it."

Kitty smiled. "How did she pass through it? How I should like to know her story!" she thought, calling to mind the unpoetic exterior of her husband, Alexei Alexandrovitch.

"I know; Stiva told me. I congratulate you. I was immensely taken with him," Anna continued. "I met him at the station this morning."

"Was he there?" Kitty asked with a blush. "What did Stiva tell you?"

"He told me the whole story. I should be delighted. . . . I travelled with his mother from St. Petersburg yesterday," she continued, "and she did not cease talking about him the whole way. He is her favourite son. I know mothers can be partial, but . . ."

"What did his mother tell you?"

"A great deal. I know she thinks a lot of him, but still he has a very chivalrous nature. . . . For instance, she told me that he wanted to give his share of the property to his brother, and that he did something wonderful when he was quite a boy . . . saved some woman from drowning. He is quite a hero, I assure you," she said with a smile, recollecting the two hundred roubles at the station.

She did not mention the incident to Kitty. She did not like thinking about it. There was something in his action concerning her that should not have been.

"The old lady asked me to go and see her," she continued; "I think I shall go to-morrow. I'm so glad Stiva is so long with Dolly," she added, to change the subject, and it seemed to Kitty that she was displeased about something.

"Let me go first! let me!" the children shouted. They had just finished tea and were tumbling over one another in their efforts to get to their Aunt Anna.

XXI

When tea-time for the elders arrived Dolly came out of her room. Stepan Arkadyevitch was not with her, evidently having left his wife's room by another door.

"I am so afraid you will be cold upstairs," Dolly remarked, turning to Anna. "I have a good mind to move you down so as to have you near me."

"Please don't bother about me," Anna said, trying to divine by Dolly's face if there had been a reconciliation.

"It would be much sunnier for you," Dolly persisted.

"My dear, I can sleep as sound as a top anywhere."

"What is it?" Stepan Arkadyevitch asked of his wife as he came in from his study.

By the tone of his voice both Kitty and Anna knew that a reconciliation had taken place.

"I want to put Anna downstairs, but the curtains ought to be changed. No one knows how to do it, so I shall have to see to it myself," Dolly replied, turning to her husband.

"I wonder if they've really made it up," Anna thought, as she listened to Dolly's cold, quiet tone.

"My dear Dolly! why all this fuss?" her husband said. "If you like, I will do it. . . ."

"They must have done," Anna thought.

"I know how you always do things," Dolly said, with a playful smile; "you give Matvey all sorts of impossible instructions, then go away and leave him in the midst of it."

"Yes, they have quite made it up. Thank God!" Anna thought, and delighted that she had been the cause of it, she went up to Dolly and kissed her.

"You really mustn't be so hard on me and Matvey," Stepan Arkadyevitch said, turning to his wife with a repressed smile.

For the rest of the evening, Dolly, as usual, treated her husband with a half-playful sarcasm, whilst he was pleased and happy, within bounds, wishing to make it evident that although he had been forgiven, he had not forgotten his sins.

About half-past nine a particularly animated and pleasant

conversation was going on at the tea-table when an incident occurred that struck every one as very strange, although it was of such slight importance. They were talking of some mutual St. Petersburg acquaintance when Anna suddenly arose.

"I have her portrait in my album," she said, "and I can show you my little Serioja too," she added with maternal pride.

It was about ten o'clock, the time when at home she usually bade her little son good-night, or sometimes tucked him into bed before going out to balls and parties. A feeling of sadness came over her that she was so far away from him. No matter what she was talking about her thoughts reverted to her curly boy, and she was seized with a desire to look at his picture and to talk about him. At the first opportunity she departed with her light, firm step to go in search of her album. The little staircase leading to her room started from the landing of the big central staircase. As she left the drawing-room there was a ring at the front door-bell.

"Who can it be?" Dolly asked.

"It is too early for any one to come for me and too late for a call," Kitty remarked.

"Doubtless some papers from the office," Stepan Arkadyevitch suggested.

When Anna passed the big staircase a servant was running up to announce the visitor, whilst the latter stood waiting in the light of the hall lamp. Anna looked down and recognised Vronsky. A strange sensation of fear and joy suddenly seized her heart. He was standing with his coat on, searching for something in one of his pockets, and when he raised his eyes and caught sight of her an expression of fear and shame came over his handsome face. Anna bowed and passed on, and soon after Stepan Arkadyevitch's loud voice could be heard asking Vronsky to come in and the latter excusing himself.

When Anna returned with the album Vronsky was gone. Stepan Arkadyevitch explained that he had come to inquire about a dinner they were giving to some newly-arrived celebrity.

"I couldn't make him come in. He seemed so strange," Stepan Arkadyevitch concluded.

Kitty blushed. It seemed to her that she alone knew the reason of his visit and why he would not come in. "He must have been at our place," she thought, "and not finding me in thought I might be here, but he did not come in because it was so late and because of Anna."

They all exchanged glances without a word and began examining Anna's album.

There was nothing strange or unusual in the fact that a man should call at a friend's house at half-past nine in the evening to inquire about a dinner and refuse to come in, but it seemed strange to them, especially strange did it seem so to Anna.

XXII

The ball had only just commenced when Kitty and her mother mounted the staircase, brilliantly lighted, decorated with flowers, and lined on either side with footmen in gay-coloured liveries. As they were standing before the mirror in the anteroom rearranging their hair and dresses a sound like the humming of a beehive reached them from the ball-room, broken by the scraping of violins tuning up for the first waltz. A little old man who stood smoothing his grey whiskers at another mirror gazed at Kitty with admiration. A beardless youth, one of those society young men whom the old Prince Shcherbatsky designated as "fops," in a very low-cut waistcoat and white tie, which he was rearranging as he walked up the stairs, bowed to them as he passed, and then came back to ask Kitty for a quadrille. She had already promised the first quadrille to Vronsky, so she had to content the youth with the second. An officer standing at the door buttoning his gloves cast a look of admiration at her and began twirling his long moustache.

Kitty had spent a great deal of thought and time over her toilet, but as she entered the ball-room in her complicated garment of white tulle with its pink tunic, she looked as if she might have been born in that mass of tulle and lace. Her hair was dressed becomingly on the top of her head, and was ornamented by a single rose.

As they were about to enter, her mother began rearranging her girdle that had got slightly out of place, but Kitty stopped her impatiently. She was looking her best and felt it. Her dress was not too tight, her lace bertha sat admirably round her shoulders, her rosettes were not crushed and showed no danger of coming off, her high-heeled pink slippers did not pinch her tiny feet, that would scarcely stand still, her massive golden hair sat firmly on her shapely head, even the buttons of her long white gloves fitted to perfection. A medallion attached to a black velvet ribbon encircled her lovely neck. This ribbon was charming. When she had looked at herself in the mirror at home she felt that the ribbon spoke volumes, whatever else might be wrong. Her bare shoulders and arms felt as cool as marble, a sensation particularly pleasant to Kitty. Her eyes sparkled, and her rosy lips parted in a smile of pleasure at her own loveliness.

She had no sooner approached a group of ladies who stood waiting for partners in all their splendour of lace, tulle, ribbons, and flowers, when Yegor Korsunsky, a stately, handsome man, came up and invited her to dance. He was married, a splendid dancer, and considered the principal cavalier of the ball-room, the master of the ceremonies. He had just left the Countess Banin, with whom he had taken a few rounds of the first waltz, when he caught sight of Kitty, and approaching her in that free and easy manner that only the chief man in a ball-room can assume, he bent over her and put his arm round her slender waist without even asking her permission. Kitty looked round for some one to whom she might confide her fan, and the hostess took possession of it with a smile.

" I am so glad you have come early," he remarked, with his arm round her waist; " it's becoming quite a fashion to be late nowadays."

Kitty placed her left hand on her partner's shoulder, and her tiny feet, in pink slippers, glided lightly and rhythmically over the polished floor.

" It is restful to dance with you," he said, falling into the slow measures of the waltz. " How lightly you do it! such precision! charming! " He invariably said the same thing to every one he happened to dance with.

She smiled at his compliments and continued studying the ball-room over his shoulder.

This was not her first ball and the faces of all present did not mingle into one enchanting impression; nor had she been to so many that she should be tired of seeing them. She was just between these two states, sufficiently excited to be pleasant, yet able to notice everything that was going on around her. In one corner a group caught her eye, composed of the very flower of society. There was Korsunsky's wife, the beautiful Lidi, in an outrageously low dress, the hostess and Krivin with his shiny bald head, who was always to be found where the flowers of society congregated. A few shy youths stood looking on, not daring to approach. A moment later her eyes fell on Stiva and the beautiful head and elegant figure of Anna clad in black velvet. And *he* was there. Kitty had not seen him since the evening when she refused Levin. She recognised him instantly, and noticed that he was looking at her.

"Shall we have a few more turns or are you tired?" Korsunsky asked, slightly panting.

"No, thank you."

"Where shall I leave you?"

"I think Madame Karenina is here; please take me to her."

"Certainly."

And Korsunsky with a measured step began waltzing straight towards the group on the left, saying as he went, "*Pardon, mesdames, pardon, pardon, mesdames.*" He steered his way skilfully through the sea of laces, tulle, and ribbons, and after one final mad turn, deposited Kitty on a chair. The train of her dress swished out and covered Krivin's knees, exposing her pale blue stockings. Korsunsky bowed and offered her his arm to take her to Anna Arkadyevna. Kitty, flushed and a trifle dizzy, gathered up her train and passed her eyes over the crowd in search of Anna. She was not dressed in violet as Kitty had hoped, but in a low cut black velvet dress, trimmed with Venetian lace, exposing her ivory shoulders, her full bust and round arms with their delicate wrists. A garland of pansies encircled her lovely black hair and a bunch of the same flowers nestled at her waist among the white lace. Her hair was dressed very simply; there was nothing remarkable about it except a profusion of little natural curls that strayed down the back of her neck and over her temples. She wore a string of pearls around her neck.

Kitty had seen a great deal of Anna during the past week and was more than ever in love with her. She had always imagined her in violet, but seeing her for the first time in black she was struck by a new and unexpected charm about her. She saw now that Anna could not have worn violet, that one of her principal charms consisted in the fact that her garments were scarcely seen on her, that they merely acted as a frame enhancing her beauty, but that she stood out, simple, natural, elegant, full of gaiety and animation.

When Kitty joined the group, Anna was standing in her usual erect attitude talking to the host, her head bent slightly towards him.

"No, I am not one to throw stones at others," she was saying to him, "although I don't understand," and catching sight of Kitty she turned towards her with an affectionate, protecting smile. She ran her eyes hastily over her toilet and gave a nod of approval, which Kitty understood.

"It seems you are unable to walk in the ball-room," she observed.

"She is splendid," Korsunsky remarked. "The princess is an ornament to any ball-room. Anna Arkadyevna, may I have the pleasure?" he asked, bending towards her.

"You are acquainted?" the host asked.

"With whom are we not acquainted, my wife and I? We are like white wolves, everybody knows us," Korsunsky replied. "Allow me, Anna Arkadyevna."

"I never dance when I can help it," she said.

"But you must to-night," Korsunsky persisted.

At this moment Vronsky came up.

"Well, come along then," she said, and taking no notice of Vronsky who bowed to her, she put her hand quickly on Korsunsky's shoulder.

"Why is she angry with him?" Kitty thought as she noticed that Anna had purposely ignored Vronsky's bow. Vronsky came up to Kitty, reminded her that she was engaged to him for the first quadrille, and expressed regret that he had only just been able to find her. Kitty stood looking at Anna waltzing and listened to him with a smile. She expected that he would ask her to dance, but he did not do so and she turned to him with a look of astonishment. He blushed and hastily invited her, but he had only just put his arm round her waist and taken a step or two when the music stopped. Kitty glanced at his face so near to hers. Long afterwards, after many years had passed, the look that she had given him, so full of love, which he did not return, tore her heart with cruel shame.

"*Pardon, pardon!* A waltz! a waltz!" Korsunsky cried from the other end of the room, and seizing the first young lady who came to hand he began to dance.

XXIII

VRONSKY took a few turns with Kitty, after which she joined her mother, but she had scarcely time to say a few words to the Countess Nordston when Vronsky came to fetch her for the first quadrille. During the dance nothing of any importance was said between them. They talked in broken snatches about Korsunsky and his wife, whom Vronsky jestingly alluded to as a couple of forty-year-old children, about private theatricals. Only once did his words touch her, when he asked if Levin was there and added that he liked him. But Kitty did not expect much from the quadrille, she was waiting for the mazurka with a beating heart. She felt that the mazurka would bring things to a crisis. The fact that during the quadrille he did not ask her for the mazurka did not in the least disturb her. She felt certain that she would dance it with him, just as she had done at former balls, and refused all other partners accordingly. The rest of the evening, until the last quadrille, Kitty passed in a sort of wonderful dream, full of gay sounds and flowers and delightful motion. She kept on dancing until she was absolutely tired out, only then asking for a moment of rest. In the last quadrille, which she danced with a tiresome youth whom she found it difficult to refuse, she found herself face to face with Anna and Vronsky. She had not seen Anna since her arrival, and again she was struck by something new and unexpected about her. Anna seemed intoxicated with success just as Kitty herself had been. Kitty recognised its symptoms in her sparkling eyes, her joyful smile, the measured grace and lightness of her movements.

"Who has caused it?" she asked herself, "all or one?" She paid no heed to the youth at her side, who was trying in vain to pick up the threads of their broken conversation and followed Korsunsky's commands mechanically as he announced the different figures. She watched the two in front of her and her heart grew heavier and heavier. "No, it can't be the admiration of the crowd that has intoxicated her so, it must be the admiration of one. And who is it? Can it be *he?*" Every time he addressed her Anna's eyes lighted up triumphantly and her rosy lips parted in a joyful smile. She seemed anxious to hide her joy, but it came out in spite of herself. "Can it be he?" Kitty looked at him and a sensation of terror came over her. What was so plainly depicted on Anna's face, she had seen on his. Where were his coolness, his calm dignity, the repose which always marked his face? He was turning towards her with his head slightly bent, as though he were ready to fall at her feet, and the expression of his face was full of submission, mixed with fear. "I would not for the world offend you," his glance seemed to say, "I only want to save myself, and how can I?" Never before had Kitty seen such an expression on his face.

They were talking about mutual acquaintances, the merest

trifles, yet Kitty felt that each word decided her fate. And, strange as it may seem, they too, while they were jesting about the way in which Ivan Ivanovitch spoke French, or talking about Miss Eletska's marriage, felt that each word was full of significance, just as Kitty had done.

For the rest of the evening Kitty felt heavy at heart. Thanks to her severe upbringing she just managed to do what was required of her, that is, to answer questions, to talk, and even to smile. It was only when the music struck up the mazurka and everybody trooped into the ball-room that Kitty was seized with despair. She had refused five partners, and now she would have to sit out. There was no hope that she would be asked again, because aware of her success in society it would never have entered any one's head that she was not dancing. She must tell her mother that she did not feel well and ask to be taken home. But she could not summon up the courage to do so. She felt absolutely heart-broken.

She escaped to another room and buried herself in an arm-chair. Her flimsy white skirt enveloped her form like a cloud. One bare delicate hand hung listlessly at her side touching the folds of her pink tunic; with the other she kept fanning herself nervously. But while she looked like a butterfly caught for a moment against some grass and ready to spread its lovely wings, her heart was oppressed with grief.

"Perhaps I was mistaken. It may not be so." And again she recalled what she had seen.

"Kitty, what is the matter?" the Countess Nordston asked, approaching her noiselessly over the carpet. "I don't understand."

Kitty's lower lip trembled. She stood up hastily.

"Kitty, aren't you dancing the mazurka?"

"No, no," she replied with a tremor in her voice.

"I heard him invite her for the mazurka," the countess remarked, knowing that Kitty would understand whom she meant, "and she said, 'Aren't you going to dance with the Princess Shcherbatsky?'"

"It makes no difference to me," Kitty replied.

No one fully understood her position. No one knew that she had refused a man whom she probably loved—refused him because she had believed in another.

The Countess Nordston went in search of Korsunsky, who was to have been her partner for the mazurka, and asked him to invite Kitty instead.

Fortunately for Kitty she was not obliged to talk, as Korsunsky was busy all the time giving directions. Vronsky and Anna were nearly opposite to her. She saw them sometimes at a distance, sometimes near, and the more she looked at them the more she became convinced that there was no further hope for her. She could see that they felt themselves alone in that crowded room. On Vronsky's face, usually so calm and composed, there was an expression of such utter humility and submission as one sometimes sees on the face of an intelligent dog who is conscious of having done something wrong. When Anna smiled, his smile responded; when Anna became thoughtful, he grew serious. An almost supernatural power seemed to draw Kitty's gaze towards Anna. She looked lovely in her simple black dress. Tnere was a sort of fascination about her beautiful round arms bedecked with bracelets, her shapely neck encircled by a string of pearls, her unruly hair, in the light, graceful movements of her hands and feet, in the very expression of her face, but there was something cruel in the charm of it all.

Kitty admired her more than ever though it was like torture to her. She was utterly crushed and her face showed it. When Vronsky chanced to brush past her, he scarcely recognised her —she was so changed.

"What a splendid ball it's been!" he remarked, merely to say something.

"Yes," Kitty replied.

Half way through the mazurka, when they were going through a complicated figure that Korsunsky had invented for the occasion, Anna walked into the middle with two gentlemen and called out two ladies, Kitty being one. Kitty approached her nervously. Anna half closed her eyes and pressed her hand with a smile, but observing the look of despair and consternation on Kitty's face she turned away from her and began talking gaily to the other lady.

"There is something strangely callous yet fascinating about her," Kitty thought.

Anna did not wish to stay to supper, but the host insisted.

"What nonsense, Anna Arkadyevna," Korsunsky exclaimed, putting her bare arm under his own. "I have such a splendid idea for a cotillon! *Un bijou!*"

He drew her on encouragingly; the host gazed at them both with a smile.

"No, I'm sorry, I can't stay," Anna said with a smile, and

the men understood by her resolute tone that it was useless to insist.

" I have danced more to-night than I generally do during a whole winter in St. Petersburg," she said, glancing at Vronsky, who was standing beside her. " Besides, I must rest before my journey."

" Are you really going to-morrow? " Vronsky asked.

" Yes, I think so," Anna replied, a little surprised at his boldness. The brilliancy of her eyes and her smile set him on fire as she said these words.

Anna Arkadyevna left before supper.

XXIV

" Yes, there must be something repulsive about me," Levin thought as he left the Shcherbatskys' and went in search of his brother. " People can't stand me. They say I'm proud, but I know I'm not. Had I been proud I should not have put myself in such a position." He pictured Vronsky to himself; Vronsky, happy, witty, and calm. He could never have placed himself in such a position. " No wonder she preferred him. I have no right to complain of any one or anything. I am the only person to blame. What right had I to think that she would unite her fate with mine? Who am I? and what am I? A good-for-nothing insignificant person whom nobody wants." With joy he suddenly thought of his brother Nikolai. " He was right in saying that the world was not worth living in. I am afraid we judged him harshly. Of course in Prokofy's eyes, who saw him drunk and in ragged clothes, he looked contemptible, but I know him better. I know his heart, and I know that we are alike. And instead of going to find him as I should have done, I went to dine with Oblonsky! "

He took out his brother's address, read it by the light of a street-lamp, and hailed a cab. On the way he tried to recall all the incidents of his brother's life. He remembered how at the university and for a year afterwards he had lived like a monk, notwithstanding the ridicule of his comrades, how severely he had obseıved all the forms of religion, services, fasts; how he had abstained from all pleasures, particularly the society of women, and then how he had been suddenly led away by falling into the company of a loose set and had entered upon a life of aimless debauchery. He remembered his conduct towards a boy whom he had taken from the country to bring up, and whom he had beaten so severely during a fit of anger that he narrowly escaped being transported for maiming. He remembered his conduct towards a sharper to whom he had lost money at cards and whom he afterwards had arrested as a swindler. It was this money that Sergei Ivanovitch had paid. Then how he had once been locked up for violence. Then the shameful lawsuit against his brother Sergei Ivanovitch about the family property, and then finally how he had taken a post somewhere in the west and had been summoned for assaulting a superior. This was all horribly disgusting, but it did not seem so disgusting to Levin as it must have done to others who did not know Nikolai, did not know his history, did not know his heart.

Levin remembered with shame the period of Nikolai's life when he had sought the aid of religion and had by devotions, fastings, and prayers tried to curb his wild, passionate nature, and others, himself among them, had teased and laughed at him, nicknamed him Noah, the monk, and how they had all turned away from him with horror and disgust when he most needed help.

Levin knew that in the bottom of his heart, in spite of the ugliness of his life, Nikolai was no worse than the people who judged and despised him. It was not his fault that he had been born with a tempestuous nature and had a hitch in his brain somewhere. He had always wanted to be good. " I will tell him everything, make him open his heart to me, and show him that I love him because I understand him," Levin said to himself, as he got out of the cab at the door of the hotel indicated on the address. It was about eleven o'clock.

" Upstairs, Nos. 12 and 13," the porter replied to his question.

" Is he at home? "

" I believe so."

The door of No. 12 was half open, and dense fumes of inferior tobacco issued from the room. Levin could hear an unknown voice, but he knew that his brother was there; he had recognised his cough.

" It all depends on how intelligently and rationally the thing is done," the unknown voice was saying as Levin reached the door.

He looked in and saw a shock-headed young man in a short coat and a sightly pock-marked young woman in a woollen dress without a collar or cuffs, sitting on a couch. His brother was not visible. Konstantin's heart was filled with pain to think what strange people his brother was surrounded with. No one heard his approach, and as he was removing his goloshes he listened to what the shock-headed young man was saying. He was talking about some undertaking.

"The devil take the privileged classes," he heard his brother's voice after a fit of coughing. "Masha, get us some supper and some wine. I think there's a little left; if not, send out for some."

The young woman arose, and as she came out into the passage she saw Levin.

"There's a gentleman here, Nikolai Dmitritch," she said.

"What does he want?" Nikolai asked angrily.

"It is I," Levin said, appearing at the door.

"Who is I?" his brother asked still more angrily. A sound could be heard of some one rising quickly and stumbling against something, and Levin saw the well-known figure of his brother standing before him, tall, thin, round-shouldered, with large scared eyes. He was struck afresh by his wild, emaciated appearance. He was even thinner than when Levin had seen him last, about three years ago. He was dressed in a short jacket, and his hands and bony frame seemed to him larger than ever. His hair was getting thin, except for the drooping moustache. He gazed at the newcomer with a strange light in his large, frank eyes.

"Why, Kostia!" he exclaimed, recognising his brother, and his eyes shone with joy. But the next instant he turned round to the young man and a hard, cruel expression came over his haggard face. He made that peculiar, convulsive motion of the head and neck so familiar to Konstantin.

"I have told both you and Sergei Ivanovitch that I wish to have nothing further to do with you. What do you want of me?"

He was different to what Konstantin had imagined him. The hardest and most difficult part of his character that made him so impossible to get on with, Levin had completely forgotten when thinking of him, but now face to face with him it came back with full force, especially when he saw that convulsive motion of the head.

"I don't want anything of you," Levin ventured timidly. "I've simply come to see you."

Levin's timidity had a soothing effect upon his brother. He bit his lips.

"And how are you?" he asked. "Well, come in and sit down. Masha, supper for three. No, wait a moment. Do you know this gentleman?" he asked, turning to his brother and pointing to the young man; "Mr. Kritsky, a friend of mine from Kiev, a very remarkable man. The police are after him because he is not a coward."

He looked round defiantly at every one in the room. "Wait, I tell you," he shouted to the young woman who was about to leave it.

Then in his muddled way that Konstantin knew so well, he began to relate Kritsky's story, how he had been expelled from the university because he had attempted to form an aid society for poor students, also a Sunday school, and how later he had been appointed teacher in an elementary school and afterwards dismissed, and finally he had been tried for something or other.

"Were you at the Kiev University?" Levin asked, to break an awkward silence.

"Yes," Kritsky replied curtly with a frown.

"And this woman," Nikolai Levin interrupted him, "is the companion of my life, Marya Nikolaevna. I took her out of the streets," he continued, with another convulsive twist of his neck, "but I love and respect her, and all who want to know me," he added, raising his voice, "must love and respect her too. She is just the same as my wife, just the same. Now you know whom you have to deal with. And if you think that you are demeaning yourself, there's the door." And again he looked around defiantly.

"Why should I be demeaning myself? I don't understand."

"All right, Masha, get supper for three, with vodka and wine. . . . No, wait. . . . Never mind, you can go."

XXV

"You see," Nikolai Levin continued with an effort. He was at a loss to know what to do or say. "Do you see?" he asked, pointing to a bundle of iron bars in a corner of the room; "those are for a new enterprise we are embarking upon, a workman's productive association. . . ."

Konstantin scarcely listened. He kept watching his face, on which the marks of consumption were plainly visible, and grew so sorry for him that he paid no heed to what he was saying.

He could see that this association was merely an anchor of safety to keep him from utterly despising himself.

"You know that capital is crushing the labourer," Nikolai Levin continued. "Our workmen and peasants bear the whole burden of the country, and things are so arranged that no matter how hard they may work they cannot escape from their awful position. All the fruits of their toil, all that could better their lot, give them leisure and consequently education, are swallowed up by the capitalists. Society is so constituted that the more they work the more they enrich the merchant and landowning classes, while they go on as beasts of burden for ever. This state of things must be altered." He finished speaking and looked at his brother.

"Of course," Konstantin remarked, observing the flush on his brother's emaciated cheeks.

"That is why we are organising a locksmiths' association, where the products, the profits, and the means of production will all be in common."

"Where is this workshop to be?" Konstantin Levin asked.

"At Vosdrem, in the Kazan government."

"But why there? I should have thought there was enough to do in the country without that."

"Because the peasants are just as much slaves as they were before emancipation and you and Sergei Ivanovitch do not like it when we want to get them out of that slavery," Nikolai Levin replied irritably.

Konstantin Levin gave a deep sigh and glanced round the gloomy, dirty room. This sigh had a still further irritating effect upon his brother.

"I know the aristocratic prejudices of men like you and Sergei Ivanovitch. I know that he is doing all he can to defend the existing evil conditions."

"That is not so, but why do you speak of Sergei Ivanovitch?" Levin asked with a smile.

"Sergei Ivanovitch? I'll tell you why," Nikolai Levin began shouting suddenly at the very mention of his name. "This is why. . . . But what's the good? What did you come here for? You despise all this, don't you? Then go away, for God's sake!" he shouted, rising from his chair. "Go away! go away."

"I don't despise it at all," Konstantin Levin said timidly. "I am not even disputing it."

At this moment Marya Nikolaevna came back and Nikolai

Levin gave her an angry look. She approached him quickly and said something in an undertone.

"My health is broken down and I am easily irritated," he explained, somewhat calmer, yet breathing with difficulty, "and then you go and talk to me about Sergei Ivanovitch and his article. It's so utterly false, such nonsense, so full of self-deception. How can a man write about justice when he does not know what it is? Have you read his article?" he asked, turning to Kritsky. He sat down by the table and cleared away the cigarettes littered on it.

"No, I have not read it," Kritsky replied, evidently not wishing to enter into the conversation.

"Why not?" Nikolai Levin asked irritably.

"I did not want to waste my time."

"But, excuse me, how did you know that it would be a waste of time? It is above the comprehension of most people, but I can see through and through his meaning. It is weak from beginning to end."

There was a moment of silence. Kritsky rose and took up his cap.

"Won't you stay to supper? Well, good-bye. Look in to-morrow with the locksmith."

As soon as he had gone, Nikolai Levin smiled and gave a wink in the direction of the door.

"In a bad way, too," he remarked, "but I see . . ."

At this moment Kritsky called him from the other side of the door.

"What more do you want?" he asked, going out to him in the corridor.

"Have you lived with my brother long?" Levin asked, turning to Marya Nikolaevna as soon as they were left alone.

"For nearly two years. He is very ill; drinks a great deal," she said.

"How do you mean?"

"He drinks vodka and it's bad for him."

"Does he drink much?" Levin asked in a whisper.

"Yes," she replied with a timid glance at Nikolai Levin who had just appeared at the door.

"What have you been talking about?" he asked, frowning and glancing from one to the other with a hunted expression in his eyes. "Eh?"

"About nothing at all," Levin replied in confusion.

"All right, you needn't tell me if you don't want to. But

you have no business to be talking with her. She is a girl of the people and you are a gentleman," he said with a nervous twist of the neck. " I see that you understand everything, have sized up everything, and look with sorrow at the error of my ways," he continued, raising his voice.

" Nikolai Dmitritch! Nikolai Dmitritch! " Marya Nikolaevna implored in an undertone, coming close to him.

" All right, all right! Well, what about supper? Ah, here it is," he said, as he caught sight of a waiter coming in with a tray. " Here, put it here," he added irritably, and taking up a bottle he filled a glass and drank it off at a gulp.

" Would you like a drink? " he asked in a gayer tone of voice, turning to his brother. " Well, let us forget about Sergei Ivanovitch. I am very glad to see you. We are still friends in spite of what people may say. Come along, have a drink. Tell me all about yourself," he continued, biting off a piece of bread and filling himself another glass. " How are you getting on? "

" I am still living in the country and looking after the estate," Konstantin replied, gazing with terror at the eagerness with which his brother ate and drank, and at the same time trying to appear unconcerned.

" Why don't you get married? "

" No luck," Konstantin replied with a blush.

" Why not? As for me, all is over. I have ruined my life. If only I had received my portion when I wanted it everything might have been different."

Konstantin hastened to change the subject.

" Do you know? I have taken Vania into the office at home," he said.

Nikolai gave a nervous shake of the head and became thoughtful.

" Tell me what is going on at Prokovsky! I suppose the old house is still there, and our school-room and the birches? Is old Philip the gardener still alive? How I remember the summer-house and the sofa! Don't have anything changed in the house, but get married soon and have it as it used to be. I'll come and see you if your wife is nice."

" Why not come now? " Levin asked. " We could arrange everything so well together."

" I would come if I was certain of not finding Sergei Ivanovitch."

" He is not there. I live quite independently from him."

"Yes, but no matter what you say, it would come to your choosing between us in the end," he said, with a timid glance at his brother. His timidity touched Konstantin.

"If it would give you any satisfaction to know, in your quarrel I have taken neither one side nor the other. You are both in the wrong. You for external reasons, he for internal ones."

"Oh! so you have found that out?" Nikolai cried joyfully.

"But I, for my part, if you would like to know, value your friendship more, because . . ."

"Why? Why?"

Konstantin did not like to say that it was because Nikolai was unhappy and needed his friendship, but the latter understood him. He frowned and turned his attention to the vodka.

"Enough, Nikolai Dmitritch!" Marya Nikolaevna implored, extending her plump hand for the bottle.

"Let go! Don't bother me or I'll strike you!" he shouted at her.

Marya Nikolaevna gave a gentle, good-natured smile which communicated itself to Nikolai as she took the bottle.

"Do you think she does not understand?" he asked. "She understands a great deal better than we do. There is something very nice and good about her, don't you think?"

"Have you been in Moscow before?" Konstantin asked, in order to say something.

"Don't say *you* to her; it frightens her. No one ever addressed her like that, except the judge, when she was being tried for escaping from a house of ill-fame. My God! how senseless everything is in this world!" he suddenly exclaimed. "These new institutions, these justices of the peace, these zemstvos, how meaningless they all are!" And he began to relate his experiences of these new institutions.

Konstantin listened to him. Although he had himself expressed similar opinions in relation to these various institutions, yet coming from his brother's lips they seemed repugnant to him.

"We shall find out everything in the next world," he said jestingly.

"In the next world? I have no love for that world! none whatever," he said, fixing his large scared eyes on his brother's face. "And yet it would be good to escape from the tangle of things, from all these horrors, both your own and other people's; but I'm afraid of death, terribly afraid." He shuddered.

"Have something to drink. Would you like champagne? Or let us go somewhere. Let us go to the gypsies. You know I love gypsies and Russian folk songs."

He began to wander in his speech, going from one thing to another. Konstantin and Masha persuaded him to stay at home, and eventually put him to bed completely drunk.

Masha promised to write to Konstantin in case of need and to try and persuade Nikolai to go to his brother.

XXVI

THE next morning Levin left Moscow and reached home that same evening. On the journey he talked with the people in the train about politics, about the new railroads, and, just as in Moscow, he was oppressed by the many conflicting issues, was displeased with himself and felt ashamed without knowing why. But when he got out of the station and caught sight of his one-eyed coachman Ignat, muffled up in the collar of his coat, his well-upholstered sledge, his horses with their plaited tails and jingling bells, that were just visible in the half-light cast by the station lamps; when Ignat began telling him all the village news, about the coming of the contractor, and how Pava the cow had calved, then the tangle began to unfold itself a little, and his shame and dissatisfaction passed away. The effect was produced merely by the sight of Ignat and his horses, but as soon as he put on his great-coat that the latter had brought for him, wrapped himself up in a rug, and began to think about the work to be done on his estate, at the same time examining the off-horse Donska, a thin, though spirited beast, that had once been his saddle-horse, then he began to look at the thing that had happened to him in quite a different light. He felt himself again and no longer wished to be a different person. He only wished to be better than he had ever been before. In the first place, he resolved to put aside all further hope of the extraordinary happiness he had expected from marriage that had caused him to make light of such happiness that he already possessed. In the second place, he resolved never to give way to such passion that had led him to make his proposal, the very thought of which tormented him. And never again would he forget his brother Nikolai, but would always keep him in sight to be there when he needed him. He felt that the time was not far off. Then the conversation with his brother about communism, which he had treated so lightly, came back to him and made him reflect. He had always looked upon any change in economic conditions as nothing short of the greatest nonsense, but had nevertheless felt the injustice of his own position as compared to that of the poor. Although he had formerly worked very hard and not lived very luxuriously, he now resolved to work harder still and live more simply than ever. It all seemed so easy to him that the whole of the way home he spent in the most pleasant illusions. With full hope for a new and better life he reached home about nine o'clock in the evening.

A light was still shining in Agafia Mihailovna's room, illuminating the little snow-covered porch before the house. Agafia Mihailovna, his old nurse, now acted as his housekeeper. She was still waiting up for him. She wakened Kusma, who, barefooted, half asleep, hurried down to open the door. Lasca the setter, almost upsetting Kusma, rushed out ahead of him, barking with delight. She rubbed herself against her master's knees, stood upon her hind legs, but dared not put her paws on his shoulders.

" You are back very soon," Agafia Mihailovna said.

" I got homesick, Agafia Mihailovna. Visiting is all very well, but there's no place like home," he replied as he went into his study.

By the dim light of the candles that Agafia had brought in, all the familiar details of the room came slowly home to him. The stags' horns on the walls, the bookshelves lined with books, the mirror, the stove with the little settle that had long been broken, his father's old couch, the large writing-table with an open book on it, a broken ash-tray, and a copy-book with some of his notes. As his eyes took in all these things he began to doubt if he could begin that new life he had dreamed of on the way. All the traces of his past life seemed to seize him in their grasp. " No, you cannot escape from us," they seemed to say. " It is useless your trying to be different from what you have always been, with your doubts, your perpetual self-dissatisfaction, your vain efforts at bettering yourself, and your everlasting expectation of happiness that does not come and never will come."

But while these external objects spoke to him thus, an inner voice kept on telling him that he need not be a slave to the past, that it was possible for a man to make what he would of himself. To gain courage he walked over to a corner of the room, picked up two dumb-bells, each weighing forty pounds, and began practising his gymnastic exercises. A sound of footsteps reached him from the other side of the door. He instantly put down the dumb-bells.

His bailiff came in and announced that, thank God, everything was well, but that the new drying-barn had burnt down with all the buck-wheat in it. Levin felt annoyed. He had himself designed that drying-barn, but the bailiff had always treated it with contempt, and now there was a secret triumph underlying his words as he announced that it was burnt down. Levin felt convinced that it had happened merely because the bailiff had neglected the necessary precautions he had a hundred times told him to observe. He grew angry and began to reprimand him. However, one piece of news pleased him very much. Pava, his very best cow, that he had paid a big price for at a cattle-show, had calved.

" Kusma, give me my coat. And will you get a lantern, please? " he said to the bailiff; " I want to go and look at her."

The cow-sheds where he kept his best cows were not far from the house. Crossing the court-yard, where the snow lay heaped up under the lilac bushes, he walked into the shed. A whiff of warm-smelling dung reached him as he pushed open the door that creaked on its frosty hinges. The cows, startled by the light of the lantern, turned over on the fresh straw. The shiny black and white back of a Dutch cow gleamed out in the half-light. Berkutt, the bull, with a ring in his nose, was about to get up, but changed his mind and snorted once or twice as they passed him. Pava, the red beauty, as big as a hippopotamus, was lying with her back to them sniffing at her calf.

Levin went into the stall, examined Pava, and lifted the red speckled calf on to its tottering legs. The mother lowed piteously, but was reassured when Levin returned the calf to her, which she began licking with her rough tongue. The calf buried its nose under its mother's side and whisked its tail.

" Bring the light here, Fiodor," Levin said, examining the calf. " It's like the mother, but the colouring is like the father's. See how long it is. Awfully pretty. Don't you think so, Vassily Feodorovitch? " he asked of the bailiff, having completely forgotten about the barn in his joy over the calf.

" Why should it not be? " the bailiff asked. " Simion the contractor came the day after you went away. It is necessary to settle things with him, Konstantin Dmitritch," he continued. "I have already spoken to you about the machine."

This instantly brought Levin back to all the business of the farm. He left the cow-shed, went straight to the office, talked things over with the bailiff and contractor; then went home and walked upstairs into the drawing-room.

XXVII

It was a large, old house, and although Levin lived alone in it yet he had it thoroughly heated throughout. He knew that this was ridiculous, that it was wasteful, and did not fall in with his new plans, but the house was a world in itself to him. It was a world in which his father and mother had lived and died, and constituted for Levin that ideal of perfection which he had hoped to renew with his wife and children.

Levin scarcely remembered his mother. The thought of her was sacred to him, and he always hoped that his future wife would be just such another ideal, charming, divine creature as she had been.

Love without marriage did not appeal to him. His first thought was of the family and then of the woman who should be at the head of it. His ideas about marriage were therefore essentially different from those held by nearly all his friends, for whom it meant nothing more than one event among many in a worldly life. For Levin it was the principal thing in life, on which depended all his happiness. And now he would have to renounce it!

When he entered the little drawing-room where tea was always served to him and sank into a chair with a book, and Agafia Mihailovna brought the tea-things and sat down in a corner with a sigh, he fully realised that he had not left his dreams behind him, that he could not live without them. "With her, or with another, but it will come." He turned his attention to the book, at the same time listening to Agafia Mihailovna's ceaseless prattle. Numerous, imaginary, disconnected pictures of his future family life floated before him. At the bottom of his heart he felt that some change was going on, some modification.

Agafia Mihailovna's prattle broke in upon him. She was telling him how Prohor had gone to the bad; how he had spent the money that Levin had given him to buy a horse with on drink, how he had beaten his wife until he had nearly killed her. He listened as he read his book, following the subject clearly. It was a book by Tyndall on heat. He remembered how he had once criticised Tyndall for his self-assurance, for the subtle way in which he produced his experiments, and for his limited philosophical outlook. Suddenly a happy thought struck him. " In two years I shall have two Dutch cows in my herd. Pava herself may still be alive with twenty of Berkutt's daughters. How wonderful! " He turned to his book again. " Well, admitting that heat and electricity are one and the same thing, but in the equation can you put the one instead of the other? The bond between all the forces of nature is felt so instinctively. . . . How nice it will be when Pava's daughter has grown into a red speckled cow and the whole herd descending from these three. . . . Splendid! And my wife and I will go out with our guests to see the herd come in, and she will say, ' Kostia and I reared that calf like a baby.' ' How can this interest you so? ' one of the guests will ask. ' Everything that interests my husband interests me,' she will answer. But who will she be? " And he remembered what took place in Moscow. " Well, what can I do? It was not my fault. Now I must begin a new life and forget the past. I must try to live better, much better than I have done. . . . " He grew pensive.

Old Lasca, the dog, who had not yet got over the delight at her master's return and had been barking about the yard to relieve her feelings, came running in, wagging her tail and bringing a gust of fresh air with her. She went up to her master and thrust her head under his arm, whining piteously for him to notice her.

" She can't speak," Agafia Mihailovna remarked, " she is only a dog, but she understands that her master has come back and is sad."

" Why sad? "

" Can't I see? It's time I knew my master's ways; I have grown up with them. No matter, sir. The Lord only give you good health and a clean conscience."

Levin looked at her attentively, astonished that she should have read his thoughts.

" Would you like some more tea? " she asked, taking his cup and going towards the door.

Lasca still nestled her head on her master's knee. He stroked her gently, and then she curled herself up at his feet, laying her

TOPOZ

head on one of her hind paws. As a sign that all was well with her she smacked her lips; then closing them over her aged teeth she settled down to a blissful repose.

"So will I!" Levin said to himself; "so will I. It's nothing. . . . All is well."

XXVIII

THE morning after the ball Anna Arkadyevna wired to her husband saying that she was leaving Moscow that same day.

"No, I really must, I really must go," she said to her sister-in-law in explanation of her change of plan. Her tone seemed to signify that she had just thought of a hundred things that must be done that moment. "No, it will be better to go to-day."

Stepan Arkadyevitch did not dine at home, but promised to be back to take his sister to the station at seven o'clock.

Kitty too did not come. She had sent a note saying that she had a headache. Dolly and Anna dined alone with the children and the English governess. The children did not care for their aunt any more and seemed to take little interest in her departure. They were either very inconstant in their affections or they instinctively felt that she was somehow different from the aunt whom they had learnt to love when she arrived and had no desire to play with her. She spent the whole morning packing, writing notes to her friends, and going over her accounts. It seemed to Dolly that Anna was not herself, that she was in some state of anxiety that Dolly knew from experience came from being dissatisfied with oneself.

After dinner Anna went to her own room to dress and Dolly followed her.

"How strange you are to-day!" Dolly said.

"Am I? Do you think so? I am not strange, I am wicked. I feel like that sometimes. I should like to have a good cry. I know it's silly, but it will pass off," Anna said quickly as she bent her flushed face over a tiny bag into which she was packing her nightcap and pocket-handkerchiefs. Her eyes shone with the tears that she could not keep back. "I was sad at leaving St. Petersburg, and now I'm sad at leaving here."

"You have done a lot of good by coming here," Dolly said, watching her closely.

Anna looked at her, her eyes glistening with tears.

" Don't say that, Dolly. I did nothing and could never do anything. I wonder why people will spoil me? What have I done? what could I have done? Your heart was so full of love that you could forgive . . . "

" Without you, God knows what might have happened. How fortunate you are, Anna! " Dolly exclaimed. " In your heart everything is serene and well."

" Most people have a skeleton in the cupboard, as the English say."

" But what skeleton can you have? Everything is so clear with you."

" I have though! " Anna said, and she smiled through her tears, a cunning, mocking smile.

" Well, they must be funny skeletons then and not gloomy ones," Dolly said with a smile.

" They are gloomy enough. Do you know why I am going to-day instead of to-morrow? This confession is hard to make, but I must make it," Anna said, dropping into a chair and looking Dolly straight in the eyes.

To her great astonishment Dolly saw that Anna had blushed to the roots of her hair.

" Yes," Anna continued; " do you know why Kitty did not come to dinner? She is jealous of me. I spoilt . . . I made the ball a torture to her instead of a pleasure. But I am really not to blame—or perhaps I am a little," she added in her soft voice, drawling out the word " little."

" Oh, how exactly like Stiva you said that! " Dolly exclaimed, laughing.

Anna felt hurt.

" No, no! I am not like Stiva," she said, knitting her brows. " I should not have told you had I for a moment doubted myself."

As soon as she had uttered these words she felt that they were not true. The very thought of Vronsky agitated her, and she was going away sooner than she had intended merely so that she should not meet him again.

" Stiva told me that you danced the mazurka with him, and that he . . . "

" You can't imagine how ridiculous it was. I merely wished to help them along and it turned out so differently. Perhaps, in spite of myself . . . " She blushed and did not go on.

" Oh, they feel these things instantly," Dolly remarked.

" But I should be in despair if I thought there was anything serious on his part. I'm convinced that he will soon forget and Kitty will leave off hating me."

"To tell you the truth, Anna, I am not very keen on this marriage. Kitty is well out of it if Vronsky can fall in love with you in a single day."

"Heavens! how absurd it would be!" Anna exclaimed, and a flush of pleasure overspread her face as she heard her thought expressed in words. "And here am I going away after having made an enemy of Kitty when I'm so fond of her. How sweet she is! You'll put it right with her, Dolly, won't you?"

Dolly could not refrain from smiling. She loved Anna and was amused at her weakness.

"An enemy? That's impossible."

"I should like you all to love me as much as I love you. And now I love you more than ever," she added, the tears coming into her eyes. "How stupid I am to-day!"

She passed her pocket-handkerchief over her face and began dressing.

Just as she was leaving Stepan Arkadyevitch arrived. He was beaming and happy and smelt of wine and cigars.

Anna's tenderness communicated itself to Dolly. She clung to her sister-in-law.

"Try and think, Anna, what you have done for me," she whispered. "I shall never forget it. Remember that I love you and will always love you as my best friend!"

"I don't know why you should," Anna said, kissing her and trying to hide her tears.

"You understand me so well. Good-bye, dearest!"

XXIX

"It's all over, thank God!" was Anna's first thought after she had said good-bye to her brother, who stood blocking up the door of the carriage even after the third bell had rung. She took her seat beside her maid and began to examine the dimly-lighted compartment. "What a blessing! To-morrow I shall see my Serioja and Alexei Alexandrovitch, and my life will assume its ordinary hum-drum course once more."

In the same state of preoccupation that she had been in all day she began to arrange herself for the journey. With an adroit movement of her little hands she opened a red bag, took out a pillow, which she laid on her knees, crossed her legs, and settled down comfortably. A lady who seemed to be an invalid was already preparing for bed. Two other ladies entered into conversation with Anna, and a stout old dame made various remarks upon the temperature as she wrapped a rug round her legs. Anna exchanged a few words with the ladies, but foreseeing no great interest in their conversation she asked her maid for a reading lamp, and fixing it on to the arm of her seat, she took out a paper knife and an English novel and settled down to read. At first she found it difficult to concentrate her thoughts on the book. The constant coming and going, the noise of the starting train, the snow-flakes beating against the window-pane, the conductor walking in and out, her fellow-passengers discussing the storm, all distracted her attention. Afterwards it grew monotonous; there was the same jolting and jarring, the same snow, the same quick changes from heat to cold and back to heat again, the same faces in the dim light, the same voices, and little by little her attention became absorbed in the book. Her maid had already gone to sleep, holding the red bag on her knees in her large, broad hands, clad in gloves, one of which was torn. Anna Arkadyevna read and understood what she read, but she found no pleasure in entering into the lives and interests of other people. She had too keen a desire to live herself. The heroine of the story was in the sick-room, nursing an invalid, and Anna wanted to be there, walking about with noiseless tread. A member of parliament was making a speech and she wanted to be making that speech herself. Lady Mary rode on horseback, teased her sister-in-law, and astonished every one by her boldness, and Anna wanted to do what Lady Mary had done. But she could do nothing. She twisted the smooth paper knife about in her little hands and tried to get still further absorbed in the book.

The hero of the novel had at last reached the summit of his English ambition, a baronetcy and an estate, and she wanted to go with him to that estate. Suddenly she felt that he must feel ashamed and that she herself was ashamed. " But why should he be? And why should I be? " she asked herself with astonishment. She put down the book, leaned back in her seat, clasping the paper-knife firmly in both her hands. She began going over her Moscow impressions. They were all pleasant and nice to think about. She recalled the ball and Vronsky with the submissive expression on his face, so full of love; she recalled her relations with him; there was nothing that she could have been ashamed of. But just at the very point when she thought of Vronsky her shame increased, " Hot, very hot, burning," an inner voice seemed to say. " Well? " she asked herself resolutely, shifting about in her seat, " what does it mean? Am I afraid to face the facts? Well? Can there really be anything more between myself and this boy-officer than exists between me and the rest of my acquaintances? " She gave a disdainful smile and took up her book again. But this time she could no longer comprehend what she was reading. She drummed on the window with the paper-knife, then laid its cool, smooth surface against her cheek. She almost laughed aloud with the joy that suddenly took possession of her. Every nerve in her was alive. She felt her eyes opening wider, her hands and feet would scarcely keep still, something caught her breath, every form and sound in the carriage struck her with an amazing clearness. She could not tell whether the train was going backwards or forwards or had come to a standstill.

" Is that Annushka sitting there beside me, or is it a stranger? What is that hanging there, a coat or an animal? And what am I doing here? Am I myself or some one else? " She was terrified at her own reflections, but could not draw herself away from them. At last she rose in order to shake them off. She put her rug on one side and took off the pelerine of her dress. A peasant in a long nankeen coat entered the compartment, and she realised that he must be the stoker who had come to look at the thermometer. She felt the gusts of wind and snow as he opened the door; then again everything became confused. . . . The long-waisted peasant seemed to be knawing something at the wall, the old dame stretched her legs the full length of the carriage and seemed to fill it like a dark cloud, then there was a terrific screech and a thump, as if some one had been torn asunder, a red, blinding light flashed before her eyes, was shut out by a blank wall, and she felt herself falling over. These sensations were not at all unpleasant to her. A man muffled up in a long coat that was covered with snow seemed to shout something into her very ear. She woke up with a start, and realised that this was the conductor, and that they had come to a station. She asked her maid for her pelerine and shawl, put them on, and went towards the door.

" Do you wish to go out? " the maid asked.

" Yes, I want to get a breath of fresh air. It's very close in here."

As she opened the door a fierce gust of wind met her and

banged it to again. It seemed like a game to her. She tried a second time and succeeded in getting out. The wind, as if it had been expecting her, whistled joyfully and tried to lift her from her feet, but with one hand she steadied herself by the icy post, while with the other she lifted up her skirts and stepped on to the platform. The wind did not seem so fierce now. With an exhilarating sensation she filled her lungs with the keen, frosty air, as she stood by the carriage, gazing up the platform at the brilliantly-lighted station.

XXX

THE storm continued raging, the wind blew in heavy gusts, moaning between the wheels of the train and shaking the posts at the corner of the station. Every visible object, people, carriages, railings, were covered with snow, which the wind kept on blowing from the same direction. There was a moment of calm, and again the storm burst out with such force that it seemed impossible to stand up against it.

Meanwhile people were running to and fro quite unconcerned, talking gaily amid a constant creaking of the platform boards, an opening and shutting of doors. The shadow of a man bent over, glided past Anna's feet, and a sound of hammering on iron reached her ears. "The despatches, quick!" an angry voice came out of the stormy darkness. "This way please!" "No. 28," other voices shouted, and people came rushing by, muffled up to the ears and covered with snow. Two men with glowing cigarettes in their mouths walked past her. She took another deep breath, drew her hand out of her muff, and was about to enter the carriage, when a man in a military coat stepped close to her, shutting out the light from the flickering lamp. She looked up and instantly recognised Vronsky. He raised his cap, bent over her, and asked if she wanted anything; if he could be of any service to her. For a moment or two she did not reply, and as she gazed at him as he stood in the deep shadow, she could see, or imagined she could see, the expression of his face and eyes. There was the same look of abandonment that had affected her so at the ball. During the last few days she had told herself repeatedly, and had done so a moment ago, that Vronsky was no more to her than the dozens of other young men she had come across, and that she would not allow herself to think of him, but now, as she met him, a sensation of joy and pride filled her heart. There was no need for her to ask him why he was there. She knew just as certainly as if he had told her that he was there to be near her.

"I did not know you were going to St. Petersburg. Why are you going?" she asked, dropping her hand with which she was about to open the door. She could not keep back the gladness that lighted up her face.

"Why am I going?" he asked, gazing into her eyes. "You know why; I am going because I want to be where you are," he said. "I can't help myself."

At this moment a terrific gust of wind blew a heap of snow from the roof of the carriage, bringing with it a sheet of iron, and the engine in front gave a deep, mournful scream. The terrible storm had an even more exhilarating effect upon her just then. He had said what her soul most desired, but her reason feared the words. She did not speak. Signs of an inner struggle could be seen on her face.

"Forgive me if I have offended you," he said humbly.

He was respectful and courteous, yet so firm and determined that for some time she could not reply.

"You should not say that; it is not well. If you are a good man I want you to forget it, just as I will forget," she said at last.

"Not a single word, not a single gesture of yours will I ever forget, and I cannot . . ."

"Enough! enough!" she cried, trying to assume a severe expression as he gazed eagerly into her face. She put her hand on the icy post, raised her foot on the step, and disappeared into the corridor leading to the carriage. Here she stopped still, trying to think what had happened. She could not recall his words or her own, but she felt that that short interchange of words had brought them close together; it gladdened and alarmed her at the same time. In a short while she went into the carriage and settled down in her place. Her agitation grew greater and greater every moment, until she felt that something must give way within her. She could not sleep the whole night. No unpleasant thought oppressed her, but a wild, unconquerable joy filled her heart. Towards the morning Anna dozed off, and when she awoke it was already broad daylight and the train was nearing St. Petersburg. Her first thoughts were of her home, her boy, her husband, the things to be done that day and the next.

As soon as the train stopped she left the carriage, and the first person her eyes fell upon was her husband. "Heavens! Why are his ears so large?" she thought as she looked at his severe, imposing figure, with his large ears protruding from under the brim of his round hat. As soon as he saw her he advanced towards her with his habitual disdainful smile playing about his lips and a weary expression in his large eyes. A disagreeable sensation came over her as she saw that determined, weary look. She had somehow expected to find him different. The sensation was not new to her. A sort of pretence characterised her relations with her husband; she had not realised it until this moment when the fact was brought painfully home to her.

"See what a kind, considerate husband I am. I was burning with a desire to see you, just as in the first year of our marriage," he said in his deliberate, thin voice, in the tone of raillery he always adopted with her.

"Is Serioja well?" she asked.

"And this is all the reward I get for my ardour!" he said. "He's quite well, quite well."

XXXI

VRONSKY did not even attempt to sleep that night. He sat staring straight before him, every now and then casting a look of amazing indifference at the people coming and going. Strangers who had on former occasions been struck by his unwonted calm would have thought him prouder and more self-composed than ever. People were of no more account to him than things. A highly-strung young man of the legal profession, who was sitting opposite to him, conceived an intense hatred for him at first sight. He asked him for a light, he spoke to him, even touched him, to make him feel that he was not an inanimate thing, but a man, but Vronsky paid no more heed to him than he did to the lamp. The young man made a grimace, feeling that he was losing complete control over himself at Vronsky's utter indifference.

Vronsky saw nothing, heard nothing. He felt himself a king, not because he believed that he had made any impression on Anna—he had not thought of that—but because the impression she had made on him filled him with pride and joy.

What would come of it all he did not know and did not even

consider. He felt that all his powers, that had hitherto been scattered and dissipated, had focussed themselves with terrific force towards one divine aim, and he was happy. He knew that he had told her the truth, that life without her had lost all meaning and purpose for him. He was glad that he had spoken. Now she knew all and was thinking about it. When he returned to his carriage, he began going over all his impressions of her, every time he had seen her, every word she had spoken, and his heart beat violently at the pictures his imagination created of a possible future.

When he got out of the train at St. Petersburg he felt as fresh as if he had just come out of a cold bath, despite his sleepless night. He remained standing at the door of his carriage waiting for her to appear. " I will see her once more," he said to himself with a smile. " I will see her graceful bearing, her smile; perhaps she will look at me, say a word to me." But it was her husband whom he saw first, politely escorted through the crowd by the station master. " Why, the husband! " It just dawned on Vronsky that he was an important factor in Anna's life. He had been vaguely conscious that she had a husband, but had not really believed in his existence until he had been brought face to face with him and saw his head, his legs clothed in black trousers, and worst of all, he saw him go up to Anna and take her hand with a calm air of possession.

The sight of Alexei Alexandrovitch with his severe, self-confident St. Petersburg air, his round hat, and slightly stooping shoulders gave him a most unpleasant sensation. He felt as if he had come to a spring after having been tortured by thirst and could not drink the water because it had been befouled by some animal. Alexei Alexandrovitch's very walk was offensive to Vronsky. He felt that no one had the right to love Anna but himself. And when she appeared, the very same as he had last seen her, his heart was filled with joy. He gave orders to his German valet who had just come up to him to see to the luggage and made his way towards her. He witnessed the meeting between husband and wife, and with a lover's intuition could feel the constraint with which she addressed her husband. " No, she does not love him, she cannot love him," he said to himself.

As he drew near to them he noticed with joy that she felt his approach and recognised him, though she went on talking with her husband.

" Did you have a good night? " he asked, coming up to them.

He bowed in such a manner as to include Alexei Alexandrovitch, leaving it open for him to acknowledge his salute or not as he chose.

" Excellent, thank you," she replied.

She seemed tired and her face had lost its habitual animation, but as she glanced at him her eyes lighted up, and although it was only a momentary flash, Vronsky was happy. She turned to her husband to see whether he knew Vronsky. Alexei Alexandrovitch looked at him with displeasure, vaguely remembering who he was. Vronsky's self-assurance had met its match in the severe self-assurance of Alexei Alexandrovitch.

" Count Vronsky," Anna said.

" I think I have the honour of your acquaintance," Alexei Alexandrovitch said coldly, extending his hand. " Departed with the mother and returned with the son," he added with precision. " Back from a furlough no doubt? " he asked, and without waiting for a reply he turned to his wife. " Well, did they shed many tears in Moscow at your departure? " he asked in his habitual playful tone, wishing to make Vronsky understand that he desired to be left alone. He raised his hat, but Vronsky turned to Anna Arkadyevna.

" I hope to have the honour of calling on you," he said.

Alexei Alexandrovitch looked at him wearily.

" We shall be delighted," he said coldly; " we receive on Mondays." Then completely dismissing Vronsky he turned to his wife again. " What a lucky thing it was that I had half-an-hour to spare to come and meet you and show you my devotion," he continued, in the same playful tone.

" You lay too much stress on your devotion for me to appreciate it," she said, in the same playful tone, at the same time listening to Vronsky's step behind them. " But what is that to me? " she thought, and began questioning her husband about how Serioja had passed his time in her absence.

" Excellently! Mariette says that he's been very good, and I'm sorry to say did not miss you; not like your husband. Thank you, my dear, for having come a day earlier. Our dear Samovar will be delighted." (Samovar was a nickname he had given to the celebrated Countess Lydia Ivanovna because she was always in a constant state of agitation about something or other.) " She inquired after you. I should advise you to go and see her to-day. You know, her heart aches over everything. And now on top of all her other troubles she has taken upon herself to reconcile the Oblonskys."

The Countess Lydia Ivanovna was a friend of her husband's and the centre of a certain circle in St. Petersburg society to which Anna belonged on her husband's account.

"But I wrote to her."

"She wants to know every detail. If you are not too tired, dear, go and see her. Well, Kondraty will see to the carriage. I have to go to a committee meeting. I shall not have to dine alone any more," he continued, this time not in jest. "You can't believe how accustomed I am to . . ."

With a long pressure of her hand and a significant smile, he helped her into the carriage.

XXXII

The first face Anna saw when she reached home was her son's.

"Mamma, mamma!" he cried, and paying no heed to his governess, he rushed wildly down the stairs and threw his arms around her neck.

"I told you it was mamma!" he shouted to his governess; "I knew it was!"

Anna's first impression on seeing her son was one of disillusionment, the same she had experienced with her husband. She had imagined him better than he really was. She was obliged to descend to the reality in order to enjoy him as he was. And he was charming, with his fair curls, blue eyes, and sturdy legs in neatly fitting stockings. Anna felt a physical pleasure in his nearness, his caresses, and a moral calm came over her when she met his trusting, loving gaze and listened to his simple, naïve questions. She unpacked the presents sent him by Dolly's children, meanwhile telling him about a little girl in Moscow named Tania, who could read and was even teaching the other children.

"Is she better than I am?" Serioja asked.

"For me you are better than any one in the world."

"I know I am," Serioja said, smiling.

Anna had hardly finished her coffee when the Countess Lydia Ivanovna was announced. She was a tall, stout woman with a bad complexion and large, dreamy, black eyes. Anna was very fond of her, but to-day, as for the first time, she seemed to see her with all her faults.

"Well, my dear, did you bring away the olive branch?" she asked as soon as she entered the room.

"Yes, it's all over. It was not nearly so serious as we had supposed," Anna replied. "My *belle sœur* is generally rather hasty."

But the Countess Lydia Ivanovna, who was always interested in things that did not concern her, had a habit of sometimes not hearing things that did concern her.

"Yes, the world is full of grief and woe," she remarked, interrupting Anna. "I am worried to death to-day."

"What is the matter?" Anna asked, containing a smile.

"I am growing weary of the ever-useless striving for truth; I feel myself quite worn out. The Little Sisters would have got on excellently were it not for these people," the countess added, with an air of ironical resignation to fate. (The Little Sisters was a religious, patriotic, philanthropic institution in which the countess was interested.) "They get hold of an idea, they mutilate it, and then they judge it so superficially. There are only two or three men, your husband among them, who know anything at all about the matter; the others are only a nuisance. Pravdin wrote to me yesterday. . . ."

Pravdin was a noted panslavist who lived abroad. The countess proceeded to tell Anna what he had said in his letter. Next she went on to tell of various schemes and snares that prevented the uniting of the churches, after which she departed in haste to some meeting of some society or other, and from there to a meeting of the Slavonic Committee.

"She has always been like that, but why have I never noticed it before?" Anna asked herself as soon as she had gone. "Or was she unusually irritated to-day? Isn't it funny? She is full of Christian virtues, yet is always angry and talking of her enemies! Enemies over Christian charity!"

In a little while another friend called, the wife of a director, and gave her all the gossip of the city. She departed at three o'clock, promising to come back to dinner. Alexei Alexandrovitch was still at the ministry. Left alone, Anna went up to be present at her boy's dinner, which he took alone; then she put her things in order, read and replied to the many notes and letters that had accumulated on her desk.

The unaccountable sensation of shame she had experienced on her journey vanished, together with her agitation. Under the conditions of her ordinary every-day life she felt firm and irreproachable.

She was amazed to think of the state she had been in yesterday. "What was it all about? Why, nothing. Vronsky said something foolish to which I replied as I should have done. To speak of it to my husband is not necessary, nor advisable. It would look as if I attached more importance to the thing than there really was in it." She recalled how once when a young man, a subordinate of her husband's, had made love to her and she had told him about it, Alexei Alexandrovitch had said that every woman in society was exposed to that sort of thing, and that he had too much confidence in her tact to ever permit himself to humiliate her by being jealous. "Then why tell? Thank God, there is nothing to tell," she said to herself.

XXXIII

ALEXEI ALEXANDROVITCH returned from the ministry at about four o'clock, but, as often happened, he found no time to see his wife. He went straight into his study to interview various petitioners who were waiting for him, and to sign various documents brought him by his secretary.

The Karenins always had at least three guests to dinner, and to-day they were an old lady, a cousin of Alexei Alexandrovitch, the director of a department with his wife, and a young man who had been recommended to Alexei Alexandrovitch for employment. Anna went into the drawing-room to entertain them, and just as the bronze clock of Peter I.'s time was striking five, Alexei Alexandrovitch joined them. He had an engagement immediately after dinner and wore a white tie with two orders glittering on his dress suit. Every moment of Alexei Alexandrovitch's time was occupied and previously arranged for. In order to accomplish all that he had to do every day he had to have recourse to the greatest regularity. "Without haste and without rest" was his motto. He greeted all the guests, smiled to his wife, and sat down.

"My solitude is over at last. You can't think how unpleasant it is to dine alone." (He laid special stress on the word unpleasant.)

At dinner he questioned his wife about Moscow, referring to Stepan Arkadyevitch with an ironical smile, but the whole conversation was of a general character, dealing with St. Petersburg official as well as society life. He spent about half-an-hour with his guests after dinner; then giving his wife another smile and pressing her hand, he departed for the council.

Anna did not go to the Princess Betsy Tverska's, who was giving a party and had invited Anna when she heard of her arrival, nor did she go to the theatre, where she had a box that evening. She did not go out because a dress that she had intended to wear was not finished. After the departure of her guests she began turning out her wardrobe. She had always been extremely clever at dressing economically, with the very best results. Before her departure for Moscow she had commissioned her dressmaker to alter three of her dresses in such a way as to make them unrecognisable. They ought to have been ready three days ago, but to her great horror she discovered that two of them had not yet been touched, while the third was altered in a way she did not like. The dressmaker came to excuse herself, and tried to persuade Anna that the dress was really better like that. Anna lost her temper and upbraided the dressmaker in a way that made her ashamed to think of it afterwards. To calm her agitation she went into the nursery, spent some time with her little boy, put him to bed herself and made the sign of the cross over him as she tucked him in. She was glad that she had not gone out and had spent the evening in such an agreeable manner. It was so quiet and restful. She now saw quite clearly that what had seemed to her of such exaggerated importance on the journey was nothing more or less than a commonplace incident in society life of which she need not be ashamed. Anna sat by the fire with an English novel waiting for her husband. At half-past nine precisely his ring was heard at the bell, and shortly afterwards he entered the room.

"At last!" she exclaimed, extending her hand. He kissed it and sat down beside her.

"I see your visit has been a great success," he remarked.

"Yes," she said, and began telling him everything, about her journey with the Countess Vronsky, her arrival, the accident at the station, and then went on to say how at first she felt sorry for her brother and afterwards for Dolly.

"I can't imagine how a man like that can be excused for that because he happens to be your brother," Alexei Alexandrovitch said with severity.

Anna smiled. She knew that he had merely said that in order to show that her being related to Oblonsky could in no way alter his opinion of him. She knew this trait in her husband's character and admired it.

"I am glad that everything has ended happily and that you

have come back," he continued. "Now tell me, what are they saying about the changes I have introduced in the council?"

Anna had heard nothing about these changes, and she could not help feeling a little conscience-stricken that she should have completely forgotten a thing that was of such importance to him.

"Here, on the other hand, they have created quite a sensation," he said with a self-satisfied smile.

Anna saw that he had something to tell her concerning this, flattering to himself, and she proceeded to help him out with questions. With the same smile of self-satisfaction he began telling her of the congratulations he had received as a result of these changes.

"Of course, I couldn't help being pleased. It shows that they are at last beginning to look at these things in a more rational light."

Having finished a second glass of tea with cream and a roll, Alexei Alexandrovitch rose to go to his study.

"I see you did not go out; were you not dull alone?" he asked.

"Oh, no!" she said, rising also and accompanying him. "What are you reading now?" she asked.

"I am reading the Duc de Lille's *Poèsiedes Enfers*," he replied—"a very remarkable book."

Anna smiled, as people smile at the weaknesses of those they love, and passing her arm through her husband's she walked with him to his study door. Anna was familiar with his never-failing custom of reading in the evening. Despite his many duties that swallowed up nearly all his time, he nevertheless considered it necessary to keep up with anything of importance that appeared in the intellectual world. She knew that he was interested in books dealing with philosophy, politics, and religion, but he also considered it his duty to read anything that had made a stir in the world of art, although art was utterly contrary to his nature. She knew that in the realms of philosophy, politics, religion, Alexei Alexandrovitch had doubts which he was always trying to solve, but on questions of art or poetry, particularly music, of which he knew nothing, he had the most set and fixed ideas. He loved to talk of Shakespeare, Raphael, and Beethoven, the importance of the new schools of music and poetry, which he classed most accurately.

"Well, God be with you," she said at the door of the study, within which some shaded candles and a jug of water were standing ready near her husband's chair; "I must write to Moscow."

He pressed her hand and kissed it.

"And, really, he's a very good, upright, honest man, quite remarkable in his own sphere," Anna said to herself on the way to her own room, as if she found it necessary to justify him, to defend him from somebody who maintained that he was not lovable. "But why do his ears stick out so? Or has he cut his hair unusually short?"

It was just on the stroke of twelve and Anna was sitting at her bureau writing to Dolly when she heard the measured step of Alexei Alexandrovitch in his bedroom slippers. He came in washed and brushed, with a book under his arm.

"It's time for bed," he said, with a peculiar smile, and proceeded to their bedroom.

"What right had he to look at him like that?" Anna thought, recollecting the look Vronsky had given him.

She undressed and went into the bedroom, but her face had lost the animation it had worn in Moscow, that had shone out in her eyes, her smile. The fire had gone out or was hidden somewhere far away.

XXXIV

On leaving St. Petersburg Vronsky had put his rooms at the disposal of his friend and beloved comrade, Petritsky.

Petritsky was a young lieutenant, not particularly distinguished, and not only not rich but head over ears in debt. He got drunk nearly every evening, was frequently put under arrest for various scrapes of an indecent character, but was nevertheless loved alike by all his comrades and superiors. When Vronsky reached home at about twelve o'clock in the morning he saw a well-known carriage standing outside. As he rang the bell he could hear the sound of men's laughter and a woman's lisping voice. "If it's any of those villains, don't let them in!" Petritsky's voice shouted. Vronsky asked the man-servant not to announce him and quietly entered the room. The Baroness Shilton, a friend of Petritsky's, in all the splendour of a lilac satin dress and her pink and white complexion, was sitting by a round table making coffee. She filled the whole room with her high-pitched Parisian accent. Petritsky in an overcoat and Captain Kamerovsky in full uniform, evidently just off duty, were sitting near her.

"Bravo! Vronsky!" Petritsky shouted, jumping up and upsetting his chair. "The master himself! Baroness, give him some coffee out of the new coffee-pot. We did not expect you. I hope you are pleased with the new ornament in your study," he said, pointing to the baroness. "You are acquainted?"

"I should think so!" Vronsky said with a gay laugh. "We're old friends."

"Are you back from a journey?" the baroness asked. "Then I'm off. Dear me! I must go home this minute if I'm in the way."

"My dear baroness, you are at home wherever you are," Vronsky said. "And how are you?" he asked, turning to Kamerovsky and shaking hands coldly.

"There! you can never say pretty things like that," the baroness remarked to Petritsky.

"Can't I? I shall do as well after dinner."

"After dinner there is no merit in it. Well, run along and get washed and I'll give you some coffee afterwards," she said, sitting down and attacking the handle of the new coffee-pot. "Pierre, give me the coffee," she said to Petritsky. She called him Pierre after his family name, and did not attempt to hide her intimacy with him. "I want to add some more."

"You will spoil it."

"No, I won't. Well, and how is your wife?" the baroness asked suddenly, interrupting Vronsky's remarks to his comrades. "We have been marrying you. Did you bring her with you?"

"No, baroness. I was born a Bohemian and I shall die a Bohemian."

"So much the better, so much the better. Give me your hand."

And the baroness, without letting him go, began jesting with him, telling him all her new plans and asking his advice.

"He will never divorce me! What am I to do? I want to bring an action against him. What would you advise me to do? Kamerovsky, do look after the coffee; it's boiling over. You see how busy I am. I must bring an action against him, because I want to get control over my own property. How stupid it all is! Under the pretext of my having been unfaithful," she said scornfully, "he wants to get entire possession of my property."

Vronsky listened with pleasure to the gay prattle of this

pretty woman, approved of what she said, gave her half-serious advice, and generally fell into the tone he usually adopted with women of her kind. In his St. Petersburg world humanity was divided into two distinct classes. The first, the lower one, a vulgar, stupid, ridiculous set, believed that a man must live with only one woman, to whom he must be lawfully wedded, that girls must be innocent and women modest, that men must be manly and temperate, that it was necessary to care for your children, earn your daily bread, and pay your debts. This was the old-fashioned, dull set. But the other, the real kind, to which he and his friends belonged, required only that men should be generous, bold, gay, should not be ashamed of their passions, and laugh at the rest of the world. Vronsky, still under the influence of his totally different life in Moscow, felt out of his element in the first few moments, but he soon slipped back into the ways of his gay and pleasant world.

The coffee boiled over after all, spoiling an expensive carpet and the baroness's dress, but it caused a good deal of laughter and merriment.

" Well, good-bye. I must be off or you'll never get washed, and I shall have the worst crime on my conscience that a human being can commit, that is, uncleanliness. So you advise me to put a knife to his throat? "

" By all means. Only in such a way that your little hand just touches his lips. He will kiss it and all will be well," Vronsky replied.

" At the French theatre this evening? " she asked, and gathering up her rustling dress she vanished.

Kamerovsky rose also, but Vronsky, without waiting for him to go, shook hands with him and went into his dressing-room. Whilst he was washing, Petritsky gave him a few graphic descriptions of the changes that had taken place in his affairs in Vronsky's absence. He had absolutely no money and his father refused to pay his debts. His tailor had threatened to put him in prison, and so had another tradesman. His colonel had told him that he must leave the regiment if these scandals continued. He was sick to death of the baroness, mainly because she was always wanting to give him money, and had discovered another wonderful creature, whom he promised to introduce to Vronsky, a wonderful Eastern beauty, " like Rebecca, you know." Then he had quarrelled with Berkoshev, who had threatened a duel, but nothing came of it. Generally, everything was very flourishing and jolly. And then, without leaving Vronsky time to worry over these details, Petritsky began telling him the various news of interest.

Petritsky's well-known stories, his familiar rooms, that he had occupied for three years, all contributed to bring Vronsky back to the current of his irresponsible St. Petersburg life, and the sensation was pleasant to him.

"Impossible!" he shouted, as he poured the water over his powerful, healthy neck. "Impossible!" He had just learned that Laura had thrown over Fertinhoff and gone to live with Milaev. "Is he still as self-satisfied and stupid as ever? And what is Busulukov doing?"

"Oh, there's such a lovely story about Busulukov!" Petritsky exclaimed. "You know his passion for balls. He never misses a single court ball. He went to the last one in a new helmet. Have you seen the new helmets? They're very nice and light. Well, he was standing . . . But you're not listening."

"Yes, I am," Vronsky said, rubbing himself with a towel.

"The grand duchess was just going by with some foreign ambassador when, as luck would have it, the conversation turned on the new helmets. The grand duchess was anxious to show him one, when she turns round and sees our dear Busulukov standing there." (Here Petritsky put himself in an imaginary pose.) "She went up to him and asked him for his helmet, and, would you believe it? he wouldn't give it to her. The fellows wink at him, make signs, scowl at him, but he does not budge! He stands as if turned to stone. You can imagine the scene! Then the ambassador, I forget his name, goes up to him and wants to take it off, still he does not stir. At last he snatches it off and hands it to the grand duchess. 'This is the new kind,' she began, but as she turned it over out came tumbling pears and sweets, about two pounds of sweets! He had taken them, my dear!"

Vronsky shook with laughter. Even later on, when they were already talking of other things, he burst into loud peals of laughter, showing all his fine regular teeth, every time he thought of the unfortunate helmet.

After he had heard all the news, Vronsky put on his uniform with the aid of his valet, and went out to report himself. Then he determined to go and see his brother, the Princess Betsy, and to make various other calls among the set where he was likely to meet the Karenins. According to his usual habit in St. Petersburg he left the house, not intending to return until very late at night.

PART II

I

TOWARDS the end of the winter a consultation took place at the Shcherbatskys' regarding Kitty's health, which was growing worse and worse as spring drew nearer. The family doctor had ordered cod-liver oil, then iron, and other things; but as none of these remedies did any good, he advised them to take her abroad. At this point a specialist was called in. He was a handsome young man, and insisted on making a careful examination of the invalid. He laughed at her girlish modesty which he said was a remnant of barbaric times, and seemed to think that there was nothing more natural than for a young man to examine a young girl's naked body. He found it natural no doubt, because he was accustomed to do it every day, and neither felt nor saw anything bad in it. The girl's shame he looked upon not merely as a barbaric instinct, but as a personal insult to himself.

But there was nothing to be done. Notwithstanding the fact that this doctor had studied at the same school and out of the same books as all the other doctors, and that many people considered him of no account, yet by the princess and her circle he was looked upon as something wonderful, as the only person in the world who could possibly save Kitty.

After a careful examination of the invalid, who felt ready to die with shame, the specialist washed his hands and went into the drawing-room to talk to the prince. The latter coughed and frowned as he listened to him. He had never been ill and had no faith in doctors. In his heart of hearts he despised the whole comedy, as he called it, and knew better than any one what was the matter with Kitty. He therefore listened with contempt to what the doctor was saying about her, whilst the latter barely disguised his disdain for this old gentleman who could not understand him. He knew, however, that the old man was of no account in the house, and that the principal person was the mother, and resolved to reserve his eloquence for her. Just then the princess entered the room accompanied by the family doctor. The prince fled so as not to let them see how ridiculous the whole thing appeared to him. The princess was beside herself and did not know what to do. She felt a little guilty in regard to Kitty.

"Well, doctor, let us know our fate," the princess said. "Tell me all." She wanted to say "is there any hope?" but her lips trembled and she could not frame the words. "Well, doctor . . ."

"In a moment, princess. Permit me to consult with my colleague. We shall then have the honour of giving you our joint opinion."

"Do you wish to be alone?"

"As you please."

The princess sighed and left the room.

As soon as they were alone the family doctor began explaining his opinion timidly, and saying that he thought it was the beginning of tuberculosis . . . etc. . . . etc. The specialist listened to him for a time, then cut him short in the middle by taking out his large gold watch.

"Yes," he said, "but . . ."

The family doctor waited respectfully.

"You know it is hardly possible to decide when tuberculosis first sets in. Until the lesions appear you can't be sure. We can only suspect the trouble at present from such symptoms as malnutrition, nervousness, etc. The only question before us now, if there is any suspicion of tuberculosis, is to keep up the nutrition."

"But you know there is always some mental trouble in these things," the family doctor ventured, with a faint smile.

"Of course!" the specialist replied, with another glance at his watch. "Excuse me, do you know if the Yansky bridge is finished yet, or is it necessary to go round?" he asked. "It's finished? Then I've twenty minutes to spare. What were we saying? Ah, yes. We thought it necessary to keep up nutrition to strengthen the nerves. You can't do one without the other."

"What do you say to a trip abroad?" the family doctor asked.

"I am opposed to these trips abroad. If there is really any tubercular trouble, of which we are not by any means certain, a trip abroad will not help it in the least. The most important thing is to see that the patient is well nourished, and a journey abroad may not do much in that direction." (Here the specialist began to talk of the ill-effects of the Soden waters, whilst the family doctor stood listening respectfully.)

" The only thing in favour of a journey abroad is that it would be a complete change, and would take her away from all unhappy associations. And then her mother wants her to go," the family doctor ventured again.

" In that case, let her go by all means. Only I'm afraid of these German quacks. They must be got to carry out my instructions. Well, let them go."

He gave another glance at his watch.

" I say! it's time I was off," he exclaimed, going towards the door.

The specialist informed the princess that he wished to see the patient a second time.

" What! another examination! " the princess cried with horror.

" Oh, no, only a few details, princess."

" Then come in, I beg of you."

She led the doctor into Kitty's room. Kitty was standing in the middle of it, her emaciated cheeks flushed with excitement and shame, caused by the doctor's visit. When she caught sight of him she blushed and her eyes filled with tears. Her illness seemed to her so absurd, so utterly ridiculous, and the remedies worse than useless. It was like attempting to piece together a broken vase. Her heart was broken. Then of what use were all these pills and powders? But she could not hurt her mother, who, she knew, blamed herself a great deal.

" Please be seated, princess," the specialist said to her.

He smiled, sat down opposite her, felt her pulse, and began going over the same stupid questions. For a time Kitty replied, then suddenly she rose impatiently.

" Excuse me, doctor, but this won't lead us anywhere. You have asked me those questions three times over."

The specialist was not offended.

" Nervous irritability," he said to the princess when Kitty went out. " However, I had finished . . . "

And he began explaining Kitty's condition in very learned terms, treating the princess as a woman of the very highest intelligence. He ended by recommending the very waters he had just condemned. When the princess asked his advice about going abroad, he became very grave, but gave his consent at last on the strict understanding that they were not to trust to German quacks, but consult him in everything.

The atmosphere grew lighter as soon as the doctor had gone. The mother felt more hopeful when she returned to Kitty, and

Kitty too pretended to share her hope. She was always pretending now.

"Really, there is nothing the matter with me, *maman*, but if you want to, let us go," she said, and in her endeavours to show what interest she took in the journey she began to speak of their preparations.

II

Soon after the doctor had gone, Dolly appeared. She knew that there was to be a consultation that day, and although she had not long left her bed after her confinement (she had given birth to a little daughter) and had a great many troubles and worries at home, she left her tiny infant and another child ill in bed and came post haste to find out what had been decided about Kitty.

"Well?" she asked, as she came into the drawing-room and removed her hat. "You all seem very merry. I suppose it's all right."

They tried to tell her what the doctor had said, but though his speech had been long, and as it seemed at the time, very clear, they were nevertheless unable to give her the gist of it. The only point of interest was the decision in regard to the journey.

Dolly gave an involuntary sigh. Here was her best friend, her sister, going away, and her life was none too happy as it was. Her relations with her husband since their reconciliation had been most humiliating to her. Anna's intervention had helped matters only for a time, and things were now as bad as they had ever been. It is true there was no definite ground for complaint, but Stepan Arkadyevitch was never at home and there was scarcely any money in the house. The suspicion that he was still unfaithful to her was a constant torment to Dolly, but remembering the agonies she had endured through jealousy she tried to put it from her. Never again would she permit herself to go through the awful fit of jealousy she had experienced in the first hours of her discovery. She did not wish to investigate his conduct too minutely, fearing that any further disclosures might completely upset their family life. So she shut her eyes to his doings, and despised him and herself for this weakness. On top of all, the cares of a large family rested upon her shoulders. At first the infant did not thrive, then the nurse left, and now one of the elder children had fallen ill.

" Well, and how are you all? " the princess asked.

" Don't ask, *maman.* There are troubles upon troubles. Lilly is not well, and I'm afraid she has scarlet fever. I just came for a moment to inquire about Kitty. If Lilly really has scarlet fever I shall not be able to go out again for a long time."

When he learnt that the doctor had gone, the old prince ventured out of his study, and after giving his cheek to Dolly and asking her a few questions, he turned to his wife.

" Well, have you decided to go? " he asked. " And what are you going to do with me? "

" I think you had better stay at home," the princess said.

" As you please."

" *Maman!* Why should not papa come too? " Kitty asked. " It would be much jollier both for him and for us."

The prince went over to Kitty and began stroking her hair. She raised her face to his and tried to smile. It always seemed to her that he understood her better than the others, although he said little. As the youngest child she was her father's favourite, and she thought that his extreme love for her gave him a better insight into her character. As she looked into his kind blue eyes gazing earnestly at her, she felt that he could see through and through her. She blushed and put her face nearer to his, expecting to be kissed, but he merely patted her head.

" Oh, these stupid chignons! You can't get down to the real daughter. It's like stroking the hair of some departed woman. Well, Dolly? " he asked, turning to his eldest daughter; " what is that hero of yours doing now? "

" Nothing, papa," Dolly replied, knowing that he was referring to her husband. " He is always out. I hardly ever see him," she could not help adding with a bitter smile.

" What! hasn't he gone down to the country to see about the sale of the wood? "

" Not yet, but he intends to."

" Does he? " the prince asked. " He must be like me. All right," he said, in answer to some remark of his wife's, sitting down. " And now, Kitty," he began, turning to his youngest daughter, " what you have to do is to get up one fine morning and say to yourself, I am quite well and happy, why not go for a walk with papa and enjoy the lovely frosty air? Eh? "

At these simple words Kitty felt as though she had been

convicted of a crime. "Yes, he knows all, he understands all, and these words mean that I ought not to allow my shame to overcome me." She was about to say something, but burst into tears and left the room.

"There! see what you have done!" the princess said to her husband, angrily. "You always . . ." and she began heaping reproaches upon him.

The prince listened quietly, but his face grew darker and darker.

"The poor dear is so unhappy, so unhappy, and you can't see that the slightest allusion to the cause of her suffering hurts her. Oh, dear! how mistaken we are in people!" the princess exclaimed, and by the change in her tone both Dolly and the prince knew that she was referring to Vronsky. "I cannot understand why there are no laws to punish such people."

"Oh, let me be!" the prince exclaimed, rising from his chair and going towards the door. "There are laws enough, my dear," he said, turning back, "but since you've brought the matter up, let me tell you that you and you alone are to blame. There are laws enough to punish such villains and there always will be. Had it not been for certain things that should never have taken place I—old man as I am—would have called that young prig out. And now you try to cure her by the aid of these humbugs."

The prince had only just begun to relieve his feelings, when the princess, as always happened on these occasions, deeply repented that she had ever embarked upon the subject and burst into tears.

"Alexandre, Alexandre," she entreated, drawing nearer to him.

The prince stopped as soon as he saw her tears.

"There, there," he said, trying to soothe her; "I know it's difficult for you, but what are we to do? After all, there is no great harm done. God is merciful. . . . Thank you, dear" . . . he said to her, as she emplanted a wet kiss on his hand, and hardly knowing what to say further he left the room.

As soon as Kitty had gone, Dolly, with her maternal instinct, would have liked to follow, feeling that a woman's advice might be of some service. She was about to go to her when she was arrested by the quarrel, and tried to stop her mother in so far as her filial respect would allow her. During her father's outburst she was silent. She was ashamed for her mother and admired her father for his kindness. He had no sooner gone, however, than she thought of the principal matter in hand—Kitty and the necessity of soothing her.

"I have long wanted to ask you, *maman*. Did you know that Levin intended proposing to Kitty when he was here last? He told Stiva about it."

"Well? I don't understand . . ."

"Perhaps Kitty refused him. Did she tell you?"

"No, she told me nothing. She has not spoken about him or the other; she is too proud. But I know that all this comes from . . ."

"Yes, but supposing she should have refused Levin because of the other one? I know she would not have done so had it not been for him, and that after all she should have been so mistaken."

The princess could not bear to think how much she was to blame for her daughter's unhappiness. She grew angry.

"It seems I understand nothing! Every one wants to be clever nowadays. Mothers are not to know anything, and this is the result . . ."

"I am going to her, *maman*."

"Very well, you may," the princess said.

III

As she entered Kitty's pretty little boudoir, just as gay and pretty as Kitty herself had been two months back, Dolly remembered with pleasure how they had both furnished it only a year ago. Her heart stood still when she caught sight of the poor girl sitting on a chair near the door staring at a corner of the carpet. She looked up on her sister's entrance, but the severe expression of her face did not change.

"I have to go home directly and you won't be able to come and see me," Dolly began, sitting down beside her. "And I do so want a talk with you."

"What about?" Kitty asked in alarm, raising her head.

"About the thing that troubles you, of course."

"I have no troubles."

"Kitty, dear. Do you think I don't know? I know everything. Believe me, it isn't worth thinking about. We have all gone through it."

Kitty was silent, the severe expression had not left her face.

"He is not worth your troubling over him," Dolly continued, making straight for the main point.

"Yes, because he slighted me," Kitty said in a trembling voice. "Don't talk about it! Don't talk to me about it!"

"But who said that? I have not heard it. I am sure he was in love with you and is still in love with you, but . . ."

"For Heaven's sake don't sympathise with me! It drives me mad!" Kitty cried suddenly flaring up. She blushed and turned away, fingering the buckle on her belt nervously.

Dolly was familiar with this trait in her sister's character, and knew that in a moment of anger she was capable of saying a great deal that she would regret afterwards. She attempted to soothe her, but it was already too late.

"What do you mean? What is it? Do you want to insinuate that I am in love with a man who does not care for me, and that I'm eating my heart out for him? And this is what my sister thinks, my sister who . . . who sympathises with me! I don't want your sympathy and your pretences!"

"Kitty, don't be unjust."

"Then why are you torturing me?"

"I? on the other hand . . . I see that you are grieved . . ."

But Kitty would not listen to her.

"I have nothing to break my heart over and don't need consolation. I am too proud to love a man who does not care for me."

"I did not for a moment suppose . . . Kitty, tell me," Dolly said, taking her hand, "tell me, did Levin speak to you?"

At the mention of Levin's name Kitty lost complete control over herself. She leapt up from her chair and threw the buckle on the floor.

"Why drag in Levin? I don't know why you're bent on torturing me. I have told you and repeat it now; I am too proud and could never, *never* have done what you did . . . go back to a man who no longer cared for me and loved another woman. I can't understand how you could bring yourself to do it! I simply can't!"

As she said these words she looked at her sister. Dolly bent her head and was silent, and Kitty, instead of leaving the room as she had intended to, sat down again by the door and covered her face with her pocket-handkerchief.

For a little while they were silent. Dolly was thinking of

herself. Her humiliation, which she always felt deeply, now seemed more cruel than ever thus referred to by her sister. She was angry with Kitty; she did not think that she could be so unkind. But suddenly she heard the rustle of a dress, a broken sob, and two arms were thrown around her neck. Kitty was on her knees before her.

" Dolly, dear, I am so unhappy! " she whispered guiltily and hid her tear-stained face in Dolly's lap.

It seemed that only the tears were needed to bring the two sisters together, but they talked only of indifferent things and not of the subject that lay nearest their hearts. Kitty felt that her unfortunate words relating to Dolly's husband had wounded her sister, but that she had been forgiven. Dolly on her side knew everything she wanted to know. She was more than ever convinced that Kitty's grief was due to the fact that she had refused Levin for Vronsky, who had deceived her, and that she was now ready to love Levin and hate Vronsky. Kitty did not say a word about this, however, she merely alluded to her mental condition.

" I have really nothing to worry about," she began, after she had calmed down a little, " but you can't think how disgusting and revolting everything seems to me—I can't endure myself! You can't imagine what horrid things I think about! "

" What horrid things can you think about? " Dolly asked with a smile.

" The most horrid, horrid things. I really can't tell you. It's neither grief nor despair, it's something worse. Everything that was good in me seems to have disappeared and nothing but the evil is left. How can I explain? " she continued, seeing the look of astonishment in her sister's eyes. " When papa spoke . . . it seemed to me that he only thought of getting me married. When mamma takes me to a ball I think it's for the same reason, that she only wants to get rid of me. I know it isn't true, but I can't escape from these thoughts. Eligible young men I simply can't endure. They seem to be always summing you up. It used to give me the greatest pleasure to go to a ball, to admire myself in my pretty frocks, but now I feel uncomfortable, ashamed. . . . What am I to do? The doctor . . . But . . . "

Kitty stopped. She wanted to say that since this change had come over her she could not bear Stepan Arkadyevitch. The most unpleasant sensations came over her every time she saw him.

"Everything seems distorted to me," she continued. "It may be due to my illness. Perhaps it will pass over."

"Don't think about it . . ."

"I can't help myself. I only feel better when I'm with you and the children."

"What a pity you can't come home with me now."

"But I am coming. I've had scarlet fever already. I'll persuade mamma to let me go."

Kitty begged so hard that she was allowed to go. All the six children went down with scarlet fever, and during the whole of their illness Kitty helped Dolly to nurse them. But Kitty's own health did not improve, and just before Easter the prince and princess took her abroad.

IV

EVERYBODY knows everybody else in the upper circle of St. Petersburg society and all are on visiting terms with one another. There are, however, distinct sets of which the upper circle is composed, and Anna Karenina had a good many friends and connections in no less than three of them. One was her husband's set, the official set, composed of his colleagues and subordinates, an incongruous set, curiously bound together by the laws of social etiquette. It was difficult for Anna to comprehend the sentiment almost of religious awe with which she had at first looked upon every individual member of it. Now she knew them all well, as well as people know each other in a small provincial town. She was familiar with all their habits and weaknesses, knew exactly where the shoe pinched, what were their relations among themselves as well as to the common centre to which they all belonged. She knew exactly what they thought of each other, and why this one had fallen out with that. But Anna was not interested in this set, in spite of what the Countess Lydia Ivanovna had to say of it, and avoided it as much as she could.

Another set, to which Anna was more closely connected, was the one through which Alexei Alexandrovitch had embarked upon his career. The head of this set was the Countess Lydia Ivanovna. It was chiefly composed of pious, virtuous, ugly old women, and clever, learned, ambitious men. One of these clever men had once talked of it as "the conscience of St.

Petersburg society." Alexei Alexandrovitch was very much attached to this set, and Anna, who could get on with most people, had in the early days of her St. Petersburg life made a great many friends among the people in it. Since her return from Moscow, however, she simply could not endure them. She found them unnatural and pretentious, their society became dull and irksome to her, and she contrived to see as little of the Countess Lydia Ivanovna as possible.

The third set in which Anna moved was the smart set, society proper, the world of balls, dinners, and brilliant toilets. This set kept fast hold on the court and affected to despise less fashionable people, whose tastes and habits were nevertheless very much the same as their own. She was connected with this set through the Princess Betsy Tversky, the wife of a cousin of hers, who enjoyed an income of twenty thousand roubles a year. On Anna's first appearance in St. Petersburg she had fallen in love with her and taken her under her protection. She was always trying to draw her into her own set, and made fun of the Countess Lydia Ivanovna.

"When I am old and ugly I shall be just like her," she would say; "but it's a shame for a young and pretty woman like yourself to be buried among that pious lot."

Anna had always tried to avoid the Princess Betsy's set, partly because it meant living beyond her means and partly because she really preferred the other. But since her return from Moscow, however, a complete change had come over her. She now fled from her more serious-minded friends and took to frequenting the great world. It was there she met Vronsky and experienced a wild joy every time she saw him. He was frequently at the Princess Betsy's, who was a cousin of his.

Vronsky on his part went everywhere where he could possibly meet Anna, and did not fail to speak of his love whenever an opportunity arose. She did not give him any encouragement, but every time she saw him a strange gladness filled her heart, just as when she met him for the first time in the railway carriage. She knew that her eyes, her smile, betrayed her, but she had not the power to hide her joy.

At first Anna sincerely persuaded herself that she was angry because he persisted in forcing himself upon her, but one evening, when she was present at a party where she had expected to meet him and he did not come, she knew by her feeling of disappointment that she had been deceiving herself. His attentions were not only not disagreeable to her, but had become the chief interest of her life.

. . . .

The famous prima donna was singing a second time, and St. Petersburg society crowded to the theatre to hear her.

Catching sight of his cousin, Vronsky, without waiting for the interval, left his seat in the stalls and went into her box.

"Why didn't you come to dinner?" she asked. "How intuitive you lovers are!" she added in a whisper, smiling. "*She also did not come.* But you must look in after the opera."

Vronsky gave her a questioning look. She nodded her head. He thanked her with a smile and took a seat beside her.

"And how you used to laugh at others!" the Princess Betsy went on, finding some special pleasure in watching over his passion. "What has become of you? You're caught at last, my dear."

"That is all I want," Vronsky said, with his quiet, good-natured smile. "To be quite honest my only complaint is that I am not caught fast enough. I am beginning to lose hope."

"What hope can you possibly have?" Betsy asked, trying to take her friend's part. "*Entendons nous. . . .*" Her eyes were full of mischief, showing plainly that she understood as well as he what hope he was referring to.

"None whatever," Vronsky said with a smile, showing his regular teeth. "Excuse me," he added, taking up her opera-glasses and looking over her bare shoulder into the opposite box, "I fear I am becoming ridiculous."

He knew very well that in Betsy's eyes and in those of her set he ran no such risk. According to their standard to be hopelessly in love with a young girl or with any unmarried woman was ridiculous in the extreme, but to conceive a passion for a married woman, to spend a lifetime in winning her, was a grand and beautiful thing to do. So Vronsky had no real fear of being thought ridiculous. He put down the opera-glasses and looked at his cousin, a proud smile playing about his lips.

"Now tell me why you didn't come to dinner," she began, gazing at him with admiration.

"I bet you couldn't guess. I was trying to make peace between a husband and a man who had insulted his wife."

"Did you succeed?"

"Almost."

"You must tell me all about it," she said, rising. "Look in during the next interval."

"I'm afraid I can't. I'm off to the French theatre."

"You're going to desert Nielson?" Betsy asked in horror, though she would not have been able to distinguish Nielson from any chorus girl.

"I can't help it. I have an engagement there in my office of peacemaker."

"Blessed are the peacemakers, for they shall be saved," Betsy said, with a vague idea that she had heard something like that somewhere. "Well, sit down and tell me something more," she said, resuming her seat.

V

"This is rather a naughty story, but so amusing that I must tell it you," Vronsky began, as he looked into her sparkling eyes. "But I won't mention any names."

"But I can guess; so much the better."

"Listen then. Two gay young men . . ."

"Officers of your regiment, of course."

"I did not say they were officers, but two young men who had lunched together . . ."

"Translated, got drunk together."

"Perhaps they had. Well, they were on their way to dine with a friend, in the most excellent spirits, when a pretty young woman in a cab suddenly passes them. She turns round and, as it seems to them, nods to them and laughs. Of course, off they go after her at full speed. To their great surprise, the lady stops at the door of the very house they were bound for. She runs up the stairs as fast as she can go. They see nothing but a pair of rosy lips under a veil and a pair of pretty little feet."

"You describe it all so well that I'm half inclined to think you were one of the party."

"What did you say to me just now? Well, the two young men go up to their comrade's rooms. He was giving a farewell dinner, and as always happens on those occasions they drank a great deal more than was good for them. They question everybody about the inmates of the house, but nobody seems to know anything about them. At last to their question, "Are there any mam'selles here?" the landlord's servant informs them that there are a great many. After dinner our two young men go down to the landlord and write a letter to the fair unknown. It was a passionate letter full of confessions, and they themselves take it upstairs in order to explain anything that might not be quite clear."

"Why do you tell me these disgusting things? Well?"

"They ring the bell. A girl opens the door. They give her the letter and assure her that they're both so much in love that they are ready to die on the spot. The astonished girl begins to remonstrate with them. Out comes a gentleman as red as a lobster, with long whiskers, who puts them out of the door, declaring that nobody lives there except his wife."

"But how did you know that he wore whiskers?"

"You shall see. I called there to-day to make peace between them."

"Well? what happened next?"

"We are coming to the most interesting part. The happy man turns out to be no other than a titular councillor. He lodges a complaint and I am obliged to enter the scene as a peacemaker! What a peacemaker too! Talleyrand, compared to me, was nobody."

"What were the difficulties?"

"I will tell you. Of course we apologised. 'We are in despair, we beg you to forget this unfortunate incident,' we said. The titular councillor begins to thaw a little. He wants to express his feelings, but as soon as he begins he loses his temper again, says the most horrid things, and I have to bring my diplomatic talents to bear upon him. 'I quite agree that they've acted very badly, but you must make allowances for their extreme youth, and then they had only just dined together. You understand; they are sorry from the bottom of their hearts and beg you to forgive them.' The titular councillor begins to thaw again. 'I quite agree with you, count; I am prepared to forgive them, but, you see, my wife . . . my wife . . . an honourable woman, is subjected to the insolences of good-for-nothing young rascals. . . .' The rascals in question being present, I had to make peace between them. Again I resort to my diplomatic powers, and am just on the point of concluding the whole thing happily when our titular councillor loses his temper again, grows red in the face, and I have to begin again from the beginning."

"We must tell you all about this," Betsy said to a lady who

at that moment came into the box. "He's been amusing me so much."

"*Bonne chance,*" she said to Vronsky, giving him the tip of one finger as she held her fan, and with a movement of the shoulders she forced down the bodice of her dress so as to expose her bosom when she took her seat in front of the box in the glaring light.

Vronsky went to the French theatre where he really had an appointment with his colonel, who never missed a single performance there. He had to see him about the peacemaking affair that had occupied and amused him for the last three days. Besides, Petritsky was involved in it, and he was very fond of Petritsky. Then another nice young fellow was mixed up in the affair—Prince Kedrov, who had lately joined their regiment. And, above all, it was an affair that concerned the regiment. They were both in Vronsky's company.

Venden, the titular councillor, had called upon their colonel and complained that two of his officers had insulted his wife. His young wife, he explained, to whom he had scarcely been married six months, had been to church with her mother, and not feeling very well, because she was in a certain condition, she had engaged the first cab that came to hand in order to get home quickly. She was chased by the officers, who had nearly frightened her to death. Venden himself had just returned from his office when he heard a ring at the bell and voices. He went out, and seeing two drunken officers with a letter he pitched them out of doors. He demanded that they should be severely punished.

"You can say what you like," the colonel said to Vronsky as he invited him to sit down, "but Petritsky is getting impossible. Hardly a week goes by without some story or other. This man won't leave things alone, he'll take further proceedings."

Vronsky knew that the thing looked bad, but a duel was out of the question. Something must be done to appease this titular councillor. The colonel had consulted him because he had a good deal of faith in his common sense, and also believed him to have the honour of the regiment at heart. After they had discussed the matter thoroughly, the colonel commissioned Vronsky to accompany Petritsky and Kedrov who were to go and apologise to Venden. They both felt that his name and epaulets of an aide-de-camp might help to soften the outraged titular councillor. The desired effect was partially produced, but, as Vronsky had related, peace was not absolutely restored.

At the theatre Vronsky took the colonel into the lobby and told him of the success, or rather lack of success, that had attended his mission. After some reflection the colonel decided that he would do nothing further in the matter, but he nevertheless took a great deal of pleasure in questioning Vronsky about all the details of the meeting, and nearly died of laughing to hear Vronsky's description of the way in which the titular councillor had stormed at them, how Vronsky had brought all the powers of his eloquence to bear upon him, and how he had finally retreated, pushing Petritsky before him.

"A wretched business this, but very funny. Kedrov can't possibly fight this man! Was he so very angry? How do you like Claire this evening? Isn't she splendid!" He was referring to a new French actress. "No matter how many times you see her there's always something fresh about her. Only the French are like that."

VI

THE Princess Betsy left the theatre before the end of the last act. She had scarcely more than time enough after reaching home to go up to her dressing-room, put some more powder on her pale, long face, and order tea to be served in the large drawing-room, when one after another the carriages began to arrive at her large house on the Bolshaya Morskaya. A portly footman opened the great glass doors noiselessly, allowing the guests to pass in. The hostess, with a glittering head-dress and renewed colour on her cheeks, entered the drawing-room at one door while the guests came in at another. It was an enormous room, with dark, sombre walls and rich carpets. On the table, which was covered with a cloth of dazzling whiteness, stood a silver samovar and a tea-service of delicate china.

The hostess sat down by the samovar and began taking off her gloves. Moving the chairs, with the help of the silent footmen, the guests arranged themselves in two groups, one near the hostess at the samovar, the other in a corner of the room around the wife of a foreign ambassador, a beautiful woman in a black velvet dress. In both groups the conversation lagged at first. The continual stream of new arrivals, greetings, and offers of tea made it impossible to fix on a common subject.

"She is remarkably handsome for an actress; you can see

that she's studied Kaulbach," remarked a diplomat in the group around the ambassador's wife. " Did you notice how she fell? "

" Oh, please don't talk of Nielson! There is nothing new to say of her," pleaded a stout fair-haired dame in an old silk dress. It was the Princess Mahkaya, who was known in the set as *l'enfant terrible* for her unsophisticated, rough manners. She was sitting between the two groups and mixed in the conversation first of one and then the other. " No less than three people have made that remark about Kaulbach to-day; the very same words, I assure you. I don't know why they should have taken such a fancy to them."

The conversation was cut short by this remark. Some one had to think of a new theme.

" Tell us something amusing, but not spiteful," the ambassador's wife said, turning to the diplomat. She was reputed to be a good conversationalist, clever at what the English call " small talk."

" They say there is nothing more difficult, that only spiteful things are amusing, but I'll try," he said with a smile. " Give me a theme. Everything depends upon the theme. If you have the theme the padding comes easy enough. I often think that the celebrated talkers of last century would have found it exceedingly difficult to hold an intelligent conversation had they been alive to-day. Everything intellectual is so dull. . . . "

" That has been said long ago," the ambassador's wife interrupted him with a smile.

The conversation was getting on nicely, but it was too nice to last. Again they came to a stop. There was nothing to be done but to resort to the never-failing subject—scandal.

" Don't you think there is something Louis XV. about Tushkevitch? " he asked, with a motion of the eyebrows in the direction of a fair, handsome young man who was standing near the table.

" So there is! He goes so excellently with the room. Perhaps that's why he comes here so often."

This topic continued, particularly as they spoke wholly in hints, it being impossible to allude openly to Tushkevitch's relations with the hostess in her own drawing-room.

Around the samovar the conversation had also fluttered between three subjects; the latest society news, the theatre, and the criticising of one's neighbours. It had stopped on the latter theme—that is, scandal.

" Have you heard that Maltishcheva, the mother, not the daughter, is having a dress made in *diable rose ?* "

" Impossible! Really, this is too funny! "

" I am surprised that with her sense—you know she's not a fool—she does not see how ridiculous she is."

Every one had something to say in condemnation of the unfortunate Maltishcheva, and the conversation grew quite lively.

The Princess Betsy's husband, a good-natured, round little man, with a passion for collecting engravings, having heard that his wife had guests, came in for a moment before going out to his club. He walked softly over the thick carpet straight towards the Princess Mahkaya. " How did you like Nielson? " he asked.

" Oh dear! how you startled me! " she exclaimed. " Don't talk to me about the opera, please. You don't know anything about music. I had better descend to your level and talk to you about your majolicas and engravings. What treasures have you picked up lately? "

" I'll show you, if you like, but I'm afraid they won't appeal to you."

" Do let me see them. I've learnt all about that sort of thing at . . . what do you call those banker people? They have a splendid collection of engravings. They showed them to us."

" Have you been to the Schützburghs? " the hostess asked from her place at the samovar.

" Yes, *ma chère*. They invited us to dinner, and I was told afterwards that the sauce at that dinner cost no less than a thousand roubles," the Princess Mahkaya said in a loud voice, feeling that every one was listening to her. " And a very poor sauce it was too—something green. Of course I had to invite them to dinner, and I made them a sauce that only cost eighty-five kopeks, but they were all quite satisfied. I can't afford thousand-rouble sauces."

" Isn't she unique! " the hostess remarked.

" Wonderful! " another person exclaimed.

The Princess Mahkaya never failed to create a sensation by her remarks. She always spoke of the most ordinary simple things in and out of season, but in the society in which she moved it had the effect of the most subtle wit. She herself never understood the reason of it, but could not help taking advantage of the fact all the same.

Making use of the silence that followed the princess's remarks, the hostess turned to the ambassador's wife in the hope of bringing the company together.

"Won't you really have some tea?" she asked. "Do come over here."

"We are quite comfortable here, thanks," the ambassador's wife said with a smile, and turned to the person she had been talking to.

Every one was enjoying the conversation. They were discussing Karenin and his wife.

"Anna seems greatly changed since her visit to Moscow. There is something so strange about her," a friend of hers was saying.

"The only change I can see about her is that she has brought back the shadow of Alexei Vronsky," the ambassador's wife replied.

"There is a story of Grimm's about a man without a shadow. I think he had it taken away from him as a punishment for something or other. I confess I always failed to see where the punishment came in, but it must be rather unpleasant for a woman to be without one."

"Yes, but women with shadows always come to grief," Anna's friend remarked.

"What dreadful people you are!" the Princess Mahkaya exclaimed at these words. "Madame Karenina is a very nice woman. I don't like her husband, but I'm very fond of her."

"Why don't you like her husband? He's such a distinguished man," the ambassador's wife observed. "My husband says there are few such statesman-like men in Europe."

"That is what my husband says too, but I don't believe him," the Princess Mahkaya remarked. "If our husbands were not so fond of talking we should be able to judge things better for ourselves. In my opinion Alexei Alexandrovitch is simply stupid. I am saying this under my breath, mind you. At one time I used to rack my brain to find out where his wit lay and thought that I was too stupid to see it. But the moment I said to myself '*He is stupid,*' it all became as clear as day."

"How unkind you are to-day."

"Not at all. I had no other alternative. One of us two must have been stupid, and you would never admit it of yourself, would you?"

"No sensible man is contented with his lot, but every man is contented with his sense," the diplomat remarked.

" That's just it," the princess turned to him hastily. " But I won't let you say a word against Anna. She is a dear, sweet woman. How can she help it if all the men are so much in love with her that they pursue her like shadows? "

" I was not blaming her," Anna's friend ventured, anxious to justify herself.

" Because no one follows us like a shadow that does not give us the right to judge others." Having completely squashed Anna's friend, she rose and followed the ambassador's wife to the other group at the table, where a general conversation was going on concerning the King of Prussia.

" Whom have you been gossiping about over there? " Betsy asked.

" About the Karenins. The princess has been summing up Karenin's character," the ambassador's wife replied with a smile as she sat down at the table.

" What a pity we were not there to hear her," the hostess said with a glance at the door. " Ah! here you are at last! " she greeted Vronsky, who was just coming in.

Vronsky not only knew all the people present, but came across them every day somewhere or other. He therefore entered the room with the calm air of a man who had only just left it, so to speak.

" So you want to know where I've come from," he said in reply to a question of the ambassador's wife; " I am ashamed to confess from the Bouffes. No matter how often I go there, I always enjoy it. It's charming. I know it shows my bad taste, but I always go to sleep at the opera, whilst at the Bouffes I can sit through to the end. This evening . . . "

He mentioned the name of some French actress, and was about to tell some story about her when the ambassador's wife interrupted him with mock horror.

" Please don't talk about that fright! "

" All right, I won't, particularly as you know all about them."

" And they would all go to see them too if it was looked upon as the thing, like the opera," the Princess Mahkaya remarked.

VII

Steps were heard at the door, and the Princess Betsy, who knew that it must be Anna, glanced at Vronsky. He was looking in the direction of the door, and a strange expression of joy, mixed with fear, came over his handsome face as Anna entered the room. He rose slowly. Holding herself erect as usual she walked quickly up to the hostess in her light, springy gait, so different from that of other society women, extended her hand with a smile, and turned to Vronsky with the same smile still on her lips.

He bowed low and offered her a chair.

Anna inclined her head slightly, blushed, and knit her brows. She instantly turned to the other guests, shook hands, then addressed herself to the hostess.

" I've just come from the Countess Lydia's. I should have been here earlier, but I was detained. Sir John was there. He was very interesting."

" Do you mean the missionary? "

" Yes. He told me a lot of interesting stories about his life in India."

The conversation, again interrupted by Anna's arrival, began to waver like a lamp that is threatening to go out.

" Sir John! Why of course I've met him. He talks extremely well. Vlaseva is quite in love with him."

" Is it true that the younger Vlaseva girl is going to marry Topov? "

" They say it's quite settled."

" I am surprised at the parents. I heard it was a love match."

" A love match! What antediluvian ideas you have! I didn't know people talked of love matches nowadays," the ambassador's wife remarked.

" What would you have? This stupid old custom has not gone out of fashion yet," Vronsky observed.

" So much the worse for those who follow it. The only happy marriages I know are those of convenience."

" Yes; but that sort of happiness breaks down at the first approach of the very passion that you refuse to recognise," Vronsky remarked.

" I should say that a marriage of convenience was one where

both the parties had already sown their wild oats. Love is like the measles; we must all go through it."

"In that case we ought to be inoculated against it, as we are against smallpox."

"When I was a young girl I was in love with a curate. That may have helped me," the Princess Mahkaya remarked.

"But, seriously, I think that in order to find love it is better to make mistakes and atone for them afterwards," the Princess Betsy observed.

"Even after marriage?" the ambassador's wife asked in fun.

"It's never too late to mend!" the diplomat remarked, quoting the English proverb.

"That just expresses it," Betsy put in. "It is necessary to make mistakes in order to mend them afterwards. What do you think?" she asked, turning to Anna, who was listening in silence with a faint smile on her lips.

"I think," she began, toying with her glove that she had taken off, "I think . . . that if there are as many minds as there are heads, then there are as many ways of loving as there are hearts."

Vronsky gazed at Anna waiting to hear what she had to say with a beating heart. He gave a sigh of relief when she finished.

Anna turned to him suddenly.

"I've had a letter from Moscow. They say that Kitty Shcherbatsky is very ill."

"I'm sorry," Vronsky said, with a frown.

Anna looked at him severely.

"You don't seem interested."

"On the contrary, I am very interested. Who wrote to you, if one may ask?"

Anna rose and went up to Betsy.

"I should like a cup of tea, please," she said, leaning against her chair.

While Betsy was pouring out the tea, Vronsky came up to Anna.

"Who wrote to you?" he repeated.

"Men have no conception of honour though they are always talking about it," Anna remarked without replying to his question. "I have long wanted to talk to you about it," she added, going towards a little corner table laden with albums.

"I don't quite understand what you mean," he said, handing her a cup of tea.

She sat down on a couch, he sat down beside her.

" Yes, I have long wanted to tell you," she went on, " you have acted badly, very badly indeed."

" Do you think I don't know it? But whose fault was it? "

" Why do you say that to me? " she asked, looking at him severely.

" You know why," he said boldly, gazing straight into her eyes.

Anna hung her head.

" It only shows that you have no heart," she said. But her look denied the words.

" What you were talking about just now was an error, a mistake, but not love."

" You forget, I have forbidden you to speak that word, that hateful word," Anna said, trembling with emotion, yet instantly realising that by the very word " forbidden " she admitted to some proprietorship over him and encouraged him to go on. " I have long wanted a talk with you," she continued, looking him straight in the eyes though her face was burning, " and I came here on purpose because I knew I should meet you. This must come to an end. I have never had cause to blush before anybody, and you somehow make me feel guilty! "

He looked at her and was struck by the spiritual beauty of her face.

" What do you want me to do? " he asked solemnly.

" I want you to go to Moscow and ask Kitty to forgive you," she said.

" You don't want that," he said, feeling that she was saying it against her will.

" If you love me as you say you do," she whispered, " then do what will give me peace."

Vronsky's face lighted up.

" Don't you know that you are my life? But I cannot give you peace, because I don't know it. I can give you myself . . . my love. I cannot think of you as apart from me. For me, you and I are one. I see no hope of peace for either of us. There is nothing but despair and unhappiness in store for us. Unless it be happiness, such happiness! Is it quite hopeless? " he asked in a scarcely audible whisper. But she understood him. She struggled with herself, tried to say the thing that she felt she ought to say, but could not. She raised her eyes to his, full of love, and looked at him silently.

" At last! " he thought, beside himself with joy. " Just when I was beginning to despair, when I had given up all hope, here it is! She loves me. She has confessed it."

" Do it for my sake, don't ever speak to me like that again, and let us be friends," her words said, but her eyes spoke differently.

" We can never be mere friends, you yourself know it, but whether we are the most happy or most miserable people in the world is for you to decide."

She was about to say something, but he interrupted her.

" I ask for nothing only the right to go on hoping and suffering, but if even that is impossible, then I will disappear if you wish me to. I will relieve you of my presence if it is painful for you to see me."

" I do not wish to drive you away."

" Then change nothing. Let everything remain as it is," he implored in a trembling voice. " Here comes your husband."

Alexei Alexandrovitch was at this moment entering the room in his quiet, awkward way. He glanced at his wife and Vronsky, then went up to the hostess and sat down at the tea-table.

" Your Rambouillet is complete—the graces and muses," he remarked in his drawling, superior tone.

The Princess Betsy could not bear this tone of his—sneering she called it—and like the clever hostess she was she soon led the conversation into a more serious channel. They began talking about the general condition of the army, and Alexei Alexandrovitch became quite heated in his defence of certain new decrees. The Princess Betsy attacked him mercilessly.

Vronsky and Anna still sat near the little table.

" This is getting rather pointed," one lady whispered with a motion of the eyebrows in the direction of Karenin, then Anna and Vronsky.

" What did I tell you? " Anna's friend said.

Not only these two ladies, but by degrees every one in the room, including the Princess Mahkaya and Betsy, began casting disapproving glances at the couple who had withdrawn themselves from the circle. Only Alexei Alexandrovitch appeared not to notice them, and did not for a moment lose the thread of his argument.

Betsy, perceiving the unpleasant impression the two were creating, seized a moment when some one else was replying to Alexei Alexandrovitch and crossed over to Anna.

" I do so admire the clear and precise way in which your husband speaks," she said. " I can understand the most transcendental questions when he is explaining them."

" Oh, yes! " Anna said, radiant with joy, though she did not understand a single word that Betsy had said. She went over to the big table and joined in the general conversation.

At the end of half-an-hour Alexei Alexandrovitch came up to her and proposed that they should go home together, but without looking at him she declared her intention of staying to supper. He took leave of the company and departed.

An old Tartar in a smart uniform, the Karenins' coachman, was trying to restrain the left off-horse standing at the wide portico. A footman held open the carriage door, while another stood at the hall-door allowing Anna and Vronsky to pass through. She was fingering the lace frills on her sleeve that had got caught on the clasp of her fur coat and listening in ecstasy to what Vronsky was saying as he led her down the steps.

" You promised nothing and I make no demands," he said, " but you know it is not friendship that I ask for. All happiness for me is contained in that one word, so offensive to your ear—love."

" Love . . . " she repeated slowly, as if speaking to herself. Then as she disentangled her lace she turned to him.

" I dislike the word because it means a great deal more to me, a vast deal more than you can possibly understand," she said, gazing into his eyes. " Good-night."

She held out her hand, and with a rapid step she passed the footman and disappeared into the carriage.

Her glance, the pressure of her hand, set him on fire. He kissed the palm of his hand where her fingers had touched, and went home happy in the thought that this evening had brought him nearer to the attainment of his dream than all the past two months.

VIII

Alexei Alexandrovitch did not see anything wrong in the fact that his wife was sitting apart with Vronsky engaged in some animated conversation, but he noticed that the others thought it wrong and therefore resolved to talk to her about it.

When he reached home he went into his study as usual, sat down in an arm-chair, and opened a book on Papistry. A paper-knife marked the page where he had left it. He read for some time, every now and again shaking his head as if to drive away some unpleasant thought. At the accustomed hour he rose and went into his dressing-room to prepare for bed. Anna had not yet returned. With a book under his arm he proceeded upstairs, but instead of being preoccupied as usual with his official duties, he was filled with an unpleasant foreboding concerning his wife. Contrary to his habit, instead of going straight to bed, he began walking up and down the room, his hands clasped behind his back. He felt it necessary to review the new situation that had been thrust upon him.

When he had first decided to speak to his wife it had seemed to him simple and easy enough, but as soon as he began to consider the matter endless obstacles seemed to stand in the way.

Alexei Alexandrovitch was not jealous. He would have considered it insulting to Anna, believing that a man should have full confidence in his wife. Why he should have such confidence that she, a young woman, would always love him, he had never stopped to consider, but the fact remained that he had never doubted her because it was against his principles to do so. Now he was in a most absurd and illogical position. At last he had come face to face with a living fact, and was at a loss to know how to act. He had always been so occupied with his official duties as never to have come in contact with real life, and now that he was confronted by it he shrank from it involuntarily. He felt like a man who, having just crossed a bridge, suddenly realises that it was crumbling to pieces and that there is a yawning abyss beneath. The abyss was life, the bridge the artificial existence he had been leading. The idea that his wife could love another man occurred to him for the first time and filled him with terror.

He did not attempt to undress, but kept walking up and down with regular steps over the echoing floors. At first he walked through the dining-room, in which a single lamp was burning, then over the carpet of the dark drawing-room, where a ray of light fell from the door on his own portrait, recently painted, that was hanging above the couch. He paced through her little boudoir, where two candles were burning, casting their dim light on the portraits of her relatives and friends, on the familiar delicate little knick-knacks adorning her writing-table. He continued as far as her bedroom door and turned back again.

Every now and again he stopped, particularly when he came to the dining-room. " Yes, this must be settled and done with. I must tell her what I think of it and what I have decided to do," he would say to himself. " But what shall I tell her?

and what have I decided to do? " he asked as he turned back to the drawing-room. But no answer was forthcoming. " After all," he continued, as he walked through his study, " what has happened? Nothing at all. She had a long conversation with him. What harm is there in that? A woman in society talks with all sorts of people. To be jealous would be humiliating to both of us," he concluded, as he reached her boudoir, but those words had lost the meaning they had once had for him. From the door of the bedroom he turned back to the hall, then through the dark drawing-room, while an inner voice was telling him that there must be something wrong, else the others would not have noticed it. " Yes, the thing must be decided and done with," he said to himself again. " But how? " he asked, going over the same ground again without striking on any new ideas. He realised this at last, passed his hand over his forehead, and sat down in her boudoir.

He glanced at her writing-table, on which an unfinished letter was lying, and his thoughts suddenly took another direction. He began to think of her, of what she thought and felt. He tried to imagine her own private life, her interests and desires, and the idea that she could possibly have an existence apart from him was so terrible that he hastened to put it from him. It was the abyss into which he dared not look. To penetrate to the very soul of another human being was beyond Alexei Alexandrovitch, and in fact he would have considered it dangerous.

" The most awful thing about it," he thought, " is that she should have sprung this upon me just now when I have the greatest need of all my mental powers, when I ought to be concentrating on my affairs." (He was thinking of the changes he had effected in the ministry.) " But what's to be done? I cannot go about in this state of anxiety. I am not one of those people who are afraid to look trouble in the face."

" I must think it over and decide what to do once and for all," he said out aloud.

" I have no right to probe into her feelings, to find out what is going on in her heart, that is a matter for her own conscience and comes into the domain of religion," he said to himself, relieved that he had at last found some law that he could apply to the disturbing circumstance. " Assuming that questions relating to her feelings," he continued, " are questions of conscience in which I have no concern, my duty lies clearly before me. As head of the family it is my duty to guide her, and as

I am in a sense responsible for her I must point out the dangers, warn her, even if I have to exercise my rights. There is nothing to be done but to talk to her plainly."

And Alexei Alexandrovitch began planning what he should say to his wife, at the same time thinking what a waste of time it was for him to be spending his intellectual powers on domestic matters. "This is what I must tell her," he said to himself, his thoughts unconsciously assuming the precise logical form of a report. "In the first place, I must point out the meaning and importance of public opinion. In the second, the religious significance of marriage. In the third place, the misfortunes that might befall her son, and lastly the misfortunes that might befall herself." Having finished, Alexei Alexandrovitch put his hands together and made the joints of his fingers crack. This gesture, a bad habit of his, was always soothing to his nerves.

The rumbling of a carriage was heard in front of the house, and Alexei Alexandrovitch stopped still in the middle of the drawing-room. He heard his wife coming up the stairs and stood ready with his speech. He twisted his fingers and waited for the sound—only one joint cracked.

He could feel her coming nearer, and although he was quite satisfied with the speech he had prepared he was nevertheless terrified at the forthcoming scene.

IX

ANNA came in playing with the tassels of her hood. Her head was slightly bent, but her face was radiant with a terrible radiance, like a fire on a dark winter's night. When she saw her husband, she raised her head and smiled as though awakening from a dream.

"Not in bed yet? What a surprise!" she exclaimed, as she took off her hood and proceeded to the dressing-room. "It is late, Alexei Alexandrovitch," she said from the other side of the door.

"Anna, I want to have a talk with you."

"With me?" she asked in surprise as she came out and looked at him. "What is it? What about?" she asked, sitting down. "Come along, since it is so important, but I would rather go to sleep."

Anna said the first thing that came into her head, astonished at her faculty for lying. It sounded so natural for her to want to go to sleep. She felt herself clad in an impenetrable armour of falsehood, as if some invisible power was helping and sustaining her.

" Anna, I must put you on your guard."

" On my guard? Why? "

She looked at him so innocently, so gaily, that any one who did not know her as well as her husband did would have detected nothing strange in her tone or her words. But for him, who knew that ordinarily, had he gone to bed five minutes later than was his wont, she would have wanted to know the reason of it, who knew that her first impulse was to tell him of her pleasures and her sorrows—the fact that she tried not to notice his condition, nor spoke a single word about herself, was a very significant one. Her heart which was always so open to him now seemed closed to him for ever. Her very tone was defiant. " Yes, it is shut," it seemed to say; " that is as it should be, as it will always be." He felt like a man who had come home and found the house locked up. " But I may be able to find the key yet," Alexei Alexandrovitch said to himself.

" I want to put you on your guard," he said in a soft tone of voice, " because I fear that your indiscretion and carelessness may lead people to talk about you. Your rather animated conversation with Count Vronsky this evening attracted attention." He pronounced Vronsky's name slowly and distinctly.

As he spoke he looked into Anna's sparkling eyes, so impenetrable for him now, and felt how utterly idle and useless were his words.

" You are always like that," she said, as though she had comprehended absolutely nothing that he had said except the last few words. " You don't like me to be bored and you don't like me to enjoy myself. I was not bored this evening—is that what is troubling you? "

Alexei Alexandrovitch trembled; he put his hands together and was about to crack the joints of his fingers.

" Don't do that, please; it goes on my nerves," Anna said.

" Anna, is this you? " Alexei Alexandrovitch asked, trying to control himself and stop the movement of his hands.

" Well, what is it? " she asked with a sincere and almost comic astonishment. " What do you want of me? "

Alexei Alexandrovitch passed his hand over his eyes and forehead, and did not say anything. He felt that instead of having warned his wife against making mistakes in the eyes of the world, he was agitated at what concerned her conscience and had come up against a dead wall, as it were.

" This is what I wished to say to you," he continued coldly, " and I beg you to listen to me. As you know, I look upon jealousy as a most offensive and humiliating sentiment which I would never permit myself to be led away by, but there are certain laws of propriety that cannot be ignored without incurring the gravest consequences. This evening I noticed, that is, it was forced upon my notice by the impression you created on the whole company, that you did not conduct yourself in a way to be desired."

" I really don't understand you," Anna said, shrugging her shoulders. " He does not care," she thought; " he is only disturbed because the others noticed it. You are not well, Alexei Alexandrovitch," she added, and rose with the intention of going to the door, but he moved a step or two forward as if he wished to detain her.

Anna had never seen his face so dark and severe. She stopped, threw back her head, and with a quick movement began taking out the hairpins from her hair.

" Go on, I'm listening," she said sarcastically. " I am anxious to know what it's all about."

She herself was surprised at the calm, natural way in which she spoke, and at the choice of her words.

" I have no right to analyse your feelings, neither do I consider it would be useful or well to do so," Alexei Alexandrovitch began. " If we probe too deeply into our hearts we often discover something that we would rather not see. Your feelings concern your own conscience, but it is my duty to you, to myself, and to God, to remind you of your obligations. Our lives are united, not by man, but by God. The bond can only be broken by a crime, and such a crime brings its own punishment."

" I don't know what you are talking about and I'm simply dying to go to sleep," she said, hunting for the remaining pins in her hair.

" Anna, for Heaven's sake, don't talk like that," he implored gently. " I may have been mistaken, but believe me I am speaking as much for your sake as for mine. I am your husband and I love you."

For a moment she hung her head and the mocking light disappeared from her eyes, but the word " love " irritated her.

" Love? " she thought; " can he love? If he had never heard of love he would never have used the word. He cannot possibly know what it means."

" Alexei Alexandrovitch, I really don't understand you," she said. " Could you be a little more explicit . . . "

" Allow me to finish. I love you, but I am not speaking for myself, my only desire is to protect our son and yourself. It is quite possible that I may be mistaken, in which case I ask your pardon, but if you have the slightest reason to think that there is some ground for my remarks, then I beg you earnestly to consider and, if your heart will allow you, to tell me everything . . . "

Alexei Alexandrovitch did not notice that he was saying something quite different from the speech he had prepared.

" I have nothing to tell you and it's really time for bed," she said, scarcely able to contain a smile.

Alexei Alexandrovitch gave a deep sigh, and without another word he went into the bedroom.

When Anna came in he was already in bed. His lips were tightly clenched and his eyes avoided hers. She lay down on her bed and waited, expecting that he would speak to her, yet dreading him to do so, but Alexei Alexandrovitch was silent. She lay motionless for a time, but soon forgot all about him. She was thinking of another. Her imagination pictured him before her and her heart was filled with a wild, guilty joy. Suddenly she heard a slow regular sound of snoring. At first Alexei Alexandrovitch was startled himself and stopped, but after a moment or two the sound continued anew with an astonishing regularity.

" How late it is! " she said to herself with a smile. She lay motionless for a long time with wide-open eyes, and it seemed to her that she herself could see how radiant they looked in the darkness.

X

FROM that evening a new life began for Alexei Alexandrovitch and his wife. Anna went into society as usual, spent a good deal of time at the Princess Betsy's, and met Vronsky wherever she went. Alexei Alexandrovitch was aware of it, but was powerless to stop it. All his efforts that might have led to an understanding she treated with the blankest astonishment, utterly beyond his comprehension. There was no outward change in their life, but their relations to one another were quite different. Alexei Alexandrovitch, a remarkable statesman, found himself utterly powerless in his own home. He bent his head submissively like an ox expecting the final blow of the axe that was hanging over him. Every time he reviewed the situation he tried to assure himself that there was still hope, that kindness and patience might yet save her and bring her to her senses again. Whenever he tried to talk to her, however, the spirit of falsehood that possessed her seemed to communicate itself to him, and he said something quite other than the thing he had intended to say. Involuntarily he assumed that bantering tone he had always adopted with her, and it was impossible to say what he wanted to in that tone.

XI

WHAT for nearly a year had been the sole desire of Vronsky's life, changing all his former desires, what had seemed to Anna so impossible, terrible, yet so fascinating, had come to pass. Pale, with quivering lips, he stood over her, begging her to calm herself, yet not knowing himself why or how.

" Anna! Anna! " he implored in a trembling voice. " Anna, for Heaven's sake . . . "

But the more intensely he spoke the lower she hung her head, once proud and gay but now humiliated. She bent lower and lower, and crouched down from the couch she had been sitting on to the floor at his feet. She would have fallen on to the carpet had he not held her.

" My God! forgive me! " she sobbed, pressing his hand to her breast.

She felt like a guilty criminal with nothing remaining for her but to humiliate herself and beg forgiveness, and as he was all that she had in the world, it was to him that she addressed her prayer. As she looked at him she felt her humiliation physically and could not utter another word. He felt exactly as a murderer feels who sees the body of his victim lying before him. The body of the victim was their love, the first period of their love There was something terribly revolting to think of the frightful price they had paid for their shame. Her shame before their spiritual nakedness communicated itself to him. But in spite of all the horror felt by the murderer in presence of the body of his victim, he must cut it in pieces, must bury it, must take advantage of his crime.

And as with fury and passion the murderer throws himself on the dead body and tears it to pieces, so he covered her face and shoulders with kisses. She held his hand and did not stir. These were the kisses she had bought with her shame. She raised his hand and kissed it. That hand that would always be hers—the hand of her accomplice. He fell down on his knees before her trying to look into her face, but she hid it from him and did not utter a word. At last, as if trying to control herself, she made an effort to rise and pushed him away. Her face was as beautiful as ever, but it was pitiful to see.

" All is over," she said. " I have nothing but you. Remember that."

" I cannot forget what is my life. For one moment of happiness like this . . . "

" Happiness! " she exclaimed with horror that involuntarily communicated itself to him. " For Heaven's sake, not a word more."

She rose quickly and drew away from him.

" Not a word more," she repeated, and with a strange expression of coldness and despair that he could not understand she took leave of him. She felt at that moment that she could not express in words the sensation of shame, horror, and joy at this entrance into a new life, and she was unwilling to speak of it, to profane the sensation by insignificant words. But even afterwards, the next day and the next, she not only could not find words to express all the complexity of her feelings, but could not even find thoughts with which to analyse what was taking place in her soul.

" No, I cannot think of it now," she kept on saying to herself; " later on when I am calmer." But that time never came. Every time she attempted to think of what she had done, of what she must do, and what would become of her, the horror of her position came upon her and she put these thoughts from her mind.

" Later on, later on, when I am calmer," she said to herself.

But in her dreams when she had no control over her thoughts the situation appeared to her in all its nakedness. One dream came to her almost every night. It seemed to her that she was the wife of both Vronsky and Alexei Alexandrovitch at the same time, and that they both lavished their caresses on her. Alexei Alexandrovitch was kissing her hands, and weeping said, " How happy we are now! " Vronsky was also there, and he too was her husband. She was amazed that she had thought this impossible, and explained to them laughing that it was much simpler, that now they would both be happy. But this dream oppressed her like a nightmare and she always woke in a fright.

XII

In the early days of his return from Moscow Levin trembled and blushed every time he thought of his rejection. " This is how I trembled and blushed," he would say to himself, " when I failed in my physics examination. I thought that the world had come to an end. And it was just the same when I made a mess of that affair of my sister's. But now that a year has gone by I am amazed to think how it could ever have troubled me. In time I shall get quite indifferent to this."

But three months had gone by and he did not feel indifferent, and could never think of it without pain. He had so long dreamt of family life, was so well cut out for it, as he thought, and here he was not married nor ever likely to be. He shared the feelings of those around him that it was not good for a man of his years to live alone. He remembered how before he had set out for Moscow he had happened to be talking with Nikolai, the peasant who looked after his cattle. " Well, Nikolai! " he had said, " I want to get married." " It's quite time you were married," Nikolai had replied hastily, as if he were referring to a thing about which there could be no doubt. But marriage now seemed farther off than it had ever done before. His heart was occupied and he could not imagine any other girl of his acquaintance taking Kitty's place. Recollections of the way in which she had refused him still tormented him. No matter how often he assured himself that he was not to blame, still every time he thought of it he could not help blushing with shame. He was more ashamed of it than of any mean thing he had ever done in his life. It was a wound that would not heal.

Time and work, however, brought their reward. The painful impressions began to fade little by little in the absorbing interests of his country life. As the weeks went by he found himself thinking less and less of Kitty, and waited impatiently for the news that she had got married, hoping that this would finally cure him.

Meanwhile spring had come, beautiful, tender, without treachery, one of those rare springs such as fills plants and animals no less than men with joy. It filled Levin with new hope, and made him desire more than ever to tear himself from the past and reorganise his life on a new basis. Although many of the plans he had made on his return home had not been fulfilled, still the most essential one, the purity of his life, had not been stained. He no longer experienced the shame he had felt after every fall, and could now look people straight in the eyes.

In February he had received a letter from Marya Nikolaevna stating that his brother Nikolai's health had got very much worse, but that he still refused to take care of himself. This letter had taken Levin to Moscow, where he had managed to persuade his brother to see a doctor and to go abroad. Levin could not help feeling pleased at the way in which he had arranged it all, and lent Nikolai money without irritating him.

Besides his reading and the work on the farm, which demanded greater attention as spring drew nearer, Levin had begun a treatise on rural economy. He set out to prove that the temperament of the labourer was equally as important as the soil and the climate, and that therefore agricultural science could no more neglect the labourer than the other two factors.

In spite of his loneliness or perhaps because of it, his life was extraordinarily full. Only every now and again a desire would come over him to share his thoughts with some one, other than Agafia Mihailovna, his housekeeper. However, he often discussed all sorts of things with her, such as physics, rural economy, especially philosophy, which was Agafia Mihailovna's favourite subject.

The spring was rather late. During the last week in Lent the weather was still clear and frosty. It thawed during the day, but at night there were seven degrees [1] of frost, and the ground was so hard that the carts could still drive over the fields. At Easter there was snow, but a day or two later a warm wind arose, the sky became overcast with clouds, and for three days and three nights a gentle rain came down. On Thursday the wind dropped and a thick, grey mist overspread the earth as if to conceal the mysteries that nature was preparing. The ice was melting everywhere, the streams were overflowing with running water. On the evening of the Sunday after

[1] Réaumur.

Easter, the mist lifted, the clouds dispersed themselves, and the spring appeared in all its glory. On the following morning the remaining ice disappeared in the hot rays of the sun, and the air seemed to tremble with the vapours rising out of the damp, warm earth. Green blades of grass began to show themselves, the buds swelled on the currant-bushes, the hazel-trees, and the birches, and around their branches a swarm of bees were humming. Invisible larks sent forth their songs of joy over the green fields, the peewits seemed to mourn for their marshes, submerged by the stormy waters, the cranes and wild geese flew high in the air with their calls of spring. The cattle lowed as they were turned out of their stalls, the young lambs gambolled about near their mothers, children played about on the paths, covering them with the footprints of their bare feet, the merry voices of women bleaching their linen could be heard at the pond, from all sides resounded the hammering of peasants repairing their ploughs and harrows.

Spring had really come.

XIII

Levin put on his heavy boots, a short coat (for the first time discarding his great-coat), and went out on the farm, stepping now in pools of water that flashed in the sunlight, now into the soft mud.

Spring is the time for plans and projects. Levin had not the remotest idea of what he would first take in hand any more than a tree knows where its young branches are going to shoot out and clothe themselves with green leaves, but he felt himself full of the most excellent schemes.

He first went to examine his cattle. The cows had been let out into the yard and were lowing piteously to be allowed out to pasture. Their smooth, speckly backs were shining in the warm sun. Levin looked at them with satisfaction; then gave orders for them to be turned out into the fields to make room for the calves. The milkmaids, lifting up their petticoats, were running to and fro in the mud with their bare feet, not yet browned by the sun, driving the frisky calves before them.

Levin was particularly pleased with this year's herd. Pava's daughter, only three months old, was nearly as big as a yearling. He ordered their troughs to be brought out, filled with hay, and placed in the hurdles, but the hurdles, never used except in winter, turned out to be in very bad repair. He sent for the carpenter, who was supposed to be mending the threshing machine, but he was discovered at work on some ploughs that ought to have been seen to months ago. Levin felt annoyed. This eternal lack of order that he was always struggling against made him angry. He was told that the hurdles had been taken to the stables, and as they were of light construction, intended only for the calves, they had got broken somehow. Besides which it turned out that the harrows and other farm implements that ought to have been mended in the winter, for the purpose of which three carpenters had been engaged, had not been touched. They were now busy on them when they ought to be in the fields harrowing. Levin sent some one to find the bailiff, but was too impatient to wait, and set off to find him himself. He discovered him coming out of the threshing barn in a light lambskin coat, twisting a straw about in his hand, as radiant as everything else on that day.

"Why isn't the carpenter at work on the threshing-machine?"

"I meant to tell you yesterday that the ploughs wanted mending. They are wanted on the fields."

"They should have been done in the winter."

"Why do you want the carpenter, Konstantin Dmitritch?"

"Where are the hurdles for the calves?"

"I gave orders to have them put up, but what can you do with these people?" the bailiff asked, waving his hands about.

"It's not the people, but the bailiff!" Levin burst out. "What do I keep you for?" he shouted, but recollecting that this would not help matters he stopped. "Well, can we get the seed in?" he asked after a pause.

"We might round by Turkino to-morrow or the day after."

"And the clover?"

"I sent Vassily and Mishka to sow it, but I don't know whether they succeeded. The ground is too hard yet."

"How many acres are being sown?"

"Six."

"Why not the whole?"

He was still more angry to learn that they were sowing only six acres with clover instead of twenty. He knew by experience as well as theory that the best time to sow clover was just before the snow went, but he could never get them to do this.

"There are not enough men. Besides, what can you do with

these people? Three of them did not turn up, and then there's Simion . . ."

"Why didn't you take them off the straw?"

"That's just what I have done."

"Then where are they all?"

"Five of them are preparing the compote" (he meant to say compost) "and four others are moving the oats so that they should not spoil."

Levin knew very well that the words "so that they should not spoil" meant that his best English oats were completely done for. Again his orders had been neglected.

"Did I not tell you to keep them well ventilated!" he cried.

"Don't worry yourself, Konstantin Dmitritch; everything shall be done in good time."

Levin threw up his arms in despair, went into the barn to examine the oats, then came back to the stables. Fortunately the oats were not yet spoilt, but the men were turning them over with their spades instead of moving them straight to the lower barn. Levin ordered the men to do this, told two of them to go down to the clover field, and little by little his anger calmed down. It was really impossible to be angry for long on such a lovely day.

"Ignat!" he shouted to the coachman who was standing near the wall with turned-up sleeves washing down the wheels of the carriage. "Saddle me a horse."

"Which one?"

"Kolpik will do."

"Right, sir."

While the horse was being saddled Levin called to the bailiff who was still within sight, so as to make his peace with him. He talked to him about the coming spring work, and about the various plans he had made with regard to the estate generally. He wanted the manure carted early so as to have it all done before the first mowing. Then the farthest field was to be ploughed and left fallow. As for the first mowing, he was to put all the labourers on it at the same time, instead of doing it bit by bit.

The bailiff listened attentively, trying to look as if he approved of what his master was saying with that familiar, irritating, hopeless expression of his. "That is all very well," it seemed to say, "if God wills."

Nothing irritated Levin more than this expression of his, but it had been common to all the bailiffs he had ever employed.

They had all treated his orders in exactly the same way, and he realised that it was no use getting vexed about it any longer. He only felt troubled at this attitude, " if God wills," that seemed to oppose him everywhere, and resolved to try and combat it more than ever.

" Will there be time to get all done, Konstantin Dmitritch? "

" Why should there not be? "

" We should want at least fifteen more hands, and you can't get them anywhere. A labourer expects to get seventy roubles for the summer nowadays."

Levin was silent. Here was the same old obstacle. However much they tried they could never get more than thirty-seven or forty labourers at a fair price. This time they had procured forty, and no more were to be found. But Levin would not be contented.

" Can't you send to Sura or to Chefirovka? If they won't come you must try and find them."

" I'll send if you like," the bailiff said dejectedly, " but you know the horses are getting feeble."

" We must get others. I know," he said with a laugh, " that you will do as little as you can, but I won't let you have your own way this year. I shall look after things myself."

" You sleep little enough as it is. We are happier under our master's eye . . . "

" Are they sowing clover down in the slope by the birches? I will go and have a look," he said as he mounted a small light bay horse that the coachman had led out.

" Don't go by the stream, Konstantin Dmitritch," the coachman shouted after him.

" All right, I'll take the road."

The little easy-going ambler snorted as he crossed the puddles and pulled at the bridle. He soon left the muddy yard behind him and came out into the open fields.

Levin had felt happy in the yard among the cattle, but here his spirits rose still more. He jolted gently up and down on his excellent horse, and drank in deep draughts of warm air as he sped his way through the wood, which was still covered by small patches of snow lying here and there. Every tree, every bud, every piece of moss filled him with joy. He left the wood behind him and came out into the open fields. They spread out before him like a green velvet carpet. Not a single bare spot or pool anywhere, but here and there just a few patches of snow. He did not feel angry when he saw the peasants' horses trampling down his green fields, and asked the first man he came across to drive them away.

"Well, Ipat, are you going to sow soon?" he asked of another peasant who came up.

"We must do the ploughing first," Ipat replied vacantly.

But even this answer failed to anger Levin. The farther he went the more his good-humour increased, and each of his new plans seemed to him better than the last. He would plant trees along the south side of the fields to keep the snow from staying too long; he would turn nine other fields into meadows; build a new cow-house in the farthest corner, and dig a new pond; he would build portable enclosures for the cattle, so as to manure the land where he wanted it; sow three hundred acres with wheat, one hundred and fifty with clover, and put one hundred under potatoes. He would not leave a single acre idle.

With such thoughts as these he picked his way carefully so as not to harm the crops till he reached the place where his men were sowing clover.

The cart with the seeds was standing in the middle of a ploughed field, and the horse was trampling down his winter corn. Two labourers were sitting on the path smoking a pipe between them. Instead of having mixed the seed with fine soil they had used great hard lumps of clay.

Seeing the master approach, the two men got up and went towards the cart. Mishka started sowing. It was all in the most hopeless disorder, but Levin rarely got angry with his men. When Vassily came up he ordered him to remove the horse to the side.

"He won't do any harm, sir," Vassily replied.

"Do as I tell you, please, and don't attempt to discuss," Levin said.

"Very well, sir," Vassily replied, taking hold of the horse. "The seed is very good, Konstantin Dmitritch," he remarked, attempting to put himself right, "but you can hardly get along. You seem to pick up a hundredweight of soil with each step."

"Why didn't you sift the soil before you mixed it with the seed?"

"We break it up as we go along," Vassily replied, taking up a handful of seed and crushing the soil.

Of course it was not Vassily's fault that the soil had not been sifted, but Levin was none the less annoyed. He looked at Mishka, who was endeavouring to shake off an enormous clod of earth that had stuck to his boot, and dismounting, went up to him and took the basket of seed from his hand.

" Where did you leave off? " he asked.

Vassily pointed to the spot with his foot and Levin began to sow the seed as best he could. The ground was so heavy as to make it very difficult to get along, and when he got to the end of the furrow he stopped and handed the basket back to Vassily.

" Well, sir, I hope you won't blame me for that furrow when the summer comes," Vassily remarked.

" Eh? "

Levin smiled, his anger having completely left him.

" We shall see in the summer. It will all come right. How well it looks over there, Konstantin Dmitritch, where I sowed last spring. I work for you just as if you were my own father, sir. I don't like to do things badly and I won't let others if I can help it. What is good for the master is good for us. See that field over there? " he said, pointing to it, " it does your heart good to look at it."

" A fine spring we are having, Vassily! "

" Yes, our old men say they have never known such a spring The elder in our village sowed a lot of land with wheat and they say you can hardly tell it from rye."

" Is it long since you've started growing wheat? "

" It was you who taught us that. You gave us two measures last year. We sold a fourth of it and sowed the rest."

" I must be off. Mind you break up the soil," Levin said as he went towards his horse, " and keep an eye on Mishka. If the crop turns out good I shall give you fifty kopeks for every acre."

" Thank you, sir. We should be content without that."

Levin mounted his horse and rode away to visit his last year's clover field, and then to the field that was being ploughed for the wheat.

The crop looked very healthy, just appearing above the stubble of last year's wheat.

The horse found it difficult to get along over the soft ground, and as for the ploughed field they could not get over that at all. The men had nearly finished and would soon be ready for the furrowing and sowing. It gladdened Levin's heart to look at it all as he turned on his homeward way. He resolved to cross the stream, hoping that the water would be lower. As he leapt across two wild ducks flew out.

"There ought to be snipe," he thought, and farther on he met the keeper, who confirmed him in his opinion.

Levin spurred his horse to get home as quickly as he could, to be in time for dinner and to prepare his gun for the evening.

XIV

LEVIN reached home in the most excellent spirits. A minute or two later a ring was heard at the front-door bell.

"That must be some one from the station," he thought; "the Moscow train was due a short time ago. I wonder who it can be? Supposing it should be Nikolai?" He had said that he might come down to him instead of going abroad. His first thought was one of annoyance that his brother should come and spoil his plans for the spring, but disgusted with the selfishness of the thought he felt ready to receive him with open arms. He turned his horse, and as he came round a group of acacias, he caught sight of the station sledge and a man in a big coat sitting in it. It was not his brother.

"If only it were some sensible person whom I could talk to," Levin thought.

"Why, it's Stepan Arkadyevitch!" he exclaimed joyfully, as soon as he recognised the visitor. "What a pleasure! I am so glad to see you!"

"I shall find out whether she is married or not," he thought.

Even the memory of Kitty was not painful to him on this beautiful spring day.

"You did not expect me," Stepan Arkadyevitch remarked, as he leapt out of the sledge. His face was splashed with mud, but he was radiant with health and pleasure. "I have come first to see you, secondly for some shooting, and thirdly to sell my wood at Yergushov."

"That's right! What do you think of the spring? Why ever did you come in a sledge?"

"It would have been worse in a cart, Konstantin Dmitritch," the driver interposed.

"Well, I am delighted to see you," Levin said with his frank, child-like smile.

He led his guest to his room where his things were brought after him, and leaving him to wash and change he proceeded to the office to give orders about the ploughing and the clover.

Agafia Mihailovna, who had the honour of the house very much at heart, stopped him in the hall with questions about dinner.

"Prepare what you like, only let us have it as quickly as possible," he said as he went in to talk to the bailiff.

When he returned Stepan Arkadyevitch, washed and brushed and beaming, was just coming out of his room. They went upstairs together.

"Well, I'm glad I've got to you at last! I can now understand the mysteries of your existence. Really, I envy you. What a house! How beautiful it all is! So sunny and light." Stepan Arkadyevitch had completely forgotten that it was not always spring, and that the days were not always bright. "And what a darling your nurse is! I should have preferred a pretty little housemaid in a white apron, but in your severe monastic style the nurse fits in better."

Stepan Arkadyevitch related all the news. Amongst other things he told Levin that his brother Sergei Ivanovitch intended to come and spend the summer with him. He did not, however, say a word about the Shcherbatskys, other than that his wife had sent her kind regards. Levin appreciated his delicacy. As usual he had stored up a fund of ideas and impressions during his solitude which he had been unable to communicate to any one. He now began pouring them all out to Stepan Arkadyevitch. He spoke of the joy he felt in the spring, of the plans he had formed and those that had failed. He mentioned all the books he had read during the last few months, and touched upon his own work on rural economy, which he said was merely a criticism of other books written on this subject. Stepan Arkadyevitch, who was always very attentive, seemed especially so on this occasion, and Levin noticed with pleasure that there was a sort of tenderness and respect in his bearing towards him.

The united efforts of Agafia Mihailovna and the cook, who were preparing a most excellent dinner, resulted in the two friends, who were half famished, sitting down to the table before it was ready and devouring bread and butter and salt fish. Levin at last called for the soup before the little pies were done, much to the disgust of the cook, who had hoped to astonish the visitor. But Stepan Arkadyevitch, though he was used to different dinners, found everything excellent. He went into raptures over the bread and butter, the mushrooms, nettle soup, roast chicken and white sauce, and the white Crimean wine.

" Excellent! excellent! " he exclaimed as he lighted a cigarette after the roast chicken. " I feel as if I had escaped from a stormy sea on to a quiet shore. So you think that the labourer's temperament should be taken into consideration in matters relating to rural economy. I don't pretend to know much about it, but I should think that the theory can't have any but a very good effect on the labourer himself."

" But, one moment, I was not talking about political economy, I meant agricultural science. I maintain that you must study the premises, the phenomena, just the same as in the natural sciences, and the labourer must be looked at from the economic and ethnographic point of view . . . "

At this moment Agafia Mihailovna came in with the desert.

" Well, Agafia Mihailovna," Stepan Arkadyevitch said, throwing her a kiss with the tips of his shapely fingers, " I must congratulate you on your cooking! Don't you think it's time to start, Kostia? " he added.

Levin looked out of the window at the sun which was setting behind the trees, still bare and leafless.

" I think it is," he replied. " Kusma, have the dog-cart brought out," he shouted, running downstairs.

Stepan Arkadyevitch followed. He removed the linen cover from his handsome case and took out a new, expensive gun of the very latest pattern. Kusma, who foresaw a generous tip, hovered around him. He helped him on with his stockings and hunting boots, and Stepan Arkadyevitch accepted his aid complacently.

" I say, Kostia, if Rabinin, the merchant, calls, tell your people to get him to wait. I am expecting him to-day."

" Are you selling the wood to him? "

" Yes. Do you know him? "

" Of course I do. I have done business with him, positively and finally."

Stepan Arkadyevitch burst into a laugh. " Positively " and " finally " were the merchant's favourite words.

" Yes, it's very funny the way he talks. She knows where her master is going," he added, patting Lasca, who was jumping and barking around Levin, licking now his hands, now his boots and gun.

A trap was standing at the door when they came out.

" I told them to harness it although it's not very far, but if you would rather walk we can."

" I would rather drive, thanks," Stepan Arkadyevitch said,

taking his seat and lighting a cigar. " How is it you don't smoke? " he asked, wrapping a rug around his legs. " To my mind a good cigar is the very height of pleasure. Now this is what I call life! How jolly! I should always like to live like this."

" What is there to prevent you? " Levin asked with a smile.

" You're a very fortunate man. You have everything you like. You like horses and you have them; dogs, you have them; hunting, you have that, and an estate too."

" Perhaps it's because I enjoy what I have and don't bother myself about what I have not," Levin remarked, remembering Kitty.

Stepan Arkadyevitch understood and looked at him without speaking.

Levin was grateful to Oblonsky, who with his usual tact had refrained from mentioning the Shcherbatskys, fearing that it might be unpleasant to him. Levin however now wished to know how matters stood, but was afraid to inquire.

" Well, how are your affairs? " he asked, suddenly realising that it was selfish to be only thinking of himself.

Stepan Arkadyevitch's eyes sparkled.

" According to your ideas it's wrong to want hot rolls when you have your allowance of stale bread, but personally I don't think life is worth living without love," he began, construing Levin's question in his own fashion. " What can I do? I was born like that. Besides, it does so little harm to other people and the pleasure that it gives more than counterbalances . . . "

" Is there some one new? " Levin asked.

" There is, Kostia. You know the Ossian type of woman . . . such as you only see in dreams. . . . These women exist in real life sometimes and they are terrible. Woman is an everlasting theme—no matter how much you study it, there is always something new about it."

" So much the better not to study it then."

" I don't agree with you. Some mathematician once said that happiness consists in searching for truth and not in finding it."

Levin listened without a word. No matter how hard he tried he could not bring himself to understand his friend nor the peculiar pleasure he took in the pursuit of women of that kind.

XV

The place where they were bound for was not very far away. It was a small grove of poplars near the stream. Levin got out of the trap and conducted Oblonsky through a mossy glade in which there was no sign of snow. He himself went back, leant his gun against a birch-tree, took off his coat, fastened a girdle round his waist, and made a few gestures with his arms to make sure that nothing should hinder his movements.

Old Lasca, following him step by step, sat down near him and pricked up her ears. The sun sank behind the wood, lighting up the few silver birches in the groves, throwing a rosy light on their hanging branches and buds that were ready to burst. From another part of the wood, where the snow had not yet melted, a faint trickling of running water could be heard. The birds were chirping and flying from tree to tree. The intervals of silence were broken by the rustling of last year's dry leaves that were moved by the thawing earth and the newly-sprouting grass.

"How nice! You can almost see and hear the grass grow!" Levin said to himself as he noticed a yellow leaf stir near some young blades of grass. He stood there listening and looking, now at the damp mossy ground, now at the watchful Lasca, now at the sea of bare tree-tops in the forest at the foot of the hill, now at the long white clouds floating in the sky overhead. A hawk flew high over the forest, another followed, and both were soon lost from view. The birds in the thicket were chirping louder and gayer than ever. An owl shrieked. Lasca pricked up her ears, took a few cautious steps, and bent her head to listen. From the other side of the stream the cuckoo's voice could be heard. It called once or twice in its usual note and then gave forth various hoarse uneven sounds.

"Why, the cuckoo has come," Stepan Arkadyevitch remarked as he appeared from behind a bush.

"Yes, I hear," Levin said, annoyed that the silence of the forest should be broken even by the sound of his own voice. "Now let us be quick."

Stepan Arkadyevitch disappeared again behind a bush and nothing more was seen of him except the flash of a match, the red glow of a cigarette, and a light bluish smoke.

"Tchik! tchik!"

Stepan Arkadyevitch cocked his gun.

" What is that noise? " he asked, attracting Levin's attention to a strange noise that sounded like a child crying.

" Don't you know what that is? It's the buck rabbit. Let us be quiet. Listen, there's something flying." Levin cocked his gun.

A faint whistle was heard in the distance, then another and another, till it changed to a hoarse cry. Levin looked up to right and left, and there straight in front, against the deepening blue sky, over the tall poplars, a bird was flying towards him. Its cry, like the noise made by a tearing cloth, rang in his ears. He soon distinguished the long beak and neck of the snipe. Suddenly a red flash shone out from behind Oblonsky's bush. The bird fluttered in the air, then attempted to go up again. There was another flash and report, and the bird flapped its wings and fell heavily to the ground.

" Did I miss? " Stepan Arkadyevitch asked, who could see nothing through the smoke.

" Here it is! " Levin exclaimed, pointing to Lasca, who with one ear cocked back and tail erect was bringing the dead bird to her master. " I am glad you had the first hit," Levin said with a slight touch of envy.

" The right barrel missed at first," Stepan Arkadyevitch said. " Sh. . . . Here's another." Shrill cries followed one after another. Two birds flew right over the heads of the sportsmen as if chasing each other. Four shots rang out, and the snipe, turning on their track like swallows, disappeared from sight.

. . . .

The sport was excellent. Stepan Arkadyevitch killed two more birds and Levin two, one of which was lost. It grew darker and darker. Venus with her silvery light appeared in the west glimmering through the birch-trees. In the east Arcturus gleamed with his sombre reddish light. Overhead Levin could distinguish the Great Bear. No more snipe appeared, but Levin decided to wait until Venus rose above the birch-trees and the Great Bear was entirely visible.

Venus was already high above the horizon, the Wain of the Bear could be seen clearly in the purple sky, and still he waited.

" Isn't it time to go home? " Stepan Arkadyevitch asked.

There was perfect stillness in the wood, not a bird moved.

" Let us stay here a little," Levin said.

" As you please."

They were standing near one another.

"Stiva," Levin began suddenly, "you have not told me whether your sister-in-law is married, or if she is going to be."

Levin felt himself so calm, so resigned, that nothing, he thought, could move him. But he did not expect Stepan Arkadyevitch's reply.

"She is not married and is not thinking of getting married. On the other hand, she is very ill and the doctors have sent her abroad. They even fear for her life."

"What did you say?" Levin cried. "Ill? What is the matter with her? How did she . . ."

While they were talking Lasca pricked her ears, raised her head aloft, then looked at them reproachfully.

"Here's a fine time for talking," she seemed to say. "There goes one, they will miss him."

But at this moment the two friends heard a shrill cry. They seized their guns and fired at once. The reports were simultaneous. The bird dropped its wings and fell to the ground.

"Well done! both together!" Levin exclaimed as he ran with Lasca to look for the bird. "What was that unpleasant feeling?" he thought. "Oh, yes, Kitty is ill. . . . What a pity! Found it? Clever dog," he said, taking the warm bird out of Lasca's mouth and putting it into the game-bag that was almost full. "I've got it, Stiva!" he shouted.

XVI

On the way home Levin questioned Oblonsky about Kitty's illness and the Shcherbatskys' plans. He could not help feeling pleased at the news, though he would not have admitted it to himself. He felt that there was still hope, and was a little glad that she who had caused him so much suffering was suffering herself. But when Stepan Arkadyevitch spoke of the cause of Kitty's illness and mentioned Vronsky's name Levin interrupted him.

"I have no right to know these family matters, and to tell you the truth, I am not in the least interested."

Stepan Arkadyevitch gave a scarcely perceptible smile when he saw his friend's face change from gay to grave.

"Have you sold your wood to Rabinin?" Levin asked to change the subject.

"Yes, the matter is quite settled. I've got an excellent price for it, thirty-seven thousand roubles. He is to pay me eight down and the rest in six years. I've been trying to get rid of it for a long time, but no one would give more than that."

"You are selling it for a mere song," Levin said severely.

"What makes you think so?" Stepan Arkadyevitch asked with a good-natured smile, knowing that Levin was in a bad humour.

"Because the wood is worth at least five hundred roubles an acre," Levin replied.

"Oh, you country gentlemen!" Stepan Arkadyevitch exclaimed jestingly. "What contempt you have for us poor town's people! But when it comes to business we come out better than you do. You may take my word for it, I have weighed the matter thoroughly. The price is a very good one. I am only afraid that our merchant may want to get out of it in the end. The timber isn't up to much after all."

Levin smiled scornfully. He was amused at these city people who come into the country about once in ten years and then imagine they know everything.

"I would not attempt to teach you your business at the office, and if necessary I might even come to you for advice, but are you sure you understand this thing quite as well? It's not so easy as you think. By the way, have you counted the trees?"

"Counted the trees!" Stepan Arkadyevitch exclaimed with a laugh, anxious to drive away his friend's ill-humour. "You might as well count the grains of sand on the sea-shore or the planets in the heavens. Only a lofty mind might . . ."

"No more lofty than Rabinin's. No merchant would buy a forest without counting the trees, unless he came across a person like you who was willing to give it him for nothing. I go to shoot in that wood of yours every year, and to my mind it's worth at least five hundred roubles an acre, cash down, whereas he is giving you only two hundred and not paying you at once. You've made him a present of thirty thousand roubles."

"How high you fly," Stepan Arkadyevitch remarked in a less assured tone of voice. "Why would no one give me that price?"

"Because the merchants are all in league with one another. He probably squared the others first. I have had to do with all of them, so I know them well. They're a most unscrupulous set. They won't put their hands to anything unless they can make at least ten or fifteen per cent., and will wait until they can buy for twenty kopeks what is worth a rouble."

"You see the worst side of everything."

"Not at all," Levin said severely as they reached the house.

A trap with two well-fed horses was standing at the door. Rabinin's red-faced bailiff, who acted as his coachman as well, was sitting in it. Rabinin himself was already in the house, and met the two friends in the hall as they entered. He was a tall, thin man of middle age with a moustache, clean shaven, prominent chin, and dull protruding eyes. He was dressed in a long blue coat with buttons low down at the back, and high boots with goloshes over them. He passed his pocket-handkerchief over his face, wrapped himself still closer in his coat, which was quite unnecessary, and greeted the two friends with a broad smile.

He extended his hand to Stepan Arkadyevitch.

"Ah! here you are!" Stepan Arkadyevitch said, shaking hands. "Very good."

"I dared not disobey your excellency's commands although the roads were so bad. I positively had to walk all the way, but here I am in time. My respects to you, Konstantin Dmitritch," he said, turning to Levin with an attempt to grasp his hand. But Levin frowned, pretended not to notice the hand extended to him, and proceeded to take out the snipe from the game-bag. "You've been having some sport I see," he added. "What kind of bird is that?" he asked, gazing disdainfully at the snipe. "Does it taste nice?" He shook his head dubiously as if doubting whether it would be worth while cooking it.

"Would you like to go into my study?" Levin asked Stepan Arkadyevitch in French, still frowning. "Go into my study and discuss your business there."

"As you please," Rabinin said with majestic scorn, as if he wished them to understand that others might find it difficult to transact business, but not he.

When they entered the study, Rabinin, by force of habit, looked around for the icon, but when he discovered it, however, he did not cross himself. With the same air of doubt and disdain with which he had looked at the snipe, he cast his eyes at the bookcases and shelves lined with books.

"Have you brought the money?" Oblonsky asked. "Sit down, please."

"There will be no trouble about the money, but I came to talk it over."

"What is there to talk over? Do sit down, please."

"Thank you," Rabinin said, sitting down and leaning against

the back of his chair with a most painful expression on his face. " You must give in a trifle, prince. It would be a sin to give so much. The money is ready to the last kopek. There will be no delay about that."

Levin, who had put away his gun and was about to go to the door, stopped when he heard the merchant's words.

" The price is cheap enough as it is," he observed. " Had he come to me sooner, we could have sold it at a different one."

Rabinin rose and looked Levin up and down with a smile.

" Konstantin Dmitritch is very close," he remarked, turning to Stepan Arkadyevitch. " You can never drive a bargain with him. I bought some wheat from him once and was compelled to pay a very high price."

" But why should I give you my property for nothing? I did not find it or steal it."

" How can you say that? It is positively impossible to steal nowadays. Everything is now done honestly and openly. Who talks of stealing? We were discussing it like honourable men. The wood is too dear, I shall make nothing out of it. I beg you to give way a little."

" Is the matter settled or not? If it's already settled, then there's no use discussing it further; if not, I'll buy the wood," Levin said.

The smile suddenly disappeared from Rabinin's face and a cruel, greedy expression came over it. He unbuttoned his coat quickly with his bony fingers, exposing his shirt and waistcoat and his watch-chain, and drew out a fat, greasy pocket-book.

" The wood is mine, if you please," he said, crossing himself quickly. " Here, take the money, the wood is mine. This is how Rabinin does business, he does not count the kopeks," he said with a frown, flourishing his pocket-book.

" I shouldn't be in a hurry if I were you," Levin remarked.

" But I've given my word! " Oblonsky said in astonishment.

Levin went out of the room banging the door behind him. Rabinin looked after him and shook his head with a smile.

" It's merely his youth; positively pure childishness. Believe me, I am buying it more for the glory than anything else, so that people should say that Rabinin and not another bought Oblonsky's wood. There is not much profit in it, I can assure you. Will you be so kind as to sign the agreement? "

An hour later the merchant, well wrapped up, with the agreement in his pocket, took his seat in the trap and started on his way home.

" Oh, these gentry! " he said to his bailiff; " they are all alike."

" That may be," the bailiff observed, pulling down his leather cap and tightening the reins, " but what about your little bargain? "

" Well, well . . ."

XVII

Stepan Arkadyevitch, his pockets bulging out with the bills the merchant had given him, promising to pay in three months time, proceeded upstairs. The wood was sold, part of the money in his pocket, the sport had been excellent, and Stepan Arkadyevitch felt in the very best of humours. He was particularly anxious to take Levin out of himself. He wanted to finish the day as pleasantly as he had begun it.

And Levin was really in a very bad mood. Notwithstanding the fact that he wished to be nice to his guest, he could not bring himself to be cheerful. The feeling of intoxication that had first come over him to learn that Kitty was not married was beginning to leave him. Kitty was not married and ill because another man had jilted her. The insult reflected somehow on him. Vronsky had slighted her, Vronsky no doubt despised him, therefore Vronsky was his enemy. These were the thoughts that floated through Levin's brain. He felt annoyed and seized upon the first thing he could to vent his annoyance upon. The sale of the wood, the way Oblonsky had been cheated in his own house, was an additional irritation.

" Well, have you finished? " he asked as Stepan Arkadyevitch entered. " Would you like some supper? "

" I won't say no. This country air does give you an appetite! Why didn't you offer Rabinin something? "

" Oh, let him go to the devil! "

" But, really, you did treat him badly," Oblonsky observed. " You wouldn't even shake hands with him. Why didn't you? "

" I don't shake hands with my butler, and he's worth a hundred of him."

" What a retrograde person you are to be sure! You don't believe in the mixing of the classes? "

" Let those who enjoy it do the mixing—I don't."

" You really are retrograde, you know."

"To tell you the truth, I have never bothered to find out what I am. I am Konstantin Levin and nothing more."

"Konstantin Levin in a very bad temper," Stepan Arkadyevitch added with a smile.

"I am certainly in a bad temper, but do you know why? Because of the stupid way in which you sold your wood, excuse the expression . . ."

Stepan Arkadyevitch made a good-natured grimace.

"Don't bother yourself about that. Nobody has ever yet sold anything without being told afterwards that it was sold too cheaply. But all the same no one offered me more. . . . You have your knife into Rabinin, haven't you?"

"Perhaps I have. But do you know why? You will call me a retrograde again or some such awful word, but it makes me furious to see how the nobility are getting poorer and poorer; yes, the nobility, to which I am happy to say I belong, in spite of your mixing of the classes. If this poverty were due to luxurious living I wouldn't say anything; that would be their own affair; every one has a right to live as he likes. Our peasants are buying up our land and I don't mind that in the least. It is only right that the man who works should take the place of the man who doesn't. But what makes me so furious is to see our nobility getting poorer, because—I don't know how to express it—because of their own ignorance. Here, a Polish merchant buys an estate from a lady who lives in Nice for less than half its worth. There, another merchant buys up land for a rouble an acre when it ought to fetch ten. And you go and give this rascal a present of thirty thousand roubles."

"What could I do? Count my trees one by one?"

"Of course you should count them. Rabinin took good care to do so. His children will have means and a good education and yours will have nothing."

"Excuse me, there is something mean in these calculations. We have our affairs; they have theirs; they must make a profit. However the thing is over and done with. Ah! here comes my favourite omelette. Perhaps Agafia Mihailovna will give us some of that delicious brandy of hers. . . ."

Stepan Arkadyevitch sat down to the table and began to rally Agafia Mihailovna. He assured her he had not eaten such a dinner and supper for an age.

"It does me good to see you enjoying your food. As for Konstantin Dmitritch, if you were to give him a dry crust of bread, he would eat it and walk away without a word."

Levin made a great effort to be cheerful, but did not succeed. He was burning to ask Stepan Arkadyevitch a single question, but did not know how and when to put it. Stepan Arkadyevitch retired, undressed, washed himself, put on his goffered nightshirt, and got into bed, but Levin still lingered in his room, talking about the merest trifles, and not daring to ask the thing that he wanted to know.

" How nicely they get up soap nowadays," Levin remarked, taking up a cake of scented soap that Agafia Mihailovna had put there for Oblonsky, but which the latter had not used. " It is truly a work of art."

" Yes, everything has reached such a state of perfection," Stepan Arkadyevitch said with a comfortable yawn. " The theatres, for instance, and these electric . . . a-a-a! " a yawn . . . " this electric light everywhere . . . a-a! "

" Yes, electric light," Levin repeated. " Do you know where Vronsky is now? " he asked suddenly, putting down the cake of soap.

" Vronsky? " Stepan Arkadyevitch asked as he ceased yawning. " He's in St. Petersburg. He left soon after you did and has not been near Moscow since. Do you know, Kostia," he continued, leaning his elbows on the table near the bed, and supporting his handsome face on his hands as he looked at Levin with his good-natured, sleepy eyes, " to my mind you alone were to blame? You were too much afraid of a rival. As I told you then, I don't know who stood the bigger chance, but why didn't you go and make a clean breast of it? I told you that . . . " he yawned, trying not to open his mouth.

" I wonder if he knows that I proposed to her? " Levin thought as he looked at him. " He must; there is something subtle, something diplomatic, about his face." He felt himself blush and looked Stepan Arkadyevitch straight in the eyes without a word.

" If there was any feeling on her side at the time, it was merely on the surface," Oblonsky continued. " You know he is such a confirmed aristocrat, and the prospects of a brilliant future no doubt had some effect both on herself and her mother."

Levin frowned. The wound that he had felt at his rejection opened afresh, but he was at home and the very walls seemed to sustain him.

" Stop! stop! " he exclaimed, interrupting Oblonsky. " You talk of aristocracy, but I should like to know what the particular aristocracy of Vronsky or of any other person of his kind consists in that it should have led them to treat me with contempt? You think Vronsky an aristocrat, but I tell you he's not. A man whose father rose to rank by all sorts of intrigues, whose mother has been the mistress of I don't know how many men. . . . That is not aristocracy. It is people like myself who are aristocrats. People who can show in the past three or four generations of honourable families, cultured in the real sense of the word—talents and intellect are another matter; people who have never cringed to anybody, have always been self-reliant like my father and grandfather before him. There are many such families. It seems mean to you that I count my trees while you give Rabinin thirty thousand roubles for nothing. But you receive rent and other things that I don't. That is why I value what my father left me and what my labour gives me. It is we who are aristocrats, and not those flunkeys whose existence depends on the great ones of this world, and whose souls you can buy for twenty kopeks."

"But whom are you angry with? I quite agree with you," Stepan Arkadyevitch said with a frank smile, even though he felt that Levin was probably including him among the people whose souls could be bought for twenty kopeks. He admired Levin's enthusiasm.

"But whom are you angry with?" he repeated. "A great deal of what you say about Vronsky may be perfectly true, still I was not talking about that. I tell you frankly, if I were in your place I should go straight to Moscow and . . ."

"I don't know whether you are aware or not, but it makes no difference, I will tell you. I proposed to Katerina Alexandrovna and she refused me. It is painful and humiliating for me to think of her now."

"Why? What nonsense!"

"Don't let us talk of it any more. I'm sorry I was so rude to you," Levin said. Now that he had unburdened himself his mood of the morning returned. "You are not angry with me, Stiva, are you?" he asked, taking his hand.

"Of course not. I have nothing to be angry about. I'm glad you told me. Do you know, it would be rather nice to take a turn with our guns early in the morning. Shall we? I should wake early in any case and I could go to the station directly afterwards."

"Very well."

XVIII

Notwithstanding the fact that Vronsky was so absorbed in his passion, the outward course of his life did not change in the smallest degree. He kept up all his social and military acquaintances, was extremely occupied with the affairs of his regiment, partly because he loved it and still more because he was so popular with every one. He was not only liked, he was immensely admired, because he, a man of such brilliant opportunities, placed the interests of his regiment and his comrades above that of mere vainglorious ambition. He was fully conscious of the sentiment that he inspired and felt it his duty to live up to it.

Of course he never spoke to any one of his passion, and was very cautious to allow no imprudent word to escape him even when he joined his comrades in some drinking bout. It must be said, however, that he never drank enough to lose control over himself. He was also extremely quick to shut up any of his comrades who permitted themselves to make the least allusion to his love. It was nevertheless common knowledge to the whole town. All the young men envied him, perhaps for the very thing that appeared most difficult—Karenin's high station and the importance which the thing assumed in the eyes of the world.

The majority of the younger society women, who had always been jealous of Anna and had grown tired of hearing her praises sung, were not sorry to have their predictions verified, and were only waiting for the sanction of public opinion to heap all their scorn and contempt upon her. They had already gathered up the mud with which to bespatter her when the time came. The elders, on the other hand, and those of high rank looked on with disapproval, dreading the scandal that was bound to follow.

Vronsky's mother was at first highly pleased when she heard of the affair. In her opinion there was nothing more calculated to form a young man than for him to fall in love with some great society lady, and then there was a great satisfaction in the thought that Madame Karenina, who had talked such a great deal about her boy, was after all neither better nor worse than most beautiful society women. But when she heard that her son had refused an important promotion so as not to leave his regiment in order to be near the lady in question, and that a certain person in high quarters was highly displeased about it, she soon changed her opinion. As far as she could gather it was not a brilliant society flirtation such as she could have approved of, but had developed into something far more serious, after the style of Werther, and she was beginning to fear that her son might commit some imprudence. She had not seen him since his sudden departure from Moscow, and sent word to him through his elder brother that she wished him to come to her.

His elder brother was also displeased. Not because he troubled himself to analyse whether his love was deep or shallow, passionate or otherwise, guilty or innocent, for although he was a married man and had children of his own, he was attached to various actresses and could therefore not be too severe on that score. He knew, however, that this love affair was looked upon with disapproval by people with whom it was best to be on good terms, and could not help blaming his brother.

Besides his military and social duties Vronsky had yet another interest—horses, of which he was passionately fond.

The officers' races were to take place this summer. Vronsky entered his name, bought himself a pure-bred English mare, and in spite of his love affair took the keenest interest in the forthcoming races.

These two passions did not interfere with one another. He needed some outside interest to counteract the violent emotions that Anna aroused in him.

XIX

On the day of the Krasno-Selo races Vronsky went to eat his beef-steak in the officers' mess-room earlier than usual. It was not at all necessary for him to limit himself, as his weight did not exceed the regulation weight of the service, but he did not wish to grow fat, so he refrained from all sweets and starchy foods. He sat down at the table, supported his head on his hands, and began turning over the leaves of a French novel that was lying on his plate. His coat was unbuttoned, displaying his white waistcoat. He was merely pretending to read, so as to avoid talking to his fellow-officers as they came in and out, because he wanted to think.

He was thinking of Anna, who had promised to see him after

the races. He had not seen her for three days, and was wondering if she would be able to keep her promise, as her husband had just returned from a journey abroad, and considering how he could best find out. He had last seen her at his cousin Betsy's country house. To the Karenins' country house he went as rarely as possible, and was now asking himself if he might venture to go there.

" I will simply say that Betsy sent me to find out if she was coming to the races. I don't see why I shouldn't go." He looked up from his book. His face shone. The thought of seeing her filled him with joy.

" Send word that I wish my carriage harnessed," he said to the servant who was bringing his beef-steak on a silver dish. He drew it to him and began to eat.

The clicking of balls could be heard from the billiard-room adjoining, and the sound of voices talking and laughing. Two officers appeared at the door. One of them was a young man with a pale, delicate face, who had recently entered the regiment from the Corps of Pages; the other a stout old man with tiny little eyes and bracelets on his arms.

Vronsky frowned as he looked at them, and went on eating and reading as though he had not noticed them.

" Preparing for work? " the elder asked, sitting down near him.

" As you see," Vronsky replied with a frown, wiping his lips and not looking at him.

" But aren't you afraid of getting fat? " the officer asked again, drawing up a chair for the younger.

" What? " Vronsky asked angrily, making a grimace and showing his even teeth.

" Aren't you afraid of getting fat? "

" Waiter! some sherry! " Vronsky called without deigning to reply, and moving the book to the other side he continued to read.

The stout officer took up the wine-list and turned to the younger.

" You choose what we're to drink," he said, handing him the card.

" Rhine wine would be nice," the young officer replied, trying to twirl his scanty moustache, and looking at Vronsky timidly out of the corner of his eye. But when he noticed that Vronsky turned away from him he stood up.

" Let us go into the billiard-room," he said.

The elder officer also rose and the two proceeded to the door.

At this moment a cavalry captain named Yashvin entered the room—a tall, handsome man. He looked down at the two disdainfully, gave them a slight salute, and went up to Vronsky.

"Ah! here you are!" he exclaimed, slapping Vronsky on the shoulder. The latter turned round angrily, but seeing who it was, his face brightened and instantly assumed its habitual friendly expression.

"That's right, Alyosha," Yashvin remarked in his loud baritone, "go on eating and have a glass with me."

"I can't eat any more, thanks."

"The inseparables!" Yashvin added with a disdainful look at the door through which the two officers had just departed. He sat down beside Vronsky, crossed his legs that seemed much too long for the chair he was sitting on, and pulled up his tight trousers. "Why didn't you come to the theatre last night? It was not at all bad. Where were you?"

"I stayed rather late at my cousin's."

"Ah!" Yashvin exclaimed.

Yashvin was a gambler and a debauchee. It could not be said that he lacked principles; he had principles, but they were immoral ones. In the regiment he was Vronsky's best friend. Vronsky admired his extraordinary physical strength, which allowed him to drink like a fish and not feel it, and do without sleep if necessary. He also admired him for the tremendous moral courage he showed in relation to his superiors and comrades alike. The latter were filled with awe and admiration at his feats, at the way he would play for large stakes, drinking all the time, and never once losing his head. He had the reputation of being the best player at the English club.

Vronsky was especially attached to him because he felt that Yashvin liked him, not on account of his wealth or his social position, but for himself alone. He was the only man of his acquaintance to whom Vronsky could have spoken of his love. He felt that Yashvin, despite the contempt he showed for any kind of sentiment, was the only person who could have understood the strength of his passion, now absorbing the whole of his life. Besides, Yashvin was above scandalmongering or idle gossip. He would see the thing in the right light, would realise that love was not a joke, but something far more important and serious.

Vronsky had not yet spoken to him of his love, but he felt that Yashvin knew all about it by the look in his eyes.

"Ah, yes," he repeated, when he heard that Vronsky had been at the Tverskys'. His black eyes sparkled, and giving way to a bad habit of his he began to bite his moustache.

"Well, and what did you do yesterday? Had any luck?" Vronsky asked.

"Oh, yes. I won eight thousand, but three are no good. I shall never get them."

"Then you'll have plenty of money to lose on me," Vronsky said with a laugh.

Yashvin had made a heavy bet on Vronsky.

"I am not going to lose. Mahotin is the only danger."

They began discussing the day's races, which was the only subject that Vronsky could think of just then.

"Come along, I've finished," Vronsky said as he rose and went towards the door. Yashvin rose also and stretched his back and long legs.

"It's too early for dinner, but I want a drink. I'll be with you in a moment. Waiter! some wine!" he shouted in his loud, commanding voice that made the windows rattle. "Never mind, I don't want it," he called again. "If you're going home, I'll come too."

They went out together.

XX

Vronsky lodged in a neat little hut that was divided in two by a partition. Petritsky lived with him even in camp. He was still asleep when Vronsky and Yashvin entered.

"Get up! you've slept long enough!" Yashvin exclaimed as he went behind the partition and shook Petritsky by the shoulder. He was lying with his nose buried in the pillow.

Petritsky jumped up and looked around.

"Your brother called," he said to Vronsky. "He woke me up, confound him. He said that he would look in again," and drawing up the blanket he buried his head in the pillow again. "Leave off, Yashvin," he said angrily, as the latter was trying to pull the bed-clothes off him. "Leave off!" He turned over and opened his eyes. "Do tell me what to take! I've such a horrid taste in my mouth that . . ."

" Vodka is better than anything," Yashvin remarked. " Tereshchenko! bring your master some vodka and cucumbers! " he shouted to the servant, delighted at the sound of his own voice.

" So you think vodka best? " Petritsky asked with a grimace, rubbing his eyes. " Will you have some too? All right, let's have it all together. Eh, Vronsky? " he asked as he got out of bed and wrapped himself up in the striped quilt. He went through the door of the partition singing in French, " There was a king in Thu-u-le."

" Vronsky, will you have a drink? "

" You can go," Vronsky said to the servant who was handing him his coat.

" Where are you off to? " Yashvin asked. " And here's the troika," he added as the carriage drew up at the door.

" I must look in at the stables and then I must see Bransky about the horses."

Vronsky had really promised to go and see Bransky, who lived about ten miles from Peterhof, in order to pay him for a horse, but the two comrades felt that this was merely an excuse.

Petritsky winked, as much as to say, " We know who Bransky is! "

" Mind you're not late," Yashvin cautioned him. " How do you like my bay? " he asked to change the subject, as he looked at the shaft-horse that Vronsky had bought of him.

" I say! " Petritsky called after him. " Your brother left a letter and a note. Wait a moment. Where did I put them? "

Vronsky stopped.

" Well, where are they? "

" Where are they? that is the question! " Petritsky exclaimed dramatically, putting his forefinger above his nose.

" Don't be silly and tell me where they are," Vronsky said with a smile.

" I haven't lighted the fire; they must be here somewhere."

" Well, come along! where is the letter? "

" I've really forgotten. Or did I see them in my sleep? Wait a moment—don't get angry. If you had drunk four bottles, as I did last night, you would not have remembered even where you had gone to bed. Let me think a moment."

Petritsky went behind the screen and lay down on his bed.

" Let me see. I was lying like this and he was standing there. Why, of course! here it is! " he exclaimed, pulling the letter out from under the mattress where he had hidden it.

Vronsky took the letter and note. He had been expecting them. The letter was from his mother, and was full of reproaches that he had not come to her; the note from his brother, saying that there was something he wished to talk over with him. Vronsky knew what that meant. " What business is it of theirs? " he thought, crumpling up the letter and thrusting it into his breast pocket in order to read it more carefully on the way.

As he got out into the passage he ran against two officers, one belonging to their regiment and the second to another. Vronsky's quarters were the haunt of all the other officers.

" Where are you off to? "

" I must go to Peterhof."

" Has your horse arrived from Tsarskoe? "

" Yes, but I've not seen it yet."

" They say that Mahotin's Gladiator is a little lame."

" Nonsense! But I wonder how you'll get on in this mud? " another remarked.

" Here are my saviours! " Petritsky exclaimed as he caught sight of the two officers. A servant was handing him some vodka and pickled cucumbers on a tray. " Yashvin advised me to have a drink in order to refresh myself."

" What a time you gave us last night," one of the officers remarked, " we didn't get a wink of sleep."

" How nobly we finished up! " Petritsky continued. " Volkov climbed on to the roof and told us that he felt sad. So I got them to play him a march—a funeral march—and there he went to sleep to the slow music."

" Go along, drink your vodka; then you must have some soda water and lots of lemon," Yashvin said, standing over him as a mother does when she is trying to persuade her child to swallow some medicine, " and then if you're good a little champagne, about a bottle."

" That sounds better. Here, Vronsky, have a drink with us."

" No, thanks, I am not drinking to-day. Good-bye, gentlemen."

" Afraid of putting on weight? Very well, we'll drink without you. Hand me the soda water and lemons."

" Vronsky! " some one called after him as soon as he had got into the passage.

" What is it? "

" You should get your hair cut. It's getting too long, especially on the bald part."

Vronsky was in fact beginning to get a little bald. He

laughed, put on his cap to cover up the bald spot on his head, and went out to his carriage.

"To the stables," he said, and took out his two letters in order to re-read them, but on second thoughts put them away again, so as to have nothing on his mind before he examined his horse. "Later will do," he said to himself.

XXI

Some temporary stables built of wood had been erected near the racecourse, where Vronsky's horse was to have been taken yesterday, but he had not yet seen her. He had not mounted her the last few days, having given her over entirely to the trainer, so that he did not know in the least what sort of a condition she was in. He had scarcely time to get out of his carriage when his groom, who had noticed him from a distance, called out the trainer. A dry little Englishman with a shock head of hair, in a short jacket and high boots, came out to meet him in the leisurely, dandified gait peculiar to jockeys.

"How is Frou-Frou?" Vronsky asked in English.

"She's all right, sir," the Englishman replied somewhere deep down in his throat. "You had better not go in," he added, raising his cap. "I have put a muzzle on her and she's rather excited. If you go in it will only upset her."

"I'm going though. I must see her."

"Come on then," the Englishman said with a frown, and led the way to the stable in his mincing gait, jerking his elbows as he went.

They entered the little court-yard leading to the stables. A smart stable-boy in a beautifully clean coat and a whip in his hand met them at the door. There were five horses in the stable, each in its own stall. Vronsky knew that Mahotin's Gladiator, a fine chestnut—his most dangerous rival—must be there, and he was more curious to see it than his own horse. It was, however, contrary to the rules of etiquette—he not only could not see it, but could not even ask any questions about it. As he was passing along the corridor the boy opened a door to the left and Vronsky got a glimpse of a powerful chestnut with white legs. He felt certain that this must be Gladiator, but turned his head away as a man would from an open letter not addressed to him, and proceeded to Frou-Frou's stall.

"That horse belongs to Ma-k . . . Mak. . . . I never can pronounce his name," the Englishman remarked, pointing to Gladiator's stall with his forefinger, the nail of which was black with dirt.

"Mahotin's? Yes, he's my only serious rival," Vronsky observed.

"I should back you if you were to ride him," the Englishman said.

"He is stronger, but Frou-Frou is more reliable," Vronsky said with a smile, delighted at the Englishman's praise.

"In steeplechasing a great deal depends on pluck," the jockey remarked.

Vronsky felt himself to be full of pluck, and what is more he was firmly convinced that no one could have more pluck than he.

"You are sure that a good sweating was not necessary?"

"Not at all," the Englishman replied. "Please don't speak so loud, she's excited," he added with a nod in the direction of the stall where the horse was heard stamping on the straw.

He opened the door and Vronsky entered the stall, dimly lighted by a single tiny window. A bay horse, muzzled, was prancing up and down on the fresh straw. Vronsky stood looking at his favourite.

Frou-Frou was a mare of medium size, none too perfect in shape. She had very slender bones, and although her chest came out well in front, it was nevertheless narrow; her crupper seemed to hang down, and her legs, especially the hind legs, were considerably bowed. The muscles of the legs were not large, but the flanks seemed enormous on account of the training she had undergone and the smallness of her belly. The bones of the legs below the knee seemed no thicker than a finger seen from the front, but were extraordinarily large when seen sideways. She gave one the impression of having been squeezed in at the sides and lengthened out, but she had one quality that made up for all her defects—she had good blood, was a thoroughbred, as the English say. Her muscles stood out under a network of veins, covered with a skin as smooth and soft as satin. Her delicate head, with her prominent, intelligent eyes, her broad, quivering nostrils that seemed suffused with blood, every part of her seemed to be full of life and energy. She looked as if she could talk if only the construction of her mouth would allow it. At any rate, it seemed to Vronsky that she understood what he was feeling as he looked at her.

When he came in she was taking deep, long breaths, rolling

her bloodshot eyes in her endeavours to shake off the muzzle, and pawing the ground nervously.

" You see how restive she is," the Englishman observed.

" Gently, my beauty, gently," Vronsky said, approaching her and trying to calm her.

But the nearer he came the more excited she grew. It was only when he began stroking her head that she calmed down somewhat and he could feel the muscles tightening under her delicate skin. Vronsky patted her powerful neck, put into place a bit of her mane that she had tossed to one side, laid his face close to her nostrils, that swelled and dilated like the wings of a bat. She snorted, pricked up her ears, and stretched out her black lips to seize the sleeve of his coat, but suddenly remembering the muzzle she shook herself and began pawing the ground again.

" Quiet, my beauty," Vronsky said, stroking her back, and pleased that his horse was in such excellent condition he went out of the stall.

The horse's excitement had communicated itself to Vronsky. The blood seemed to rush to his heart. He felt restive and wanted to be moving. It was a sensation strange and pleasant at the same time.

" Then I may count on you," he said. " Be on the spot at half-past six."

" All right, sir," the Englishman replied. " But where are you going, my lord? " he asked suddenly. He rarely used the expression " my lord."

Vronsky raised his head in astonishment and looked at him haughtily. He was amazed at the audacity of the question, but instantly realised that the Englishman looked upon him just then more as a jockey than his master.

" I am going to Bransky's and will be back in an hour," he replied. " How many times have I been asked that question to-day! " he said to himself and blushed—a rare occurrence with him.

The Englishman looked at him carefully.

" The most important thing is to keep quite calm before the race. You mustn't be worried or upset yourself about anything." He cautioned him just as if he knew where Vronsky was going.

" All right! " Vronsky said with a smile, and stepping lightly into his carriage he ordered the man to drive to Peterhof.

As soon as they started, the sky which had been overcast with clouds since the morning, grew more threatening and a torrent of rain came down. "That's bad," Vronsky thought, raising the hood of his carriage. "It was muddy enough before, but now it will be like a quagmire."

In the privacy of the carriage he drew out the two letters his brother had left and began to read them.

It was the same old story. Both his mother and brother had thought it necessary to interfere in his love affairs. He grew angry—a most unusual thing for him.

"What business is it of theirs?" he thought. "Why do they all consider it their duty to look after me? Why don't they leave off worrying me? Only because they see that this is something they cannot understand. Had it been one of those vulgar society intrigues they would have left me alone. They can feel that this is different somehow; that I am not merely playing; that this woman is dearer to me than life. That is why they are annoyed. Whatever may be our fate, we ourselves have made it and shall not complain," he said to himself, including Anna in the word "we." "But no, they want to teach us how to live. They, who have not the remotest idea of what happiness means. They do not know that without our love happiness and unhappiness would not exist for us, that life itself would have no meaning."

The thing that really annoyed him was the fact that his conscience told him that they were right. He knew very well that the love that bound him to Anna was not a mere attraction of the moment, that would pass away like an ordinary society intrigue without leaving any other trace behind than some pleasant or perhaps unpleasant recollections. He felt all the torture of their position, all the difficulties in the eyes of the world, from whom they had to conceal their love by means of lies and deceptions. He knew how hard it was to go on lying and deceiving, perpetually pretending to be occupied with outside things while all the time they could do nothing, think of nothing, but their love.

He went over all the situations in which he had been compelled to lie and dissemble—a thing so contrary to his nature. He could feel over again the sensation of shame—never once noticed in her—the overwhelming shame that had come over him on those occasions.

A strange feeling of disgust would come over him every now and again which he could not possibly define. He felt it now. Was it for Alexei Alexandrovitch, himself, or the entire world?

He could not tell. But he always tried to banish such thoughts.

He shook himself.

" Yes, at one time she was unhappy, but proud and calm. Now she cannot be calm, however hard she may try to appear so. We must put an end to it," he said to himself.

For the first time the idea of cutting short this life of deception appeared to him quite clearly, and he felt that the sooner it was over and done with the better.

" We must leave everything, we two together, and go and bury ourselves somewhere with our love," he said to himself.

XXII

THE shower was of short duration, and when Vronsky reached his destination, his shaft-horse at full trot and the other two galloping along beside it without reins, the sun had come out again, lighting up the lime-trees on either side of the road, the dripping leaves, and the roofs of the houses from which the water was pouring down the gutters. He was no longer annoyed that the shower would spoil the race-course, but was glad that, thanks to the rain, she was sure to be at home and alone, as Alexei Alexandrovitch, who had recently returned from a visit abroad, would not have left St. Petersburg while it lasted.

Anxious to avoid attracting attention as much as possible, he got out of the carriage before they crossed the little bridge, walked the rest of the way, and entered the garden by a side entrance.

" Is your master at home? " he asked of the gardener who was standing there.

" No, sir, but madame is. Will you go round by the front door, please; they will let you in there."

" No, thanks, I'll go through the garden."

He now felt certain that she was alone and was eager to surprise her, as she probably did not expect him before the races, having said that he would see her later. He walked cautiously along the gravel path bordered with flowers, holding his sabre so that it should make no noise until he reached the terrace near the house. The depression and anxiety he had experienced on the journey now left him; he thought only of her. He would see her again, not in imagination only but in reality, such as she was—alive. He was ascending the steps of the terrace as gently as possible when he suddenly remembered the most painful feature of his relations with her, a fact he was always forgetting — her boy. Vronsky could not bear his hateful, inquisitive look.

This boy stood in their way more than any other being. When he was present Vronsky and Anna not only refrained from speaking of anything that might not be said before all, but would not even permit themselves to hint at anything that the boy must not understand. There had been no understanding on the point between them, the thing had happened spontaneously. They would have been ashamed to deceive the child, and treated each other as mere acquaintances before him. But nevertheless Vronsky often felt the boy's scrutinising, suspicious eyes upon him. Sometimes he was strangely timid, sometimes affectionate, and at others extremely cold. It seemed as if the child felt that there was some mysterious relation between this man and his mother that he could not understand.

The boy, indeed, often made futile efforts to find out how he ought to behave to this man. He could see with the peculiar instinct of a child that his father, his governess, and his nurse not only did not like Vronsky, but looked on him with the utmost disfavour, and that his mother treated him as her best friend.

" What does it mean? Who is he? Must I love him? If I don't understand it must be my own fault, because I am a bad, naughty child," the little boy would think. This was the cause of his timidity, his distrust, his changeableness, that were so perplexing to Vronsky.

The boy's presence invariably aroused in Vronsky that feeling of disgust he had been subject to of late.

The sensation he aroused both in Vronsky and Anna might be compared to that of a seafarer who can see by the compass that his vessel is drifting away in the wrong direction and that he is powerless to stop it. Every moment sees him getting farther and farther, with nothing but ruin before him. The child was the compass that showed them what they knew only too well, but refused to recognise.

This time the boy was not at home. Anna was sitting on the terrace waiting for him. He had been caught in the rain whilst out for a walk, and she had sent a man and a maid to look for him. She was clad in a white embroidered gown, and did not hear Vronsky approach as she sat in a corner of the terrace concealed by flowers. Her dark curly head was bent as she pressed her brow against a cool watering-can standing on the balustrade that she was holding with her beautiful hands laden with rings, so familiar to him. Her lovely figure, her shapely head, neck, arms, struck Vronsky by their extraordinary beauty, as though he had seen her for the first time. He stopped and looked at her in ecstasy. She instinctively felt his approach, and as he was about to take a step towards her she turned to him with a burning face.

"What is the matter? Are you ill?" he asked in French, drawing near to her. He wanted to rush up to her, but recollecting that people might be about, he looked towards the door of the balcony, blushing with shame that anything should make him deceitful and afraid.

"No, thanks, I am quite well," she replied, rising and pressing the hand that he held out to her. "I did not expect you."

"What cold hands you have!" he said.

"You startled me. I am alone, waiting for Serioja. He has gone for a walk. They will come back from that way."

Although she tried to be calm her lips trembled.

"Forgive me for coming, but I could not bear to go through the day without seeing you," he continued in French, thus avoiding the rather cold "you" and the dangerous "thou" of the Russian.

"There is nothing to forgive. I am glad you have come."

"But you are not well, or are you worried about something?" he continued, still retaining her hand and bending over her. "What were you thinking about?"

"About the same thing," she replied with a smile.

She had spoken the truth. At any moment of the day when she might have been asked that question she could safely have made the same reply. She was always thinking of her happiness and her misfortune. At the particular moment when he arrived she was wondering why others, Betsy, for example, whose relations with Tushkievitch she knew about, could treat so lightly what was such torture to her. This thought often occurred to her now.

She questioned him about the races, and seeing that she was upset about something he tried to divert her mind by telling her all the little details in connection with the preparations.

"Shall I tell him or not?" she thought, gazing into his calm, caressing eyes. "He is so happy with his races that he probably will not understand the importance of the thing I have to tell him."

"But you have not told me yet what you were thinking when

I came," he said suddenly, cutting short his stories. " Come, tell me."

She did not speak, but bent her head and gave him a searching look with those sparkling eyes of hers. Her hand, in which she was holding a leaf that she had torn off, trembled. He noticed this, and that expression of humility, absolute devotion, that had captivated her in the early days, came over his face.

" I fear something has happened. Can I be calm for a single moment when I know that you have some grief that I do not share? For God's sake tell me what it is! " he implored.

" Yes, but I shall never forgive him if he fails to comprehend the full significance of what I must say to him. Better not; why should I risk it? " she thought, as she looked at him. She could feel that her hand holding the leaf was trembling more and more.

" For Heaven's sake! " He took her hand.

" Shall I tell you? "

" Yes, yes, yes . . . "

" I am about to have a child," she whispered slowly.

The leaf trembled violently, but she did not take her eyes off his face; she wanted to see what effect her avowal had had upon him. He turned pale, opened his lips to speak, but stopped, dropped her hand, and hung his head.

" Yes, he realises the importance of this," she thought, and pressed his hand gratefully.

But she was mistaken when she thought he felt as she, a woman, did. The sensation of disgust and horror that had been familiar to him of late now came upon him with full force. He realised that the crisis he had so much desired had arrived at last; that it was no longer possible to keep things from her husband, and that the unnatural situation must somehow come to an end. He gave her a fond, submissive look, kissed her hand, and began pacing up and down the terrace without speaking.

" Of course," he began at last resolutely, approaching her, " we neither of us looked upon our relations in the light of an amusement, but now our fate is sealed. We must put an end to the false situation in which we live."

" Put an end? But how, Alexei? " she asked softly.

She had grown calmer and her face was bathed in a tender smile.

" You must leave your husband and unite your life with mine."

" It is united with yours as it is," she said in a scarcely audible whisper.

" Yes, I know, but I mean completely, completely."

" But how, Alexei? tell me how? " she asked with a bitter smile at the hopelessness of the situation. " What escape is there? What about my husband? "

" There is some way out from any situation. We must decide definitely," he said. " Anything would be better than the position in which we are living. Do I not see how you torment yourself about your husband, your boy, society, everything? "

" Not my husband, I beg of you," she said bitterly. " I don't know, but I never think of him, he doesn't exist."

" You are not speaking sincerely. I know you well. You are constantly tormenting yourself about him."

" He does not know," she said, and suddenly she blushed to the very roots of her hair and tears of shame stood in her eyes. " Do not let us speak of him," she implored.

XXIII

VRONSKY had on several former occasions attempted to make her consider their position, though perhaps not in the same definite way, but he had invariably met with the same superficiality of judgment with which she tried to put him off now. It seemed as if she could not bring herself to face the facts; at the very mention of the subject the real Anna disappeared, giving place to another strange, unfamiliar being, ever resisting him, whom he feared but could not love. To-day he decided to have a complete explanation.

" Whether he knows or not," Vronsky began in his habitual calm tone, " does not make the least difference to us. We cannot . . . you cannot go on like this, especially now."

" Then what do you think we should do? " she asked in the same tone of light raillery. She who had feared that he would treat her avowal lightly was now annoyed that he made it an excuse for definite action.

" You must tell him everything and leave him."

" Very well; supposing I tell him," she began, " do you know what will come of it? I know so well beforehand what he will say." A wicked light flashed in her eyes, a moment ago so gentle. "Oh, so you love another and have entered into illicit relations with him." (She tried to imitate Alexei Alexandrovitch, and laid special stress on the word *illicit*, just as he would have done.) "I warned you of the consequences that would follow from the point of view of religion, society, and the family, but you would not listen to me. I will not allow my name to be dragged through the mire . . ." She was about to add "my son," but could not bring herself to do so. "In a word, he will tell me in his precise, official manner that he will not let me go and will take measures towards avoiding a scandal. And he will do exactly as he says. That is what will happen. He is not a man, but a machine, and a remorseless machine when he is roused," she added, recollecting all the details of his person and his manner of speaking. At that moment she tried to see only his bad points, and could not forgive him for the wrong that she had done him.

"But, Anna," Vronsky began in a firm yet persuasive tone of voice, trying to soothe her, "you must tell him all the same; we will know better how to act afterwards."

"What! elope?"

"Why not? It is impossible to go on living like this. Not for myself only; I can see how you suffer."

"Elope and become your mistress openly," she said bitterly.

"Anna!" he said reproachfully.

"Yes," she continued, "become your mistress and ruin everything."

Again she wished to pronounce the name of her son, but could not bring herself to do so.

Vronsky could not comprehend how she, with her proud, upright nature, could accept the false position in which she was placed without wishing to escape from it. He did not guess that the principal cause was her boy, whose name she could not bring herself to pronounce.

"I beg you, I implore you," she began suddenly in quite another tone, sincere and gentle, "don't ever speak to me of this."

"But, Anna . . ."

"Never, never. You must leave it to my judgment. Believe me, I fully understand all the indignity of my position, but it is not so easy to decide as you think. Trust me and don't ever speak to me of this again. Will you promise? Never, never; promise me!"

"I promise anything you wish, but I cannot help being

anxious after what you have told me. I cannot be at peace while you are not . . ."

"I?" she repeated. "Yes, I sometimes torment myself, but it will pass off if you never mention this again. I cannot bear to hear you speak of it."

"I don't understand," he said.

"I know how your honest nature abhors lying. I am sorry. It often occurs to me that you have ruined your life on my account."

"And I too have thought how you have sacrificed everything for me. I can never forgive myself that you are unhappy."

"I, unhappy?" she asked, drawing closer to him and gazing up at him in ecstasy. "I feel like a starving man who has been given food. His clothes are in rags and he may be cold and ashamed, but he is not unhappy. I, unhappy? Here is my happiness . . ."

She could hear the voice of her boy, and casting a hurried look around she rose quickly. Her eyes were on fire. With a rapid movement she took his head between her beautiful hands, gazed into his eyes, then drawing her smiling face close to his, she kissed him on the lips and pushed him away from her. But he would not let her go.

"When?" he whispered, looking at her with rapture.

"To-night, at one o'clock," she replied softly, and with a deep sigh she walked away quickly to meet her son.

Serioja had got caught in the rain in the park and had taken refuge with his nurse in the summer-house.

"Good-bye," she said to Vronsky. "I must get ready for the races. Betsy promised to come for me."

Vronsky looked at his watch and hurried away.

XXIV

When Vronsky had looked at his watch on the Karenins' veranda he was so disturbed and preoccupied that though he plainly saw the hands and figures on the face he could not tell what time it was. He walked along the muddy road till he reached his carriage. He was so absorbed in Anna that he had completely forgotten his visit to Bransky. He vaguely remembered that he had decided to do something, and it was only outward things that recalled to his mind what it was. He woke the coachman who was asleep on the box, while the horses were standing in the shade of the lime-trees with swarms of midges buzzing round them, jumped into his carriage, and ordered him to drive to Bransky's. It was only after they had gone about seven miles that he recollected himself sufficiently to look at his watch and realise that it was half-past five, and that he was late for the races.

There were to be several races that day. First the convoys', then the officers' two-mile race, then a four mile, and the last, that in which he was to take part. There was still time to get to the race-course before his own race was due, but if he went to Bransky's first he ran the risk of getting to the grounds after the court had arrived, which would not be in good form. However, he had given Bransky his word, so he ordered the coachman to whip up and not to spare the horses.

He spent about five minutes at Bransky's and started off again at full speed. The quick motion soothed him. All his depression, the uncertainty regarding his relations with Anna that their conversation had produced in him, suddenly left him. He looked forward to the race with the keenest delight, was glad that he would be in time after all, and the thought of seeing Anna that night thrilled him through and through.

He got more into the atmosphere of the races as one by one he overtook other carriages coming from St. Petersburg and the surrounding country on their way to the race-course.

When he reached home no one was there except his valet, who stood waiting for him at the door. All the others had already departed. While he was changing his clothes his valet told him that the second race had begun, that several people had called to ask for him, and that they were getting anxious at the stables.

Vronsky dressed leisurely—he hated to hurry and never lost his self-command—then he gave orders to drive to the stables. From there he could see a whole sea of carriages, pedestrians, and soldiers, surrounding the racecourse, and masses of people in the pavilions. The second race must have begun, for as he drew near he could hear the sound of a bell. Mahotin's white-footed chestnut, Gladiator, was being led out, covered with a gorgeous caparison of orange and blue.

"Where is Cord?" he asked of the stable-boy.

"In the stables, saddling the mare."

Frou-Frou stood in her stall already saddled. Cord was about to lead her out.

"Am I late?"

"All right! all right! don't get excited," the Englishman cautioned him.

Vronsky cast another look at the beautiful creature, who was trembling in every limb, and scarcely able to take his eyes off her he left the stables. He got to the pavilion at a very propitious moment, when no one was likely to notice him. The second race was drawing to a close, and all eyes were fixed on a guardsman and a hussar who were riding with all their might towards the goal. From all sides people crowded to the winning post, and a group of cavalry soldiers and officers gave forth a triumphant shout in honour of their successful comrade.

Vronsky joined the throng at the very moment when a bell announced that the race was over, and the victor dropped the reins and sprang from his saddle, his grey cob panting and dripping with sweat.

The animal had pulled up with difficulty and the guardsman, as though waking from a dream, looked around with a smile. He was immediately surrounded by friends and strangers.

Vronsky purposely avoided the fashionable crowd who were walking to and fro near the pavilion. He knew that Anna would be there, and Betsy and his brother's wife, and not wishing to distract his attention, he kept away from them. Various acquaintances stopped him every now and again, gave him the details of the other races, and wanted to know why he was late.

While the prizes were being distributed at the pavilion, and every one was hurrying in that direction, Vronsky's elder brother Alexander came up to him. He was a short man with a ruddy face, squarely built, like Alexei, only rather more handsome. He was dressed in the uniform of a colonel, his nose was red, and his face was flushed with wine.

"Did you get my note?" he asked. "One can never find you in."

Alexander Vronsky, despite his debauchery and life of dissipation for which he was notorious, was a most diplomatic man. Knowing that all eyes would be fixed upon them he tried to appear as natural and unconcerned as though they were jesting about the most trifling matters instead of discussing a most painful subject.

"Yes, I got it, but I really don't see what you have to worry about," Vronsky replied.

"I am worried because I've been told that you were seen in Peterhof on Monday."

"There are certain things that concern only those who are directly interested, and the matter you are meddling with now is one of them."

"That's all very well; but you'll have to leave the service . . ."

"I must ask you to mind your own business." Alexei Alexandrovitch turned pale and his lower jaw trembled. He was a man of a kindly heart and rarely got angry, but when he was once roused he was dangerous, as Alexander Vronsky knew. The latter laughed.

"I only wanted to give you mother's letter. You can write to her. Don't upset yourself before the race. *Bonne chance*," he added with a smile as he left him.

His brother had no sooner gone than another friendly greeting arrested Vronsky.

"Won't you recognise your friends? How are you, *mon cher?*"

It was Stepan Arkadyevitch, who was no less gay and animated in the fashionable St. Petersburg crowd than he had been in Moscow. He was beaming all over.

"I arrived yesterday and shall be delighted to witness your triumph. When shall we meet?"

"Come to our mess-room to-morrow," Vronsky said, and apologising for having to leave him he pressed his arm and walked towards the centre of the racecourse, where they were leading out the horses for the steeplechase.

The dripping horses who had run in the last race were led away, and one after another fresh ones appeared for the next. They were English horses for the most part, well caparisoned, with their sunken bellies, looking for all the world like some weird, enormous birds. To the left Frou-Frou appeared. She looked beautiful and seemed to tread as if she were on springs. A little further on they were removing Gladiator's horse-cloth, exposing his long ears. The magnificent, powerful cob, with his splendid crupper and his broad hoofs, attracted Vronsky's attention. He was about to go up to Frou-Frou when another acquaintance stopped him.

"Ah! there is Karenin! He is looking for his wife. She's in the pavilion. Have you seen her?"

"No, I haven't," Vronsky replied, and without so much as a glance in the direction where his friend said Anna was, he turned to his horse.

He had scarcely time to examine and rearrange the saddle when those who were to compete in the race were summoned up to the pavilion to receive their numbers. With stern, solemn faces seventeen officers approached, some of them deadly pale. Vronsky's number was seven.

" Mount! " some one cried.

Feeling that all eyes were fixed upon them, Vronsky, despite his excited condition, walked up to his horse calmly and slowly.

Cord, in honour of the occasion, was dressed in his best. He wore a black coat, tightly buttoned, a large stiff collar that came up to his cheeks, a round black hat, and jack-boots. He was calm and solemn as usual, and stood next to Frou-Frou holding the reins. The mare trembled feverishly. She looked at Vronsky coming towards her with her fiery eyes. He put his finger under the saddle. The mare showed her teeth and pricked up her ears. The Englishman grinned at the idea that there could be any doubt as to his skill in putting on a saddle.

" You had better mount. It will make you less nervous.

Vronsky took a last look at his rivals, knowing that when once they started he would not see them again. Two of them were already at the starting point. Galitsin, a friend of Vronsky's and another dangerous rival, was walking round and round his bay cob, who would not let him mount. A little hussar, in tight trousers, was coming along at full gallop, crouching over his horse like a cat, in his efforts to imitate the English. Prince Kusovlev, deadly white, was sitting on his thoroughbred mare, which an Englishman was leading by the bridle. He was well known to Vronsky and all the other officers for his awful conceit and his highly-strung nerves. He was afraid of everything, afraid of riding a front-rank horse, but just now, because of the very horror of the thing, because it meant broken necks and that at every obstacle a surgeon and nurse were stationed, he had made up his mind to ride. Vronsky caught his eye and gave him an encouraging nod. Only Mahotin and Gladiator were not to be seen.

" Don't be in a hurry," Cord remarked, " and remember this: when you come to a jump, don't urge her on, but let her choose her own course."

" Very good," Vronsky said, taking the reins.

" Get ahead at first if you can, but don't get discouraged till the last moment if you happen to be behind."

The mare had barely time to stir when Vronsky, with a quick movement, put his foot in the stirrup and sprang lightly into the saddle that creaked beneath his weight. He took the reins between his fingers and Cord let go his hold. Frou-Frou stretched out her neck, pulled at the reins, and started off in her springy gait, balancing her rider on her flexible back. Cord quickened his steps to keep up with them. The excited mare jumped from right to left, as if trying to take her rider off his guard, and pulled violently at the reins. Vronsky said a few soothing words to her and patted her neck. They were approaching the starting point at the river bank. There were riders on all sides, some in front, others behind. Vronsky suddenly heard the clatter of hoofs at full gallop in the mud, and Mahotin came by on Gladiator. He smiled as he passed Vronsky showing his large teeth, but Vronsky looked at him angrily. He had never liked Mahotin personally, and now looked upon him as his most dangerous rival. His riding up suddenly and frightening Frou-Frou annoyed him. The mare set off at a gallop, made two bounds, then annoyed at the restraint of the curb she settled down to a trot which shook her rider. Cord frowned and ran along to keep up with them.

XXV

THERE were seventeen officers competing in the steeplechase. The course was elliptical in shape, stretching in front of the pavilion, making a circuit of four miles. There were nine jumps in all, the river, then a barrier of about five feet in height, a dry ditch, a ditch full of water, a steep slope, an Irish bank. (This was the most difficult of all. It was composed of dry brush-wood, sticking straight up, with a ditch on the other side which the horse could not see, so that the animal would have to take two jumps at once at the risk of its life.) Then there was still another dry ditch and two full of water, and lastly the winning post by the pavilion. The race began at some distance to one side of the ellipse, with the river, about eight feet across, as the first jump. The rider could either leap it or ford it as he chose.

Three times the horsemen got into line, but some horse or other would start off before the appointed time and the men had to draw up again. At last, for the fourth time, when Colonel Sestren, the starter, was beginning to get impatient, the signal was given and the men started.

All eyes, all field-glasses, were directed towards the racers.

"They're off! There they go!" was heard on all sides.

Everybody began moving from place to place in order to get a better view. At first the group of horsemen separated, and one after another, by twos and threes, they drew near the river. For those looking on they seemed one indistinguishable mass, but the short distances dividing them had a tremendous significance for each.

Frou-Frou, excited and too nervous, lost ground at first, and several of the others got ahead of her, but Vronsky, before he got to the river, spurred on and overtook three of those who had gained on him. There was still Mahotin's Gladiator in front, and ahead of them all the beautiful Diana, who was carrying Kusovlev, more dead than alive.

During the first few moments Vronsky could not control either himself or his horse.

Gladiator and Diana leapt the river together. With one bound they crossed over to the other side. Frou-Frou followed as if on wings. But as she leapt in the air, Vronsky suddenly got a glimpse of Kusovlev struggling with Diana at his very feet. (Kusovlev had dropped the reins after Diana had jumped, and the horse had stumbled and pitched him on his head.) Vronsky learnt all the details later, but now there they lay and Frou-Frou might get entangled with them as she got her feet to the ground. But like a cat she saw the danger, made a tremendous effort while in the air, and bounded past them.

" You beauty! " Vronsky thought.

As soon as they crossed the river he gained complete control over his horse and even held her back a little, meaning to take the next jump behind Mahotin and to overtake him when they reached the next clear space.

The big barrier was right in front of the royal pavilion. The emperor, the court, and the whole crowd were watching breathlessly as they measured the distance between the two horsemen. Vronsky felt all eyes fixed upon him, but he could see only Frou-Frou's neck and ears, the ground flying under him, and Gladiator's flanks and white feet beating the ground in cadence and maintaining the same distance between them. Gladiator leapt in the air, cleared the barrier, and whisking his short tail disappeared from Vronsky's view.

" Bravo! " some one cried.

At this moment the planks of the hurdle flashed before his eyes. Without a moment's hesitation the horse went over, but Vronsky heard a loud crash behind him. Frou-Frou, excited by Gladiator, had leapt too soon and struck the hurdle with her hind hoof. Her speed did not slacken, however, and Vronsky, his face splashed with mud, could see that the distance between him and Gladiator had not increased. There were his flanks, short tail, and white feet that flew like the wind. Now was the moment for overtaking him and Frou-Frou, as if divining her master's thought, quickened her speed and made for the most advantageous side, near the rope. But Mahotin would not let her pass. It occurred to Vronsky to try the outer side, when Frou-Frou, again divining his thought, changed her course. Her shoulder, darkened with sweat, came up level with Gladiator's flanks. For several paces they rode side by side, but just before they got to the next jump, Vronsky, to avoid the outer line, began pulling at the reins and got ahead of Mahotin down the big slope. He got a glimpse of his face as he passed; it was covered with mud, and it seemed to Vronsky that he smiled. But Mahotin came on close behind him. Vronsky could hear the regular rhythm of Gladiator's feet and his quick breathing.

The next two jumps, a ditch and a hurdle, were easily passed, but Vronsky could hear Gladiator's gallop and puffing coming nearer. He spurred his horse and could feel with joy how she quickened her speed, and the distance between her and Gladiator was again increased.

He now had the lead as he had desired and as Cord had recommended and felt certain of success. His excitement, his joy and tenderness for Frou-Frou increased. He wanted to look back, but dared not, and tried to calm himself and not to spur his horse too much, so as to reserve her energy. The most difficult jump was still before him; if he could clear that first he was sure to win the race. They drew near to the Irish bank. Both he and Frou-Frou could see it from a distance, and each felt a moment of hesitation. Vronsky noticed the hesitation in his horse's ears, but instantly felt that she regained her confidence and knew exactly what to do. She made a tremendous effort, rose in the air, and with one bound cleared the bank and the ditch together and went on without changing the measure of her pace.

" Bravo, Vronsky! " the crowd shouted. He recognised his regiment and friends who were standing near the obstacle, and could distinguish Yashvin's voice although he did not see him.

" You darling! " he said inwardly to Frou-Frou, at the same time trying to hear what was going at the back of him. " He's over! " he thought as he heard Gladiator's gallop behind. There remained only a ditch full of water, about five feet across.

Vronsky scarcely heeded it. Anxious to come in far ahead of the others he began to pull on the reins and move the horse's head up and down in time to the beat of her hoofs. Frou-Frou was straining herself to the utmost. She was dripping with sweat and drawing short, sharp breaths. But Vronsky felt certain that she would hold out for the remaining short distance that lay between him and the goal. Only because he felt himself so near the ground and by the remarkable smoothness of her motion did he realise how she had increased her speed. She flew over the ditch like the wind, scarcely noticing it, but at this moment Vronsky felt to his horror that instead of swaying his body to the motion of the horse, for some unexplicable reason he made a false motion backwards on the saddle. His position suddenly changed, and he felt that something terrible had happened. He could not tell exactly what it was, but he got a glimpse of the white feet of a chestnut cob close by and Mahotin dashed past him. One of Vronsky's feet touched the ground and his horse fell on it. He had scarcely time to extricate it when the mare rolled over on her side, panting heavily. She stretched out her neck, dripping wet, and made one fearful effort to rise, but fell back at his feet like a wounded bird. Vronsky's awkward movement had broken her back. He did not realise it all until much later. Now he could only see Mahotin shooting on ahead, while he stood dazed on the muddy ground with Frou-Frou panting at his feet, gazing up at him with her beautiful eyes. Too dazed to realise what had happened he pulled at the reins. The poor animal struggled like a fish, tried to raise herself on her fore-legs, but fell on her side exhausted. Vronsky, white as a sheet and trembling with rage, kicked her in the belly to make her rise, but the poor creature did not stir. She gave her master one beseeching look and dropped her head to the ground.

"Oh! what have I done?" Vronsky cried in despair, seizing her head in both his hands. "I've lost the race! and it was all my own fault! Stupid! unpardonable! And the poor creature is done for! Oh, what have I done?"

He was immediately surrounded by a crowd of people, the doctor and surgeon and the officers of his own regiment. The horse's back was broken and she had to be shot. Vronsky did not answer any of the questions that were put to him, he could not bring himself to speak to any one. He turned away, and not troubling to pick up his cap that had fallen off his head he left the racecourse, not knowing where he was going. He was in despair. For the first time in his life a misfortune had happened to him—an irremediable misfortune for which he alone was to blame.

Yashvin hastened after him with his cap and took him home In about half an hour Vronsky was quite himself again, but for a long time afterwards this race was one of the most cruel and bitter remembrances of his life.

XXVI

THERE was no outward change in the relations between Alexei Alexandrovitch and his wife, except perhaps that he was now more occupied than he had ever been before. It was his habit to go abroad in the early part of the spring for a water-cure to repair his health after a strenuous winter. He had just returned as usual in the middle of July and resumed his duties with new energy. His wife had gone down to their country house and he remained in St. Petersburg.

Since their conversation after the reception at the Princess Tverskaya's he had said nothing further to Anna about his suspicions and his jealousies. The light tone of raillery which he always adopted with her now came in particularly useful. His manner towards her was perhaps rather more cold. It seemed as if he had a slight grievance against her for shirking the explanation of that night, but nothing more. There was a shade of displeasure in his intercourse with her. "You would not come to an understanding with me," he seemed to say, "then so much the worse for you. A time may come when you may beg for an explanation, but I shall not listen to you." His attitude towards his wife might be compared to that of a man who in his vain efforts to put out a fire loses all patience and says, "Burn away then, if you like! I shall not interfere with you!"

He, a man intelligent and shrewd enough in matters concerning his official duties, failed to see the absurdity of such an attitude. He could not bring himself to face the real facts of the situation and tried to stifle the affection he felt for his wife and child. Towards the end of the winter he grew singularly cold to the boy, and would talk to him in the same ironical way that he used towards his mother. "Ah, young man!" he would greet him whenever he saw him.

Alexei Alexandrovitch told every one that he had never had

so many important affairs on his hands as that year. It was perfectly true, but he would not have admitted it, even to himself, that he had expressly invented a good many of these important affairs in order to keep him occupied and prevent him brooding over his wife and boy. He wanted to drive away all troublesome thoughts about them which grew worse and worse the more he tried to evade them. If any one had assumed the right to ask Alexei Alexandrovitch what he thought of his wife's conduct, then this gentle, peaceful man would have flown into a rage and refused to answer. There was something severe and proud in his expression when any one inquired after his wife's health. Alexei Alexandrovitch wished to banish all thoughts about his wife's conduct and inner life, and he succeeded in doing so.

The Countess Lydia Ivanovna usually spent her summers at Peterhof near the Karenins, where she could see a good deal of Anna. This summer she declined to go there and had not once been to visit her. She tried to throw out a few hints about her intimacy with Vronsky, expressing her disapproval, but Alexei Alexandrovitch stopped her severely, saying that his wife was above suspicion. Since then he avoided the countess as much as possible. He tried to shut his eyes to the fact that many people looked at his wife with disfavour, and did not attempt to analyse the reasons that had led her to insist on moving to Tsarskoe where Betsy lived, not far from Vronsky's camp. He did not allow himself to think of these things; nevertheless, without even admitting it to himself, and without any other proof than the merest suspicion, at the bottom of his heart there was a feeling that his wife was unfaithful to him, and he suffered horribly.

How many times during the eight years they had lived happily together had he marvelled at other men placed in exactly the same position he was in now? "How could they ever bring themselves as far as that? Why don't they free themselves from such a frightful position?" he used to ask himself, but now that the misfortune had befallen him, he not only made no attempts to free himself from the situation, but would not even admit that it existed, because he felt it to be too unnatural, too terrible.

Since his return from abroad he had been down to their country house twice, once to dinner and another time he had brought some friends to spend the evening. He did not spend the night there as he had been in the habit of doing formerly.

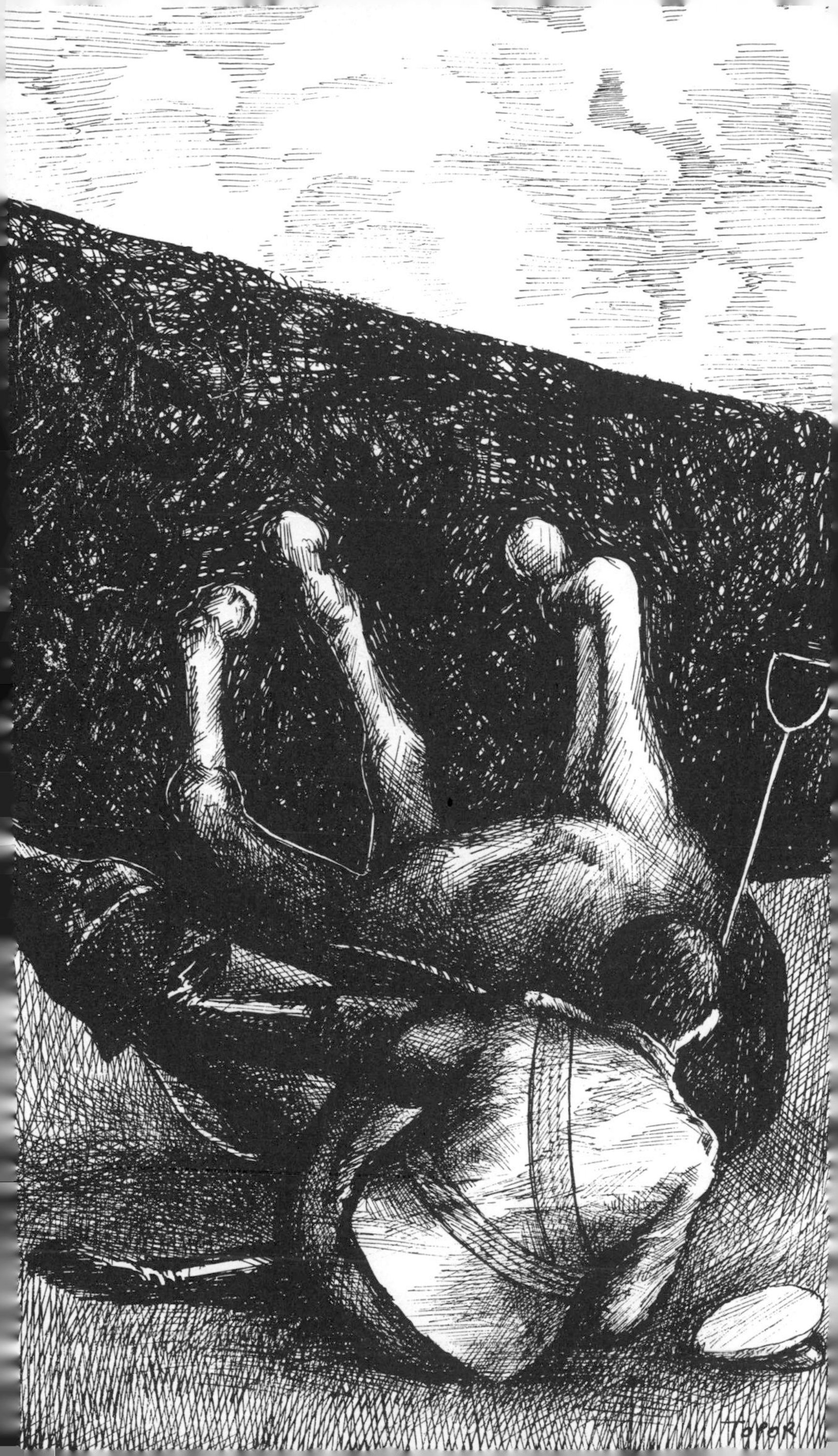
TOPOR

The day of the races was a very busy one for Alexei Alexandrovitch, but when in the morning he made his plans for the day, he decided that he would run down and see Anna after an early dinner and then go on to the races, as the whole court would be there, and it would not do for him to absent himself. For the sake of propriety he had decided to visit his wife at least once a week. Besides which it was the fifteenth of the month, and on that day he usually gave her the allowance for the household expenses.

With his immense power of concentration that allowed him to regulate his thoughts, he considered these details, but did not permit himself to enter into any further analysis concerning her feelings.

The morning was a very busy one. The Countess Lydia Ivanovna had sent him a pamphlet the evening before, together with a note introducing the author, who had travelled a good deal in China, as a very useful and interesting man. Alexei Alexandrovitch had not been able to get through the pamphlet in the evening, so he finished it the first thing in the morning. Then came various petitions, reports, visits, dismissals, distribution of rewards, pensions, salaries, correspondence, the ordinary routine work that consumed so much time. Then came private business, a visit from his doctor and steward. The steward was easily dispensed with. He merely gave Alexei Alexandrovitch a brief report of the condition of his affairs, which showed a deficit this year on account of the heavy expenses and numerous journeys. The doctor, on the other hand, a famous St. Petersburg specialist, who was on friendly terms with Karenin, took a considerable time. Alexei Alexandrovitch had not expected him, and was the more surprised when he began to ply him with questions and carefully examine his lungs and liver. Alexei Alexandrovitch was not aware that his friend, the Countess Lydia Ivanovna, who had been anxious about the state of his health for some time, had asked the doctor to go and see him. "Do it for my sake," she had said.

"I will do it for Russia, countess," the doctor had replied.

"Invaluable man!" the countess exclaimed.

The doctor was very much disturbed at Alexei Alexandrovitch's state. His digestion was bad, his liver very much enlarged, in fact his condition was generally poor. He ordered plenty of exercise, as little brain-work as possible, and told him to avoid anything of a worrying nature. The latter precaution was not so easy to fulfil. He went away leaving Alexei

Alexandrovitch with the painful impression that something was radically wrong with him that could not be put right.

As he got outside the doctor ran against Sludin, Karenin's chief secretary. They had been at the university together, and although they rarely met now, still they were very good friends and admired each other immensely. The doctor would not have spoken so freely about his patient to any one as he did to Sludin.

"I am so glad you've seen him," Sludin said. "He does not appear at all well, and I think. . . . What is the matter with him?"

"You see," the doctor began, making a sign to his coachman to draw up and pulling on his kid gloves, "if you strain a string to its utmost the merest touch will break it. What with his sedentary life and too conscientious labour, he is strained to the utmost limit, and besides there's a great deal of pressure from another direction," he concluded, with a significant motion of the eyebrows. "Shall you be at the races?" he asked, taking his seat in the carriage. "Yes, yes; of course, it takes too much time," he said in reply to some remark of Sludin's that he did not quite catch.

As soon as the doctor had gone the celebrated traveller arrived, and Alexei Alexandrovitch by the aid of the pamphlet he had just read, and the previous information he had obtained on the subject, impressed the visitor by his remarkable knowledge and broad-mindedness. At the same time the marshal of the nobility from one of the provinces was announced. He had just come to St. Petersburg, and Alexei Alexandrovitch had some business to talk over with him. When they left he had to settle various matters with his chief secretary, and then he went to pay a call on some important personage to talk over some very serious undertaking. It was five o'clock when he returned to dinner, which he took with Sludin, whom he afterwards invited to come down with him to Peterhof and to the races afterwards. For Alexei Alexandrovitch felt it necessary to have a third person present in his interviews with his wife.

XXVII

Anna was standing before the mirror putting the finishing touches to her toilet by the help of Annushka, her maid, when she heard the sound of wheels in front of the house.

" It is too early for Betsy," she thought, and looking out of the window she saw a carriage and the black hat and large ears of Alexei Alexandrovitch, so well known to her.

" What a nuisance! I hope he's not going to stay the night," she thought. She was so terrified at the idea of what might happen if he did that she would not stop to think about it. She quitted the room hastily and went out to meet him with a smiling face. She felt herself possessed of a spirit of falsehood so familiar to her of late, and abandoning herself to it said the first thing that came into her head, without knowing why.

" How nice of you to come! " she said, extending her hand to her husband and greeting Sludin with a smile. " I hope you are going to stay the night? " was the first thing she was prompted to ask. " We can go to the races together. What a pity I asked Betsy to come! She promised to call for me."

" I would not for the world separate the inseparables," Alexei Alexandrovitch said in his habitual jesting tone. " I shall go with Mihail Vassilevitch. The doctor ordered me plenty of exercise, so I think we'll walk. I shall try and persuade myself that I'm still taking the waters."

Alexei Alexandrovitch frowned when Betsy's name was mentioned.

" There's no hurry," Anna remarked; " would you like some tea? "

She touched the bell.

" Let us have some tea, and tell Serioja that Alexei Alexandrovitch is here," she said to the servant who answered it. " Well, and how are you? " she asked. " I don't think you've been here before, Mihail Vassilevitch," she said, turning to Sludin; " look how nice it is from the veranda."

She spoke simply and naturally, but rather too much and too quickly. She felt conscious of it herself, especially when she caught Mihail Vassilevitch's eye observing her curiously. Sludin immediately went out on the terrace and Anna sat down beside her husband.

" You are not looking at all well," she remarked.

" Oh, yes, the doctor came to-day and took up a whole hour of my time," he said. " I suppose one of our friends must have sent him, so precious do they consider my health . . . "

" What did he say? "

She questioned him about his health and his work, and tried to persuade him to take a holiday and join her at Peterhof.

She said all this gaily and with a peculiar light in her eyes, but Alexei Alexandrovitch attached no importance to her tone. He took everything she said literally and replied simply, though half jestingly. There was nothing particularly important about their conversation, but afterwards Anna could never recall this scene without pain.

Serioja came in accompanied by his governess. If Alexei Alexandrovitch had cared to, he might have noticed the timid, disconcerted look with which the boy regarded him and then his mother, but Alexei Alexandrovitch did not wish to notice anything and saw nothing.

" Well, young man, how are you? He has grown. Will soon be grown up in fact."

He extended his hand to the scared child.

Serioja had always been shy with his father, but since he had taken to calling him young man, and the boy had begun to wonder whether Vronsky were a friend or an enemy, he kept more aloof from him than ever. He turned to his mother as if asking for her protection. He felt at ease only with her. Meanwhile Alexei Alexandrovitch began talking to the governess with his hand on the boy's shoulder. Serioja was so terrified that Anna could see he was going to cry.

She had blushed when the boy came in, and when she noticed his discomfort she jumped up, released him from Alexei Alexandrovitch, and kissing him led him out on the terrace. She came back shortly.

" It is time we started," she observed, glancing at her watch; " I wonder why Betsy doesn't come? "

" By the way," Alexei Alexandrovitch remarked as he rose and cracked the joints of his fingers, " I've also come to bring you some money. No doubt you need it, for nightingales don't live on songs."

" I don't need any, thanks. . . . Yes, I do though," she added, not looking at him and blushing to the roots of her hair. " Shall you come back here after the races? " she asked.

" I think so," he replied. " Ah, here comes the pride of Peterhof," he added as a smart English carriage drew up at the door. "What elegance! beautiful! I suppose we had better go too."

The princess did not leave her carriage. A footman in livery leapt down and rang the bell.

"Good-bye, I am going," Anna said. She kissed her son and extended her hand to Alexei Alexandrovitch. "It was so good of you to come!"

Alexei Alexandrovitch raised her hand to his lips.

"Well, good-bye. You'll come back to tea, won't you?" she said, and went out smiling and radiant. But as soon as she had left his presence, she shuddered with repugnance as she still felt his kiss on her hand.

XXVIII

When Alexei Alexandrovitch got to the racecourse Anna and Betsy were already ensconced in the grand pavilion where the cream of society had gathered. Anna espied her husband from afar. These two men, her husband and her lover, were the two main springs of her life; she could feel their approach instinctively. And so she felt him coming when he was still some distance off, and her eyes followed his progress through the crowd involuntarily. He drew near to the pavilion. She saw him bow condescendingly to some, affably to others, while his eye tried to catch the glances of the great ones of the earth, to whom he paid his respects by removing his large, round hat that came down to the tops of his ears. Anna was familiar with his various ways of greeting people, and they were equally distasteful to her. "Nothing but ambition—a desire to get on, that is the only thing he cares about," she thought. "As to his high ideals, his passion for culture, religion, they are only means to success."

He was looking straight into the pavilion trying to find his wife amidst a sea of muslins, ribbons, feathers, parasols, and flowers, but she pretended not to see him.

"Alexei Alexandrovitch!" Betsy called to him, "your wife is here!"

He smiled with his habitual cold smile.

"There is so much brilliance here that it quite dazzles the eye," he remarked as he entered the pavilion.

He smiled to Anna as a husband who had only seen her a

moment ago, greeted the princess and other acquaintances, exchanging a few jesting remarks with the ladies and merely nodding to the men.

A certain general was standing a little lower down whom Alexei Alexandrovitch admired very much, an extremely cultured man, well known for his wit. He joined him and they entered into conversation. It was during an interval between two races, so that they could talk quite freely. The general condemned racing as an amusement, Alexei Alexandrovitch defended it. Anna listened to his precise, thin voice that grated on her ear, and did not miss a single word he said. When the steeplechase began she leaned forward, not letting Vronsky out of her sight for an instant. She saw him approach and mount his horse, her husband's voice still grating on her ear. She was filled with apprehension for Vronsky, and was all the more irritated at the sound of this voice, every intonation of which she knew.

" I am a bad, wicked woman," she thought, " but I hate lying and pretence. He " (meaning her husband) " can't live without them. He sees and knows everything, how can he go on speaking so calmly? If he were to kill us both I should have some sort of respect for him, but all he cares about is pretence, propriety."

Anna did not exactly know what she would have liked her husband to be, and did not realise that her irritation was merely due to her agitated condition. Alexei Alexandrovitch felt the need of some mental exertion to drown all thoughts about his wife and Vronsky that would arise in her presence, especially when his name was constantly mentioned, just as a child contracts its muscles and goes on playing to prevent it crying when it has hurt itself. Talking came just as naturally to him as playing to the child.

" It seems to me that the element of danger in these cavalry races is the main thing," he observed. " If England can boast of glorious deeds of valour performed by her cavalry, she owes it solely to the daring she has developed in her men and her horses. Sport, in my opinion, has a deep significance, and we, I am sorry to say, treat it only superficially."

" That is hardly true when one officer has broken two of his ribs," the Princess Betsy remarked.

Alexei Alexandrovitch gave a faint smile, but did not say anything.

" I must admit, princess, it was more than superficial in this case," he said after a pause, " but the point is," he turned to the general again and continued seriously. " We must not lose sight of the fact that those taking part in these races are military men. They have chosen it as their calling, and every calling has two sides. This is part of their military duty. Prize-fighting and Spanish bull-fights are indications of barbarism, but specialised sport is a sign of development."

" No, I won't come another time, it's too upsetting," the Princess Betsy remarked. " Don't you think so, Anna? "

" Yes, but it is so fascinating," another lady remarked. " Had I been a Roman I should have spent all my days at the circus."

Anna did not speak. She held her glasses and was looking intently towards one particular spot.

At this moment a tall general walked past the pavilion. Alexei Alexandrovitch, breaking off his discourse abruptly, rose with dignity and made a low bow.

" Why are you not racing? " the general asked jestingly.

" My race is a more difficult one," Alexei Alexandrovitch replied respectfully. There was nothing very astonishing in the remark, but the general looked as if he had just heard something very witty from a very clever man and fully appreciated *la pointe de la sauce.*

" There are two distinct elements in this thing," Alexei Alexandrovitch continued; " you have the participator and the spectator. A passion for such spectacles always points to a low state of development, but . . . "

" Princess, a wager! " The voice of Stepan Arkadyevitch was heard from below addressing Betsy. " Whom will you back? "

" Anna and I back Kusovlev," Betsy replied.

" I bet you a pair of gloves that Vronsky wins."

" There they go! "

" Aren't they beautiful? "

Alexei Alexandrovitch did not speak while this conversation was going on. When they had finished he began anew.

" I quite agree, but manly games . . . "

At this moment the horsemen started and every one ceased speaking. They stood up looking eagerly towards the river. Alexei Alexandrovitch, however, not being interested in the race, cast his eyes vaguely over the spectators till they rested on Anna.

Her face was pale and serious. She seemed to see nothing but one horseman. She clutched her fan feverishly and held her breath. Alexei Alexandrovitch turned away from her and began examining the other faces.

"Here is another lady who seems very much excited, and so are all the others; it is only natural," he tried to assure himself. He did not wish to look at Anna again, but his gaze was irresistibly drawn towards her face, on which he read with horror what was so plainly written on it, the very thing he had been trying not to see.

When Kusovlev fell in crossing the river the excitement was general, but Alexei Alexandrovitch saw quite clearly by Anna's pale, triumphant gaze that he who fell was not the one on whom her eyes were riveted. And when Mahotin and Vronsky had leapt the great barrier and the officer following was pitched on his head and picked up for dead and a shudder of horror ran through the crowd, Alexei Alexandrovitch could see that Anna did not even notice it, and could scarcely make out what the people around her were saying. He hardened his heart and kept on looking at her. Anna, absorbed as she was in Vronsky's course, could feel her husband's cold gaze fixed upon her. She turned to him for a moment, gave him a questioning look, frowned, and turned away again.

"I don't care," she seemed to say, and paid no further attention to him.

The race was disastrous. Out of seventeen men more than half were thrown. Towards the end the general excitement grew tremendous, all the more so as the emperor was displeased.

XXIX

All were expressing their disapproval. "You only want the lions to make the circus complete," was heard on all sides. When Vronsky fell the general horror was so great that Anna's cry caused no astonishment. But the expression of her face, the anxiety she betrayed, was beyond the bounds of propriety. She lost complete control of herself. She struggled like a bird in a cage. She wanted to rise, to get away.

"Let us go, let us go!" she implored of Betsy.

But Betsy did not hear her. She was leaning over and talking to a general who had just come up.

Alexei Alexandrovitch approached Anna and offered her his arm.

"We can go if you wish," he said in French. But Anna did not heed him. She was straining to hear what the general was saying, and paid no attention to her husband.

"He has broken his leg they say," the general remarked. "This is really too bad."

Anna made no reply to her husband, but picking up her glasses she gazed at the place where Vronsky had fallen. It was so far off and so many people had crowded there that it was impossible to distinguish anything. She dropped her glasses and was about to go out, but at this moment an officer came running up with news for the emperor. Anna leant over trying to catch what he said.

"Stiva! Stiva!" she called to her brother, but he did not hear her. Again she rose to go out.

"Here is my arm, if you wish to go," Alexei Alexandrovitch repeated, touching her hand.

She shrank from him with aversion.

"No, no, leave me alone, I want to stay," she said, without looking at him.

At this moment she saw an officer coming at full speed from the place of the accident to the pavilion. Betsy waved to him. The officer told them that the rider was uninjured, but that the horse had broken her back.

At this news Anna sank back in her seat and covered her face with her fan. Alexei Alexandrovitch could see that she was crying. She could no longer restrain the tears, nor the sobs that heaved her breast. He stepped in front of her to shield her from the public gaze so that she might have time to recover herself.

"For the third time I offer you my arm," he said, turning to her at the end of a few moments. Anna looked at him not knowing what to say. But the Princess Betsy came to her aid.

"Excuse me, Alexei Alexandrovitch, I brought Anna and I promised to take her back."

"I am sorry, princess," he said politely, meeting her gaze firmly, "but I see that Anna is not very well and I want her to come home with me."

Anna looked round in terror, then rose submissively and put her arm through her husband's.

"I will try and find out how he is and will let you know," Betsy whispered to her.

As they left the pavilion Alexei Alexandrovitch spoke to the acquaintances they met in his habitual tone. Anna too was compelled to speak and to answer, but she was not herself, and passed along on her husband's arm as in a dream.

"Is he hurt or not? Was it true what the officer said? Will he come? Shall I see him to-night?" she kept asking herself.

In silence she took her seat in the carriage, and in silence they rode away from the throng of vehicles standing outside the racecourse. In spite of what he had just seen, Alexei Alexandrovitch still refused to consider his wife's real condition. He was only concerned about outward appearances. She had not conducted herself properly, and he felt it his duty to speak to her of it. He opened his lips and was about to begin, but involuntarily he said something quite different.

"I don't know what pleasure we find in these cruel spectacles," he observed. "I noticed . . ."

"What? I don't understand," Anna said contemptuously.

He was hurt, and instantly began saying what he had wished to.

"I am obliged to tell you," he began.

"Now for the explanation," Anna thought in terror.

"I am obliged to tell you that your conduct to-day has been extremely improper."

"Why? what have I done?" she asked, turning towards him quickly and looking him straight in the eyes. She no longer tried to hide her feelings under a mask of gaiety, but fixed her gaze on him boldly and tried to conceal the terror which she felt in her heart.

"Be careful," he cautioned her, pointing to the open window behind the coachman's back.

He got up to shut it.

"What was there improper about my conduct to-day?" she asked again.

"The despair which you did not conceal when one of the horsemen fell."

He waited for her to speak, but she was silent and sat looking straight before her.

"I have already asked you to behave in such a way before the eyes of the world as to leave no room for the gossip of evil tongues. There was a time when I spoke of your inner feelings. I now say nothing about them. I am only speaking about outward appearances. You have conducted yourself with impropriety, and I sincerely hope that it will not happen again."

She barely listened to him as she sat there in terror, wondering if it was really true that Vronsky had not hurt himself. She smiled disdainfully when he had finished, but made no reply, as she had not heard what he had said. Alexei Alexandrovitch began quite boldly, but when he realised the thing he was talking about, the terror that she felt communicated itself to him. He noticed her smile and tried to delude himself.

"She is amused at my suspicions. She will tell me that they are utterly groundless, absurd, as she did then."

Now that the truth hung over him he would have been ready to believe anything, and was longing for her to tell him in her light, disdainful tone that his suspicions were groundless and ridiculous. He could not bear to hear the truth; it was too terrible. But the expression of her gloomy, frightened face bespoke no further falsehood.

"I may be mistaken," he ventured to say, "in which case I hope you will forgive me."

"No, you are not mistaken," she said slowly, looking into his solemn face with an expression of despair, "you are not mistaken. I was in despair; I could not help it. I am listening to you and thinking of him. I love him, I am his mistress, and I am afraid of you, I can't bear you, I hate you. . . . Do what you like with me."

She withdrew into a corner of the carriage, covered her face with her hands, and burst into tears. Alexei Alexandrovitch did not stir, he sat staring straight before him. His face assumed a death-like rigidity, which remained unchanged for the rest of the journey.

"I must insist upon the preservation of appearances," he said to her in a trembling voice as the carriage stopped at the door, "at any rate until I take the necessary measures to vindicate my honour, which I will communicate to you."

He stepped down first and helped her out. As the servants were there he shook hands with her in the ordinary way, re-entered the carriage and returned to St. Petersburg.

He had no sooner gone than a footman came bringing a note from the Princess Betsy.

"I sent to Alexei to find out how he was," it said, "and he tells me that he is perfectly sound, but in despair."

"Then he will come!" Anna thought joyfully. "What a good thing I told him everything."

She looked at her watch. There were still three hours to wait. The recollection of their last meeting set her on fire.

"Heavens! how light it is! It is terrible, but I love to see his face, and I love this fantastic light. . . . But my husband? Thank God all is over between us."

XXX

As in all places where people congregate, so in the little German town where the Shcherbatskys had gone to take the waters society crystallised itself, so to speak, apportioning each his particular place according to the social status that he occupied. As every drop of water crystallises in the cold and assumes its particular form, so every new arrival dropped into his particular place.

" *Fürst Shcherbatsky, samt Gemahlin und Tochter,*" both by the apartments they occupied, their name, and acquaintances they made, soon fell into their apportioned sphere.

That year a genuine German princess honoured the waters by her presence, and society was even more rigidly divided up than usual. The Princess Shcherbatsky was eager to introduce Kitty to her, and this ceremony took place two days after their arrival. Kitty, dressed *très simple*, that is to say, in a gorgeous Parisian gown, made a deep, graceful courtesy.

" I hope the roses will soon return to her cheeks," the princess had been gracious enough to say. From that moment the Shcherbatskys found themselves in that walk in life from which it is impossible to descend. They also made the acquaintance of an English titled lady, a German countess and her son, who had been wounded in the wars, a Swiss professor, and M. Canut and his sister. The people they saw most of, whether they would or not, were Moscow people. There was Marya Yevgenevna and her daughter, whom Kitty took a dislike to because her illness was also due to a love affair. Then a certain colonel whom Kitty remembered since she was a child, invariably dressed in his uniform and epaulets. He seemed ridiculous here with his tiny little eyes and coloured cravat, and tired her to death, particularly as she could not get away from him.

When they had settled down she began feeling very bored, the more so as her father departed for Carlsbad and she was left alone with her mother. Her former acquaintances did not interest her as she could find out nothing new about them, so her principal amusement consisted in studying the people whom she had never seen before. It was in accordance with her character to see only the best side of people, particularly when they were strangers, and so she imbued all the people she met with the most excellent and perfect qualities.

She was particularly interested in a Russian girl who had

come to the little town with an invalid lady, also a Russian, of good family, whom everybody called Madame Stahl. This Madame Stahl was very ill, and was only taken out on rare days in a bath-chair. It was not only on account of her illness but her pride that she refused to have any connection with the other Russians, the princess explained. The girl looked after Madame Stahl and made friends among the many invalids who had come to take the waters. She tried to be of service to them in the most natural manner.

It seemed to Kitty that this girl could be neither a relation of Madame Stahl's nor a hired nurse. Madame Stahl called her Varenka, and others addressed her as Mademoiselle Varenka. Kitty felt extremely attracted to her, and whenever they chanced to meet she was pleased to see that Mademoiselle Varenka liked her too.

Mademoiselle Varenka, though still quite young, seemed to lack youthfulness. She might have been any age between nineteen and thirty. If you examined her features carefully she was rather good-looking than otherwise in spite of her bad complexion. Her figure too might have been considered perfect had she not been so thin, and her head was rather too large for the smallness of her stature. She was not a girl men would have been attracted to, and reminded one of some beautiful flower which, though still preserving its petals, had lost its colour and scent. She lacked too what Kitty possessed in such abundance, a keenness in life and a consciousness of her own attractiveness.

She was always absorbed in her duties and seemed to have no time for anything else. That was why Kitty felt so drawn towards her. It seemed to her that Varenka was leading exactly the kind of life that she, Kitty, had been seeking—a life of interests other than the stupid intercourse between young girls and young men of her set, that now appeared to her so vulgar and horrible. It was like an exhibition of wares offered to the highest bidder. The more Kitty observed her unknown friend, the more convinced she became that Varenka was exactly the perfect being she had imagined her to be, and she longed to make her acquaintance.

The two girls would pass each other several times during the course of a day. "I wonder who you are and what you are like?" Kitty's glance seemed to say. "What a charming person you must be! But for Heaven's sake don't imagine that I wish to force my acquaintance upon you. I merely wish to admire you and to love you."

"I also love you and think you very, very charming. I would love you much more if I had time," Varenka's glance would reply. And really Kitty could see that she was always busy. She was either taking some Russian children home from the baths or trying to amuse some invalid, or choosing some sweets for another's coffee.

One morning, soon after the Shcherbatskys' arrival, a couple appeared who became the object of some rather unfriendly criticism. The man was tall and round-shouldered with enormous hands, and was clad in an old coat much too small for him. There was a hunted expression in his large, innocent black eyes. The woman was pock-marked, but she had a pleasant face in spite of her shabby, dowdy clothes. Kitty could see that they were Russians, and began weaving a touching romance about them, but when her mother found out from the *Kurliste* that they were Nikolai Levin and Marya Nikolaevna she soon explained to her what a bad man he was and her dream vanished. It was not merely what her mother told her, but he was Konstantin's brother, and this fact alone made them both extremely repulsive to her. This man with the strange way he had of moving his head, produced a feeling of disgust in her. His large, wild eyes, that followed her about persistently, seemed to her to be full of mocking hatred, and she tried to avoid meeting him.

XXXI

It was a wet day; the rain came down steadily all the morning and the invalids crowded to the gallery carrying umbrellas.

Kitty was with her mother and the Moscow colonel, happy in showing off his new European coat that he had bought in Frankfort. They were walking on one side of the gallery trying to avoid Levin who was on the other. Varenka, in a dark dress and black hat that shaded her face, was acting as guide to a little blind Frenchwoman, and every time she passed Kitty they exchanged friendly glances.

"Mamma, can I go and speak to her?" Kitty asked, looking after her unknown friend. She had just approached the spring, and it would have been a favourable moment for doing so.

"Certainly, if you like. I will inquire about her and make her acquaintance first," the princess replied. "What do you see in her? She is only a lady's companion. If you like I can speak to Madame Stahl. I knew her sister-in-law," she added with a touch of pride.

Kitty knew that her mother was hurt at Madame Stahl's refusing to notice her, so she did not insist.

" Isn't she charming! " she exclaimed as she watched Varenka hand the little Frenchwoman a glass of water. " She's so simple and natural."

" Your *engouements* are very amusing," the princess remarked. " I think we had better turn back," she added as she saw Nikolai Levin and Marya Nikolaevna coming towards them, accompanied by a German doctor, with whom Nikolai Levin was speaking in sharp tones.

They turned to go back when suddenly they were arrested by loud, angry cries. Nikolai Levin had stopped and was shouting at the doctor, while the latter too grew heated. A crowd collected round them. The princess and Kitty drew away as quickly as possible, and the colonel went up to find out what had happened. He joined them again in a few minutes.

" What was the matter? " the princess asked.

" Disgraceful! " the colonel exclaimed. " It makes one afraid to meet these Russians abroad. The tall man quarrelled with his doctor for not attending to him as he wished. He abused him dreadfully, and even threatened him with his stick. Perfectly disgraceful! "

" How very unpleasant! " the princess said, horrified. " How did it all end? "

" Fortunately, that girl . . . in the mushroom hat, a Russian, I think, came along and put them right," the colonel replied.

" Mlle Varenka? " Kitty asked with interest.

" Yes. She was the first to interfere. She went up to the tall man, took him by the arm, and led him away."

" You see, mamma! " Kitty exclaimed, " and you wonder why I am so enthusiastic about her."

The next morning Kitty noticed that Mlle Varenka had taken Nikolai Levin and Marya Nikolaevna under her wing and treated them just the same as she did her other *protégés*. She would go up and speak to them and act as interpreter to the woman, who did not know any language besides her own.

Kitty again implored her mother to let her become acquainted with Mlle Varenka. Though it was unpleasant to the princess to seem to be making advances to Madame Stahl, who considered herself very superior for some reason or other, she made a few inquiries about the girl, and satisfying herself that there was nothing objectionable about her, she was the first to go up and speak to her.

She met Varenka outside a confectioner's when Kitty was at the spring.

" Allow me to introduce myself," she began with an affable smile. " My daughter has simply fallen in love with you. Perhaps you don't know who I am, I . . . "

" It is quite mutual, I assure you," Varenka said hastily.

" It was splendid of you to help our unfortunate fellow-countryman yesterday," the princess observed.

Varenka blushed.

" I hardly remember; it seems to me that I did nothing at all," she said.

" Why of course you did! You saved that Nikolai Levin from a very unpleasant affair."

" Oh, yes, *sa compagne* called me and I did my best to calm him. He is very ill and the doctor annoyed him. I am so used to looking after invalids."

" I believe that you live at Mentone with your aunt, Madame Stahl. I used to know her sister-in-law."

" Madame Stahl is not my aunt. I always call her *maman*, but I am not related to her. She brought me up," Varenka replied with another blush.

It was said so simply, with such a frank expression on her pleasant face, that the princess began to understand why Kitty was so attracted to her.

" Well, what is this Levin going to do? " the princess asked.

" He is going away," Varenka replied.

At this moment Kitty came up beaming when she saw her mother talking to her unknown friend.

" Well, Kitty, your ardent desire to know Mlle . . . "

" Varenka," the girl added, with a smile. " Everybody calls me so."

Kitty blushed with pleasure. She did not speak, but pressed the hand of her new friend for a long time. Varenka's hand lay limply in hers, but her face was lighted up with a glad, subdued smile, exposing her large but fine teeth.

" I have long wanted to meet you," she said.

" But you are always so busy . . . "

" On the other hand, I have nothing whatever to do," Varenka replied. But at this moment she was obliged to leave them as two Russian children, two little girls of an invalid mother, came running up to her.

"Varenka! Mamma wants you!" they cried.

And Varenka followed them.

XXXII

The particulars that the princess learnt of Varenka's past life and her relation to Madame Stahl were the following:

Madame Stahl was a very delicate woman with highly-strung nerves. Some people said that she tormented the life of her husband; others that he tormented her by his loose conduct. However, they were divorced, and soon after Madame Stahl gave birth to her first child, that died as soon as it was born. Knowing her emotional nature her friends were afraid that the shock might kill her and substituted in place of the dead child another that was born on the same night in her own house, the daughter of a cook, who was a serf. This child was Varenka. Madame Stahl learnt the truth later, but continued to take charge of her, the more willingly as her real parents died shortly after and left her quite alone in the world.

It was now more than ten years since Madame Stahl lived abroad in the south, scarcely ever leaving her bed. Some people said that she was posing as an extremely charitable, religious woman; others that she really was a highly virtuous woman, who lived only for the sake of others, that she was, in a word, the woman that she seemed to be. No one knew whether she was a Catholic or Protestant, or whether she belonged to the Orthodox Church, but one thing alone was certain—that she was on friendly terms with high dignitaries of all churches and creeds.

Varenka lived with her constantly, and every one who knew Madame Stahl also knew and loved Mlle Varenka, as she was called.

And so the princess saw no reason why her daughter should not make her acquaintance, especially as her manners were excellent and she was well educated and spoke French and English perfectly. Above all, she brought her a message from Madame Stahl, expressing her regret that she was unable to see people on account of her illness.

Kitty was delighted with her new friend, and every day she discovered some new charm about her.

One day, having learnt that Varenka could sing, the princess invited her to come and spend the evening with them.

" Kitty plays and there is a piano at our place. Not a very good one, I must say, but it will give us great pleasure to hear you sing," she said with a forced smile. This smile was particularly distasteful to Kitty, as she could see that Varenka did not wish to sing.

She came in the evening and brought her music.

The princess had invited Marya Yevgenevna and her daughter and the colonel to meet her. Varenka was not in the least abashed that there were strangers present and walked straight up to the piano. She could read very well, but could not accompany herself, and so Kitty, who was an excellent pianist, played for her.

" You have a great deal of talent," the princess said to Varenka when she finished the first song, which she had sung admirably.

Marya Yevgenevna and her daughter thanked her and were full of praise.

" Come and see what a large audience you have," the colonel said as he looked out of the window. And, really, quite a crowd had collected outside to listen to her.

" I am glad you liked it," Varenka said quite simply.

Kitty felt proud of her friend. She was charmed with her voice, her art, her face, and, above all, her manner. She evidently attached no importance to her singing and seemed quite indifferent to the compliments paid her. " Shall I sing some more, or is it enough," her glance seemed to say.

" How proud I would be if I could sing as well as that! " Kitty thought. " How delighted I would have been to see that crowd outside! And she seems quite indifferent. She is only anxious to please *maman*. What is there in her? What gives her that power of self-reliance and extraordinary calm? How I should like to learn of her, to be like her! "

The princess asked for another song, and Varenka sang that as well as the first, with the same care and perfection, beating time with her little brown hand. The next song in her music-book was in Italian. Kitty played the prelude and turned to her.

" Let us skip that," Varenka said, blushing.

Kitty, in surprise and wonder, fixed her eyes on Varenka's face.

" Very well, another one then," she said hastily, turning over the leaves and feeling that there was some association connected with this one.

" No, let us try that," Varenka replied, laying her hand on the music with a smile. And she sang that just as she had done the others, with equal self-possession.

They all thanked her when she finished and went into the dining-room to take tea. The two girls went into the garden.

" That song brings some association back to you," Kitty said. " You need not tell me about it," she added hastily; " I merely wished to know if I was right."

" Why should I not tell you? " Varenka asked simply, and continued without waiting for a reply. " Yes, there is an association, and it was very painful for me to think about at one time. I was once in love with a man to whom I used to sing it."

Kitty, with wide-open eyes, gazed at Varenka with emotion.

" We loved each other, but his mother did not approve of me, so he married another. He lives quite near us and I see him sometimes even now. Don't imagine for a moment that there was anything very romantic about it," she added, and her face lighted up for a moment. She looked beautiful. Kitty imagined that at one time she must have always looked like that.

" Why not? If I were a man I could not have loved any one after knowing you. I simply can't understand how he could have given you up, made you unhappy, merely to please his mother. He must have been heartless."

" Oh, no, he was a good man and I am not unhappy. On the contrary, I am very happy. Shall we sing any more this evening? " she asked, turning towards the house.

" How good you are! how good you are! " Kitty exclaimed, kissing her. " If I could only be a little like you! "

" Why should you be like anybody? You are very nice as you are," Varenka said with her sweet, sad smile.

" No, I am not at all nice. Tell me now. . . . Don't go yet, sit down a while," she said, drawing her down on the seat beside her. " Tell me, don't you think it humiliating for a man to scorn your love, to jilt you? "

" He did not jilt me. I know he loved me, but he was a dutiful son."

" Yes, but supposing his mother had nothing to do with it, that he himself . . . " Kitty felt that she had betrayed her secret by her words as well as her face, which had flushed a deep red.

" Then he would have behaved badly and I should not have

regretted him," Varenka replied, realising that the thing they were talking about did not concern her but Kitty.

"But the insult?" Kitty went on. "You can't forget the insult. It is impossible," she said, remembering the look she had given Vronsky at the ball.

"What insult? You did not do anything wrong."

"It was worse than that, it was shameful!"

Varenka shook her head and laid her hand on Kitty's.

"But why shameful? You surely did not go and tell a man who was indifferent to you that you loved him?"

"Of course not; I never said a single word, but he knew. By my look and manner . . . no, no, I shall never forget it if I live to be a hundred!"

"Now what is it? I don't understand. The question is, do you love him now or not?" Varenka asked, who liked to talk plainly.

"I hate him and can never forgive myself."

"Why?"

"For the shame, the humiliation."

"Why, if every one were as sensitive as you are . . ." Varenka began. "Every girl goes through that sort of thing. It is not so important after all."

"Then what is important?" Kitty asked, looking into her face with astonishment and curiosity.

"Oh, many things," Varenka said with a smile.

"What are they?"

"There is so much that is more important," she replied, hardly knowing what to say.

"Kitty, it's getting chilly," the princess's voice was heard at this moment from the window. "You must either wrap yourself up or come in."

"I really ought to be going," Varenka said, rising. "I have to look in on Madame Berthe; she asked me to come."

Kitty held her hand and gazed at her with a look full of curiosity and supplication. "What are these important things? What gives you so much calm? You know. Tell me," her glance seemed to say, but Varenka did not understand. She could think of nothing but that she had to go and see Madame Berthe and get back home to tea with *maman* by twelve o'clock. She went in, gathered up her music, took leave of everybody, and turned to go out.

"May I have the pleasure of accompanying you?" the colonel asked.

"Of course, you mustn't go alone at night," the princess said. "I meant to send Parash."

Kitty saw that Varenka could scarcely contain a smile at the idea that some one must take her home.

"No, thanks; I always go about alone and nothing ever happens to me," she said, putting on her hat. She kissed Kitty a second time and walked away with a firm step, carrying her music under her arm. She soon disappeared in the semi-darkness of the summer night, taking the secret of her calmness and her dignity with her.

XXXIII

Kitty also made the acquaintance of Madame Stahl, and both this lady and Varenka had a great influence over her and consoled her in her grief. Through them a new world opened out before her, having no connection with her past life—a world, sublime and beautiful, from the height of which she could look down calmly on that past. She discovered that besides the life of instinct that she had always led, there was yet another, a spiritual life. This life was reached by religion, not the religion to which Kitty had been accustomed since her infancy, which consisted in going to church, visiting charitable institutions where she could meet her acquaintances, or learning Slavonic texts by heart, but a lofty, mystic religion that was bound up with her purest thoughts and feelings. She could believe in this religion, not because she was told to, but because she loved it.

Kitty learnt all this, but not through words. Madame Stahl would speak to her as to a child, whom she had grown fond of, who reminded her of her own youth. Only once did she allude to the consolation that was brought by faith and love and to the compassion of Christ, to whom no human sorrow was insignificant. But in every movement of hers, in every word, in every blessed look of hers, as Kitty would say, and through the story of this lady's life, which Varenka told her, did Kitty discover "those important things" that she had known nothing of till now.

Despite Madame Stahl's lofty character, touching story, and the gentleness of her speech, Kitty could not help noticing certain things about her that troubled her. One day when she happened to inquire about some relative of hers, Madame Stahl smiled disdainfully, a thing not in keeping with Christian charity. And once when a certain Catholic priest came to see her, Kitty noticed that she kept her face carefully in the shade of the lamp and that there was a peculiar smile on her lips. They were both trifling incidents in themselves, but Kitty was troubled and began to lose her faith in Madame Stahl. Varenka, on the other hand, without any friends or relatives, with her sad disappointment, regretting nothing, desiring nothing, seemed to Kitty the most perfect being she had ever met. It was Varenka who taught her that if she wanted to be happy and calm she must forget herself in her love for others. Kitty longed to be like her. And when once she understood clearly what the *more important* things were she did not hesitate, but gave herself up to the new life that opened out before her. Varenka told her various things about the life of Madame Stahl and others whom she named, and Kitty began drawing up a plan for her own future. She would be like Aline, Madame Stahl's niece, about whom she had heard. She would seek out the most unfortunate people, no matter where she was, and devote herself to them. She would distribute the gospel, read the New Testament to the sick and the dying and to criminals. The idea of reading to criminals, a thing Aline had done, appealed to her more than anything. Kitty kept all these thoughts to herself and said nothing about them either to her mother or to Varenka.

However, while waiting to carry out her schemes on a larger scale Kitty found plenty to do now. At the waters the sick and unfortunate are easily found and she did what Varenka did. The princess soon noticed how completely Kitty had fallen under the influence of her *engouement,* as she called Madame Stahl and particularly Varenka. She saw how Kitty not only imitated her in her activities, but quite unconsciously adopted her manner of walking and blinked her eyes in the peculiar way that Varenka did. Later she discovered that Kitty was passing through some spiritual phase quite independent of the influence of her friends.

In the evenings she would read the New Testament in a French edition that Madame Stahl had given her, a thing that she had never done before. Then she avoided worldly acquaintances and mostly spent her time with the invalids whom Varenka had taken under her care, particularly with the family of a poor artist named Petrov. She was proud to fulfil the duties of a sister of mercy in this household.

Topor

That was all very well and the princess had nothing against it, particularly as the artist's wife happened to be an extremely nice woman and the German princess praised Kitty for her activities and called her a ministering angel. However, it occurred to her after a time that Kitty was going to extremes and decided to speak to her on the subject.

" *Il ne faut jamais outrer,*" she said to her one day. But her daughter made no reply. She merely wondered how any one could go to extremes in a religion that bade you offer the other cheek, and when a man asked you for your cloak to offer him your coat also.

But the princess disapproved of these extremes and felt unhappy that Kitty no longer confided in her. For, in fact, Kitty kept all these new thoughts and feelings hidden from her mother. It was not because she did not respect her, but for the very reason that she was her mother. She would sooner have opened her heart to a stranger than to her.

" I wonder why Anna Pavlovna has not been to see us for so long? " the princess asked one day, referring to the artist's wife. " I asked her to come, but she seems offended about something."

" I haven't noticed it, *maman,*" Kitty said with a blush.

" Have you been there lately."

" We are going for a walk on the mountains to-morrow," Kitty replied.

" Oh, very well," the princess said, looking attentively at her daughter and trying to make out the cause of her confusion.

Varenka came to dinner in the evening and announced that Anna Pavlovna had changed her mind about the walk to-morrow. The princess noticed that Kitty blushed when she heard this.

" Kitty, has anything unpleasant happened between you and the Petrovs? " the princess asked when they were left alone. " She never comes to see us now, nor sends the children."

Kitty told her that nothing had taken place between them, but that for some reason or another Anna Pavlovna seemed annoyed with her. It was perfectly true. She did not know and could only guess at the reason why Anna Pavlovna had changed towards her. But she could not tell her mother what was in her mind. She dared not even confess it to herself, so painful and humiliating would it have been had she been mistaken.

One by one she recalled all the incidents of her relations with this family. She remembered the joy that shone on Anna

Pavlovna's round, good-natured face whenever they met, and all their secret consultations about the invalid; how they had thought of scheme after scheme of taking him away from his work that had been forbidden him. She recalled the affection of the youngest boy, who called her " my Kitty " and would never be put to bed without her. How nice it all was! Then she recalled the emaciated figure of Petrov, with his long neck stretching out of his brown coat, his thin, curly hair, his blue eyes that had seemed to her so terrible at first, the feverish efforts he made to try and appear bright and happy in her presence. She remembered how in the early days of their acquaintance she used to try and overcome the disgust he aroused in her—the disgust she could not help feeling for all consumptives—and how she racked her brain to invent all sorts of things to say to him. She recalled the timid, grateful glance that he would fix upon her and the strange feeling of compassion and awkwardness that came over her, followed by a consciousness of her own charitableness. How nice it all was in those early days! But now everything was changed. Anna Pavlovna would greet her with a forced amiability and did not cease watching her and her husband.

Could it be that the touching joy he expressed at seeing her was the cause of Anna Pavlovna's coolness?

" Yes," she said to herself, " there is something unnatural in her manner. She is not at all like the good, kind creature she used to be." And she recalled a thing that happened about two days ago when she went to see them.

" You see, he has been waiting for you. He would not drink his coffee till you came, although he is so weak," Anna Pavlovna had said sharply when Kitty entered.

" I dare say it was disagreeable to her when I handed him his rug. It was such a natural thing to do, but he would keep on thanking me till it made me feel quite uncomfortable. And then that portrait of me which he painted so well and his gentle, confused glance. Yes, it must be that! " she said to herself in horror. " No, it can't be, it's impossible! He's so pitiful! " she added afterwards.

XXXIV

JUST before the end of the season Prince Shcherbatsky joined them. After Carlsbad he had been to Baden and Kissingen, where he went to see some Russian friends, " to get a breath of Russian air," as he said.

The prince and princess had conflicting ideas upon the subject of living abroad. The princess was delighted with everything. Notwithstanding the fact that she occupied an important position in Russian society, she tried to put on the airs of a European lady, quite unbecoming to her, as she was Russian through and through. The prince, on the other hand, thought everything abroad horrid, hated the European life, clung to his Russian habits, and purposely tried to make himself appear even less European than he really was.

He came back in the most excellent spirits though he looked thinner, and was delighted to see how much Kitty had improved. When he heard of her friendship with Madame Stahl and Varenka and the princess's account of some change she was going through, the prince grew disturbed. A feeling of jealousy came over him that Kitty might be drawn away from his influence into spheres that were beyond him. But even this disagreeable news could not drown the gaiety and good-humour he always carried with him—a characteristic which the waters at Carlsbad had increased.

On the morning after his arrival, the prince, in a long coat, with his Russian wrinkles and puffed cheeks standing out above his stiff collar, accompanied Kitty to the spring in the gayest possible humour.

It was a beautiful day. The bright, neat little houses, with their tiny gardens, the jolly, ruddy German servants, working merrily in the brilliant sunlight, all delighted the heart. But as they drew nearer the springs they met more and more invalids, who looked so out of keeping in those well-ordered German surroundings. Kitty was not struck by the incongruity. For her the bright sun, the green trees, the sounds of the music seemed to form a natural framework for those faces, whose changes for the better or worse she had been watching eagerly. But for the prince, this bright June morning, the orchestra playing a merry waltz, the robust-looking German servants, were all somehow desecrated by the sight of these half-dead looking people who had gathered there from all the corners of Europe. The pride he felt in walking along with his favourite daughter, who always made him feel young again, was somehow marred by the sight of these people. With his firm step and powerful figure, he felt awkward and guilty in their midst, as a man who had been stripped naked in a crowd.

" Introduce me to all your friends," he said to his daughter as he pressed her arm. " I am beginning to like this awful place for the good it has done you. Only it is so depressing here. Who is this? "

Kitty told him the names of all the acquaintances and strangers they met on the way. At the entrance of the garden they came across the little blind Frenchwoman, Madame Berthe, who was walking along with a guide. The prince was struck by the joyful expression that lighted up her face when she recognised Kitty's voice. With exaggerated French politeness she complimented the prince upon having such a charming daughter, whose merits she praised to the skies, declaring that she was a treasure, a pearl, a ministering angel.

" Then she must be angel number two," the prince responded with a smile, " for she tells me that Mlle Varenka is angel number one."

" Oh, Mlle Varenka! She is a real angel. *Allez,*" Madame Berthe said enthusiastically.

In the gallery they came upon Varenka herself. She was walking quickly towards them, carrying an elegant red handbag.

" Here is papa come back," Kitty said to her.

Varenka greeted him simply, making a half-curtsey, and entered into conversation with him quite naturally.

" Of course I know you, I've heard a great deal about you already," the prince said with a smile, by which Kitty was delighted to see that he liked her new friend. " Where are you hurrying to? "

" *Maman* is here," she said, turning to Kitty. " She did not sleep the whole night, so the doctor ordered her to come. I am bringing her work."

" So this is angel number one! " the prince said as soon as Varenka left them.

Kitty could see that he would have liked to make fun of Varenka, but did not know what to pitch upon. She had obviously pleased him.

" You must take me to all your friends, even Madame Stahl, if she will deign to recognise me," he said.

" Do you know her, papa? " Kitty asked, in alarm, as she noticed a peculiar twinkle in his eye at the mention of her name.

" I used to know her husband and her also a little, in the days before she grew so pious."

" What do you mean by pious, papa? " Kitty asked, horrified that any one should talk like that of Madame Stahl, whom she admired so much.

" I can't exactly say, my dear. I only know that she thanks God for all her misfortunes, even for her husband's death. It seems rather funny, particularly when you know they didn't get on together. Who is this? What a sad face! " he added as he caught sight of a rather short man in a brown coat and white trousers, that hung in strange folds around his thin, emaciated legs. He was sitting on a seat and raised his straw hat as they passed, showing his thin curly hair and feverish-looking forehead.

" That is Petrov, an artist," Kitty replied, blushing. " And that lady is his wife," she added, with a motion in the direction of Anna Pavlovna, who at their approach purposely turned away to one of her children who was playing about on the path.

" Poor man! What a nice face he has! " the prince said. " Why didn't you go up to him? It seemed to me as if he wanted to speak to you."

" Very well, let us go back," Kitty said, turning back resolutely. " How do you feel to-day? " she asked Petrov.

Petrov rose, leaned on his stick, and gazed at the prince timidly.

" This is my daughter," the prince began, " allow me to introduce myself."

The artist bowed. A smile spread over his face showing his brilliant white teeth.

" We expected you yesterday, princess," he said to Kitty.

He staggered as he said this, then to conceal the fact that it was involuntary he repeated the motion.

" I would have come, only Varenka told me that Anna Pavlovna said you were not going."

" Why did she say that? " he asked, flushing red and beginning to cough. " Annetta! Annetta! " he cried, looking round for his wife, while the veins stood out like cords on his thin, white neck.

Anna Pavlovna came up.

" Why did you send to the princess to say that we were not going? " he whispered irritably, in gasps.

" Good morning, princess! " Anna Pavlovna greeted Kitty, with a forced smile, so unlike her former self. " I am so pleased to meet you," she said, turning to the prince. " Your family have been long expecting you."

" But why did you send to the princess to say we were not going? " the artist demanded still more angrily, in a hoarse voice. He was still more irritated because he could not express himself as he wished.

" Merely because I thought we were not going," his wife replied with some annoyance.

" But why? when . . ." A fit of coughing seized him and he made a gesture with his hand.

The prince raised his hat and walked away with his daughter.

" Poor people! " he said with a sigh, " poor people! "

" Yes, papa," Kitty began, " and you must know that they have three children, no servants, and no means. He gets a trifle from the academy," she continued eagerly, anxious to conceal the emotion that Anna Pavlovna's strange manner had aroused in her.

" And here is Madame Stahl," she said as she caught sight of a bath chair and a mass in grey and blue lying smothered in cushions under a parasol. This was Madame Stahl. A severe, powerful-looking German who was wheeling her, was standing at the back. A fair-haired Swedish count, whom Kitty named, was standing beside her. Several of the other invalids lingered near this chair, wondering at the extraordinary creature within.

The prince approached her. Again Kitty noticed that peculiar twinkle in his eye. He addressed Madame Stahl in excellent French that few are able to speak so well now, and was extremely polite and friendly.

" I dare say you do not remember me, but it is my duty to intrude upon you in order to thank you for your kindness to my daughter," he said, removing his hat and standing bare-headed.

" Prince Alexander Shcherbatsky," Madame Stahl pronounced, raising her glorious eyes, in which Kitty noticed a shade of displeasure, " delighted to meet you again. I have grown so fond of your daughter."

" I am sorry to see your health is still bad."

" Oh, I have grown accustomed to it now," Madame Stahl remarked, then introduced him to the Swedish count.

" You are very little changed," the prince observed. " It is now ten or eleven years since I last had the honour of seeing you."

" Yes, God gives us the cross and the strength to bear it. I often wonder to what purpose my life is still dragging on. . . . Put it on that side! " she said crossly to Varenka, who was trying to arrange the rug round her feet.

" To do good, of course," the prince remarked with a merry twinkle in his eye.

" It is not for us to judge," Madame Stahl observed, noticing the expression on the prince's face. " You will send me that book, my dear count? " she asked, turning to the young Swede. " Thank you so much."

" Ah! " the prince exclaimed as he caught sight of the Moscow colonel standing close by, and bowing to Madame Stahl he and Kitty joined him.

" This is our aristocracy, prince," the colonel remarked scornfully. He was a little piqued that Madame Stahl refused to have anything to do with him.

" She is just the same as ever," the prince observed.

" Did you know her before her illness, prince? I mean before she became a complete invalid? "

" Yes, it happened since I knew her."

" They say she has not walked for ten years."

" She does not walk because one of her legs is shorter than the other. She has a very bad figure . . . "

" It's impossible, papa! " Kitty cried.

" Evil tongues say so, my dear. I dare say your Varenka has a great deal to put up with," he added. " Oh, these invalid ladies! "

" Oh, no, papa," Kitty said vehemently, " Varenka adores her. And then, think of all the good she does! You can ask any one you like. She and Aline Stahl are known to everybody."

" That may be," he said, pressing her arm with his elbow, " but it would be better to do good in such a way that people knew nothing about it."

Kitty was silent, not because she had nothing to say, but because she was reluctant to reveal her thoughts even to her father. But strange to say, although she had decided not to yield to her father; not to let him penetrate to her innermost sanctuary; she could not help feeling that the divine image of Madame Stahl that she had carried so sacredly in her heart for the past month had vanished, as an imaginary figure seen in a garment thrown down by chance vanishes when one really sees how the garment is lying. There remained only a little lame woman who stayed in bed to conceal her deformity and tormented poor Varenka because her rug was not properly arranged. Her imagination was powerless to bring back the former Madame Stahl.

XXXV

The prince's high spirits infected his household, all their acquaintances, and even their German landlord with whom they lodged.

When he returned home with Kitty, after having invited Marya Yevgenevna, the colonel, and Varenka to come and take coffee with them, he ordered lunch to be laid in the garden under the chestnut-tree. The landlord and servants fulfilled his commands with alacrity, knowing his generosity. In less than half an hour a Hamburg doctor, an invalid, who lodged upstairs, was looking down enviously at the jolly group of healthy Russians gathered together under the shade of the chestnut-tree. At one end of the table, covered with a white cloth, whereon were placed the coffee service, bread, butter, cheese, and cold game, sat the princess, in a bonnet with lilac ribbons, handing round the cups and sandwiches. At the other end sat the prince, eating heartily and talking with great animation. He had spread out before him all the purchases he had made in the various towns he had been to. There were little carved wooden boxes, tiny ornaments, and paper-knives of all sorts. He amused himself by distributing them among his guests, not forgetting Lieschen, the maid, nor the landlord. He chaffed the latter in his comic, bad German, and assured him that it was not the waters that had cured Kitty, but his excellent cooking, particularly his prune soup. The princess laughed at her husband's Russian manners, but was happier that day than she had been during the whole of her stay in the little town. The colonel as usual smiled at the prince's jokes, but when it came to questions of European custom he was on the princess's side, feeling that he had studied them carefully. The good-natured Marya Yevgenevna laughed till the tears rolled down her cheeks, and even Varenka, to Kitty's great astonishment, was infected with the general merriment.

All this delighted Kitty, but she could not help feeling worried. She had not yet solved the problem which her father had unconsciously opened out before her by the light way he had spoken of her friends and the life that she had learned to love. Added to this, there was the unpleasant change in relations to the Petrovs, which had struck her so forcibly and unpleasantly to-day. She felt conscience-stricken that she could not be merry like the rest. It was rather like the feeling she had experienced in her childhood, when, having been shut in her room as a punishment, she could hear her sisters enjoying themselves outside.

"Why did you buy all those things?" the princess asked with a smile, handing her husband a cup of coffee.

"What would you have? You are out for a walk and go into a shop and they ask you to buy. '*Erlaucht, Excellenz,*' they begin on you, '*Durchlaucht.*' When they get to *Durchlaucht* I can no longer resist and my ten thalers are gone."

"Then it was only because you were bored?"

"Bored, my dear? I should think so. I didn't know what to do with myself."

"How can you be bored, prince? There are so many interesting things in Germany nowadays," Marya Yevgenevna remarked.

"Yes, I know all your interesting things — prune soup, sausages. I know them all."

"Say what you like, prince, but their institutions are very interesting."

"What do you find interesting about them? They are so mighty self-satisfied, they've conquered the world. But what is that to me? I have not conquered anybody I only know that I have to take off my own boots and even stand them outside my door. You get up in the morning and have to hurry into your clothes in order to go and drink bad tea in the dining-room. How different it is at home! There you can wake up when you please; grumble at some one if you feel like it; have plenty of time to collect your thoughts, so that you can think things out clearly; there is no need to hurry about anything."

"But think of the time — the money," the colonel remonstrated.

"Why? There are times when you would be glad to give away a whole month for a song, and others when you would not sell a single half-hour for love or money. Isn't that so, Kitty, dear? Why do you look so sad?"

"I? oh, it's nothing."

"Going so soon? why not stay a little longer?" he asked, turning to Varenka.

" I must go home," Varenka said, rising and bursting into a merry peal of laughter. She pulled herself up suddenly, took leave of everybody, and went into the house to get her hat.

Kitty followed her. Even Varenka seemed to her different now. She was not less good, but different from what she had imagined her.

" I haven't laughed like this for a long time," Varenka said as she took up her parasol and bag. " What a dear your papa is! "

Kitty was silent.

" When shall I see you? " Varenka asked.

" *Maman* wanted to go and see the Petrovs. Shall you be there? " Kitty asked, trying to sound her.

" Oh, yes," Varenka replied. " They are leaving and I promised to help them pack."

" Then I'll come too."

" I should not if I were you."

" But why? why? why? " Kitty asked, opening her eyes wide and taking hold of Varenka's parasol so as to detain her. " Don't go, tell me why."

" Simply because your papa has come home, and then they don't feel at ease with you."

" No, you must tell me plainly why you don't want me to go to the Petrovs. You don't want me to; do you? Why? "

" I did not say so," Varenka replied calmly.

" But tell me, please! "

" Shall I tell you the whole truth? " Varenka asked.

" Yes, yes, everything! " Kitty implored.

" You see," Varenka began with a smile, " Mihail Alexaevitch " (that was Petrov's name) " a few weeks back was ready to leave here any time, but now he does not want to go."

" Well! well! " Kitty demanded, looking at Varenka severely.

" And Anna Pavlovna says that he does not want to go because you are here. Of course there is no foundation for it, but at any rate you were the cause of a family quarrel and you know how irritable these invalids can be."

Kitty was silent, while her face grew darker than ever. Varenka went on speaking, trying to pacify her. She saw a storm gathering, but did not know whether it would vent itself in tears or words.

" It would be better for you not to go there. . . . You quite understand, don't you? "

" And I deserve it all! I deserve it! " Kitty exclaimed,

snatching the parasol from Varenka's hand and not looking at her.

Varenka felt like smiling at her friend's childish rage, but she was afraid of hurting her feelings.

"But why?" she asked. "I don't understand."

"I deserve it because it was nothing but hypocrisy and pretence. What business had I to interfere in the affairs of a stranger? And now I have been the cause of a quarrel, because I would meddle where I was not wanted. And all because of my hypocrisy, hypocrisy, and pretence!"

"But why hypocrisy?" Varenka asked gently.

"Oh, how stupid, how horrible it is! There was no need for me. . . . It was all hypocrisy!" she went on vehemently, opening and shutting the parasol.

"But what reason had you to be hypocritical?"

"I did it to appear better to others, to myself, to God, to deceive everybody. But I will not fall so low again. It is better to remain bad as I am than to lie and be a humbug!"

"But who is a humbug?" Varenka asked reproachfully. "You speak as if . . ."

But Kitty was beside herself and would not allow her to finish.

"I was not speaking of you at all. You are perfection itself. Yes, yes, I know how perfect you are, but what can I do if I am wicked? This would not have happened if I had not been wicked. I will be what I am and give up all this deceit. What have I to do with Anna Pavlovna? Let them live as they like and I will live as I like. I can't make myself different. . . . Besides it's not the thing, not the thing . . ."

"What is not the thing?" Varenka asked, puzzled.

"Everything. I can only live by my heart, but you live by your principles. I loved you, but you have merely been trying to save me, to teach me."

"That is hardly fair," Varenka said.

"I was not referring to the others; I only meant myself."

"Kitty!" her mother's voice called, "come here and show papa your corals."

Kitty took up a little box of corals and walked out with a dignified air, without becoming reconciled to her friend.

"What is the matter? How flushed you are!" her father and mother called out in one voice.

"Oh, it's nothing," she replied. "I will be back in a moment," and she ran into the house again.

"She is still here," Kitty thought. "What shall I say to her? Heavens! what have I done? What have I said? Why did I hurt her? What shall I do? What shall I say to her?" she asked herself again and again as she stopped by the door.

Varenka, with her hat on, was sitting by the table examining her parasol which Kitty had broken. She raised her head.

"Varenka, forgive me, forgive me!" Kitty whispered, drawing near to her. I did not know what I was saying. I . . ."

"I did not mean to hurt you," Varenka said with a smile.

Peace was restored.

But with her father's homecoming the world in which Kitty lived changed for her. She realised that she had been deceiving herself, that she could not be what she had wanted to be. It was all like a dream. She could see now that without hypocrisy she could not have remained in the heights that she wanted to reach. Besides which, all the sorrows that surrounded her—all these sick, dying people, weighed too heavily on her mind. The efforts that she used to make to overcome her disgust now appeared to her terribly difficult, and she longed to be in the fresh air, in Russia, in Pokrovska, where she had heard that Dolly had gone with the children.

But her love for Varenka did not change. When she took leave of her she tried to persuade her to come and stay with them.

"I shall come when you are married," Varenka said.

"But I shall never marry."

"Then I shall never come."

"In that case I shall marry for your sake. Mind you don't forget your promise!" Kitty said.

The doctor's predictions turned out correct. Kitty returned home to Russia completely cured. She was not quite so gay and careless as she had been formerly, but her calmness was restored. Her Moscow sorrows became only a memory.

PART III

I

Sergei Ivanovitch Kosnishev needed a rest after his mental labours, and instead of going abroad, as he usually did towards the end of May, he decided to go and stay with his brother in the country. In his opinion country life was better than anything, and so he departed to his brother's to enjoy it. Konstantin Levin was very pleased to see him, particularly as he no longer expected his brother Nikolai that summer. But in spite of his love and respect for Sergei Ivanovitch, Konstantin Levin was not altogether at ease with him in the country. His brother's attitude towards the country annoyed and irritated him. For Konstantin Levin the country was the place for life—for joys, sorrows, labours. For Sergei Ivanovitch, on the contrary, the country was a place to rest from labour. He looked upon it merely as an antidote after the effects of town life, that he took with pleasure, fully realising its usefulness. For Konstantin Levin the country was the more beautiful because it offered him work of unquestionable utility; for Sergei Ivanovitch it was the more delightful because there he need not work at all. And then his attitude towards the peasantry was also offensive to Konstantin. Sergei Ivanovitch declared that he loved and understood the people and would often talk with the peasants—a thing he knew how to do very well, but he always drew some favourable conclusion from these talks to show that he had not been mistaken in his judgment. Such superficial deductions annoyed Konstantin. For him the peasant was the main factor in the general scheme of toil, and though he respected and loved him with a sort of kindred love—a love he had drawn in with his nurse's milk, as he was wont to say—still he was not blind to his vices. Though sometimes going into rapture over his strength and gentleness and fairness, at others he could not help feeling annoyed at his carelessness, slovenliness, drunkenness, and his capacity for lying. Had Konstantin Levin been asked if he loved the people, he would have been at a loss to know what reply to make. For in some ways he loved them; in others he did not. He lived amongst them and all his interests were bound up with theirs. He felt himself to be so much part of them that he could not look at them from a detached point of view, nor consider their particular merits or demerits. And though there existed the closest relations between the peasants and himself, as their fellow-worker, landlord, mediator, and adviser—for the peasants would come for his advice from miles around—he expressed no definite judgment about them, and had he been asked if he understood them, would have found it just as difficult to reply as to the question did he love them. For to say that he knew and understood the peasants would have been in his opinion like saying that he knew and understood certain people. He was in the habit of studying and observing all kinds of people, peasants or otherwise, whom he considered interesting and would be constantly discovering new characteristics about them which would cause him to reconsider his former ideas. As for Sergei Ivanovitch he loved the people as he loved the country, because it meant an escape from something that was disagreeable to him. In his methodical mind there were definite ideas about peasant life and customs, only partly arrived at through observation, but he never changed them, just as his feelings towards the people never changed.

In the many discussions that arose between the two brothers on this subject, Sergei Ivanovitch always came out the victor because of the very definiteness of his views; while Konstantin Levin, whose opinions were constantly being modified, would be accused of inconsistency.

Sergei Ivanovitch looked upon his brother as an excellent fellow whose heart was *bien placé* as he expressed it in French, but whose mind, though quick and active, was apt to be carried away by the impressions of the moment. With the condescension of an elder brother he would sometimes try and explain things to him, but could find no pleasure in discussing with him because he was too easily vanquished.

Konstantin Levin on his side looked upon his brother as a man of vast intellect and learning, honourable in the highest sense of the word, and endowed with the gift of being able to work for the public good. But the older he grew, the more he learnt to know him, doubts would arise in his heart as to whether this capacity of work for the public good, which he himself did not possess in the smallest degree, was a blessing or a curse. Not because it did not involve desires, aspirations, honour, good taste, but because it seemed to point to a certain weakness, preventing a man from choosing one course out of a thousand and following it at all costs. And the more he observed the more he felt that Sergei Ivanovitch and all those other people who were busy working for the public good, did so, not through the dictates of their hearts, but for some intellectual conclusion that made them consider it the proper thing to do. It seemed to him that his brother was no more concerned about questions relating to human welfare, to the immortal soul, than he was about a problem of chess or the clever construction of some new machine.

Besides all this there was yet another reason why Konstantin Levin felt uncomfortable with his brother in the country, particularly in the summer, his most busy time when he scarcely found the days long enough to get through all that had to be done. His brother would be resting. And though he was resting now, that is, not occupied with his literary work, his mind was too active to be idle. He loved to express his ideas in his logical, elegant manner, and loved to have some one to listen to him. And, of course, his most natural auditor was his brother. And notwithstanding their friendly relations Konstantin did not like to leave him too much alone. Sergei Ivanovitch loved to lie on the grass basking in the sun, talking lazily.

"You can't imagine," he said to his brother one day, "how I enjoy this laziness. I have not a single idea in my head. It's perfectly empty."

But Konstantin was tired of sitting and listening to him. He knew that in his absence the men would spread the manure on the wrong fields or put it on anyhow. Or they would purposely loosen the nuts of the ploughshares to make them come off in order to be able to say that his new English plough was a stupid invention and not so good as the old-fashioned kind that Andraev used, and so on and so on.

"You should not walk about too much in this heat," Sergei Ivanovitch said.

"I'm only going to run into the office for a moment," Levin replied and he hurried away to the fields.

II

ONE day in June Agafia Mihailovna, the old nurse and housekeeper, was going into the cellar with a pot of mushrooms she had just pickled, when she slipped and dislocated her wrist. The local doctor, a voluble young man who had recently taken his degree, came and examined the arm, declared it was only a sprain, and applied fomentations. He remained to dinner, and proud of finding himself in the society of so distinguished a man as Sergei Ivanovitch Kosnishev, he began expounding his enlightened ideas by relating all the gossip of the neighbourhood and complaining of the rottenness of things in general.

Sergei Ivanovitch listened attentively. Animated by the presence of a new auditor he likewise talked, and his smart weighty remarks were eagerly treasured up by the young doctor. Konstantin Levin noticed that his brother was in one of his lively moods, that a brilliant conversation never failed to produce in him. After the doctor had gone he proposed that he should go down to the river for some fishing. Sergei Ivanovitch had a passion for fishing, and seemed rather proud of the fact that so stupid an occupation could amuse him. Levin, who was anxious to get to the fields, offered to drive him down.

It was at that stage in the summer when the prospects of the coming crop could be estimated, and it was already time to begin thinking of autumn sowing and the harvest. The rye, still green, was swaying gently in the breeze, and the oats were peeping out irregularly over the late-sown fields. The buckwheat covered the ground in profusion. The fallow fields had been trodden hard by the cattle, showing numerous little paths running all over them, and the smell of manure mingled with the smell of decaying weeds lying in heaps. It was the lull before the harvest, the great yearly event that required everyone's strength and time. The crops promised to be magnificent, and there were beautiful hot days followed by short dewy nights.

The brothers had to go through the wood in order to get to the fields, and Sergei Ivanovitch went into raptures over its beauty. He would point first to the tall lindens whose leaves were beginning to turn, then to the bright green saplings of that year's growth. But Konstantin Levin did not like to talk about the beauties of nature; words for him spoilt the effect of what he saw. He merely nodded every now and again and went on thinking of something else. As they left the wood his attention was drawn to some fallow land on a hill covered with decaying weeds along which a line of carts was moving. Levin counted them to assure himself that the work was being properly done. A little farther on at sight of the fields his thoughts turned upon the hay-making. A feeling of exhilaration always came over him when he thought of it. He stopped his horse when they reached the meadow. The thick long grass was still wet with dew, and Sergei Ivanovitch, afraid of the damp for his feet, asked his brother to drive him as far as the clump of laburnums on the other side. Though he disliked to trample down his grass, Levin drove him across. The tall grass entwined itself round the horse's legs and wheels of the trap, leaving the seed sticking to the damp spokes.

Sergei Ivanovitch sat down under the laburnum and cast his line while Levin tied up the horse and went to examine the grey-green meadow that stretched out like a sea before him. In the more marshy places the grass came up to his waist. When he got out into the road he came across an old man carrying a swarm of bees in a basket.

"Halloa! did you catch them, Fomitch?" he asked.

"How, Konstantin Dmitritch? They are mine. This is the second time they've gone off. Had it not been for the children I should not have found them. I see you've already begun ploughing."

"Do you think it's time to cut the hay, or would it be better to wait a little?"

"Well, we think it better to wait till St. Peter's Day, but you always cut yours earlier."

"What about the weather?"

"That is in the Lord's hands. Perhaps it will be fine."

Levin returned to his brother.

Sergei Ivanovitch had not caught anything, but was in the most excellent humour. Animated by his conversation with the doctor he wanted to talk. Levin was anxious to get back home to decide definitely and make all arrangements about the hay-making about which his mind was full just now.

"Well, shall we start back?" he asked.

"What is the hurry? Let us stay a little longer. How wet you are! It is pleasant here, though I haven't caught anything. Look at this beautiful steely water and these green banks! It makes me think of that old riddle, you know, the one where the grass says to the water, 'We are rolling on and on together!'"

"I don't think I know it," Levin replied dejectedly.

III

"I WAS thinking about you just now," Sergei Ivanovitch remarked. "I've told you all along, I think it very wrong of you not to attend the Assembly meetings and keep in touch with what is going on. From what that young doctor told me, and he is no fool, things down here seem to be pretty bad. If all decent people withdraw themselves from the Council, what can you expect? We pay our rates, but there are no schools, or doctors, or midwives, not even a dispensary. The money seems to be entirely spent on salaries."

"I kept on as long as possible," Levin replied unwillingly, "but I couldn't do anything."

"Why couldn't you? I confess I don't understand. It can't be through lack of capacity or indifference; isn't it simply laziness?"

"It is not that nor the first nor the second. I have tried and feel quite certain that I could do nothing," Levin replied.

He was scarcely listening to what his brother was saying. He stood looking across the river at a field that was being ploughed. Some dark-looking object attracted his attention in the distance, but he could not make out whether it was merely a horse or his bailiff on horseback.

"But why? You make one or two attempts and when they don't turn out to your satisfaction you abandon everything. I wonder you have not more pride."

"Pride!" Levin exclaimed, stung to the quick by his brother's remarks, "I don't see what that has to do with it. Had I been told when I was at the university that others understood the integral calculus while I did not, that would have touched my pride. But as for the thing we are talking about, you have first to make up your mind whether you are cut out for that kind of work and then consider whether it's worth doing."

"Don't you think it is?" Sergei Ivanovitch asked, hurt that his brother should consider a thing of no importance that interested him so much and still more because he noticed that he was only half listening.

"No, I don't. It does not appeal to me. I can't help it," Levin replied, now certain that the object in the distance was the bailiff who had probably come to dismiss the men. He saw them turn the ploughs over. "Have they finished already?" he thought.

"Listen to me," his brother began, his fine handsome face growing a shade darker, "there are limits to everything. It is all very well to be original and outspoken, and to hate falsehood, but what you say has no sense at all, or a very bad sense. Do you really mean to tell me that it does not matter whether these people whom you love, as you assert—" ("I never asserted any such thing," Levin thought)—"should die without aid? Coarse peasant women act as midwives; people are wallowing in ignorance at the mercy of every unscrupulous letter-writer, and it is in your power to remedy it all; but you refuse to do it because you don't consider it worth while."

In a word his brother was accusing him of being either too stupid to see the great things he could do, or too selfish to do them. Levin felt annoyed. He must either say nothing or attempt to defend himself.

"I don't quite see how you could do all that," he said resolutely.

"Why not? You could institute a public medical service if the funds were watched more carefully."

"Personally, I think it impossible. Our country is too scattered, and what with our floods and storms, bad weather and busy seasons, a public medical service would be impractical. Besides I have no great faith in medicine anyway."

"Really, you are unjust. . . . I could name you a thousand cases. . . . But what about schools?"

"What use are they?"

"What! There surely cannot be any doubt as to the advantages derived from education? If it is good for you, why not for others?"

Konstantin Levin felt himself driven into a corner, and in his irritation he involuntarily gave expression to the real cause of his indifference.

"May be it's a good thing, but why should I bother about medical dispensaries that I should never use, nor schools where I should never send my children? Besides, I am not so sure that the peasants want to send their children to them either, nor whether it's wise to send them in any case."

Sergei Ivanovitch was disconcerted for a moment at this unexpected point of view, but he instantly thought of a new scheme of attack. He drew out his fishing-line, cast it again, then turned to his brother with a smile.

"As for your first point," he began, "we have this very day sent for the country doctor to come and see Agafia Mihailovna."

"Her wrist will never be right again anyhow."

"That remains to be seen. And as for your second point, surely a workman who can read and write is worth more to you than one who can't?"

"Not at all; you can ask any one you like," Levin replied resolutely. "A workman who can read and write is hopeless. He will think it beneath him to mend the roads, and if you put a bridge across he will be sure to steal the planks."

"But that is hardly the point," Sergei Ivanovitch said with a frown. He could not stand contradiction and hated jumping from one subject to another and bringing in irrelevant arguments. "Do you or do you not admit that education is good for the people?"

"Yes, I do," Levin replied without thinking, but instantly realised that he had not said what was in his mind and if he confessed as much would be accused of talking nonsense. He waited for his brother to bring this up against him, feeling certain that he would bring the most logical arguments to bear to try and prove his inconsistency. However it happened much more simply than he had expected.

"If you do, then I fail to see how as an honest man you can help working for it."

"But I do not admit that it is good," Levin objected in confusion.

"Why, you have only just said . . ."

"I neither admit it to be good nor practical."

"You can hardly tell until you've tried it."

"Well, let us admit for the sake of argument that education is good for the people, but still I do not quite see why it should be my duty to bother about it."

"How do you mean?"

"Since we have touched on the point explain it to me philosophically."

"I don't see what philosophy has to do with it," Sergei Ivanovitch observed in a tone which seemed to cast some doubt as to whether his brother was competent to judge of philosophy. This irritated Levin.

"There is a direct connection though," he began with some warmth. "To my mind all action is based on personal interest. Now I see nothing in our county institutions that contributes in any way to my personal well-being. The roads are no better and cannot be made so; besides, my horses carry me even on bad roads. The doctor and the dispensary are of no use to me, nor is the justice of the peace. I have never had occasion to go to him nor do I ever expect to go. As for the schools, they are not only useless to me, but I consider them even dangerous. I am merely compelled to pay a rate of eighteen kopeks for every acre of land, to spend a night in town sometimes to be eaten by vermin and listen to people talking vulgar nonsense. All this in no way affects my personal interests . . ."

"One moment," Sergei Ivanovitch interrupted him with a smile; "we were not actuated by personal motives when we worked for the emancipation of the serfs, but we accomplished it."

"I don't agree with you," Levin said, becoming still more heated. "The emancipation was quite another matter, and I maintain that personal interest was involved in it. All decent people were anxious to throw off the yoke that was oppressing us all alike. But to be a member of a town council and have to decide the number of night-watchmen necessary, or how to lay drains in a place where I do not live, or to sit on a jury and judge a peasant for stealing a ham, and listen for six whole hours to all the rubbish that the defendant and prosecutor may utter and as president to have to ask my old friend Aliosha if he pleads guilty to having stolen the ham . . ."

Konstantin Levin was quite carried away and began enacting the scene between the president and Aliosha, the idiot. He could not see that he had got away from the point. But Sergei Ivanovitch merely shrugged his shoulders.

"What exactly do you mean?"

"I mean that I am always prepared to defend the rights that concern me, touch my personal interests; just as when the police came to search us students and read our letters I was ready to defend our right to instruction, to liberty, with the last drop of my blood. I can take an interest in military service because it concerns the fate of my children, my brothers, myself; but to decide on the spending of forty thousand roubles of district money, or to judge Aliosha the idiot, that I cannot do."

Konstantin Levin spoke as if the flood-gates of his eloquence had been opened. Sergei Ivanovitch smiled.

"Supposing you were to be tried to-morrow would you prefer the old criminal court?"

"I shall not be tried. I am not likely to commit a murder. Do you know?" he continued, again diverging from the point, "our provincial institutions put me in mind of the little sprigs of birch we stick into the ground on Trinity Sunday and make believe that it is a real European forest. I have no faith in these sprigs and cannot for the life of me water them."

Sergei Ivanovitch shrugged his shoulders as much as to say that he really could not see what sprigs of birch had to do with the subject they were discussing, though he understood quite well what his brother meant.

"You can't get at the truth of the matter that way," he remarked.

Konstantin Levin was anxious to justify his indifference to public affairs—an indifference he had himself admitted again and again.

"No activity can be sound," he continued, "unless it is founded on personal interest; that is a common philosophical truth." He laid special stress on the word philosophical as if challenging any one to say that he had no right to talk of philosophy.

Sergei Ivanovitch was amused. "Even he has a philosophy for the benefit of his inclinations," he thought.

"You had better not talk of philosophy," he said. "The great problem that philosophy has in all ages tried to solve has been to discover the essential bond existing between the individual and common welfare. But that is getting away from the point, though I have a word or two to say about your comparisons. The birches are not stuck in the ground as you said—some are planted, others are sown and they should be treated tenderly. The only nations that have a future before them, the only nations that can be called historic, are those who have been able to see the good in their institutions and have known how to value and preserve them."

And Sergei Ivanovitch, to bring home to his brother the error of his judgment, drew the discussion into the realms of history and philosophy where the latter was unable to follow him.

"As to your dislike of public affairs, excuse me for saying so, but I put it down merely to your fastidiousness and indolence, a characteristic common to most Russians. I have no doubt it will pass off."

Konstantin Levin was silent. He felt himself beaten all round, but was nevertheless conscious that his brother had not understood him. He did not know exactly whether it was because he was unable to express himself clearly, or because his brother did not wish to understand or could not understand him. He did not, however, try to fathom this question, and without attempting to contradict what his brother had said, he became absorbed in entirely different thoughts connected with his work.

Sergei Ivanovitch rolled up his line, unfastened the horse, and they drove away.

IV

WHILE he was talking with his brother, Levin was thinking about an incident that had occurred the year before. One day during the hay-making he had fallen into a passion with his bailiff, and to soothe his nerves he had taken the scythe out of a peasant's hand and begun mowing. He had enjoyed the work so much that he had tried it several times afterwards. He had cut the grass in front of the house and this spring he had made up his mind to spend whole days mowing with the peasants. With the arrival of Sergei Ivanovitch, however, he grew doubtful. In the first place he did not like to leave him alone for days at a time, and in the second he feared that his brother would laugh at him. But when they crossed the meadow, the impression of last summer came back to him, and he decided that he would go after all, particularly after their conversation that had irritated him so much.

" I must have some physical exercise or I shall be absolutely no good, " he said to himself, and was determined to go hay-making with the peasants no matter what either they or his brother might think.

That very evening Levin went to his office, gave some directions about the work to be done, and sent to the surrounding villages for some mowers in order to begin on his field at Kalinov, the largest and best field of all.

" And will you get Tit to put my scythe right and let me have it by the morning—I may come along and mow too," Levin said, trying to hide his confusion.

" Very well," his bailiff replied with a smile.

At tea in the evening he determined to tell his brother.

" The weather seems quite settled, I think I shall begin the hay-making to-morrow."

" I love this work," Sergei Ivanovitch remarked.

" So do I. I think I shall go down and mow the whole day with the peasants."

" How? work with the peasants all day long? "

" Yes, it's very enjoyable," Levin replied.

" It's a splendid form of physical exercise, but will you be able to stand it? " Sergei Ivanovitch asked quite seriously.

" I have tried it. At first it's rather difficult, but you get used to it after a time. I think I shall stand it all right."

" But what do the peasants think of it? It must amuse them no doubt."

" I don't think so. The work is so jolly and at the same time so hard, that they have no time to think about it."

" But what shall you do about dinner? They could hardly bring you a bottle of wine and a roast turkey down there."

" I shall come home when they knock off for dinner."

On the following morning Levin got up earlier than usual, but various other duties in connection with the farm detained him, and when he got down to the field on which they were hay-making the men had already finished the first row.

From the foot of the hill at some distance away Levin could see the shady part of the field that had already been cut, with here and there a pile of coats that the men had thrown off. The men were moving along in a straight line, some in coats, some in their shirt-sleeves. Levin counted them. There were forty-two in all. They followed one after the other slowly at the lower part of the field where there was an old dam. Levin recognised some of them. There was old Yermil in a long white smock, bending over his scythe; there was young Vaska, who had been Levin's coachman, and Tit, a thin little peasant who had taught him to mow. He was walking erect in front and wielding his scythe like a toy.

Levin tied up his horse and went up to Tit who immediately got a second scythe that was lying near a bush and handed it to him.

" Here it is, sir. As sharp as a razor; it will cut of itself," he said with a smile, removing his cap.

Levin began trying his scythe. The merry hay-makers having finished their line came back one after another and greeted the master as they passed. No one ventured to speak until a tall old man with a clean-shaven wrinkled face, dressed in a sheep-skin coat, turned to him.

" Look here, sir, if you begin on the work you must not leave off," he turned to him jestingly, and Levin could hear the suppressed laughter of the others behind.

" I will try not to," he replied, taking his place behind Tit, and waiting for the signal to begin.

" 'Tention! " the old man cried.

Tit led the way and Levin followed. The grass was short and tough, and Levin, who had not used a scythe for a long time and was rather constrained by the watchful eyes of the men, made very bad work of it at first, though he expended a good deal of energy. Voices could be heard behind him.

"He does not hold his scythe right. Look at the handle! and see how he's bending over."

"He should press more firmly on the handle," another remarked.

"That's nothing; he'll improve all right," the old man said. "Look at him now! He's swinging out too much. He'll soon get tired at this rate. It does not matter how the master works for himself! Look at that now! We should have got beaten for such work."

The grass became less tough and Levin, making no reply to these remarks, did his best and followed Tit. They had advanced about a hundred paces. Tit kept on without showing the least fatigue, but Levin was so tired that he began to doubt whether he could hold out much longer. He was about to ask Tit for a rest when the latter stopped of his own accord, and picking up a handful of grass, he wiped his scythe and began sharpening it. Levin straightened himself and looked round with a sigh of relief. A peasant at the back of him was evidently also tired, for without waiting to come up to him he stopped and began to sharpen his scythe. When Tit had sharpened both his own and Levin's they started again.

At the second attempt it was just the same. Tit advanced a step at every swing of the scythe; Levin did his best not to lag behind; while the work became harder and harder every moment. When he felt that he could not have gone another step, Tit stopped again.

And so they went on till they got to the end of the first row. The long stretch was very hard for Levin. But when Tit slung his scythe over his shoulder and began to retrace his steps, Levin, following behind, felt a sensation of pleasure and pride coming over him at the idea that he would be able to stand it after all. He was dripping with perspiration and his pleasure was slightly marred by the thought that his work was not as good as that of the others. "I must not swing out so much with the arm, but must work more with the body," he thought, as he compared the straight line over which Tit had gone with his own uneven one.

Tit had gone rather quickly over the first row, perhaps in

order to see what his master could do, but afterward he went more leisurely. Levin, however, had to work with all his might to keep up with the others. To work well and not to lag behind was the one idea that absorbed him. He heard nothing save the swish of scythes behind him, saw nothing but the tall erect figure of Tit in front and a semi-circle of grass and flowers falling over as he went, while ahead was the end of the line, promising a rest.

Suddenly he felt a pleasant sensation of coolness on his shoulders. He glanced up at the sky while the scythes were being sharpened and saw that it was overcast by a heavy cloud. Soon a heavy shower came down. Some of the men went to get their coats; others, like Levin, were glad to feel the cool rain upon their shoulders.

The work went on and on. Levin lost all idea of time and did not know whether it was early or late. There was a noticeable change in the quality of his work that afforded him great pleasure. There were moments when he completely forgot what he was doing. He seemed to be less tired and his line was nearly as even as that of Tit's. But as soon as he began thinking of his work and trying to improve upon it, his line would grow less straight and a terrible feeling of fatigue would come over him.

They had reached the end of another line, and Levin was about to start again when Tit stopped and, going up to the old man, whispered something to him. They both looked up at the sun. "What are they talking about? Why don't they go on?" Levin thought, completely forgetting that the men had already been working for four hours, and that it was time for their breakfast.

"Breakfast, sir," the old man said.

"What! already! Very well, then."

Levin handed his scythe to Tit, and together with the peasants, who were walking towards their coats to fetch the bread for their morning meal, he walked over the mown grass, slightly moistened by the shower, towards his house. He suddenly realised that his predilections about the weather had not been correct.

"The hay will be spoiled," he observed.

"Not at all, sir. Mow in the rain, rake in the sun!" the old man replied.

Levin untied his horse and rode away home to take coffee.

Sergei Ivanovitch had only just got out of bed. Before he

was dressed and down in the dining-room, Levin had finished his coffee and was back in the field again.

V

When he returned to work after breakfast Levin found himself between the old man, who had asked him to be his neighbour, and a young peasant, who had got married lately and was mowing for the first time that summer.

The old man walked on in front with long regular strides. He swung his scythe with the same ease with which a man swings his arm when walking. It seemed as if his scythe cut of itself.

Young Mishka followed behind Levin. His head was encircled by a plait of freshly cut grass and his handsome, youthful face looked strained with the effort of wielding his scythe. He smiled when any one looked at him. He would sooner have died than confessed that the work was too hard for him.

The work seemed lighter to Levin during the heat of the day. His clothes were dripping wet and gave him a sense of coolness, while the sun burning his back, his head, and his arms, with the sleeves rolled up to the elbow, gave him new force and energy. There were moments of complete oblivion when he lost all consciousness of what he was doing and the scythe seemed to cut of itself. These were happy moments. Still more delightful was the time when they got to the river and the old man would take up a handful of grass, wipe his scythe and dip it into the water, then fill a can and hand it to Levin.

" How do you like my kvass? " he would ask with a wink.

And really it seemed to Levin that he had never tasted anything better than that warm water in the rusty tin, with the bits of grass floating about on the top.

And then came the blessed moment when, after reaching the end of a line, they would walk back with their scythes over their shoulders. There was time to wipe the perspiration from the face, to take a deep draught of the fresh air, gaze at the long line of hay-makers in front and at the woods and fields around.

The longer Levin worked the more frequently the moments of oblivion would come over him when his hands no longer wielded the scythe. It seemed to be possessed of a self-conscious body of its own, which worked on in a sort of enchantment. They were indeed joyful moments. It was only difficult when he had to interrupt this unconscious activity to mow round a little hillock, or to cut down a clump of sorrel. The old man accomplished these things lightly. When he came to a little mound he would change the action of his scythe and go round it with short, sharp strokes. He was constantly watching for things that might be hidden underneath the long grass. Every now and again he would pick some berry or other which he would either eat himself or hand to Levin, or he would move a branch out of the way with the end of his scythe, or uncover a nest of young quails whose mother would come flying out from almost under the scythe. Or some insect would attract his attention. He would dig the scythe into it like a fork, show it to Levin, then throw it away.

But for Levin and the young fellow behind him, anything that required a change of motion was difficult. They were quite unable to observe the things around them and could only repeat the same regular movement.

The time flew without his noticing it, and when it seemed to Levin that they had been working only about half an hour it was already dinner-time. The old man drew his attention to the little girls and boys, half concealed by the tall grass, who were coming from all sides bringing the men their bread and jugs of kvass.

"Here they come," he said, pointing across the field and shading his eyes from the sun with his hand.

They did another couple of lines and then the old man stopped.

"Well, sir, it's time for dinner," he said resolutely.

The men walked back to the river where their coats were lying and the children were waiting with their little bundles. They sat down, some under the shade of the cart, others under the lilac-bushes, where they spread some newly-mown hay. Levin sat down near them; he did not wish to go home.

All constraint in the presence of the master had disappeared. The men were preparing to eat their dinners. Some washed themselves, while the little ones were paddling about in the water, others untied their bundles and drew out the corks from their bottles, while others were preparing a place on which to lie down and rest after the meal.

The old man crumbled his bread into a basin, poured some water over it, cut off some more bread, and sprinkling the whole with salt he turned to the east and said his grace.

"Have some dinner with me, sir," he said to Levin as he knelt down before his basin.

Levin found his mess so palatable that he decided not to go home to dinner. While they were eating he asked the old man many questions about his domestic affairs, and took the keenest interest in his answers. He also told him anything about his own affairs that he thought would be interesting to him. He felt more intimate with him than he had ever felt with his brother Sergei Ivanovitch, and could not help smiling at him affectionately. When they had finished, the old man got up, prayed again, then lay down under the bush with a bunch of grass for a pillow. Levin followed his example, and notwithstanding the numerous flies that were buzzing all round him, he went off sound asleep and did not wake till the sun had gone over on the other side of the bush and was shining full on his face. The old man was already awake and making toy scythes to amuse the little children.

Levin glanced around, but could scarcely recognise the spot; everything was so changed. The enormous field, nearly all cut, stretched in front of him with its rows of sweet-smelling hay, while the oblique rays of the evening sun seemed to endow it with a new glory. The bushes and the river that had been hidden by the tall grass could now be seen in all their beauty. The steel surface of the water glistened and sparkled. The men were moving to the part of the field that had not yet been mown; a vulture flew high over the bare field—it all looked new to Levin.

He stood up and began calculating the work that had been done and the possible amount that might still be done that day. The work accomplished by the forty-two men was considerable. It used to take thirty men two full days on an average to cut that field, and now they had nearly finished the whole of it. But very little remained to be done. Levin was anxious to have more done that day and felt annoyed that the sun was already sinking. He did not feel in the least bit tired and was eager to go on.

" Do you think we could do Mashkin Hill to-day? " he asked the old man.

" If God wills; the sun is getting low. Will there be a little vodka for the boys? "

About tea-time, when they sat down for a rest, the old man announced that if they did Mashkin Hill there would be vodka.

" Come along then! " some one cried. " Here, Tit! let us look sharp about it. We can eat in the evening! " And without waiting to finish their bread, they set off again. "Look alive, boys!" Tit said, running along in front.

"Come along! come along!" the old man cried, hastening after them. "Take care! I shall cut you!"

Both old and young worked like fury. Yet with all their haste the work was properly done and the grass lay in regular even lines. They finished what remained to be done in the first field in about five minutes. The last mowers had scarcely reached the end of their line when the first had already slung their coats over their shoulders and were hurrying along to Mashkin Hill.

The sun was already behind the trees as they went through the little wood on the way to Mashkin Hill. Their cans rattled as they walked along. In certain places, the soft, tender grass dotted all over with pansies came up to their waists.

After a short consultation to decide whether to begin on the field crossways or lengthwise, an old peasant, Prohor Yermilin, also an experienced mower, took the lead. He cut one row by himself and the others joined him as he came back. They were working along the foot of the hill, skirting the wood. The sun had already sunk behind the trees and the dew was falling. Only the mowers on the hill were in the sunlight; those below were in the deep shade. It was getting cooler and a heavy mist was rising. Still the work went on.

The sweet-smelling tall grass fell in heavy rows under the swish of the scythe. The mowers came close together where the rows converged, rattling their cans, sometimes clicking their scythes together. There were merry shouts and laughter.

Levin still kept his place between his two companions. The old man, who had put on his sheep-skin coat, was just as lively as he had been earlier in the day. Nearer the wood the grass was strewn with mushrooms which the mowers cut down as they went along. The old man, however, every time a mushroom caught his eye, would pick it up and put it in his breast. "Another little present for my old woman," he would say.

Though the grass was damp and easy to cut it was difficult to ascend and descend the steep slopes of the hollow. For the old man, it made no difference. He swung his scythe just as lightly and strode on with his firm step, not letting a single blade of glass or a mushroom escape him, nor ceasing to joke with the others. Levin, walking behind him, felt as if he would drop at every instant. The hill would have been difficult to climb even without a scythe. But he persevered all the same. Some inner strength seemed to sustain him.

VI

Mashkin Hill was finished; the men put on their coats and walked merrily home. Levin took leave of them regretfully, mounted his horse, and rode away. From the top of the hill he turned to look back, but the men, hidden by the dense mist, were lost from view. He could only hear their merry voices and laughter and the clicking of scythes.

Sergei Ivanovitch had already dined and was sitting in his room drinking iced lemonade as he looked through the papers and reviews that had just arrived by post, when Levin rushed in. His hair was matted and clinging to his forehead, his condition generally was one of wild disorder, but he was in the gayest of moods.

"We finished the whole field!" he exclaimed as he burst in. "It has been so jolly! And what have you been doing all day?" he asked, their unpleasant conversation of yesterday quite forgotten.

"Heavens! what a sight you are!" Sergei Ivanovitch exclaimed, glancing at his brother with disapproval. "Shut the door! shut the door quickly! You must have let in at least a dozen!"

Sergei Ivanovitch could not bear flies and always closed his windows and door at night to keep them out.

"Not a single one, and if I have I shall catch them myself. You can't think how jolly it was! What did you do?"

"Oh, I was all right. But did you really mow the whole day long? You must be as hungry as a wolf. Kusma has everything ready for you."

"No, I am not hungry; I had something to eat there. I shall just go and wash myself."

"All right, I'll join you presently," Sergei Ivanovitch said, shaking his head as he gazed at his brother. "Go along! make haste!" he added with a smile, as he collected his papers and prepared to follow him. He was infected by his brother's good-humour and wanted to be with him all the time. "And what did you do during the rain?" he asked.

"What rain? Oh, yes, there were a few drops. Very well then, I'll be back directly. You weren't dull, were you? That's right!" And Levin went to dress.

In a little while the brothers were together again in the dining-room. Levin imagined that he was not hungry and sat down to the table merely for the sake of pleasing Kusma. When he began, however, everything seemed to him extraordinarily appetising. Sergei Ivanovitch looked at him with a smile.

"Oh, by the way, there's a letter for you. Will you bring it up, Kusma? But take care to shut the door."

It was a letter from Oblonsky, written from St. Petersburg. Levin read it aloud. "I have just heard from Dolly; she is at Yergushov, and everything seems to have gone wrong there. Do go and see her and give her your advice. You know everything. She will be so glad to see you, poor thing, she is quite alone. Her mother and the others are still abroad."

"I shall be delighted," Levin said. "Why not go together? She's a splendid woman; don't you think?"

"Are they far from here?"

"About thirty or forty miles, but the road is excellent. We could get there in no time."

"I shall be pleased to come," Sergei Ivanovitch said with a smile. The sight of his brother made him feel happy. "What an appetite you have!" he exclaimed, as he looked at his sunburnt face and neck bending over his plate.

"Haven't I? You can't think how good this sort of thing is for you. I am going to enrich medicine with a new term —*Arbeitskur*."

"You are hardly in need of it, I should think."

"It would be an excellent cure for nervous diseases."

"Yes, it ought to be tried. I wanted to go down and see you hay-making, but the heat was so unbearable that I didn't get farther than the wood. I sat and rested there a while, then I went on to the village. I came across your old nurse and questioned her as to what the peasants thought of you. According to her they do not approve of your working in the fields. 'That is not work for the gentry,' she said. As a general thing the peasantry have very definite ideas as to what is and what is not becoming for the gentry to do, and they don't like them going outside certain fixed limits."

"That may be so, but I've never enjoyed anything more in my life. And what harm is there in it?" Levin asked. "It's not my fault if they don't like it. Besides, it really doesn't matter either way."

"On the whole you seem to be very pleased with your day," Sergei Ivanovitch observed.

"Of course I am. We finished the whole field. And then

I made friends with such a dear old man! You can't imagine how nice he was!"

"You are satisfied with your day and I with mine, too. I solved two chess problems—one was splendid; I must show it you. And then I've been thinking over our conversation of yesterday."

"What conversation?" Levin asked as he finished his dinner and leant back in his chair. He remembered nothing about it.

"I came to the conclusion that you were partly right. Our only point of difference appears to be that you assume personal interest to be the moving power in all our actions; whereas I maintain that any man who has reached a certain stage of intellectual development must place the public good above everything. For all that you may be right. Activity with a personal motive behind it may be preferable. You are too *primesautier*, as the French say; you must either expend terrific energy or do nothing at all."

Levin listened to his brother, but did not take in the meaning of what he was saying. He did not try to understand, and was merely afraid that Sergei Ivanovitch might ask him some question by which it would become evident that he was not paying any attention to his remarks.

"What do you think?" Sergei Ivanovitch asked, laying his hand on Levin's shoulder.

"Why, of course; I don't set much store on my own opinion," Levin replied, smiling like a child conscious of having done something naughty. "What was it we disagreed about?" he thought. "Of course, I am right and he is and everything is delightful. Only I must go and see to things in the office." He stood up and stretched himself.

Sergei Ivanovitch was also smiling.

"Are you going? Then I'll come too," he said. He did not wish to part from his brother, who seemed to exhale freshness and vigour. "I'll come with you to the office if you like."

"Dear me!" Levin exclaimed so loudly that his brother was startled.

"What is it?"

"How is Agafia Mihailovna's arm? I had completely forgotten her."

"It's much better."

"I must go and see her though. I shall be back before you've time to get your hat." And he clattered down the stairs.

VII

While Stepan Arkadyevitch had set off for St. Petersburg to perform the most natural and essential duty of reminding the ministry of his existence—a duty so familiar to officials, yet so incomprehensible to outsiders and without which there is no possibility of serving—and while he was enjoying himself at the races and his friend's country houses, having taken with him nearly all the ready money in the house, Dolly and the children went down to stay at Yergushov to cut down expenses as much as possible. Yergushov was a piece of property that had formed part of her dowry—the wood that was sold in the spring had belonged to it. The estate was situated about fifty miles from Pokrovsky, Levin's village. The old house at Yergushov had long been in ruins, and even in the prince's time the whole of it had not been inhabited. The family had lived mostly in a new wing built about twenty years ago, when Dolly was quite a child. This wing stood with its back to the main avenue and faced due south. Though it had once been spacious and comfortable, it was now damp and out of repair.

When Stepan Arkadyevitch had gone down there in the spring Dolly had asked him to look over the house and have any necessary repairs made. Like all guilty husbands, Stepan Arkadyevitch was very solicitous about the comforts of his wife. When he got there, he decided that the furniture wanted recovering, the pictures rehanging; the garden had to be put right, lots of flowers planted, and a new bridge had to be built across the pond. As for the more essential things, they had entirely escaped his notice, much to Dolly's discomfort when she came to live there.

Notwithstanding the fact that Stepan Arkadyevitch did his very best to be a considerate husband and father, he was for ever forgetting that he had a family, and his tastes remained those of a bachelor. On his return to Moscow he assured Dolly with great pride that he had seen to everything and that the house was in perfect order. He advised her to go down there as soon as possible. For Stepan Arkadyevitch, her going was a most desirable arrangement from every point of view. Expenses would be decreased, the children would enjoy the country, and, above all, he would be more free.

As for Dolly, she considered it essential to go into the country for the summer for the sake of the children's health, particularly as the little girl was very slow in recovering from the effects of scarlet fever. Besides which, she would be freed from the worry of tradesmen, who were clamouring for their bills to be paid. Moreover, she had some thoughts of persuading Kitty to join her, as the doctors had ordered her plenty of out-door bathing. To her great joy, Kitty had written from abroad saying that nothing would please her more than to spend the rest of the summer with her and the children at Yergushov, a place so full of pleasant memories for both of them.

At first Dolly found life in the country very difficult. She had lived there when she was a child, and viewed in the light of early recollections she had expected it to be a refuge from the troubles and trials of town life. She knew it would not be very gay or elegant; still it would be less expensive and the children would be happier. When she got there, however, things turned out quite otherwise.

It poured in torrents on the first day of her arrival. There was a leak in the roof and the water dripped through into the corridor and nursery, so that the little beds had to be carried into the drawing-room. It was impossible to find a cook, and out of the eight cows they possessed, Dolly learnt that some were going to calve, others had calved, and the rest were either too young or too old to give milk. Consequently there was not a drop of milk for the children. There were no eggs and no hens; they had to boil and roast all the tough old roosters. Not a woman was to be found to do the scrubbing, as all the peasant women were working in the fields. They could not drive because one of the horses was restive and would not be harnessed. Bathing was impossible because the banks of the river had been trodden into a quagmire by the cattle; besides which it was too conspicuous from the road. Even walking was not pleasant, as the tumble-down fences admitted the cattle into the garden, and the children were in terror of a bull who was always bellowing. There were no cupboards in which to hang dresses, or such as there were either had no doors, or the doors opened of themselves as you walked past them. There were no pots or pans in the kitchen and no tubs or ironing boards in the laundry.

This astounding poverty, as Dolly looked upon it, nearly drove her to despair at first. She worked from morning till night to get things in order, and could scarcely hold back the tears when she realised the hopelessness of the situation. Her manager, formerly a sergeant, whom Stepan Arkadyevitch had raised to the dignity of footman on account of his impressive appearance, did absolutely nothing to help her. "It is impossible," he said, "the people are no good." That is all she could get out of him.

There was one member in the Oblonsky household, however, as there are in most well-regulated houses, who did not give way to despair. That was the indispensable Marya Filimonovna. She tried to comfort her mistress and assured her that everything would come right in the end. And she went on working patiently, without any fuss or bother. She immediately made friends with the manager's wife, took tea with them in the garden on the first day of her arrival, and proceeded to talk things over. Very soon a sort of club was formed under the acacia trees, consisting of Marya Filimonovna, the manager, the bailiff, and the man from the office; they all put their heads together to see what could be done. By degrees the roof was mended, a cook was found, chickens were procured, the cows began to give milk, the garden fence was mended, the carpenter made a few things for the laundry and put catches to the cupboard doors so that they no longer flew open. An ironing board covered with military cloth was reposing on a chest of drawers and a smell of hot irons came from the kitchen.

"You see, everything has come right," Marya Filimonovna said to her mistress as she pointed to the board triumphantly. Even a little thatched bathing hut was constructed so that they could all bathe. Dolly's hope of a comfortable if not a peaceful country life was almost realised. Peace with six children was next to impossible. One would fall ill, another would threaten to fall ill, a third was in need of something, a fourth began to show signs of a bad disposition, and so on, and so on. A period of rest and quiet rarely came. But all these worries and anxieties were in a sense Dolly's only consolation. Had she not been so absorbed in these little daily cares, she would have become a prey to thoughts about her husband who no longer loved her. Besides, these same children who worried her by their faults and ailments were a constant source of happiness to her in other respects. Her joys were so small that they were almost invisible, like gold among sand. In trying moments she saw only the sand—her sorrows—but at others she was rewarded by a sight of the pure gold.

In the quiet of the country her joyful moments were more frequent. No matter how often she accused herself of a mother's partiality, she could not help admiring her children. It seemed to her that they were the most charming children you could wish for—the whole six of them, each in its own particular way —and she was proud and happy in possessing them.

VIII

TOWARDS the end of May when everything was beginning to improve, Dolly received a letter from her husband in reply to the various complaints she had made about her domestic troubles. He excused himself profusely for not having thought of everything and promised to go and see her at the first possible opportunity. The opportunity had not presented itself, and in June Dolly was still living alone.

On Sunday, during the feast of St. Peter, she took all her children to holy communion. When discussing spiritual or philosophical matters with her sister, her mother, or her friends, Dolly would often surprise them by her independent views regarding religion. She had a curious religion of her own that had little in common with church dogmas. She was very punctilious, however, about observing the forms of the church, both for the sake of her family as well as the needs of her own soul. She was genuinely concerned that the children had not been to communion for a whole year, and with Marya Filimonovna's approval she decided to take them now.

For several days beforehand she planned what the children were to wear. Their clothes were all altered, mended, and washed, and were now lying all ready to the last ribbon. Tania's dress alone had caused Dolly a good deal of anxiety. The English governess who had undertaken to alter it had completely spoiled it. However, thanks to Marya Filimonovna, it was made wearable, and a quarrel with the governess was avoided.

At about ten o'clock in the morning—the hour that the priest had been asked to fix the service—the children, dressed in their best and radiant with joy, were standing near the carriage in front of the house waiting for their mother. As a result of Marya Filimonovna's intervention the restive horse had been dispensed with and one of the bailiff's put in its place.

At last Dolly came out dressed in a robe of white muslin. She had taken a considerable amount of pains over her toilet. There was a time when she liked to dress well for her own sake, because it made her look pretty and attractive, but later on it became irksome to her, for she grew conscious how much her appearance had altered for the worse. To-day, however, she took special pains over the way she dressed herself, not for the sake of enhancing her own beauty, but for the sake of her lovely children. She did not wish to spoil the general impression of the whole scene. When she took a final glance in the mirror she felt satisfied. She looked pretty. Not with the sort of prettiness that had once inspired admiration at a ball, but with another kind more in keeping with her present purpose.

Besides peasants and peasant women there was no one else in the church. It seemed to Dolly that every one looked at them with admiration. The children were pretty in their Sunday frocks and behaved charmingly. Aliosha, to be sure, was not all that could be desired; he kept turning round to look at the back of his coat, but he was sweet all the same. Tania the eldest looked after the younger ones, and the youngest, Lily, was fascinating in her simple childish delight at everything she saw. No one could contain a smile when, after she had received the communion, she cried out, " Please some more! "

When they returned home the children felt that something very solemn had taken place and were unusually quiet. Everything seemed to go well until lunch-time, when Grisha began to whistle, and what was worst of all, he refused to obey the English governess. He had to be sent away without his pudding. Had she been alone, Dolly would probably not have resorted to punishment on that day, but she had to support the governess who insisted upon it. The event somewhat spoiled the general good-humour.

Grisha wept bitterly and said that Nikolinka had also whistled, and yet he remained unpunished. He tried to explain that he was not crying about the pudding, but because they had not been fair to him. This was too much for Dolly, and after a word or two with the governess she decided to forgive Grisha, and went out to find him. But as she passed through the drawing-room she witnessed a scene that brought such joy to her heart that the tears came to her eyes.

Grisha was sitting on a window-sill in a corner of the room, and Tania was standing beside him with a plate. Under the pretext of wanting some dinner for her dolls she had asked the governess to let her take her tart to the nursery and had brought it straight to her brother. Grisha, still crying over the unfairness of the punishment, was eating the tart. " Have some too. Let us eat it together," he said to Tania through his tears.

Tania, who had at first felt sorry for her brother, was now overcome by her generous action, and the tears rose to her eyes. She did not, however, refuse her portion.

When they caught sight of their mother they grew frightened, but seeing by the expression of her face that she was not displeased, they burst out laughing, their mouths crammed with tart, and began wiping their faces, besmeared with jam and tears, with the sleeves of their garments.

"Heavens! Your new white dresses! Tania! Grisha!" Dolly exclaimed in her efforts to save the dresses, but a glad smile lighted up her face.

The new dresses were speedily removed and replaced by tunics for the boys and blouses for the girls. The trap was harnessed again, much to the disgust of the bailiff and the delight of the children, who set off to bathe and gather mushrooms.

A basket was soon filled; even little Lily found a mushroom. At first Miss Hull had to point them out to her, but in a little while she discovered one by herself. There was a shout of triumph, "Lily has found a mushroom!"

When the basket was quite full they went down to the part of the river that had been screened off for bathing. Tarenty, the coachman, tied up the horses, and while they were battling with the flies he lay down under the shade of a birch-tree and lighted his pipe. A hum of merry children's voices reached him from the river.

Though there was a considerable amount of trouble in looking after all these children; though it was difficult not to mix up their various shoes, stockings, knickers for so many different legs, and to fasten and unfasten so many strings and buttons—still Dolly, who was fond of bathing herself and thought it good for the children, was never happier than when she was playing about with them in the water. She loved to pull the stockings on their plump little legs or to take a naked little body in her arms and hear its shouts of joy and fear as she dipped it into the cold water. Nothing gave her greater pleasure than to see their breathless, jolly faces.

When about half the children were dressed, some peasant women in Sunday attire came by and stopped by the bathing-shed. Marya Filimonovna called to one of them and gave her a towel and a shirt that had fallen into the water to dry while Dolly entered into conversation with the others. They were somewhat shy at first and tried to hide their amusement, but in a little while they grew bolder and completely won Dolly's heart by their sincere admiration of the children.

"Isn't she a beauty! as white as milk!" one of them said, pointing to Tania. "What a pity she's so thin."

"She's been very ill."

"And did you bathe too?" another asked of the baby.

"Oh no! he's only three months old," Dolly replied proudly.

"Is that all?"

"Have you any children?"

"I had four, but only two are left, a boy and a girl. I weaned her just before Lent."

"How old is she?"

"Two years."

"Why did you nurse her so long?"

"Oh, that's our way. We leave off when Lent comes round a third time."

Dolly became engrossed in their conversation. She asked them all about their children, their various ailments, where their husbands were and if they often saw them. Their interests were so much in common that Dolly could scarcely tear herself away from these women. She was pleased to see how they were filled with admiration because she had so many and such lovely children. They made her laugh and hurt Miss Hull's feelings because she was evidently the cause of their laughter.

One of the younger women stared at the unfortunate Miss Hull who was dressing after having finished with the last child, and when she saw her put on her third petticoat she could no longer contain herself. "Why, look at her! she has not finished yet!" she exclaimed, and they all burst out laughing.

IX

Dolly, with a kerchief over her head, surrounded by all the six children with dripping hair, was just approaching the house when the coachman said, "A gentleman is coming; the one from Pokrovsky I think."

Dolly turned round and was delighted to see Levin's familiar figure in a grey hat and coat coming towards them. She was always glad to see him, but was now especially glad, because he saw her in all her glory. No one could understand her greatness better than Levin.

As he looked at her she reminded him of one of the many pictures his imagination had conjured up of his future domestic life.

"You are just like a broody hen, Darya Alexandrovna," he greeted her.

"Oh, I am so glad to see you!" she said, extending her hand.

"Then why didn't you let me know you were here? I should not have known had not Stiva written and told me. My brother is staying with me just now."

"You heard from Stiva?" Dolly asked in surprise.

"Yes. He wrote saying that you had come down here and asked me to see if I could help you in anything," Levin replied. He felt confused as he said this and for some time walked in silence by the side of the trap, pulling off small linden shoots and biting them. His embarrassment arose from the fact that he felt it might be unpleasant for Dolly to accept the aid of a stranger in matters that her own husband should have attended to. And indeed Dolly disliked her husband's way of burdening other people with their family affairs. She saw at once that Levin understood her feeling. It was precisely for this extraordinary delicacy and quickness of perception that Dolly liked him.

"Of course," Levin went on, "I knew he merely meant that you wanted to see me, and I was very glad. I can quite understand that after the town you find things very wild here. Should you happen to need anything, I am entirely at your service."

"Nothing at all, I assure you," Dolly said. "It was rather inconvenient at first, but now everything is all right. Thanks to our old nurse," she added, pointing to Marya Filimonovna, who understood that they were talking about her. She gave Levin a friendly smile. She knew him and knew also that he would be a good match for the young lady, and was anxious for them to marry.

"There is room here," she said, "won't you take a seat? We can squeeze up a little."

"No, thanks, I prefer to walk. Children, let us race the horses."

The children knew Levin very little and hardly ever recognised him when they saw him, but they did not show towards him that strange feeling of bashfulness and dislike that they frequently experienced before grown people who made attempts to descend to their level, and for which they sometimes suffered so painfully. Pretence in anything whatsoever may deceive the cleverest and most penetrating mind, but the dullest child will see through it and turn away in disgust, no matter how artfully it is concealed. Whatever Levin's faults might have been, there was not an atom of pretence about him, and so the children felt the same sort of confidence in him that they could read on their mother's face. In response to his invitation, the two eldest instantly jumped down and ran with him, just as they would have done with their nurse, Miss Hull, or their mother. Even Lily begged to go to him. Dolly handed her down and Levin put her on his shoulder, and they started off together.

"It's all right, Darya Alexandrovna, don't be afraid," he called merrily to the mother. "She is quite safe; I won't let her fall."

And looking at his powerful form and agile, cautious movements, the mother felt reassured and smiled at him approvingly.

Here, in the country with the children and with Darya Alexandrovna who was so sympathetic, Levin fell into that childishly merry mood that sometimes came over him—a mood that Dolly liked so about him. He ran with the children, taught them gymnastic tricks, amused Miss Hull with his bad English, and told Dolly about his occupations in the country.

After dinner, when they were sitting alone on the veranda, Dolly began talking to him about Kitty.

"Do you know Kitty is coming to spend the summer with me."

"Is she?" he said blushing. "Shall I send you two cows?" he asked to change the subject. "If you really insist on paying for them, then let me have five roubles a month for each cow, though you ought to be ashamed to mention it."

"No, thanks, we don't need them now; we can manage with our own."

"In that case I must have a look at them, and if you will permit, I will tell your people how to feed them. It all depends on the feeding."

And Levin, to keep from talking about Kitty, began expounding the theory of dairy farming, pointing out that a cow was only a machine for turning food into milk and so on and so on.

He was longing to hear news of Kitty, yet was afraid to ask. He was in terror lest his peace of mind so dearly earned should again be destroyed.

" Yes, but some one has to see to all these things, and who is to do it here? " Dolly replied reluctantly.

She had entrusted everything to Marya Filimonovna's care and was loath to have anything altered. Besides she had little faith in Levin's knowledge of farming. She was somewhat suspicious of the theory that a cow was merely a machine for producing milk. It seemed to her that theorising of this kind must be bad for farming in general. In reality it was all much simpler. You had only to tell Marya Filimonovna to give the speckled cow more food and water and for the cook not to take the dish-water to the laundress's cow. This was quite clear, whereas speculations about grain and grass feeding led to nowhere. Besides she was anxious to talk about Kitty.

X

" Kitty writes to tell me that there is nothing she desires so much as solitude and quiet," Dolly remarked after a pause.

" How is she now, better? " Levin asked in agitation.

" Thank God, she has quite recovered. I never could believe that there was anything the matter with her lungs."

" I am glad to hear it," Levin said. There was something touching and helpless about the expression of his face as he spoke and also when he looked at Dolly in silence.

" Now, Konstantin Dmitritch," she began, with her good-natured, though somewhat sarcastic smile, " why are you angry with Kitty? "

" I? Not at all," he replied.

" Yes, you are. Why didn't you come to see us when you were in Moscow? "

" Darya Alexandrovna," he said, blushing to the roots of his hair, " I am surprised that with your goodness you do not feel the situation. How can you be so unkind when you know . . ."

" What do I know? "

" That I proposed to Kitty and she refused me," he replied.

All the tenderness that a moment ago he had felt for Kitty suddenly changed to a feeling of anger for the insult he had endured.

" What made you think that I knew? "

" Because everybody knows."

"You are quite mistaken; I did not know though I guessed."

"Well, you know now."

"I knew there was something that tormented her dreadfully, about which she asked me never to speak to her. Since she did not tell me, she has not told anybody. Come, what was there between you?"

"I have already told you."

"When did it happen?"

"The last time I called on you."

"Do you know," Dolly said, "I am very, very sorry for her. You are only suffering from injured pride . . ."

"That may be," Levin interrupted her, "but . . ."

Dolly would not allow him to finish.

"Now I understand everything. I feel dreadfully sorry for her, poor thing."

"You really must excuse me, Darya Alexandrovna," he said, rising. "I must go. Good-bye."

"No, don't go yet," she said, taking hold of his arm. "Wait a little, sit down."

"Then don't let us talk about this, please," he implored as he sat down again. A hope that he had thought dead and buried rose and stirred in his heart.

"If I was not so fond of you," Dolly went on, as the tears came into her eyes, "if I did not know you so well . . ."

The revived hope showed more signs of life and took possession of Levin's heart.

"Yes, I understand everything now," Dolly continued. "You cannot understand it. To you men who are free to make your choice, it is always clear whom you love. But a girl in the attitude of expectancy, with her maidenly bashfulness, a girl who can only look at you men from a distance and believes every word that is said to her, may not always be able to define her feelings or know what to say."

"Yes, if the heart does not tell . . ."

"Oh, yes, it does, but just consider for a moment. You men become attracted to a girl; you call on her, get to know her, wait your chance, and if you find her to be what you thought her, and are sure that you love her, you propose . . ."

"It does not work out exactly like that."

"All the same, you propose when your love has matured, or when the scale has come down on one of two choices. But the girl is not asked. You want her to choose for herself, but she cannot choose; her function is merely to answer 'yes' or 'no.'"

" And the choice was between me and Vronsky," Levin thought bitterly, and the hope that was brought back to life died out again and tore his heart with pain.

" Darya Alexandrovna," he said, " people choose dresses like that, or anything else that they want to buy, but not love. The choice has been made—so much the better. . . . It cannot happen again."

" Oh, pride! nothing but pride! " Dolly exclaimed, as though despising him for the baseness of that sentiment in comparison with another, that only women can feel. " At the time you proposed to Kitty she happened to be in such a position that she could not answer. She was wavering between you and Vronsky. She saw him every day, while you she had not seen for a long time. Had she been a little older—for me, for instance, there could not have been any doubt. I always hated him, and so it ended."

Levin recalled Kitty's reply, " *No, it cannot be.*"

" Darya Alexandrovna," he said dryly, " I esteem the confidence you place in me, but I think you are mistaken. Whether right or wrong, this pride that you despise so much makes every thought of Katerina Alexandrovna impossible for me—you understand, quite impossible."

" There is one other thing I should like to add; you know I am speaking of my sister whom I love as much as I do my own children. I do not say that she loves you. I only wanted to say that her refusal at that moment meant nothing."

" I am not sure," Levin said, jumping up, " if you realise how much you pain me! It is just as though you had lost a child, and people kept on telling you how nice he would have been were he alive and what joy he would have given you. And you know all the time that he is dead, dead, dead. . . ."

" How funny you are," Dolly said, with a sad smile as she looked at Levin's agitated face. " Yes, I understand everything perfectly now," she continued pensively. " Shall you not come to see us when Kitty is here? "

" No, I shall not. Of course I shall not run away from Katerina Alexandrovna, but I will try and relieve her from the unpleasantness of seeing me whenever I can."

" You really are funny," Dolly said, gazing into his face affectionately. " Very well, let us forget that we have ever spoken of this. What do you want, Tania? " she asked in French, turning to her eldest child who had just come in.

" Where is my spade, mamma? "

" I spoke to you in French and you should answer in French."

The child wanted to do so, but could not remember the French word for spade. Her mother helped her out and told her in the same language where to find it. The scene was unpleasant to Levin. In fact everything in Dolly's house and in her children seemed to him not so nice now as a short while ago.

" Why does she talk French to the children? " he asked himself. " It's so affected and unnatural! Even the children feel it. They are taught French and insincerity," he thought, not knowing that Dolly herself had thought it over about twenty times, and at the risk of insincerity had considered it necessary to teach the children in this manner.

" Why are you in such a hurry? Stay a little longer."

Levin remained until tea, but his gay mood had left him and he felt ill at ease.

After tea he went out to order his horses to be harnessed, and on his return he found Dolly in a disturbed, excited condition, with tears in her eyes. During his absence an event had occurred that had destroyed all the pride and happiness she had felt in her children that day. Grisha and Tania had come to blows over a ball. Hearing cries in the nursery, Dolly had run out to see what was the matter and was met by a terrible sight. Tania had hold of Grisha's hair and he, his face distorted with rage, was striking at her with his fists wherever he could. A pain shot through Dolly's heart when she saw them. Her life seemed to be suddenly enveloped in darkness. She became conscious that those children of hers, of whom she had been so proud, were not only most ordinary, but even naughty, badly brought-up children with the most brutal animal instincts.

She could neither speak nor think of anything else, and could not help telling Levin of her misfortune.

Levin saw that she was unhappy and tried to console her, saying that it proved nothing bad, that all children were in the habit of fighting. However, in his heart he thought, " No, I will not talk French to my children; my children will not be like these. Children should not be pampered or spoiled and then they are sure to be good. No, I will not have such children."

He said good-bye and departed; Dolly made no attempt to detain him.

XI

About the middle of July the elder of the village belonging to Levin's sister came to bring Levin a report of the mowing and affairs generally. The village was situated some twenty miles from Pokrovsky, and the principal income derived from it was from the hay of the low-lying meadows under water in winter. In former years the peasants used to buy the standing hay at twenty roubles an acre, but when Levin undertook the management of the estate he decided that it was worth more and fixed the price at twenty-five roubles. The peasants would not pay so much and Levin suspected them of keeping off other purchasers. Then Levin went there himself and made arrangements about mowing the fields, partly by hired labour and partly by payment in shares. The peasants opposed this new scheme as hard as they could, but matters went well, and in the very first year almost a double sum was realised. Last year, which was the third, they still kept up their opposition, but the harvest went on in the same order. That summer the peasants had agreed to do all the mowing for a one-third share. The elder had come to inform Levin that, fearing rain, they had invited the clerk and in his presence had divided eleven of the ricks. From the vague replies to his questions as to how much hay the largest meadow had yielded, from the whole tone of the peasant, Levin grew suspicious that something was wrong in this division of the hay; he decided to go down there himself and find out what had actually happened.

He arrived in the village at dinner-time and went straight to the cottage of an old peasant, a friend of his and husband to his brother's nurse. There he tied up his horse and went out to the old man who was among his bees to find out all the details of the hay-making. The talkative, respectable peasant, Parmenitch, was delighted to see Levin. He showed him his farm, told him all about his bees, and how many swarms he had had that year, but when it came to answering questions about the hay-making he was very guarded and indefinite. This confirmed Levin in his suspicions. He went down to the meadows to examine the ricks. There could not have been fifty loads in each of them. To catch the peasants, he ordered one of the ricks to be carted into the barn. It turned out that it contained only thirty-two loads in all. In spite of the elder's assurances about the lightness of the hay and its having settled in the ricks, in spite of his oath that everything had been done in an honest way, Levin stuck to his own opinion, and maintained that as the division had been made without his orders, he would not accept this hay as being fifty loads to the rick. After a long dispute it was decided that the peasants should take the eleven ricks for themselves, counting them at fifty loads apiece, and that the estate share should be made out anew. All these arguments and the division of the cocks lasted until supper time. When the last of the hay was divided up, Levin entrusted the supervision of the rest to the clerk and sat down on a cock marked with a stick, to take a last look at the meadow, astir with people.

In front of him, in the bend of the river beyond a little bog, a line of gaily-coloured peasant women moved along the grey rows of hay over the bright green of the after-grass. Following them came peasants with pitchforks and the long rows were speedily changed to broad, high cocks. To the left where the meadow had been cleared, several carts rumbled along, and one after another the cocks disappeared, giving place to heavy waggon-loads of fragrant hay, pressing against the backs of the horses.

" If you can get it all up in good weather, it will make fine hay," an old man remarked, sitting down beside Levin. " It is more like tea than hay! See how quickly they're picking it up," he added, pointing to the growing stacks. " They've done a good half since dinner."

" Is that the last? " he shouted to a young lad who was standing on the box of a cart and whipping the ends of his hempen reins as he drove past.

" Yes, father," the lad replied as he drew in his horse and turned with a smile to a ruddy woman beside him who was also smiling. They drove on further.

" Who is that? your son? " Levin asked.

" My youngest," the old man replied with a kindly smile.

" What a splendid fellow he is! "

" Yes, he's not bad."

" Is he married? "

" Yes, he got married during the fast of the Advent three years ago."

" Has he any children? "

" Indeed not! For a whole year he did not know a thing; besides he's so bashful," the old man replied. " What splendid hay! " he added to change the subject.

Levin turned his attention to Vanka Parmenov and his wife who were loading not far from him. Vanka was standing on the cart receiving, arranging, and pressing down the huge masses of hay that his pretty wife was handing up to him, first in armfuls and then on the pitchfork. The young peasant woman moved about lightly and merrily. The coarse hay that had settled down was difficult to get on to the fork. At first she spread it out somewhat, then stuck her fork in, and pressing all her weight against it, with an adroit movement she raised it aloft and threw the hay on to the cart. The curve of her back, encircled by a red belt, looked wonderfully graceful as she bent down, and so did her full bosom under the thin white kerchief as she straightened herself up again. Vanka, evidently anxious to save her as much trouble as possible, caught the bundle quickly and spread it over the cart. After having handed up the last stray pieces with a rake, the woman shook off the chaff that had fallen at the back of her neck, and adjusting the red kerchief over her white forehead, she crawled under the cart to tie it up. Vanka had taught her how to do this. He burst out laughing at some remark she made. Both their faces expressed vigorous, youthful, newly-awakened love.

XII

THE cart was tied up. Vanka jumped down and led the good-natured, well-fed horse by the bridle. The woman threw her rake on to the cart and with a brisk gait, waving her arms about, she joined the other women who had assembled for the singing. Vanka reached the road and joined a long procession of carts. The women, with rakes over their shoulders, sparkling in their bright colours, followed the carts, singing in their merry, ringing voices. One wild, coarse voice started a song and sang it as far as the refrain, while fifty other voices, young, fresh, and powerful, took it up from the beginning and continued to the end.

They drew near to Levin, swelling like a cloud of tumultuous joy. It seemed to envelop him and the hay-cock he was sitting on, the loaded carts, the whole field and the fields in the distance. Everything blended together and trembled with the measure of this wild, mirthful song and the shouting and whistling and clapping. Levin grew envious of this lusty mirth; he too would have liked to take part in the expression of this joy of life, yet he could do nothing but lie there and listen. When they were lost from view, and he could no longer hear their lively song, all the consciousness of his loneliness came upon him. He grew depressed at the sense of his own indolence and his hostility to the world at large.

Some of the very peasants with whom he had quarrelled about the hay—those he had insulted and others who had wanted to cheat him—these same peasants bowed to him merrily as they passed, evidently feeling no resentment towards him, and no regret or even recollection that they had intended to cheat him. All was swallowed up and forgotten in the sea of joyous communal toil. God had given the day and God had given the strength. And the day and the strength were devoted to the work in which they found their reward. And for whom was the work? What fruits would it yield? These were unimportant, irrelevant considerations.

Levin had frequently admired this life and had often envied the people who lived it. To-day, however, under the influence of the sentiment aroused in him by Vanka Parmenov and his young wife, the thought struck him clearly for the first time that it depended solely on him to change that oppressive, indolent, artificial, selfish life he had been leading for this pure, simple, delightful life of work.

The peasants had dispersed themselves; even the old man who had been sitting with him had gone home long ago. Those who lived near by had departed to their cottages, and others from a distance who were going to spend the night in the meadow were preparing their suppers. Levin still lay on the hay-cock, unnoticed by the peasants. He was watching them, listening and thinking. They hardly slept at all during that short summer night. They talked and laughed merrily over their evening meal, after which they sang songs again.

Their long, hard day's work had left no other trace behind than gaiety. Before daybreak all grew quiet. No other sound was heard than the incessant croaking of frogs in the marsh and the snorting of the horses in the rising mist. Coming to himself, Levin arose and, gazing up at the stars, realised that the night was over.

"Well, what shall I do? How shall I do it?" he asked himself, trying to give expression to what he had thought and felt during the short night. All his sensations and thoughts seemed to have run in three different directions. One was the renunciation of his former life and his utterly useless education.

This idea afforded him great pleasure, as it was easy and simple. His other thoughts had reference to the new life that he wanted to lead now. It seemed to him that in the conditions of this new life, in purity and simplicity, he would find that resignation, contentment, and dignity the lack of which he felt so painfully now. The third line of thought brought him to the question of how to effect the transition from the old life to the new. Here, nothing definite presented itself to his mind. " I must have a wife and work. And there must be an incentive to work. Or shall I give up Pokrovsky? buy land? join some commune, or marry a peasant girl? How can I do all this? " he asked himself again, but no answer was forthcoming. " I have not slept all night and my ideas are not very clear," he continued; " I shall reduce them to order later on. One thing is certain; this night has settled my fate. All my former dreams of domestic life were utter nonsense, not the right thing. This is much simpler and better. . . ."

" How beautiful! " he thought, gazing up at a fleecy cloud, the colour of mother-of-pearl, that had stopped just overhead in the middle of the sky. " How lovely everything is on this glorious night! And when did that shell have time to form? It is only a moment ago since I looked at the sky and there was nothing on it but two streaks of light. And my views on life have changed just as imperceptibly."

He left the field and walked down the high road into the village. A light wind had risen and it grew grey and gloomy. It was the gloom before the dawn that brought into stronger relief the complete triumph of light over the darkness.

Levin shivered with cold. He walked on quickly, his eyes fixed on the ground. " What is that? Who is that coming? " he thought, raising his head as he heard the tinkling of bells. About forty paces away a carriage with luggage, drawn by four horses, was driving towards him along the grassy road. The shaft horses pressed against the shafts to avoid the ruts, but the coachman, sitting sideways on the box, cleverly kept the shaft along the rut so that the wheels ran on the smooth road.

This was all Levin noticed. Without considering who it might be, he glanced absently into the carriage.

An old lady was dozing in one corner whilst at the window sat a young girl, evidently just awakened, playing with the strings of her bonnet. Bright and pensive, filled with a refined, complex, internal life foreign to Levin, she looked past him at the glow of the morning sky.

At the very instant that this vision flashed by, he caught a glimpse of her frank eyes. He recognised her and a gleam of unexpected pleasure lighted up his face.

He could not be mistaken. There were no other eyes like those in the world. There was only one being in the world for him around whom centred all the light and meaning in life. It was she, it was Kitty. He realised that she was on her way to Yergushov from the railway station. And everything that had been agitating Levin during that sleepless night, all the resolutions he had made vanished instantly. The thought of marrying a peasant girl now filled him with disgust. Only there, in that rapidly receding carriage that had crossed over to the other side of the road, was there a possible solution to the riddle of his life that had weighed on him so heavily of late.

She did not look out again. The sound of the springs was no longer heard and the bells grew fainter and fainter. The barking of dogs told him that the carriage had passed the village. And now nothing remained but the empty fields, the village in the distance, and he, a stranger to all, alone and solitary, walking along the deserted road.

He looked up at the sky in the hope of seeing the mother-of-pearl cloud that had seemed to him the symbol of his thoughts and feelings of the past night, but it was no longer there. In the unattainable height a mysterious change had already taken place. Not a trace was to be seen of the shell-like cloud. A fleecy carpet, moving and dispersing itself, covered half the heavens. The sky grew bluer and brighter and replied to his entreating glance with the same tenderness, but also with the same inaccessibility.

"No," he said to himself; "however good this simple life of work may be, I cannot return to it. I love *her*."

XIII

None but those nearest to Alexei Alexandrovitch were aware that this seemingly cold and calculating man had one weakness that was not at all in keeping with the general composition of his character. Alexei Alexandrovitch could not look on the tears of a child or a woman with indifference. The sight of tears completely unmanned him and deprived him of the ability to reflect. His secretaries knew this and always warned women petitioners not to allow their feeling to overcome them if they did not wish to spoil their chances. " He will get angry and won't listen to you," they would say. And indeed, it was perfectly true. The spiritual confusion produced in Alexei Alexandrovitch by tears expressed itself in hasty anger. " I can't, I can't do anything for you! Please go away! " he usually cried under these circumstances.

When, on their way back from the races, Anna had informed him of her relations with Vronsky, and covering her face with her hands had burst into tears, Alexei Alexandrovitch, despite the resentment she aroused in him, was stirred by that deeper feeling that the sight of weeping always produced in him. Knowing this, and knowing also that to give expression to the sentiment he felt would be incompatible with the situation, he endeavoured to repress in himself every manifestation of life, and so did not stir or look at her. Hence arose that strange expression of death-like rigidity that had so startled Anna.

When they reached home, he helped her out of the carriage, and mastering himself by a supreme effort he bade her good-bye with his customary politeness, and pronounced those words that did not bind him to anything—that he would let her know his decision on the morrow.

His wife's words confirmed his worst suspicions and caused a keen pain in his heart. It was made even keener by that strange sensation of physical compassion he felt for her at the sight of her tears. But when he was left alone in the carriage, to his surprise and joy, he experienced a complete liberation from this compassion as well as from the doubts and pangs of jealousy that had been tormenting him of late.

He felt much like a man who had had a tooth pulled out that had been bothering him for a long time. After an excruciating pain and a sensation as if something enormous, something larger than the head itself had been torn out of his gum, the patient, scarcely believing his own happiness, feels that what has been poisoning his life for so long has ceased to exist and he can once more live, think, and interest himself in something other than his tooth. Such was Alexei Alexandrovitch's feeling. The pain had been strange and terrible, but now that it was over he felt that he could live again and think of something other than his wife.

" Without honour, without heart, without religion; a corrupt woman! I have known it and seen it all along, though I have tried to deceive myself out of pity for her," he said to himself.

And, indeed, it really seemed to him that he had seen it all along. He went over all the details of their past life. Things that had never appeared wrong to him before were now brought up against her to prove how corrupt she was. " I made a mistake in uniting my life with her's," he went on; " but I have done nothing wrong and therefore cannot be unhappy. It is not I who am guilty, but she. But that is no concern of mine. She has ceased to exist for me. . . ."

Whatever might befall either Anna or his son, to whom his feelings had changed, just as they had done towards her, no longer interested him. The only thought that occupied him now was the question how best to shake off the mud she had bespattered him with in her fall. He was anxious to clear himself in the most correct, convenient way possible, which for him could only be a just way, so as to pursue his own honourable, active, useful career.

" I will not allow myself to be made miserable because a contemptible woman has committed a sin; I must merely find the best way out of the difficult position she has placed me in. And I will find it," he said to himself, his face growing darker and darker. " I am not the first, nor the last." And without counting historical examples, beginning with the fair Helen of Menelaus—his memory had lately been refreshed by reading about her—a whole series of contemporary cases in high life, of women who had been unfaithful to their husbands, arose in Alexei Alexandrovitch's imagination. " Daryalov, Poltavsky, Prince Karibanov, Count Paskudin, Dram. . . . Yes, even Dram . . . such a fine, active man . . . Simionov, Chagin, Sigonin," Alexei Alexandrovitch kept on recalling. " It is true these men have always been open to a certain senseless ridicule. I never could see why. I have always looked upon it as a misfortune and pitied them," he said to himself, though this was not quite true. He had never sympathised with misfortunes of this kind, but had always thought more highly of himself whenever a case arose of a woman deceiving her husband. " It is a misfortune that may happen to anybody. It has happened to me. The main question is how best to extricate oneself from the situation." And he called to mind the different ways in which other men in a similar position had acted.

" Daryalov fought a duel. . . ."

When he was a young man the idea of a duel had fascinated Alexei Alexandrovitch, for the very reason that he was not a strong man and was conscious of it. He could not think of a

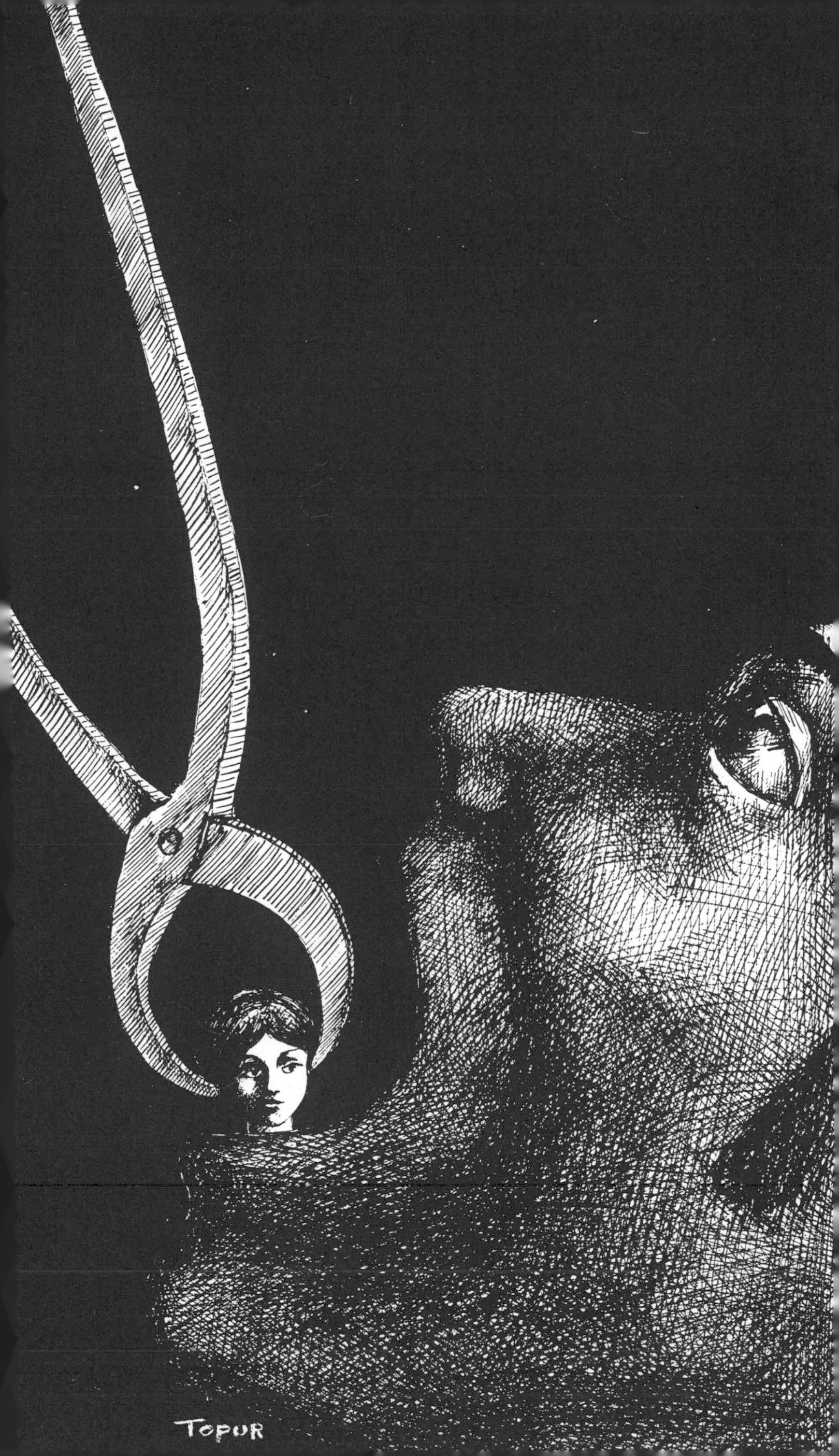
TOPUR

pistol aimed at himself without a feeling of terror and had never handled a weapon in his life. This terror had frequently caused him to dwell on duels in his youth and imagine himself in situations in which he would have to expose his life to danger. Afterwards, when he grew successful and attained a firm position in society, these impressions died away, but the habit of the sentiment prevailed. The terror he felt at his timidity became so strong that he found himself considering the question of a duel from every possible point of view—he fondled the idea, as it were, though he knew all the time that he would not fight.

"Our society is still so barbaric (not at all as in England) that a great many" (among these Alexei Alexandrovitch included people whose opinions he valued) "would look upon a duel with approval. But what good would it do? Supposing I call him out," he went on, vividly picturing to himself the sort of night he would pass after the challenge and the pistol directed against himself. He shuddered and realised that he would never do it. "Supposing I challenge him," he continued; "supposing I learn how to shoot. . . . They will put us in position and I will press the trigger," he said to himself closing his eyes. "And supposing it should turn out that I kill him." Alexei Alexandrovitch shook his head to drive away such foolish thoughts. "What sense is there in killing a man in order to define one's relation to a sinful wife and her boy? It will not solve the question as to what I am to do with her. But what is far more likely, in fact, what is almost sure to happen, is that he would either kill or wound me. I, an innocent man, will be the victim. That would be more senseless still. Besides, would it be honourable on my part to call him out, knowing beforehand that my friends would never allow me to fight? They would never permit the life of a statesman whom Russia needs to be exposed to danger. What would be the result? It would look rather as if I were anxious for the sort of glory that a challenge would give me, knowing quite well that the duel could not come off. That would be dishonest, an attempt to deceive others as well as myself. A duel is out of the question and nobody expects it of me. What I have to do is to clear my reputation so that I can continue my work unhampered." His official activity had always been of immense importance to Alexei Alexandrovitch, but now he seemed to endow it with a special significance.

Having completely disposed of the duel, Alexei Alexandrovitch began to consider the possibility of a divorce—another issue that had been resorted to by some of the men he could think of. He went over all the divorce cases he knew of (and there were many in the very highest circles with which he was familiar), but could not fix on one where the motive had been such as he had in view. In nearly every case the husband relinquished or sold his unfaithful wife, and the very person who on account of her guilt had no right to enter into wedlock, assumed so-called legal relations with her paramour. But Alexei A exandrovitch saw that in his case the attainment of a legal divorce, that is, one whereby the guilty wife could be cast off, was impossible. He knew that the complex conditions of his life, the very refinement of it, made it out of the question to supply the coarse brutal evidence that the law demanded in order to prove a woman guilty. And he knew also that such evidence, even if he could collect it, would probably lower him more than her in the eyes of the world.

An attempt to secure a divorce would only result in a shameful lawsuit that his enemies and scandalmongers generally would not be slow in making use of to injure his high position in society. The main object, that of arranging things with as little disturbance as possible, would not be secured through a divorce. Besides, a divorce, or even the preliminaries towards obtaining it, severed all connection between husband and wife and united her to her lover. In the bottom of his heart, Alexei Alexandrovitch, despite the scorn and indifference that he affected towards his wife, had one keen feeling regarding her—an unwillingness to give her the opportunities for uniting her lot completely with Vronsky, and thus letting her profit by her own guilt. The very thought of it so agitated Alexei Alexandrovitch that he groaned as with an inner pain. His face grew darker, he shifted about in the carriage, and settling down again he wrapped a fluffy rug around his chilly, bony legs.

Another course lay open to him. Instead of resorting to a formal divorce he might follow the examples of Karibanov Paskudin and even honest Dram, who had all merely separated from their wives. He grew calmer as he continued these thoughts. He tried to imagine all the disgrace and shame that would fall upon them even by this latter course, and decided that in a way it would be nearly as bad as the divorce itself. And besides, it would still throw her into Vronsky's arms. " No it is impossible, impossible! " he exclaimed aloud, shifting about in his seat again and drawing the rug closer around him. " I cannot be unhappy, but they ought not to be happy."

The feeling of jealousy that had tormented him during the period of uncertainty had passed away with his wife's words. It had been like having a bad tooth pulled out. But that feeling had given place to another. He was filled with a desire that she should not triumph, but be punished for her guilt. He would not have admitted this feeling to himself, but in the bottom of his heart he longed for her to suffer as a retribution for having destroyed his peace of mind and honour. And again going over the disadvantages of a duel, a divorce, or a separation, Alexei Alexandrovitch came to the conclusion that there was only one course open to him. He must keep her and screen things from the eyes of the world, at the same time adopting every possible measure to cut short her illicit relations with Vronsky. This latter was merely for the sake of punishing her, though he would not have acknowledged it. "I must let her know my decision. I must tell her that, having carefully considered the difficult situation in which she has placed our family, all other issues would be worse for both of us than a nominal *status quo,* and that I am prepared to observe it if she on her part will break off her relations with her lover."

Having made this resolution, Alexei Alexandrovitch began thinking of arguments in favour of it. "That is the only solution in keeping with religion," he said to himself. "I am not merely casting off a sinful woman, but I am giving her the chance of mending her ways. And however hard it may be for me, I will devote my powers to her regeneration and salvation."

Though Alexei Alexandrovitch knew that he could have no moral influence over his wife, and that his attempts at converting her would prove nothing but illusory, though, in his most difficult moments, it had not once occurred to him to seek a guide in religion; now that his decision coincided with what he thought to be the demands of religion, he felt a certain sense of peace and satisfaction. He was glad to think that even in such an important matter as this no one would be able to say that he had acted contrary to the demands of that religion whose banner he had always carried aloft in the midst of the universal apathy and indifference. In considering further details Alexei Alexandrovitch could not see why his relations with his wife could not continue almost the same as ever. Of course he could never respect her again as he had done, but there was no reason why he should ruin his life merely because she had been a bad, unfaithful wife.

"Yes, in time, I do not see why our relations should not be as of old," he said to himself. "That is, things will so arrange themselves that I shall not feel the disorder that has broken into the current of my life. Of course she will not be happy, but that is not my fault. I have done nothing wrong and therefore cannot be unhappy."

XIV

WHEN he reached St. Petersburg, Alexei Alexandrovitch had not only decided on this solution, but had even mentally composed the letter that he would send to his wife. He glanced at the documents and papers from the ministry as he entered the hall and ordered them to be brought to his study.

"Tell them to unharness the horses, and don't receive any one," he said to the porter, with a certain sense of pleasure, showing a happy frame of mind. He laid special stress on the words "don't receive any one."

When he got to his study, Alexei Alexandrovitch walked up and down it once or twice; then stopped before an enormous writing-table on which stood six lighted candles that a footman had brought in. He cracked his fingers, sat down, and began fingering the writing materials. For a moment he remained thoughtful, his elbows resting on the table, his head on his hands; then he began to write, not stopping for a single moment. He did not address her by name in the letter, which he wrote in French, in order to escape from the word "you," that sounded so cold in Russian.

"In our last interview I expressed the intention of communicating to you my resolution concerning the subject of our conversation. Having carefully considered everything, I write to you for the purpose of carrying out my promise. This is my decision: No matter what your acts may be, I do not consider that I have the right to break those bonds by which we have been united from above. The family cannot be broken up by the caprice, the arbitrariness, or even by the guilt of one of the parties concerned. Our life must go on as it has always done. This is necessary for my sake, for you, and for the sake of our child. I feel convinced that you have repented and regret the act that has given rise to this letter, and that you will aid me to destroy absolutely the cause of our estrangement and to forget the past. Otherwise you can well imagine what awaits you and your son. I hope to discuss this more fully at our next interview. As the summer is coming to an end, I would ask you to return to St. Peterburg as soon as possible; in any case not later than next Tuesday. I will see that the house is prepared for you. I beg you to observe that I attach a special importance to the execution of my request.

" A. KARENIN.

" P.S.—I enclose some money that you may need for your expenses."

When he had finished, he read the letter over and was completely satisfied, particularly because of the happy thought of sending the money. There was not a cruel word or a reproach, neither did it savour of leniency. The main thing was the golden bridge for her return. He folded the letter, smoothed it down with a large ivory paper-knife, put it in an envelope with the money and rang the bell. He felt a sense of pleasure that the handling of his perfectly arranged writing materials always gave him.

" Give this letter to the courier to take to Anna Arkadyevna to-morrow," he said, rising.

" Yes, your excellency. Will you have tea in here? "

Alexei Alexandrovitch ordered tea to be brought to him, and playing with the paper-knife he walked over to an arm-chair near which a lamp stood prepared. A French book on the Eugubian inscriptions that he had begun, lay on the table. Above the chair hung an oval portrait of Anna in a gilt frame, painted by a famous artist. Alexei Alexandrovitch fixed his gaze upon it. She looked down at him with those bold, penetrating, mocking eyes of hers, just as she had done on the night of their first explanation. The exquisite piece of black lace on her head, so beautifully painted by the artist, seemed to him especially callous and provoking; so did her lovely white hands covered with rings. Alexei Alexandrovitch shuddered as he looked at the portrait and turned away hastily. He seated himself in the arm-chair and opened his book. He attempted to read, but could not revive the former interest he had felt in the Eugubian inscriptions. His thoughts wandered away, but he was no longer thinking of his wife. His mind was trying to unravel a complication that had arisen in some important matter connected with his official duties that had been bothering him of late. He felt that he had at last penetrated to the very root of the difficulty and could claim without self-conceit that the idea which had taken birth in his mind would save the situation. He would be certain of promotion in his official career, his enemies would be defeated, and at the same time he would be rendering a great service to the state.

As soon as the footman who brought him tea had left the room, Alexei Alexandrovitch went over to his writing-table. He pulled the portfolio containing his current business papers towards him, and with a faint smile of self-satisfaction he took a pencil out of the stand and buried himself in the documents relating to the complication under consideration.

The case was this: the distinguishing trait in Alexei Alexandrovitch's character as a statesman, the thing that separated him from all other government officials, that contributed to his success no less than his honesty, moderation, and self-confidence, was his utter detestation of "red tape." He avoided unnecessary writing as much as possible, and went straight for the business in hand with the greatest expedition and economy.

It happened that in the famous commission of the 2nd of June a question was raised regarding the irrigation of the fields in the province of Zarai, that was under the jurisdiction of Alexei Alexandrovitch's ministry, and formed a striking example of the fruitlessness of "red tape" and undue expenditure. Alexei Alexandrovitch knew that the thing was necessary. The irrigation was begun by his predecessor's predecessor, had already cost a great deal of money, foolishly spent, and yielded no results. When Alexei Alexandrovitch had first taken office he could see at once that the thing was no good and was eager to investigate the matter, but as it involved too many interests and he was not yet sure of his position, he decided to leave it alone. Later on, he became so engrossed in other matters that he forgot all about this. Like most cases of a similar kind, it continued of itself, by the power of inertia so to speak. A great many people earned a living by it, and it was especially useful to a highly respectable, musical family, in which all the girls played on some instrument or other. Alexei Alexandrovitch knew this family well and had given one of the elder daughters away on her marriage.

For a hostile ministry to raise this case did not seem quite the thing to Alexei Alexandrovitch. In every ministry there were cases of this kind which no one dreamt of touching, because it was contrary to the rules of official etiquette. But now that they had thrown down the gauntlet, he took it up boldly and demanded the appointment of a special commission for examining and verifying the work of the commission that dealt with the irrigation of fields in the province of Zarai. And he showed no mercy to these gentlemen. He also demanded a second commission to inquire into the conditions under which alien tribes lived. The question relating to aliens had been raised accidentally in the committee of the 2nd of June and Alexei Alexandrovitch had given it his most energetic support, on the ground that the thing could not be put off, owing to the pitiful condition under which these people existed. This called forth a good deal of opposition from some of the other ministries. The one hostile to Alexei Alexandrovitch tried to make out that the alien tribes were in the most flourishing condition possible, and that any attempt to alter things would only upset them. Besides, if anything was wrong, it was entirely due to the ministry of which Alexei Alexandrovitch was the head, as they could not have carried out the necessary measures prescribed by law. Alexei Alexandrovitch intended to demand, in the first place, that a new commission be appointed, whose duty it would be to investigate the conditions of these aliens on the spot. Secondly, in case their condition be found such as the official data in the hands of the committee represented, that a still further commission be appointed, consisting of learned men, whose duty it would be to go into the causes of this sad state of things with a view to bettering them. They would have to investigate the matter from the following standpoints: (*a*) the political, (*b*) the administrative, (*c*) the economic, (*d*) the ethnographic, (*e*) the material, and (*f*) the religious. Thirdly, the hostile ministry should be requested to furnish information as to what measures had been taken during the last ten years towards alleviating the grievous situation in which these wretched tribes were placed. And, finally, the ministry should be called upon to explain why they had acted in direct opposition to the fundamental and organic law, vol. ——, art. 18, and note to art. 36, as the data in the committee's possession under numbers 17,015 and 18,308 proved them to have done, for a period dating from the 5th of December 1863 to the 7th of June 1864.

A flush of animation spread over Alexei Alexandrovitch's face as he hastily wrote down a summary of these thoughts. After filling a whole sheet of paper, he rose, rang the bell, and sent a note to his secretary asking for certain necessary information. He walked up and down the room, and as his glance fell upon Anna's portrait he frowned and gave a scornful smile. He resumed his book on the Eugubian inscriptions with renewed interest, and at about eleven o'clock he retired. As he lay in bed he recalled the interview with his wife, but it no longer appeared to him in the same gloomy aspect.

XV

THOUGH Anna had been stubborn and resentful in her contradiction of Vronsky, when he had said that her situation was an impossible one, yet in the bottom of her heart she loathed all its falsehood and dishonesty and desired nothing more than to put an end to it. She had been so agitated when returning from the races that in an unguarded moment she had told her husband everything, and in spite of the pain it had caused her she was glad of having done so. When her husband left her, she kept on assuring herself that she was glad, that now at least everything would be clearly defined, and there would be no more lies and deception. The new state of things might be worse, but at any rate there would be nothing underhand about it. The pain that she had caused herself and her husband by her words would be compensated, she thought, by the fact that some definite step would have to be taken. She saw Vronsky that evening, but did not tell him what had happened between herself and her husband, though she ought obviously to have done so if the position was to be made clear.

When she awoke the next morning, the first thing that presented itself to her mind was the words she had spoken to her husband. They seemed to her so terrible now that she could not understand how she could have brought herself to utter anything so strange and brutal. She was at a loss to know what would possibly come of it. But the words had been said and Alexei Alexandrovitch had left without making any reply.

"And I have seen Vronsky and did not tell him. At the moment he was going I wanted to call him back and inform him of everything, but I couldn't. It would have seemed so strange that I had not spoken when he first came in. Why didn't I tell him since I wanted to do so?" And in answer to this question a hot flush of shame spread over her face. She realised why she had not been able to speak—shame had prevented her.

Her situation, which had appeared to her so clear and defined yesterday, now seemed more hopeless than ever. She grew terrified at the disgrace about which she had not thought until now. The very idea of what her husband might do filled her with horror. It seemed to her that any moment their steward would arrive and order her out of the house, and her shame would be proclaimed to the whole world. She asked herself where she would go if she were driven away, but could find no answer.

When she thought of Vronsky, it seemed to her that he no longer loved her, that he was getting tired of her. She felt that she could not go and offer herself to him, and a keen resentment rose in her heart towards him. It seemed to her that the whole world had heard the words she had spoken to her husband, and she kept on repeating them to herself again and again. She had not the courage to meet any of the people in the house. She could not bring herself to ring for her maid, still less to go downstairs and be confronted by her boy and his governess.

The maid, who for a long time had been listening at her mistress's door, at last entered the room. Anna gave her a frightened, questioning look and blushed with shame. The girl excused herself, saying that she thought she had heard the bell. She brought Anna's garments and a note. The note was from Betsy, who informed her that she was expecting Liza Merkalova, the Baroness Stolz, and their admirers, together with old Stremov for a game of croquet that morning. "Be sure to come if only to study manners. I shall expect you," she concluded.

Anna read the note and gave a deep sigh.

"I don't want anything, I don't want anything," she said to Annushka, who was arranging the bottles and brushes on her dressing-table. "You can go away! I shall dress immediately and come down."

Annushka went out, but Anna made no attempt to dress herself. She remained sitting in the same posture with her arms hanging down and head bent. Every now and again she shuddered all over. She wished to make some gesture, to speak, but she merely trembled again. "My God! my God!" she kept on repeating, but the words had no meaning for her. Though she had never doubted the faith in which she had been brought up, the idea of turning to religion for guidance in her present situation was just as much out of the question for her as appealing to Alexei Alexandrovitch himself. She knew beforehand that the consolation offered by religion was possible only by the complete renunciation of that which had grown dearer to her than life. She was not only depressed, but she was seized also by terror at this new mental state of hers that she had never before experienced. Something began to stir in her soul; she seemed to see two sides to everything. Did she fear or desire the past or the future? She could not tell. She did not know what she desired.

" Oh, what am I doing? " she said to herself, suddenly feeling a pain on either side of her head. When she came to herself she realised that she was holding her hair at the temples in both hands and pulling it as hard as she could. She jumped out of bed and began walking up and down the room.

" Coffee is ready, madame, and mamselle and Serioja are waiting," Annushka said, returning and finding her mistress in the same condition.

" Serioja? What about Serioja? " Anna asked suddenly, waking up as the thought of her son struck her for the first time that morning.

" He has been naughty, I think," Annushka replied with a smile.

" What has he done? "

" He stole a peach out of the corner room."

The recollection of her son suddenly roused Anna from the hopeless state she had been in. The sincere though somewhat exaggerated rôle of the devoted mother that she had taken upon herself of late years came back to her mind, and she thought with pleasure that, despite the unbearable situation, she had something peculiarly her own, irrespective of Vronsky or her husband. This was her son. No matter what might happen to her, she could never leave him. Let her husband disgrace her, or turn her out of the house, let Vronsky cease to love her and go on living his own independent life (she again thought of him with reproach and resentment), she would never leave her son. She had an aim in life. And she had to act, to act at once, to secure him, to make quite sure that he would not be taken from her. She must take her boy and go away. That was the one thing she had to do now. She needed calm; she must escape from this torture. The very thought of any step in reference to her son, the thought of going away with him, no matter where, at once soothed her.

She dressed hastily, and with a firm resolute step she went downstairs into the drawing-room where coffee was usually served and Serioja and the governess were waiting for her. Serioja, dressed all in white, was bending over the table under the mirror and with a strained, serious expression, that always reminded Anna of his father; he was busying himself with some flowers that he had brought in.

His governess looked unusually severe.

"Mamma!" Serioja called out in his shrill voice and stopped in indecision. He could not make up his mind whether to abandon the flowers and go to his mother, or finish the wreath he was making and take it to her.

The governess greeted her and began a long circumstantial account of Serioja's wicked deed, but Anna was not listening to her. "Shall I take her too?" she was thinking. "No, I won't. Serioja and I will go alone," she decided.

"It was very naughty," she said aloud, putting her hand on Serioja's shoulder. She looked at him not sternly, but timidly. The boy was confused and delighted as she kissed him. "Will you please leave us together," she said to the astounded governess, and not leaving go of Serioja's hand she sat down at the table where coffee was waiting.

"Mamma! I . . . I . . . I did not. . . ." He attempted to speak, trying to judge by her expression what he might expect for the peach.

"Serioja," she began, as soon as the governess had gone, "it was very naughty of you, but you won't do it again, will you? You love me, don't you?"

She felt the tears coming into her eyes. "As if I can help loving him!" she thought, gazing at his bewildered though delighted face. "And will he be on his father's side and punish me too? Will he not pity me?" The tears were running down her cheeks; in order to conceal them she rose hastily and ran out on the terrace.

Since the last few stormy days the weather had grown cold and clear. In spite of the sun shining through the leaves that were newly washed by the rain the air was keen and chilly.

She shivered both with cold and a new terror that had seized her in the open air.

"Go to Mariette," she said to Serioja who was coming out after her, and began pacing up and down the straw matting that covered the veranda.

"Will they never forgive me? Can they not understand that I could not help myself?" she asked inwardly.

As she stopped to look at the tops of the aspens shaking in the wind, with their bright leaves sparkling in the cold sun, she understood that they would not forgive, that everything and everybody would be just as pitiless to her as that sky and that green foliage. The terrible mood of the early morning took possession of her again.

" I must not think, I must not think," she said to herself. "I must get ready to go. But where? When? Whom shall I take with me? I could go to Moscow by the evening train. I must take Annushka and Serioja and a few necessary things. But I must write to them both first."

She walked quickly into the house, went straight to her boudoir, sat down at a table, and began a letter to her husband.

" After what has happened I can no longer remain in your house. I am going away with Serioja. I do not understand the law and therefore do not know which of us two has the right of keeping him, but I am taking him with me, because I cannot live without him. Be generous and let him stay with me."

Up to this point she wrote quickly and naturally, but her appeal to his magnanimity that she had never acknowledged in him, and the necessity for concluding the letter in a touching manner, arrested her. " I cannot speak of my guilt and repentance, because . . ."

Again she stopped, not being able to connect her thoughts.

" No," she said to herself; " it is not necessary." And tearing up the letter, she wrote another without any reference to his magnanimity.

Another letter had to be written to Vronsky. " I have told my husband," she began and for a long time could not bring herself to go on any further. That was so coarse, so unfeminine. " Besides, what can I say to him? " she asked herself. A flush of shame overspread her face as she recalled his calm self-possession. She felt angry with him and tore the piece of paper on which the sentence was written into tiny shreds. " It is not necessary," she said to herself, and putting away her blotting case she went upstairs, informed the governess and domestics that she was going to Moscow, and began to pack her things.

XVI

In every room of the house, porters, footmen, and gardeners were hurrying to and fro carrying things out. Cupboards and drawers stood open, newspapers were scattered over the floors, and twice some one had been sent to the little shop for packing string. Two trunks, bags, and a bundle of rugs were standing in the hall. A carriage and two coachmen stood at the door. Anna, who during the work of packing had forgotten her inner trouble, was standing by the table in her boudoir putting the last few things into her travelling-bag when Annushka directed her attention to the rumble of an approaching carriage. Anna looked out of the window and saw Alexei Alexandrovitch's courier ringing the bell at the front door.

"Go and see what he wants," she said, as she sat down with a look of resignation and folded her hands over her knees.

A footman brought her a fat packet addressed in Alexei Alexandrovitch's hand.

"The courier has been ordered to wait for an anwser," he said.

"Very well."

As soon as he had gone, she tore open the envelope with trembling fingers. A roll of new bank-notes with a band round them fell out of it. She took out the letter and began reading it at the end. "I will see that the house is prepared for you . . . I attach a special importance to the execution of my request," she read. She went on further, then began from the beginning and read it twice over. She grew cold when she had finished and felt as if some terrible, unlooked-for misfortune had befallen her.

In the morning she had regretted having told her husband and desired nothing more than that the words might be taken back again. And here was a letter that gave her what she had wanted, that looked upon her words as unsaid, yet it appeared to her more terrible than anything she could have imagined.

"He is right! he is right!" she said. "Of course, he is always right. He is a Christian, magnanimous! Yes, a base, low-minded man! Nobody knows it but me, yet I cannot tell any one. They say he is a religious, moral, honest, clever man, but they have not seen what I have seen. They do not know how for eight years he has been crushing every atom of life out of me—every living thing about me—that during all those years he has not once thought of the fact that I am a living woman who needs love. They do not know how he has insulted me at every step and remained completely self-satisfied. Have I not tried my very hardest to find some sort of justification for my life? Did I not try to love him? And my boy, when it became impossible to love his father? But a time came when I knew I could no longer deceive myself, that I was a living human being, who could not exist without love. It is not my fault, God made me like that. And now? Had he attempted to kill me, to kill him, I could have endured it, I could have forgiven. But no, he . . ."

"How could I not foresee what he would do? He will always act in keeping with his despicable character. He will remain in the right and I, poor lost woman, will sink lower and lower . . . 'You can well imagine what awaits you and your son,'" she recollected these words in his letter. "That is a threat to take Serioja away from me, and I dare say according to their stupid laws he has the power to do it. Do I not know why he says that? He does not believe that I love my boy; he has always made fun of and despised my feelings for him. But he knows that I will not forsake him, that I cannot leave him, that life without him would be meaningless to me even with the man I love. He knows so well that in running away and leaving my son I should be acting like a low abandoned woman, and that I have not the courage to do it."

"Our life must go on as it has always done," she recalled another phrase in his letter. "That life was painful enough before; it has been like torture of late; what can it possibly be like in the future? And he knows everything. He knows that I cannot regret what I have done; that I must love just as I must breathe. He knows too that nothing but lies and deception can come of it, but he must go on tormenting me. I know him. He loves to wallow in lies like a fish in water. But I will not let him have that pleasure. I will tear down the cobweb of lies into which he wants to ensnare me. Come what may, anything is better than lies and deception!"

"But how shall I do it? My God, my God! Was there ever a woman more unfortunate than I am? No, I will tear it down! tear it down!" she cried jumping up and trying to hold back her tears. She went up to her writing-table in order to write him another letter. But in the depths of her heart she knew that she had not the courage to tear anything, nor the strength to emerge from her situation, no matter how false and dishonest it might be.

She sat down at the table, but instead of writing, she placed her arms on the table, put her head on them, and began to cry, as only children can cry, her whole body shaking with sobs. She wept because her dream of putting an end to her hopeless situation was destroyed for ever. She knew quite well that everything would go on as before, would, in fact, be worse than before. She felt the position she occupied in society, that had seemed so insignificant to her in the morning, was dear to her after all, and that she would never have the strength to exchange it for the disgraceful one of a woman who had abandoned her husband and child in order to go to her lover. And she knew that no matter how hard she might try she could never be stronger than she was. She would never know what it meant to love freely, but would always remain an unfaithful wife in terror of being disgraced any moment, and would go on deceiving her husband for the sake of a perfect stranger with whom she could never join her fate. She knew that it would be so, but it was so terrible to think of that she could not even imagine how it would all end. And so she wept without restraint, as children weep who have been punished.

The footman's approaching steps brought her to herself. She turned her face away and pretended to be writing.

" The courier is waiting for an answer," the footman said.

" Is he? Well, let him wait. I will ring when I am ready," Anna replied.

" What shall I say to him? " she thought. " What can I decide by myself? What do I know? What do I want? What do I love? " The uncertainty of the morning returned again. The sensation terrified her and she seized upon the first excuse to do something in order to take her out of herself. " I must see Alexei " (thus she always thought of Vronsky); " he alone can tell me what I ought to do. I will go to Betsy's; perhaps I shall see him there," she said to herself, completely forgetting that he had told her the night before that he would not be there as she had not intended to come. She went up to the table and wrote to her husband. " I have received your letter.—A.," was all she said. She rang the bell and gave the note to the footman who answered it.

" We shall not go to-day," she said to Annushka who entered.

" Not at all? "

" No. You need not unpack until to-morrow. I shall want the carriage, I am going to see the princess."

" What dress shall I get ready? "

XVII

THE croquet party to which the Princess Betsy had invited Anna consisted of two ladies and their admirers. These two ladies were the representatives of a select St. Petersburg clique, known as "*Les sept merveilles du monde*" in imitation of another imitation of something else. It is true they belonged to one of the highest circles, but it was quite hostile to the circle in which Anna moved. Besides, old Stremov, an exceptionally influential St. Petersburg personage, and Liza Merkalova's admirer, was, in his official capacity, an enemy of Alexei Alexandrovitch. That was why Anna was not anxious to go, and the hints in Betsy's note had reference to her refusal to come. But now Anna intended going after all, in the hope of seeing Vronsky.

She arrived there before the other guests. At the door she ran across Vronsky's valet, with his well-groomed whiskers, that gave him the air of a page of the bedchamber. He took off his cap, stood on one side, and let her pass. Anna recognised him and immediately recollected that Vronsky had told her he would not be there. Probably he had sent a note excusing himself.

As she took off her cloak in the hall she overheard the valet, who even pronounced his *r*'s like a page of the bedchamber, saying, "From the count to the princess," as he handed the footman a note.

She wanted to ask him where his master was. She wanted to go back and send him a letter, asking him to come to her or go to him herself. But it was impossible to do any of these things. The bell had been rung to announce her arrival, and a footman was already standing at the open door waiting for her to pass into the inner apartments.

"The princess is in the garden; I will tell her immediately."
"Would you like to go into the garden?" a second footman asked in the next room.

She was just in the same state of indefiniteness and uncertainty as she had been in at home—rather worse if anything. She could do nothing here; she could not even see Vronsky; yet she would have to stay there among people so out of keeping with her present mood. But she was dressed in a robe that she knew was becoming to her, and she was not alone. She was surrounded by the usual luxury so familiar to her, and after the first moment she felt more at ease than she had done at home. She had not to consider what she should do next; here everything went on of itself. When she saw Betsy coming towards her in an elegant white gown, Anna greeted her with a smile, as she always did. The princess was walking with Tushkevitch and a girl relative of hers, who much to the delight of her parents had come from the provinces to spend the summer with the famous princess.

There must have been something strange about Anna, for Betsy immediately noticed it.

" I had a bad night," Anna replied, in answer to her question, as she gazed at the footman who was coming towards them with what she thought was Vronsky's note.

" I am so glad you've come," Betsy said. " I feel very tired and would like to have a cup of tea before the others arrive. Won't you take Masha and try the croquet lawn where the grass has been cut? " she said, turning to Tushkevitch. " And you and I will have a cosy chat over our tea, won't we? " She turned to Anna again with a smile, pressing the hand in which she held her parasol.

" I shall be delighted, particularly as I can't stay long. I promised to call on old Madame Vrede; it's ages since I was there," Anna said. Lies, so foreign to her nature, had become not only simple and natural in society, but even pleasant. She could not have explained how she came to say those words; they had not occurred to her until that moment. But Vronsky would not be there; she had to secure her freedom at all costs and try and see him somehow or other. Why she had fixed upon the old maid-of-honour, Madame Vrede, with whom she had no more business than with anybody else, she would have been at a loss to say, but it turned out later that she could not have chosen a better means of meeting Vronsky.

" No, I won't let you go on any account," Betsy replied, gazing fixedly into Anna's face. " Really I should feel quite hurt if I did not love you so much. It seems as though you were afraid that my company might compromise you in some way. Tea in the small drawing-room," she said to the footman, half closing her eyes, as she always did when she spoke to her servants.

She took the note and read it.

" Alexei has disappointed us," she observed in French; " he writes to say that he can't come." She said this in the most simple, natural tone, as if it would never have entered her head to think that Vronsky could be anything more to Anna than merely a partner in a game of croquet. Anna was certain that Betsy knew everything; she only doubted whenever she heard her talk of him in her presence.

"Oh!" Anna said indifferently, as though taking little interest in the matter. "How can your society possibly compromise anybody?" she asked with a smile.

Anna, like most women, enjoyed this play of words, this concealing of a secret. There was no necessity for concealing, nor was there any object gained by it, but the process of concealing itself had a special charm for her.

"I cannot be more Catholic than the pope," she continued. "Stremov and Liza Merkalova are the very cream of society. Then, they are received everywhere, whereas *I*" (she laid special stress on the *I*) "have never been severe or what you may call over-particular. Besides I have no time."

"Don't you care to meet Stremov? Let him break lances with Alexei Alexandrovitch in committee, that does not matter to us. In society he is the most charming man I know and an excellent croquet player. You will see for yourself. In spite of his ridiculous position as Liza's old lover, you should see how well he carries it off. He's perfectly delightful. Do you know Sapho Stolz? Quite a new type."

While Betsy was speaking, Anna could see by her animated intelligent glance that she had divined her situation and was trying to think of a way out. They were in a small boudoir.

"I think I had better drop a line to Alexei," Betsy said, and sitting down at a writing-table she hastily wrote down a few words on a sheet of paper and enclosed it in an envelope. "I am asking him to come to dinner, otherwise one of my ladies will be left without a partner. See if it sounds convincing enough. Excuse me for a moment, I have something to see to. Perhaps you'll be kind enough to seal it and send it off," she added from the door.

Without considering for a moment, Anna sat down at the table, and not reading what Betsy had said she wrote underneath: "I must see you. Come to Madame Vrede's garden; I shall be there at six o'clock." She sealed the envelope and Betsy on her return gave it to a footman in Anna's presence.

And indeed while they were having tea, which was served on a tray-table in the small, cool drawing-room, the two women entered into a cosy chat such as the princess had promised.

They were discussing the various people who were expected The conversation came round to Liza Merkalova.

"She is very nice; I've always liked her," Anna said.

"You ought to; she simply raves about you. She called after the races yesterday and was in despair not to find you here. She says that you are a real heroine out of a novel, and that if she were a man she would commit a thousand follies for your sake. Stremov says that she commits them in any case."

"But tell me, I have never been able to understand," Anna began after a pause, in a tone which showed clearly that she was not putting an idle question, but one that was of greater importance to her than it ought to have been. "Tell me, what are her relations to Prince Kalujsky—Mishka I think every one calls him? I come across them very little. What is there between them?"

Betsy's eyes sparkled; she looked at Anna attentively.

"It is a new fashion," she said. "They've all adopted it lately. They've thrown their caps over the windmill, but there are fashions and fashions in throwing them away."

"But what are her relations to Kalujsky?" Anna persisted.

Betsy burst into a peal of merry laughter, a thing that rarely happened with her.

"You are getting like the Princess Mahky. It is the question of an *enfant terrible*," she said, trying to restrain her laughter, but again breaking into loud merry peals, characteristic of people who rarely laugh. "You should ask them," she added, the tears running down her cheeks.

"You are laughing at me," Anna said, involuntarily becoming infected with Betsy's gaiety, "but I have never been able to understand. What part does the husband play in it all?"

"The husband? Liza Merkalova's husband carries her wraps for her and is always at her beck and call. That is all that we need know, beyond that does not concern us. Just as no one ever dreams of talking about certain details of the toilet in good society, so it is with this."

"Shall you be at the Rolandakys' garden party?" Anna asked to change the subject.

"I don't think so," Betsy replied, and without looking at her companion she began to fill the tiny, transparent cups with fragrant tea. She handed one to Anna, and taking a cigarette she put it into a silver holder, lighted it, and began smoking.

"You see," she continued, quite seriously this time, as she held the tiny cup in one hand, "I am in a most fortunate position. I can understand both you and Liza. Liza is one of those simple natures who can no more understand the difference between right and wrong than a child. At any rate she could not when she was younger. Now I suppose she feels that simplicity is becoming to her and probably does not understand on purpose," Betsy added with a faint smile. "Still, it suits her just the same. Don't you see, you can look at a thing too seriously and make a sort of tragedy out of it, or you can take it quite simply and light-heartedly. Perhaps you are a little given to the tragic side."

"How I should like to know others as well as I know myself," Anna said pensively. "I wonder if I am better or worse? Worse I should think."

"What a child you are! A veritable child!" Betsy remarked. "But here they come."

XVIII

STEPS were heard and a man's voice, then a woman's voice and laughter, and immediately the expected guests made their appearance. Sapho Stolz came in with a young man, brimming over with health, who was known under the name of Vaska. It was evident that a diet of beef, trifle, and Burgundy had agreed with him. Vaska bowed to the ladies, but did not pay any attention to them. He had followed Sapho into the drawing-room and kept following her about in the drawing-room, as though he were tied to her. His brilliant eyes were fastened upon her ready to devour her. Sapho Stolz was a blonde with dark eyes. She came in with a quick rapid step in her high-heeled shoes, and shook hands with the other ladies energetically, like a man. Anna had not yet met this new celebrity, and was struck alike by her beauty, the extravagance of her toilet, and the boldness of her manner. Her head was a veritable scaffolding of false and natural hair of a delicate golden shade, that made it seem in proportion to her full well-shaped bosom, very bare in front. The impetuosity of her motion was such that at every turn the shape of her knees and the upper part of her legs could be seen clearly beneath her garments. In looking at her one wondered where, in that bolstered, wavy mass, her real, shapely little body was hidden.

Betsy hastened to introduce her to Anna.

" What do you think, we nearly ran over two soldiers on the way," she began, smiling and throwing back her train that had got a little to one side. " I was driving with Vaska. . . . Why, of course, you don't know him." She introduced the young man with a blush and laughed at her own mistake in having talked of him by the familiar name of Vaska to a stranger. Vaska bowed to Anna a second time, but did not say a word to her.

" I've won the bet," he said, turning to Sapho; " we got here first. Come, pay up, please," he added with a smile.

Sapho laughed more gaily than ever.

" Not now, surely," she said.

" All right, I'll take it later on."

" Very well. Oh, yes, I've quite forgotten! " she exclaimed, suddenly turning to the hostess. " I've brought you a guest. And here he is."

The unexpected young guest whom Sapho had brought and forgotten, turned out to be such an important person, in spite of his youth, that both the ladies rose to receive him.

He was a new admirer of Sapho's, and like Vaska he followed at her heels.

Soon after Liza Merkalova arrived with Kalujsky and Stremov. Liza Merkalova was a slender brunette with an indolent eastern type of face and glorious, unfathomable eyes. Every one raved about those eyes of hers. The whole tone of her dark toilet struck Anna as being absolutely in keeping with her style of beauty. She was just as soft and languid as Sapho was hard and compact.

But to Anna's taste Liza was much more attractive. Betsy had said of her that she was always trying to act the simple child, but when Anna saw her she felt that this was not true. She really was a sweet, innocent, gentle creature, but frightfully spoiled. It is true she had the same manner as Sapho and, like Sapho, was followed by two admirers, one young and the other old, who seemed to devour her with their gaze, but there was something about her that made her stand out from her surroundings—she shone like a diamond amidst glass. It came out in the sparkle of her beautiful, unfathomable eyes. The weary though intense look in those eyes, surrounded by a dark ring, struck one by its absolute sincerity. A single look into those eyes of hers seemed to reveal her through and through, and you could not help loving her. A glad smile lighted up her face when she saw Anna.

" Oh, I am so glad to see you! " she exclaimed going up to her. " I was just about to go and speak to you at the races yesterday when you went away. And I did so want to see you! Wasn't it awful? " she said, looking at Anna with that glance that revealed her whole soul.

" Yes, I never thought it would be so exciting," Anna said, blushing.

They all rose to go out into the garden.

" I don't think I shall come," Liza said with a smile, sitting down beside Anna. " You won't go, will you? I can't see the fun in playing croquet."

" But I like it," Anna remarked.

" Now tell me, how do you manage to keep so bright? It does one good to look at you. I am bored while you seem all alive."

" You bored? Why, you are the jolliest company in St. Petersburg," Anna said.

" Perhaps those who are not of our company are even more bored still, but we, at any rate I, am not at all jolly; I am horribly, hopelessly bored."

Sapho lighted a cigarette and went out into the garden with the two young men; Betsy and Stremov remained at the tea table.

" How can you say that? " Betsy exclaimed.

" Sapho says that they spent the jolliest evening possible at your house yesterday."

" Oh, it was awful! " Liza said. " They all came back with me after the races. The same everlasting crowd, doing the same everlasting things. We sat about on sofas all the evening. What is there jolly about that? No, you must tell me what you do to keep from being bored," she said, turning to Anna again. " It is enough to look at you and you see at once that here is a woman who may be happy or unhappy, but who never feels bored. Tell me how you do it? "

" But I don't do anything," Anna said, confused by these persistent questions.

" That is much the best way," Stremov remarked. He was a man of about fifty, slightly grey, though still fresh, very ugly, but had a powerful, intellectual face. Liza Merkalova was his wife's niece and he spent every moment of his spare time in her company. Like the man of the world that he was, he tried to be particularly amiable to Anna, the wife of his enemy Alexei Alexandrovitch.

" To do nothing," he said with a faint smile, " is by far the best means. I have told you all along," he added, turning to Liza, " that in order not to feel bored you must not think about it, just as you must not be afraid of not going to sleep when you are troubled with insomnia. That is what Anna Arkadyevna meant."

" Indeed, I should have been proud to have inferred that; it is not only clever, but true," Anna observed with a smile.

" No, you must tell me why we can't fall asleep and why we can't help feeling bored."

" To sleep you must work, and to be happy you must work."

" But how can I work when my work is of no use to anybody? I can't pretend and wouldn't on any account."

" You are incorrigible," Stremov said, not looking at her, but turning to Anna again. He rarely met Anna and could not therefore talk of any but the most superficial things to her. He asked her when she was returning to St. Petersburg, told her what a great deal the Countess Lydia Ivanovna thought of her, and all with an air that showed how much he wanted to be agreeable to her, to express his respect and even more than respect.

Tushkevitch came in and announced that they were all waiting for them to come and play croquet.

" Oh, don't go yet," Liza Merkalova implored when she heard that Anna was leaving. Stremov joined her.

" The contrast is too great," he said, " between our company and that of old Madame Vrede. Besides, for her you will be only an object for slander; while here you awake very different sentiments."

Anna was undecided for a moment. The flattery of this witty man, the naive childish sympathy shown her by Liza Merkalova, the pleasant social atmosphere was so different from what awaited her, that she hesitated. Could she not postpone the terrible moment of explanation? But remembering what was in store for her when she reached home, alone, without having come to some definite decision, recollecting how in the morning she had clutched her hair in both her hands, she took leave hastily and departed.

XIX

VRONSKY, in spite of the seemingly frivolous, worldly life he led, was a man who hated disorder. When still a youth in the Corps of Pages, he had once suffered the humiliation of being refused a loan he had asked of a friend when short of money, and since then had determined never to place himself in such a position again.

For the purpose of keeping his affairs straight he withdrew himself about four or five times a year, according to circumstances, in order to clear them up. He called it " putting his house in order," or "*faire la lessive.*"

On the morning after the races, Vronsky awoke late, and without shaving or taking his bath he got into his dressing-gown, put all his money, accounts, and letters on the table and set to work.

Petritsky knew that on these occasions his comrade was not in the best of tempers, and when he awoke and saw him sitting at the writing-table, he dressed quietly and went out so as not to disturb him.

Every man who is familiar with the complexity of the conditions surrounding him, and is capable of mastering them, has a feeling somewhere that both the conditions and the capacity are peculiarly his own. He seems to think that others would not have been able to extricate themselves from the difficult situations he has experienced, completely overlooking the fact that others, like him, have their own personal complexities and difficulties. So it seemed to Vronsky. And not without a certain inward pride, nor entirely without reason, did he feel that any other man in his position would have made a mess of things generally.

That day he felt it more essential than ever that he should put his affairs in order. First, because the easiest thing to do, he began going over his accounts, to ascertain his financial position. In his fine hand he wrote down his various debts on a sheet of paper, and on adding them up discovered that they amounted to seventeen thousand and some odd hundred roubles. He dispensed with the latter so as to have a clear round sum to deal with. After counting his ready money and the amount still remaining at the bank, he found that there were only eighteen hundred roubles left, and no prospects of getting any more before the new year. He glanced over his debts again and divided them into three different lists. In the first he wrote down all the debts that had to be paid at once, or at any rate as soon as they were asked for. They amounted to about four thousand roubles. Fifteen hundred for a horse and two thousand five hundred as security for his young comrade Venevsky, who had lost it to a cheat in Vronsky's presence. Vronsky had wanted to pay the money then on the spot, as he had it about him, but Venevsky and Yashvin insisted that they would pay it, as Vronsky had not been playing at all. That was all very fine, but Vronsky knew that though he had only verbally agreed to stand as security for Venevsky in that rascally affair, he must have the money ready to pay that cheat so as to finish with him completely. The four thousand roubles in the first list were absolutely necessary. The second list, not so important, mounted up to some eight thousand roubles. Most of this was owing to the stables, the hay dealer, the Englishman, the harness-maker, and so on. Of this, too, some two thousand would have to be paid immediately to clear his mind. The last list, consisting of tradesmen's and hotel bills, did not worry him in the least. In all six thousand roubles for current expenses were absolutely necessary, and he had only about one thousand eight hundred.

For a man with an income of one hundred thousand roubles a year, at which Vronsky's fortune was estimated by everybody, such trifling debts would seem to be nothing, but the trouble was, that he was far from having that income. His father's huge estate, that brought in about two hundred thousand roubles a year, had been divided between the two brothers. When the elder, laden with debts, married the penniless daughter of a Dekabrist, the Princess Varia Chirkov, Alexei yielded him his share of their father's inheritance, reserving only an income of twenty-five thousand roubles a year for himself. He told his brother that it would be sufficient for his needs till he married, and that that was never likely to happen. His brother, colonel of one of the most expensive regiments in the service, who had just taken upon himself the further expense of a wife, could not refuse the gift. Their mother, who had some property of her own, used to allow Alexei another twenty thousand roubles a year, but he always spent the whole of it. Lately, having quarrelled with him about his relations with Anna and his sudden departure from Moscow, she left off sending him money. In consequence of this, Vronsky, who had arranged his life on a scale of forty-five thousand roubles a year, found himself suddenly reduced to twenty-five. Hence his embarrassing situation. He was too proud to ask his mother for money. In yesterday's letter she had been particularly irritating. She had intimated that she was ready to help him in his career and in the service, but not to lead a life that scandalised all decent society. His mother's attempt to bribe him had wounded him to the depths of his soul, and he felt more coldly towards her than ever.

He could not take back the promise he had given his brother, though he felt now, in view of his rather uncertain relations with Anna, that it had been given too hastily. He could well see that even though he was a bachelor the hundred thousand roubles a year might stand him in good stead. But there was nothing to be done. He had only to think of his brother's wife, that dear sweet Varia, who never lost an opportunity of letting him know how much she appreciated his generosity, to realise how impossible it was to take back what he had given. It would have been as bad as striking a woman, stealing, or lying. There was only one thing he could do, and he decided upon it without a moment's hesitation. He would borrow ten thousand roubles from a money-lender, a thing that could be done easily enough. Further, he would cut down his expenses in general and sell his race horses. Having decided upon this, he immediately wrote a note to Rolandiky who had more than once offered to buy his horses. After that he sent for the Englishman and a money-lender, and apportioned the ready money he had according to the list. This done, he wrote a sharp, cold reply to his mother's letter. Then he took out Anna's last three notes from his pocket-book, read them over, and burned them. Recollecting their conversation of yesterday, he grew pensive.

XX

VRONSKY's life was peculiarly happy, because he had formed a code of rules by which he regulated all his actions, so that he always knew what to do and what not to do. This code embraced only a limited circle of duties; but as they were strictly determined, and Vronsky never had occasion to go outside this circle, he was never uncertain as to the course of action he had to take. The code prescribed that it was essential to pay a gambling debt, but not a tailor; that it was wrong to lie to men, but allowable to women; that it was wrong to deceive any one except a husband; that an insult should not be endured, but that you had a right to insult others, and so on, and so on. All these rules might be senseless and bad, but they were indubitable, and in observing them Vronsky felt that he could hold his head high. Later, however, on account of his relations to Anna, he began to feel that this code did not embrace all conditions of life, and that in the future doubts and perplexities might present themselves to which it did not apply.

His present relations to Anna and her husband were perfectly clear and simple. They were precisely determined in the code of rules by which he was guided. She was an honourable woman who had given him her love and he loved her. That alone gave her every right to his respect, even more than if she had been his legal wife. He would sooner have given his right hand than permit himself to hurt her by word or deed, or by not showing her all the esteem and regard to which a woman might feel she was entitled.

His relations to society were also quite clear. All might know or suspect his intimacy with Anna, but no one must dare to speak of it. At the first hint he was prepared to silence the talker, to make him respect the imaginary honour of the woman he loved.

Clearest of all were his relations to her husband. From the moment that Anna gave him her love, Vronsky began to look upon her as his very own; the husband was merely a superfluous person, horribly in the way. Of course he was to be pitied, but what could be done about it? He was always at liberty to demand satisfaction with a weapon in his hand if he chose, and Vronsky had been prepared for that from the first moment.

Latterly something new had cropped up in his relations to Anna that frightened Vronsky by its uncertainty. Yesterday she had told him that she was pregnant, and he felt that this news, and what she expected of him, demanded something that was not fully defined in the code of rules by which his life was guided. He had been completely taken off his guard, and in the first moment, when she had informed him of her situation, his heart had prompted him to ask her to leave her husband. Now, on reflection, he felt that it would be better to do without that, yet while assuring himself of it, he could not help feeling that it was a little mean.

" If I asked her to leave her husband, that meant that she

was to come to me. Am I prepared for it? How can I take her away now when I have no money? Of course I could get some, but how can I go away with her whilst I'm in the service? I have asked her and must be prepared. I must get the money and resign my commission."

He became thoughtful. The question of resigning his commission brought him to another question, known to no one but himself, that formed the principal interest of his life.

Ambition had been the dream of his boyhood and youth—a dream that he never acknowledged even to himself, but it was nevertheless so strong that it fought with his love. His entrance into society and the army had been extremely promising, but two years ago he had made a serious blunder. Wishing to show his independence, in spite of the fact that he wanted promotion, he refused a position that was offered to him, imagining that his refusal would enhance his value. But it turned out quite otherwise. His action had proved too bold, and since then he had been neglected. Having unwittingly gained the reputation of an independent man, he tried to carry it off as well as he could, and bore himself as if he felt no grudge against any one and was only anxious to be left in peace, because life was so jolly. In reality he had left off being jolly even before his journey to Moscow. The reputation he had gained of an independent man, who could do anything and chose to do nothing, was wearing off, and a great many people were beginning to think that he could do nothing more than be a jolly good fellow. His connection with Anna, that had caused so much stir and directed universal attention to him, had for a time lulled the gnawing worm of ambition within him, but about a week ago it had been rudely awakened.

Serpuhovsky, the friend of his childhood, belonging to his own circle, his schoolmate, who had graduated with him and had been his rival in the class-room, in the gymnasium, in his pranks and ambitions—this same Serpuhovsky had just returned from Central Asia, where he had been twice promoted, and had received honours rarely accorded to such young generals.

His appearance created quite a sensation in St. Petersburg, and people began to talk of him as a rising star of the first magnitude. He, Vronsky's chum and messmate, was already a general, expecting an appointment that would give him great influence in the affairs of the country, while Vronsky, despite his independence and success in society, and the fact that he was loved by a beautiful woman, was merely a captain, permitted to remain as independent as he pleased.

" Of course I don't envy Serpuhovsky, but his case proves that a man like me has only to wait for the propitious moment, and his career may be made in a short time. Three years ago he was in exactly the same position in which I am now. By resigning my commission I burn my own ships. Remaining in the army I lose nothing. And she told me herself that she did not wish to change anything. With her love I cannot envy Serpuhovsky." He twirled his moustache slowly, rose from the table, and began walking up and down the room. His eyes sparkled with a peculiar lustre; he was conscious of that calm, joyful state of mind that always came over him after putting his affairs in order. He had a cold bath, shaved, dressed, and went out.

XXI

" I HAVE come to fetch you," Petritsky greeted him, coming in. " Your house cleaning lasted a long time to-day. Have you finished? "

" Quite," Vronsky replied, with a twinkle in his eye, as he continued slowly twirling his moustache. It seemed as though he felt that any quick, rash action might destroy the effects of his work.

" After this performance you always look as if you've come out of a bath," Petritsky remarked. " I've come from Gritsky's " (that was how they called their colonel), " they are waiting for you."

Vronsky made no reply, but continued looking at his comrade and thinking of something else.

" Does that music come from his place? " he asked, as he caught the sound of brass instruments playing a waltz. " What is going on there? "

" Serpuhovsky has arrived."

" Really? " Vronsky said. " I didn't know."

His eyes sparkled more than ever. Having decided once and for all that he would sacrifice his ambition to his love, Vronsky was no longer envious of Serpuhovsky. He did not feel in the least bit annoyed that he had not come to him first. Serpuhovsky was an old friend and he would be delighted to meet him again.

" I am very glad," he said.

Demin, their colonel, occupied a large manor-house. The whole company was assembled on the spacious veranda when Vronsky got there. What first caught his eye as he reached the courtyard were the singers in blouses, standing near a barrel of vodka, and the jolly figure of the colonel surrounded by officers. He was standing on the first step of the veranda, shouting and gesticulating to some soldiers at the side. His voice could be heard above the band, playing a quadrille of Offenbach's. A group of soldiers, a sergeant-major, and several under officers walked up to the veranda at the same time as Vronsky. The colonel approached the table, came back with a glass in his hand, and proposed the toast, "To our late comrade and brave general, Prince Serpuhovsky. Hurrah!"

Serpuhovsky, smiling and holding a glass in his hand, came out after the colonel.

"Why, Bondarenka, you are getting younger than ever!" he said to the sergeant-major, a ruddy-cheeked soldier, serving his second term, who was standing right in front of him.

Vronsky had not seen Serpuhovsky for three years. He looked more manly, having allowed his whiskers to grow, but was just as slender and striking, not so much by the beauty of his features as by a certain gentleness and nobility in his whole bearing. There was one change that Vronsky observed in him, and that was a soft happy radiance, generally seen on the faces of successful men sure of having their importance recognised by everybody. Vronsky was familiar with this trait, and instantly noticed it in Serpuhovsky.

As he came down the steps, Serpuhovsky caught sight of Vronsky and a glad smile lighted up his face. He nodded and waved his glass to him, meaning to show that he could not go to him until he had disposed of the sergeant, who had already straightened himself and composed his lips for a kiss.

"Why, here he is!" the colonel exclaimed. "And Yashvin said you were in one of your bad moods."

Serpuhovsky kissed the dashing sergeant on his moist, fresh lips, and wiping his own with his pocket-handkerchief he went up to Vronsky.

"I am glad to see you!" he said, pressing his hand as he drew him to one side.

"Look after him," the colonel called to Yashvin, pointing to Vronsky, as he walked down the steps to join the soldiers.

"Why were'nt you at the races yesterday?" Vronsky asked, taking stock of Serpuhovsky; "I had hoped to see you there."

"I got there rather late. I'm sorry. Please divide this among the men," he added turning to an adjutant. He hastily drew out of his pocket-book three one-hundred rouble notes and handed them to him, his face flushing red.

"Vronsky, would you like anything to eat or drink?" Yashvin asked. "I say, quick there! get something ready for the count! And drink this, will you?"

The revelling at the colonel's lasted for a long time. They drank a great deal. Serpuhovsky was swung and tossed in a blanket. The same performance was repeated on the colonel, who afterwards danced with Petritsky in front of the singers. When he grew rather tired he sat down on a seat outside and began a long discussion with Yashvin on Russia and Prussia, trying to prove the former's superiority, especially in cavalry charges. The revellers became quiet for a moment. Serpuhovsky went into the house to wash his hands and discovered Vronsky there sponging himself with water. He had removed his shirt and with his head under the tap was rubbing his powerful neck. Having finished their ablutions they sat down on a couch and entered into a conversation of great interest to both of them.

"I've heard all about you from my wife," Serpuhovsky began. "I'm glad you've seen a good deal of her."

"She is a friend of Varia's and they are the only two women in St. Petersburg whom I care to see," Vronsky said with a smile. He smiled because he foresaw the subject the conversation was drifting towards, and it gave him a sense of pleasure.

"The only ones?" Serpuhovsky asked, smiling also.

"I have heard about you, too, from others besides your wife," Vronsky said, ignoring the hint with a stern expression on his face. "I was glad to hear of your success and was not at all surprised. I expected even more."

Serpuhovsky smiled. He felt flattered, but did not wish to show it.

"On the other hand, to tell you the truth, I did not expect so much. Still, I am very glad. I confess I am very ambitious. It is a great weakness of mine."

"You would probably not have confessed it had your ambitions not been realised," Vronsky observed.

"Perhaps not," Serpuhovsky replied. "I don't say that life would not be worth living without success, but it would be extremely uninteresting. Of course, I may be mistaken, but it seems to me that I possess the qualities necessary in the sphere of action that I have chosen, and that power of any kind would be better entrusted in my hands than in those of many people I know," he continued, beaming with self-satisfaction. " On that account the nearer I get to what I want the more pleased I am."

" It may be true for you, but not for everybody. I used to think the same at one time, but I find there are other things in the world besides ambition."

" There you are! " Serpuhovsky said with a smile. " I've heard about your refusal. . . . Of course I agreed with you, but there is a way of doing everything. The thing itself was not bad, but you did it tactlessly."

" What is done can't be undone, and you know I never regret my actions. Besides, I'm quite happy as I am."

" Yes, for a time, but you will not always be. You are not like your brother. He is a dear child just like our host. There he is! " he added as a shout of " hurrah! " reached them from without. " He goes about enjoying himself, but that will hardly satisfy you."

" I did not say I was satisfied."

" Besides, that is not the only thing. Men like you are needed."

" By whom? "

" By whom? By society, by Russia. Our country needs men, needs a party, otherwise everything will go to the dogs."

" What do you mean? Something like Bertenev's party against the Russian communists? "

" Oh, no," Serpuhovsky said with a frown, annoyed that any one should have accused him of such foolishness. " *Tout ça est une blague*. That has always been and always will be. There are no communists. Intriguing people must always invent some dangerous party. That is an old trick of theirs. What I mean is a powerful party consisting of independent men like you and me."

" But what for? " Vronsky named several men in power. " Are they not independent? "

" Yes, in a way. Only they have not always been independent. They have no families; they were not born near the sun as we were. They can be bought by money or flattery. To keep in power they have to invent some sort of policy, usually a bad one. They themselves have no faith in it, but they carry it out because their salaries depend on it. *Cela n'est pas plus fin que ça* when you study their game. It may be that I am worse and more stupid than they, though I do not see why I should be. You and I have this important advantage over them—it is harder to buy us. And such men are needed now more than ever."

Vronsky listened attentively. It was not so much the contents of his words that held him, as the fact that Serpuhovsky was already battling with the powers that be, that he was beginning to have his sympathies and antipathies in the great world, while for him there existed only the interests of his squadron. He felt what a powerful figure Serpuhovsky would make with his fine understanding, his clear-headedness, and his gift of oratory, so rarely met with amongst the people with whom he lived. And do what he would he could not help feeling envious.

" But you see, I lack the one important thing," he said, " the desire for power. I once had it, but it is gone."

" Excuse me, that is not true," Serpuhovsky said with a smile.

" Oh, yes, it is! just now at any rate," Vronsky added, " to be quite frank."

" That is another matter. *Now* does not mean for ever."

" Perhaps not," Vronsky replied.

" You seem in doubt about it," Serpuhovsky continued, divining his thought, " but I know it for certain. That is why I wanted to see you. You acted as you should have done, but I don't think you ought to persevere in that course. I only ask you to give me *carte blanche* . . . I am not patronising you, though I have a perfect right to do so; you have patronised me often enough! But I hope our friendship is above that. Come," he said with a smile as tender as a woman's, " give me *carte blanche*, leave your regiment, and I will draw you in imperceptibly."

" But don't you see, I want nothing more than that things should remain as they are."

Serpuhovsky rose and confronted him.

" Of course I know what that means, but listen to me. We are both of the same age, though perhaps you have known women for longer than I have . . ." Serpuhovsky's smile and gesture seemed to say that Vronsky need have no fear that he would touch the sensitive spot rudely. " But I am married, and as some one or other has written, the man who loves and knows his wife understands women better than if he had known a thousand."

" In a minute," Vronsky said to an officer who had looked in at the door to say that the colonel wanted them. He was now eager to hear what Serpuhovsky had to say to him.

" Here is my candid opinion. Women are the principal stumbling-block in the way of a man's activity. It is difficult to love a woman and do something at the same time. There is only one way to love with comfort and without hindrance, and that is—marriage. How can I explain what I mean? " Serpuhovsky asked, who was fond of metaphor. " I have it. Supposing you had to carry a *fardeau* and wanted your hands free, you could only get that by having the *fardeau* tied to your back. So it is with marriage. I only discovered it after I married. My hands suddenly became empty. But if you attempt to carry this *fardeau* without marriage you will find that your hands are so full that you cannot do anything else. Just look at Masankov and Krupov. They have ruined their careers over women."

" And such women! " Vronsky put in, recollecting a certain Frenchwoman and an actress who had been the mistresses of these two men.

" Unfortunately, the higher a woman's position in society the worse it is. Pulling the *fardeau* away from another man is perhaps more difficult than carrying it yourself."

" You have never loved," Vronsky said softly, as he gazed straight before him and thought of Anna.

" Perhaps not, but try and remember what I've told you. There is one other thing; women are more material than men. We make something immense out of love, but they are always *terre-à-terre*."

" All right, coming," he said, turning to a footman who had entered. But the man had not come to summon them, he had brought a note for Vronsky.

" From the Princess Tversky," he said, handing it to him.

Vronsky tore open the note and blushed.

" My head aches; I think I'll go home," he said to Serpuhovsky.

" Well, good-bye. You'll give me *carte blanche*, won't you? "

" We'll talk it over later. I shall look you up in St. Petersburg."

XXII

It was nearly six o'clock. Anxious to get to his appointment in time without using his own horses that were well known to everybody, Vronsky got into Yashvin's hired carriage and ordered the coachman to drive as fast as possible. It was a spacious old vehicle with room for four. He sat down in one corner, stretched his legs on the seat opposite, and began to think.

The dim consciousness of having put his affairs in order, together with the recollection of Serpuhovsky's friendship and flattery, and above all the coming interview, all combined to make him feel a keen sense of the joy of living. The sensation was so strong that he smiled involuntarily. He removed his legs from the seat, crossed one knee over the other, passed his hand over the calf of the leg he had hurt in the fall yesterday, and leaning back drew in several deep draughts of the fresh air.

"Good, very good," he said to himself. He had frequently felt the delightful consciousness of his own body, but never before had he loved himself as he did now. It gave him pleasure to feel the slight pain in his powerful leg, and he liked the sensation of his chest heaving as he breathed. The same clear, cool, August day that had so depressed Anna seemed to him wonderfully bracing. It refreshed his face and neck, that still glowed from the reaction of the wash. The odour of brilliantine from his moustache was pleasant to him in the fresh air. Everything that he saw from the carriage window, in the pale light of the dying day, appeared to him just as fresh, happy, and strong as he himself. The roofs of the houses shining in the setting sun, the sharp outlines of fences and corner buildings, the forms of occasional pedestrians and carriages, the motionless leaves, the green grass, the fields with their straight rows of potatoes, the slanting shadows from the houses, trees, and bushes—everything was beautiful, like an exquisite landscape fresh from the artist's hand.

"Faster, faster!" he said to the coachman, putting his head out of the window and handing him a three-rouble note that he had taken out of his pocket-book. The coachman's hand was heard fumbling near the lamp, there was a loud crack of a whip, and the carriage flew over the smooth, even road.

"I want nothing, nothing but this happiness," he said to

himself, with his gaze fixed on the bone bell-push between the two windows, while his imagination pictured Anna as he had last seen her. "The more I know her the better I love her. Here is Vrede's house and garden. But where is she? Where? Why did she appoint a meeting here? And why did she write on Betsy's note?" he thought, as these things struck him for the first time. But there was no time to think. He gave a sign to the coachman to stop before they reached the drive, and springing out of the carriage while it was still in motion, he went up the avenue that led to the house. The avenue seemed deserted, but turning to the right he caught sight of Anna. Her face was covered by a thick veil, but with joy he immediately recognised her characteristic gait, the slope of her shoulders, the poise of her head. An electric current ran through him. With new intensity he felt conscious of his own body, of every movement he made. When they drew close to each other Anna pressed his hand.

"You are not angry that I asked you to come? It was essential that I should see you," she began, and her lips, sternly set together, that he could see through her veil, completely changed his mood.

"I angry? But how did you get here and where are you going?"

"Never mind," she said, taking his arm, "come, I have something to tell you."

He felt that something had happened and that their interview would not be a happy one. He had no will of his own in her presence. Without knowing the cause of her agitation it involuntarily communicated itself to him.

"What is the matter? What has happened?" he asked, pressing her arm with his elbow and peering into her face to read her thoughts.

She walked a few steps in silence to gain courage, then suddenly stopped.

"I did not tell you last night," she began, breathing quickly, "that on my way home with Alexei Alexandrovitch I told him everything. . . . I told him that I could no longer be his wife, that . . . I told him everything."

He listened, bending over her tenderly as though he wished to lighten the difficulty of her position. As soon as she finished he drew himself up and his face assumed a stern, proud expression.

"Yes, yes, it's a thousand times better. I understand how

hard it must have been," he said. But she was not listening to his words; she was watching the expression of his face. She did not know that the expression arose from the first thought that occurred to him, about the inevitableness of a duel. The idea of a duel never entered her mind, and so she interpreted the sudden severity otherwise.

With the receipt of her husband's letter she had known in the depths of her heart that she would not be strong enough to give up her position, to abandon her child, in order to go to her lover. The morning spent at the Princess Betsy's had confirmed her in this. Still, the meeting was of great importance to her. She had hoped somehow that this interview would change their position and save her. If upon hearing these news he had said with determination and passion, without a moment's wavering, "Leave everything and come away with me," she would have gone. But the news produced an effect that she had not expected. He seemed to be offended about something.

"It was not at all hard; it happened of itself," she said irritably. "Here is . . ." She produced her husband's letter.

"I know, I know," he interrupted her. He took the letter, but did not read it. "The one thing I wanted, the one thing I prayed for," he went on trying to comfort her, "was to put an end to this situation and devote my life to your happiness."

"Why do you say that?" she asked. "Can I doubt it? If I were not sure . . ."

"Who is that coming?" Vronsky asked, indicating two ladies who were walking towards them. "Perhaps they know us!" He drew her hastily down a side path.

"Oh, it makes no difference to me," she said, her lips trembling. It seemed to him that her eyes looked at him from behind the veil with a peculiar resentment. "That has nothing to do with it. I cannot doubt that. But see what he writes. Read the letter." And again she stopped.

Just as in the first moment when he heard of the rupture with her husband, Vronsky, while reading the letter, again abandoned himself to the sensations aroused in him by the injured man. As he held the letter in his hand, he instinctively thought of the challenge he would find at his house either to-day or to-morrow, and of the duel itself. He pictured to himself how with a cold and haughty mien he would stand in front of his adversary, and after having fired into the air would await the fatal shot of the outraged husband. The thought of what Serpuhovsky had told him about not involving himself, and his own reflections of the morning, flashed across his mind. But he could not communicate these thoughts to Anna.

When he finished the letter he raised his eyes to hers, but there was no firmness in his glance. She felt at once that he had thought it over before. She knew that no matter what he might tell her, he would not say all that was in his mind. Her last hope was shattered. It was not what she had expected.

"You see what kind of a man he is," she said, her voice trembling; "he . . ."

"Forgive me, but I am glad of it," Vronsky interrupted her. "For Heaven's sake, let me explain," he begged, with an imploring glance. "I am glad because things cannot possibly remain as he wants them to."

"Why not?" Anna asked, trying to restrain her tears. It was evident that she no longer attached importance to his words. She felt that her fate had been decided.

Vronsky wanted to add that after the inevitable duel the position could not last, but he said something different.

"It cannot possibly continue. I hope that now you will leave him. I hope . . ." He became embarrassed and blushed. "I hope that you will allow me to arrange and plan our future life together. To-morrow . . ."

She did not allow him to finish. "But my child?" she cried. "You see what he writes! It will mean leaving him and I cannot and will not do it."

"But, for Heaven's sake, what is better, to leave your boy or to continue this humiliating situation?"

"Humiliating for whom?"

"For everybody concerned and more than all for yourself."

"Humiliating. . . . Don't say such things. Such words have no meaning for me," she said in a trembling voice. She longed to hear him speak what was absolutely in his mind. Only his love was left to her and she wanted to go on loving him. "You must understand that everything changed for me from the day I first loved you. I have nothing left in the world but your love. So long as it is mine I feel myself so high and firm that nothing can be humiliating to me. I am proud of my position, because . . . proud of . . . proud . . ." She could not finish. Tears of shame and despair choked her voice. She burst out crying.

He too felt a lump rising in his throat. For the first time in his life he was ready to cry. He would not have been able to say what had touched him so. He was sorry for her; he could not help her and at the same time he felt conscious that he was the cause of her unhappiness, that he had done something wrong.

" Is not a divorce possible? " he asked faintly.

She shook her head, but made no reply.

" Why can't you take your boy and leave him? "

" That depends on him. I must return to him now," she said dryly. Her presentiment that everything would remain as of old had not deceived her.

" On Tuesday I shall be in St. Petersburg and everything will then be decided."

" Very well," she said. " Don't let us talk of this any more."

Anna's carriage that she had dismissed and ordered to come back for her at the gate of Madame Vrede's garden, drove up at this moment. She took leave of Vronsky and departed for home.

XXIII

On Monday the general meeting of the commission of the 2nd of June took place. Alexei Alexandrovitch entered the committee-room, exchanged greetings with the members and chairman as usual, sat down in his seat and put his hand on the papers spread out before him. Among them lay the necessary references and hasty notes of the proposals he intended introducing. He had little need of them. He remembered everything and did not even feel it necessary to consider what he should say beforehand. He knew that when the time came, and he was confronted by the face of his adversary endeavouring to assume an expression of indifference, his speech would flow much more freely than if he had prepared it. He felt that the contents of his speech would be so great that every word would have a special significance. But as he sat there listening to the reading of the customary report, he wore a most harmless, innocent expression. No one would have dreamt by looking at his white hands with the veins standing out, the long fingers of which were playing with the edges of the sheet of white paper in front of him, nor by his head, bent a little to one side with an expression of fatigue, that in a few minutes his lips would pour forth a speech that would create a terrible storm, cause the members to interrupt each other rudely, and the chairman to call for order.

When the report was finished Alexei Alexandrovitch announced in his quiet, thin voice that he had a few suggestions to make regarding the condition of alien tribes. All attention was directed towards him. Alexei Alexandrovitch cleared his throat, and without looking at his adversary, according to his habit he selected the person nearest him, who turned out to be a little, meek old man, who never had a word to say for himself, and began expounding his views. When he reached the subject of the fundamental and organic law, his adversary, no longer able to contain himself, jumped up and began a series of objections. Stremov, who was also a member of the commission, was touched to the quick and sought to justify himself. In general the session proved to be extremely stormy. But Alexei Alexandrovitch triumphed. His proposition was accepted and three new commissions were appointed. On the following day, in a certain St. Petersburg circle, nothing else was talked of but this meeting. Alexei Alexandrovitch's success was greater than he had himself anticipated.

When he awoke on Tuesday morning he was pleased to recall the victory of yesterday and could not help smiling, though later he tried to appear indifferent when his secretary, in order to flatter him, informed him of the rumours afloat about the occurrence in the commission.

While busy with his secretary Alexei Alexandrovitch completely forgot that it was Tuesday, the day he had fixed for Anna's return, and was both surprised and pleased when a servant came to inform him of her arrival.

Anna got to St. Petersburg early in the morning. A carriage had been sent in response to her telegram. When she reached home, Alexei Alexandrovitch did not come out to meet her. On being informed that he was occupied with his secretary, she gave orders that he was to be told of her arrival and went up into her boudoir to unpack her things, expecting him to come to her any moment. But an hour passed and there were no signs of him. She went down to the dining-room under the pretext of giving some orders, and purposely spoke in a loud tone of voice so that he might hear her, but still he did not come. She heard him accompany his secretary to the door and knew that he would soon be starting for his office. She was eager to see him before he went, so that their relation to one another might be determined.

She crossed the hall and walked resolutely towards his study. When she entered he was sitting by a little table, dressed in his uniform, apparently ready to depart. His elbows were resting on the table and he was looking straight before him, with a melancholy expression on his face. She saw him before he noticed her and felt that he was thinking of her.

Becoming aware of her presence he wanted to rise, but changed his mind. A deep blush spread over his face, a thing that Anna had never observed in him before. He rose hastily and came towards her, looking not into her eyes, but above them, at her forehead and hair. He took her hand and asked her to sit down.

" I am very glad you have come," he said, sitting down beside her. He wanted to add something more, but hesitated. He tried to speak again and again, but could not. Though Anna, in preparing herself for this interview, had been ready to despise and blame him, now she pitied him and did not know what to say. For some time they were both silent.

" Is Serioja well? " he ventured at last and without waiting for a reply he added, " I shall not dine at home to-day; I must go directly."

" I wanted to go to Moscow," she said.

" No, you did much better in coming home," he replied, and was silent again.

" Alexei Alexandrovitch," she began, seeing that it was beyond his strength to go on. Her eyes did not drop under his gaze that was still concentrated on her hair. " I am a bad, guilty woman," she continued, " but I cannot help myself. I have come to tell you that I cannot change anything."

" I did not ask you about that," he said, looking resolutely into her eyes with an expression of hatred, " but I presumed it would be so." Under the influence of anger he apparently regained control of his faculties. " But as I told you and wrote to you, I am not obliged to know anything about that. I ignore it. Not all wives would have been in a hurry to communicate such very *pleasant* news to their husbands." He laid special stress on the word " pleasant." " I ignore it so long as the world does not know, so long as my name is not dishonoured. But our relations must be the same as they have always been, and I warn you that in the event of your compromising yourself I shall have to take other measures to clear my honour."

" But our relations cannot be the same," Anna ventured timidly, looking at him in a state of alarm.

As she saw once more his calm gestures, heard his thin, child-like, sarcastic voice, a feeling of loathing for him destroyed her former compassion. She was afraid of him, but she wanted a clear understanding of the situation at any cost.

" I cannot be your wife, when I . . ." she began.

He gave a cold, bitter laugh.

" It seems that the course of life you have chosen is becoming reflected in your ideas. I respect or despise both so much . . . I respect your past and despise your present to such an extent that I was far from inferring the interpretation you have given to my words."

Anna gave a sigh of relief and hung her head.

" However, I do not understand," he continued, " how a woman as independent as you are, who is not afraid or ashamed of informing her husband of her infidelity, can possibly object to fulfilling the duties of a wife."

" Alexei Alexandrovitch, what do you want of me? "

" I don't want to meet this man here, and I want you to conduct yourself in such a way that neither the *world* nor even the *servants* can have anything to say against you. . . . I want you to leave off seeing him. It seems a little thing to ask. And for that you will enjoy the privileges of an honourable wife without fulfilling the duties of one. I have nothing more to say. I must go now. I shall not dine at home."

He rose and walked towards the door.

Anna rose also. He bowed to her in silence and let her pass.

XXIV

THE night Levin had spent on the hay-cock did not go by without leaving its trace. The work of his estate not only lost all interest for him, but grew even irksome. In spite of the excellent harvest, he had never had, or at any rate so it seemed to him, so many misfortunes, nor known so much hostility between the peasants and himself as during the present year. And the cause of it all was now perfectly comprehensible to him. The love he had had for the work itself, the close contact with the peasants as a result of it, the envy that took possession of him when he saw the lives they led, the desire he had felt to lead such a life himself, which on that memorable night in question had not been merely a dream, but a fixed intention, all combined to change his views on the management of his farm. Still he could not take the same interest in it as before, and could not help seeing that all the trouble between himself and the peasants arose from their utterly false relations to one another.

A herd of pure bred cows like Pava, all in excellent condition, his well-ploughed land, nine fields of equal size hedged in by willows and ninety acres well manured, the new machinery, and so forth, would all have been beautiful had he accomplished the work himself, or by the aid of people who had an equal interest in it. He now saw clearly (his work on rural economy, in which the labourer was to be the main factor, may have helped him to this conclusion) that his present method of farming was one cruel struggle between himself and his men. On the one hand, there was a constant striving towards improvement; on the other, a clinging to the natural order of things. As a result of this struggle nothing was accomplished, the farm was carried on anyhow, expensive implements were spoiled, and the excellent cattle and land ruined. The energy wasted over it all was simply enormous and he could not help feeling that it was wasted for an unworthy purpose. After all, what was the cause of this struggle? He fought for every penny of his own and could not very well do otherwise. The slightest relaxation of energy on his part would mean that he would not make enough with which to pay his labourers. They on their part were only anxious to work as quietly and as pleasantly as possible, that is, to work in the way they had always been accustomed to work. It was to his interest that every man should do as much work as possible and do it intelligently, taking care not to break his winnowing-machines, horse-rakes, and threshers; while the men were anxious to take it as easy as possible and not have the trouble of worrying and thinking. It had been brought home to Levin at every step during this summer.

He had sent the men to mow the clover, selecting the worst fields, not intended for seed; but instead they mowed the best ones, excusing themselves by saying that the bailiff had told them to do those, and that it would make excellent hay, while all the time Levin knew that they had merely chosen those because they were the easiest to do. He next sent out the tedder to turn up the hay, but they broke it in the first rows, because the peasant sitting on the box got tired of the flapping wings. All the answer he received was, "Don't worry, the women will do it all right." The ploughs were condemned, because it never entered the head of the peasant working them to let down the coulter, thus wearing out the horse and himself and spoiling the ground. Still they asked Levin not to worry. The horses strayed among the wheat because not one of the men would act as night watchman. In spite of the repeated orders to the contrary they would take it in turn to watch at night, and naturally after a hard day's work they would fall fast asleep. When Vanka had been caught in the act once, all he said was, " Do as you please with me." Three of the best calves had died of over-feeding, having been let out on the clover without any water. All the consolation Levin got was to be told that some one else had lost one hundred and twelve in three days in the same way.

All this was done without the slightest intention of harm either to his farm or to himself. On the contrary, he knew that he was loved and regarded as a " simple-minded master," the highest praise they could bestow. They merely wished to work merrily and carelessly, and his interests were not only strange and incomprehensible to them, but were directly opposed to their own. For a long time Levin had been feeling a growing sense of dissatisfaction with his system of farming, but he had never been able to acknowledge where the essential difficulty lay. Now he could no longer deceive himself. It had not only become uninteresting to him; it had actually begun to disgust him and he could no longer continue it.

Added to this, Kitty Shcherbatsky was only thirty miles off and he could not see her.

Darya Alexandrovna had encouraged him to call. She wanted him to propose to Kitty again and had led him to understand that this time he would be accepted. From the glimpse he had caught of Kitty, Levin realised that he had not ceased to love her, but he dared not go to Dolly's house whilst she was there. Her refusal had placed an insurmountable barrier between them. " I cannot ask her to be my wife merely because she could not be the wife of the man she wanted," he said to himself. This thought made him cold and hostile towards her. " I shall not have the strength to talk to her without a touch of reproach, nor look at her without a feeling of resentment—and she will hate me more than ever. Besides, how can I possibly go there after what Darya Alexandrovna told me? Can I possibly help showing what I know? I shall arrive there in the capacity of the magnanimous, forgiving lover! Why did Darya Alexandrovna tell me? I might have met her accidentally and everything would have taken place naturally, but now it's impossible, impossible! "

Darya Alexandrovna sent him a note asking for the loan of a saddle for Kitty. " I was told that you had a lady's saddle," she wrote, " and hope you will bring it along yourself."

This was more than he could bear. How could a refined, intelligent woman so humiliate her sister! He wrote about ten notes, tore them all up, and eventually sent the saddle without an answer. To say that he would come was out of the question; to say that he could not because something prevented him was even worse. And so he sent the saddle without a reply, at the same time feeling that he had done something mean. On the following day he left everything in charge of his bailiff and departed to a distant county on a visit to his friend Sviajsky, whom he had long ago promised to go and see. The snipe marshes near Sviajsky's place had always been an attraction to Levin, but he had kept on putting off his visit on account of his duties on the farm. Now he was delighted to get away from it all, especially from the neighbourhood of the Shcherbatskys. He looked forward to the shooting with pleasure. It always proved an excellent remedy for all his troubles.

XXV

THERE was no railway or post road to Surov, the county Levin was bound for, so he travelled in his own coach.

In the middle of the journey he stopped to feed his horses at the house of a rich peasant. A bald fresh-looking old man with a red beard that had turned slightly grey opened the gates and stood on one side to let the troika in. He showed the coachman a place under a shed in his large, tidy yard, with its clean ploughs, and invited Levin to enter the house. A neatly dressed young woman with goloshes on her bare feet was scrubbing the floor in the passage. She was startled by Levin's dog who came in with him and gave a cry of alarm, but instantly laughed at herself when she realised that the dog would not hurt her. She made a sign with her wet hand for Levin to enter the parlour, and bending down again hid her pretty face as she continued scrubbing.

" Would you like a samovar? " she asked.

" Yes, please."

The room into which Levin entered was a large one with a Dutch stove and a partition. Beneath the image stood a table, ornamented with a coloured design, a bench, and two chairs. Near the door was a small cupboard with dishes. The shutters were closed; there were scarcely any flies and everything was so clean that Levin fearing that Lasca, who had been running along the dusty road and bathing in every puddle, should soil something, made her lie down in a corner. Having inspected the room, Levin went out into the back yard. The pretty young woman in goloshes, swinging her empty buckets on a yoke, was running towards the well to fetch water.

"Be quick!" the old man shouted after her merrily, and turned to Levin. "Well, sir, are you on your way to Nikolai Ivanovitch Sviajsky? He stops here too, sometimes," he began garrulously, as he leaned his elbows on the balustrade of the porch. In the middle of the old man's story about his acquaintance with Sviajsky, the gates creaked again and in drove the farm hands from the fields with their ploughs and harrows. The horses drawing them were in good condition and looked well fed. Two of the men were evidently members of the family, young fellows in coloured cotton shirts; the other two, an old man and a lad, in hempen shirts, were hired labourers.

The old man left Levin to attend to the horses.

"What have they been ploughing?" Levin asked.

"The potato fields. We also have a little land of our own. Fedot, don't let out the gelding, but put him to the trough. We can put in another horse."

"Father, I told them to take the ploughshares out, did they bring them in?" a tall sturdy young fellow asked, evidently the old man's son.

"Yes, they're in the sleigh," the old man replied, winding up the reins he had taken off and throwing them down on the ground. "Fix them on while they are eating their dinners."

The pretty young woman in goloshes made her appearance again, weighed down by two buckets of water. After her came other women, some young, some old, some good-looking, some otherwise, some with children, others without. The samovar was hissing under the chimney; the farm hands and the family, having attended to the horses, went to eat their dinners. Levin took his provisions out of his carriage and invited the old man to take tea with him.

"I have had tea already," he said, evidently delighted to accept the invitation, "but I will have some more for company's sake."

At tea Levin learnt all about the old man's farm. For ten years he had rented one hundred and twenty acres of land from a lady, and last year he had been able to buy it. Since then he had rented another three hundred acres from a neighbouring landowner. A small part of the land, the worst of it, he let, and forty acres he ploughed himself, with the help of his own family and two hired labourers. He complained that things were not going well, but Levin could see that he did so only as a matter of course, and that his farm was in a very flourishing condition. Had it not been he would hardly have been able to buy land for five hundred roubles, marry off three sons and a nephew, nor rebuild his house twice after it had been burnt down, making it larger each time. In spite of his complaints the old man was evidently proud of his prosperity, proud of his sons, his nephew, his daughters, his horses, his cows, and the fact that he was able to keep up the farm. From his conversation Levin gathered that he was not averse to modern improvements. He had planted a good many potatoes, and Levin had noticed in passing the fields that they had already flowered and were beginning to dry up; whilst his own were only just beginning to flower. He ploughed his potatoes with a new kind of plough that he borrowed from a neighbouring landowner. He sowed wheat. What particularly struck Levin was the fact that when he weeded out the rye he fed his horses with it, a thing that Levin had wanted done again and again, but for some reason or another it was always wasted. And this peasant had accomplished it and could not praise this kind of fodder sufficiently.

"The women have not much to do; they take the heaps on to the road and the carts pick them up."

"As for us proprietors, we can do nothing with the hired men," Levin observed, handing the old man a glass of tea.

"Thank you," he said, taking it, but declining the sugar as he pointed to a nibbled piece in front of him. "It's ruinous work to get along with hired men. Take Sviajsky, for example. We know what soil he has, but his crops are not good. And all from lack of care."

"But you have hired men too."

"Yes, but that's another matter. We are peasants and do everything ourselves. If a man turns out no good, off he goes and we do the work without him."

"Father, Fenogen wants the tar," a woman in goloshes said to him as she entered the room.

"That's how it is," the old man said, rising and crossing himself many times. He thanked Levin and left the room.

When Levin went to the back premises to call his coachman, he found all the men-folk of the family at table while the women were serving them. The sturdy, young son, with his mouth full of porridge, was relating something, and every one burst out laughing. The young woman in goloshes laughed particularly loud and merrily as she poured some hot soup into a bowl.

Her pretty face may have had a good deal to do with creating that sense of orderliness that Levin carried away with him from the old peasant's house. The impression was so strong that for the rest of the way to Sviajsky he kept recurring to it again and again as to something demanding special attention.

XXVI

SVIAJSKY was the marshal of the nobility for his district. He was five years older than Levin, and had been married for some time. His sister-in-law—a very nice young girl whom Levin liked very much—lived in his house. Levin knew that both Sviajsky and his wife were anxious that he should marry her. He knew just as certainly as most eligible young men know these things, though no one had ever told him. He knew also that, notwithstanding the fact that he was anxious to marry, and that she was a most attractive girl who would make an excellent wife, he could no more marry her than fly, even if he were not in love with Kitty Shcherbatsky. This knowledge somewhat marred the pleasure he had hoped to derive from his visit.

When he had received Sviajsky's letter inviting him for the shooting, he had immediately thought of this girl and hesitated about going, but having decided that the Sviajskys had not invited him with any ulterior motive, he resolved to go in the end. Besides, in the bottom of his heart, he was eager to test himself, to see the effect the girl would produce upon him. The Sviajskys' domestic life was extremely attractive to him, and Sviajsky himself was a very interesting man, highly devoted to the affairs of his province.

Sviajsky belonged to the type of men so surprising to Levin, whose consistent, though never independent thought, goes on of itself, while their lives, extremely fixed and definite in their tendencies, also go on of themselves as a rule diametrically opposed to their reasoning. Sviajsky was very liberal in his views. He despised the nobility and accused the majority of them of being secret adherents of serfdom, too timid to express their opinions openly. He regarded Russia as a wretched country no better than Turkey, and was so contemptuous of the government as never to permit himself to discuss its actions seriously. He served nevertheless, and was a model marshal of the nobility, though he always put on a red-brimmed cap with a cockade whenever he travelled. He held that a decent life was only possible abroad, where he made his escape whenever an opportunity offered, yet at the same time he had a huge model estate that he watched over with the greatest interest, and was always well informed of what was going on in Russia. He looked upon the Russian peasant as in the transitional stage between monkey and man, yet at elections was the first to shake a peasant by the hand and listen to his opinions. He believed neither in God, nor the devil, nor in death, but was much concerned about improving the conditions of the clergy, interested in the division of parishes, and used all his influence to retain the church in his own village.

In the woman question he was on the side of the extremists who advocated the fullest liberty for women, especially in their right to work, but he lived with his wife in such a manner that all admired their friendly, childless domestic life; and arranged things so that she did nothing and could not possibly do anything else than share her husband's care of how to spend the time in the best and jolliest way.

Had Levin not been accustomed to look at people from their best side he would have had no difficulty in explaining Sviajsky's character. He would simply have put him down as a fool or a rogue. But Sviajsky was neither the one nor the other. Far from being a fool, he was an extremely cultured man who bore his culture with the greatest simplicity. There was hardly a subject with which he was not familiar, yet he never displayed his knowledge unless the occasion demanded. The epithet of rogue applied to him still less, for he was an unquestionably honest, kind, sensible man. He did everything he had to do cheerfully, was respected by every one who knew him, and had never consciously done anything wrong, nor ever could do.

Levin always tried, but invariably failed, to understand him, and looked upon him as a sort of living riddle. They were great friends, so that Levin permitted himself on occasions to question Sviajsky in his efforts to fathom his views upon life, but he endeavoured to do so tactfully. Every time Levin attempted to penetrate into the inner regions of Sviajsky's mind, he would always draw into his shell. It seemed as though he feared that Levin would really understand him, and he put him off in a jocular, good-natured way.

Now, after the disillusionment in connection with his farm, Levin took a particular pleasure in his visit to the Sviajskys'. He loved the society of these two happy doves, who were contented with themselves and with everybody and liked the comfort of their cosy, well-ordered nest. He would have given anything to get at the secret that gave Sviajsky such a clear, definite, and happy life. Besides, Levin knew that at their house he would be sure to meet the neighbouring landowners, and there would be an opportunity to talk about crops, the hire of labour, and so forth, subjects which, though considered vulgar, were of exceeding interest to him. "These things may not have been worth considering during the time of serfdom, when the conditions were so different, nor in England, but with us, now, when everything has been turned upside down and things are only just beginning to shape themselves, such questions are very important," he thought.

The shooting did not turn out so well as Levin had expected. The marshes had dried up and there were hardly any snipe. He went out for a whole day and brought back only three birds, but was compensated by a ravenous appetite, capital spirits, and a certain mental stimulus that violent physical exercise always produced in him. And during the sport, when he seemed not to be thinking of anything, the old peasant and his family would crop up in his imagination and demanded a solution of something that seemed in some way connected with them.

At tea in the evening two neighbouring landowners called about some guardianship and they entered into the kind of discussion that Levin had been looking forward to.

Levin was sitting near the hostess at the tea-table and was obliged to carry on a conversation with her and her sister, who sat opposite to him. The hostess was a little, round-faced, fair-haired woman, beaming with her dimples and smiles. Levin tried to solve through her the riddle that her husband presented to him, but he could not think clearly because he felt extremely ill at ease. His embarrassment was caused by the fact that the sister was arrayed in a beautiful gown, put on expressly for him, as he thought. It was cut in a square, rather low in front, and the whiteness of her bosom deprived him of the full liberty of thought. It seemed to him, perhaps wrongly so, that the dress had been cut low for his especial benefit. He tried not to look at it, and felt himself to blame in some way. He felt as though he were deceiving some one, and that he ought to explain, but to do so was impossible. He kept on blushing, was extremely restless and uncomfortable. The sister too shared his discomfort. But the hostess seemed to observe nothing and tried to draw her into the conversation.

" Strange that you should think my husband does not take an interest in Russian affairs," the hostess said. " On the contrary, though he likes being abroad, he is never so happy as when at home. He feels more in his own sphere. He is so busy, and has a gift for interesting himself in everything. Oh, by the way, have you seen our school? "

" Yes, I have. It's the little house covered with ivy, is it not? "

" Yes, that is Nastia's work," she said, with a gesture in the direction of her sister.

" Do you teach there yourself? " Levin asked, trying not to look at her bosom, but feeling that no matter where he looked he should still see it.

" Oh, yes, but we have an excellent teacher besides. We've introduced gymnastics lately."

" No, thanks, I won't take any more tea," Levin said, rising with a blush. He felt it was rather rude, but he was absolutely unable to keep up the conversation any longer. " I hear they are discussing something very interesting," he added, as he moved over to the other end of the table, where the host was seated with his two guests. Sviajsky was half turned towards the table, twirling his cup about with one hand and stroking his beard with the other. Every now and again he would raise the cup to his nose as though smelling it. His bright, black eyes were fixed on one of his guests with a keen sense of amusement. He was a man with a grey moustache who had become quite heated in his complaints about the peasantry. Levin saw that Sviajsky could have completely squashed the man's objections had he chosen, but as he could not very well do so in his own house, he listened with amusement to his absurd remarks. The man was evidently a staunch upholder of serfdom and an enthusiastic farmer of the old style. Levin could see signs of it in his old-fashioned, shiny coat, in his frowning intelligent look, in his characteristic Russian speech, in his slow, authoritative manner, in the imperative gestures of his fine, sunburnt hand, ornamented by a wedding ring.

XXVII

"IF it were not a pity to abandon what has cost so much labour, I would turn my back upon everything and go abroad to hear 'Helen,' like Nikolai Ivanovitch," the old man said, while a pleasant smile lighted up his intelligent face.

"But as you don't, there must be some reason for it," Nikolai Ivanovitch Sviajsky observed.

"The only reason is that I live at home, in a house that I have neither bought nor hired. Besides, you always go on hoping that the people will come to their senses. Just look at them now! Nothing but debauchery and drunkenness! Everything has been changed; they have no horses, no cows. They are dying of hunger, but if you engage a man as a labourer he will only spoil everything you possess and end by bringing you before a justice of the peace."

"But you can also lodge a complaint if you like," Sviajsky ventured.

"I lodge a complaint! Nothing on earth would induce me. I should never hear the end of it! At the mill, for instance, the men made off with the earnest-money and the justice of the peace acquitted them. Your only chance is to go to the elder of the district. He gives them a thrashing at any rate. If it were not for that you would have to leave everything and run away to the very ends of the earth."

The old man was evidently teasing Sviajsky, but the latter was not annoyed; he was merely amused.

"We manage our estates without these measures," he said, indicating Levin and his second guest.

"Oh, yes, Mihail Petrovitch manages his affairs, but ask him how. Is that a rational method of farming?" the old man asked, evidently proud of the foreign word "rational."

"Thank God, my farming is quite simple," Mihail Petrovitch put in. "My only care is that the money should be ready in the autumn for the taxes. Peasants come to me saying, 'Help us out, father!' Well, what can I do? They are my neighbours and I pity them. I advance them the first third and tell them that when the time comes for the sowing or haymaking or harvesting they must lend me a hand too, and so I come to some arrangement with each family. There are some without consciences of course. . . ."

Levin, who was familiar with these patriarchal methods, exchanged glances with Sviajsky and turned to the old man with the grey moustache.

"Then what are your ideas? How would you manage an estate?" he asked.

"Just as Mihail Petrovitch is doing. You must either give or let half of your land to the peasants, but that is the very reason the country is getting so poor. My land is not bringing me in a third of what it used to before the emancipation. Yes, I'm afraid the emancipation has been the ruin of Russia."

Sviajsky looked at Levin with a twinkle in his eye, but Levin did not find the old landowner's words funny; he understood them better than he understood Sviajsky himself. Much that the old man said appeared to him to be true and incontrovertible. He seemed to be expressing his own honest thought, a thing very rarely met with. He was not merely saying these things for the sake of talking; he had been driven to these conclusions by long observation of country life, and seemed to have considered the questions from every point of view.

"The fact is, you see, that all progress is achieved by force," the landowner went on, evidently wishing to show that he was not averse to culture. "Take the reforms of Peter, Catherine, and Alexander; take European history itself; the improvement of agriculture; even potatoes; iron ploughs were introduced to us by force. Before the emancipation we landowners had almost brought farming to a state of perfection. We had kilns, winnowing machines, and all the necessary implements that we introduced because we had the power. The peasants at first opposed us and then imitated us. Now that the power has been taken from us, our estates, which had been raised to such a high level of culture, must sink back again to the primitive methods of long ago. That is my view of the matter."

"But why? It seems to me you could farm just as rationally with hired labour," Sviajsky remarked.

"Not without the power. How are you to do it, allow me to ask?"

"There is the main point—the force of labour, the chief element in farming," Levin thought.

"With the help of labourers of course."

" But the labourer does not want to work well, nor does he want to use decent implements. He can only get as drunk as a hog and spoil everything you give him. He will only ruin your horses, spoil your harness, take off your tires and spend them on drink, and break up your winnowing machines. He hates to see anything that is not like his own. That is why the standard of farming has gone down. The land is neglected and given over to weeds or the peasants. Where you could once have raised a million bushels of wheat, you can now get only about a hundred thousand. The national wealth is diminishing. If the same thing had been done sensibly . . ."

And he proceeded to expound a method by which the serfs could have been liberated without all these direful consequences. This did not interest Levin, and when he had finished he returned to his first point, in the hope of inducing Sviajsky to express a serious opinion about it.

" It is true that the level of our agriculture is growing lower and lower, and that with our present relations to the labourer it is impossible to farm in a rational manner," he observed.

" I don't agree with you," Sviajsky said seriously. " The thing that strikes me is that we don't understand how to farm. As for agriculture having been on a high level before the emancipation, on the contrary, I think it was on a very low one. We have not the necessary machinery, nor the cattle; we have no idea of management and no sense of keeping accounts. Ask any one of our landowners; he does not know what is profitable and what is not."

" Italian book-keeping! " the old man said disdainfully. " You can count as much as you like; they'll muddle everything and you'll make nothing out of it in the end."

" But why? They will break one of your miserable Russian threshing machines, but they won't break my steam one. They will harm one of your wretched little hacks, that you have to pull by the tail, but provide yourselves with good *Percherons* and they won't harm those. And so it is with everything. We must raise the standard of agriculture all round."

" That's all very well, but how are we to do it, Nikolai Ivanitch? It's right enough for you, but I have a son to maintain at the university and several little ones at school. How can I afford to buy *Percherons ?* "

" There are banks for that purpose."

" So that they can sell you up afterwards down to the last

threshing machine? No, thanks! I would rather not resort to that method!"

"I'm afraid I don't agree that it's either necessary or possible to raise the standard of agriculture," Levin remarked. "I work at my own farm all the time and I have the means, but I can't accomplish anything. And as for banks, I don't see the use of them. No matter how much money I spend it only ends in loss, whether it's spent on cattle or machines."

"That's perfectly true," the old landowner confirmed with a smile of pleasure.

"And I am not the only one," Levin continued; "every man who carries on his farm in a rational manner is doing so at a loss. And yet you tell me that farming is profitable. Do you really think so?" he asked, and immediately noticed the fleeting expression of fear that always passed over Sviajsky's face whenever he tried to penetrate into the inner recesses of his mind.

This question was a little unfair on Levin's part. The hostess had only just informed him at tea that they had engaged a special German accountant from Moscow, who on verifying the accounts of the estate, discovered that there had been a loss of something like three thousand roubles for the year. She could not remember the exact figures, but the German had added it up to the last kopek.

The old landowner smiled at the idea of Sviajsky, their marshal of the nobility, farming at a profit.

"Perhaps not," Sviajsky replied, "but that proves nothing. It only shows that I am either a very poor farmer, or that I spend my capital in increasing my rental value."

"Rental value!" Levin exclaimed scornfully. "There may be such a thing in Europe where the land is better for the work that has been spent upon it, but with us it is quite the contrary. Our land gets worse the more work we spend upon it, that is, because we exhaust it so."

"But there must be rental value; that is a law."

"Then we are outside it. Rental value has no meaning for us; it only confuses us. I should like you to explain how the theory of rental values can . . ."

"Would you like some curds?" Sviajsky asked. "Masha, get them to bring some curds and raspberries," he added, turning to his wife. "It is wonderful how long the raspberries have lasted this year."

Sviajsky rose and walked away in the most excellent spirits, evidently thinking that the conversation had come to an end, when for Levin it was only just beginning. He went on talking to the old landowner, endeavouring to prove to him that the whole trouble arose from the fact that we made no attempt to understand the character and habits of our labourers. The old landowner, like all people who live much alone and are accustomed to thinking for themselves, found it difficult to enter into the thought of another and clung firmly to his own opinions. He maintained that the Russian peasant was no better than a pig, who preferred living like one, and that nothing but force could drive him out of his piggishness. He lamented that the traditional rod should have been changed for lawyers and prisons, where the good-for-nothing, filthy peasant was fed on good soup and given his cubic feet of fresh air.

" Why do you think it impossible to find that true relation to the labourer that would make work profitable? " Levin asked, anxious to bring him back to the point.

" You can't do anything with the Russian peasant; you no longer have the power," the old landowner replied.

" But new conditions may be found," Sviajsky put in. He had just finished his curds, lighted a cigarette, and joined the disputants.

" All possible relations to labour have been studied and tried. That relic of barbarism, the primitive commune, where each man is responsible for everybody else, is falling to pieces of its own accord, the serf law is abolished, there remains only free labour in its various forms, the farm hand, the day labourer, the farmer—you cannot get away from that."

" But Europe is not satisfied with these forms. They are dissatisfied and looking for new ones, and will no doubt find them."

" That's what I say; why should we not discover new forms on our side? " Levin put in.

" Because it would be much the same as pretending to discover new methods of constructing railways. They are all ready, all thought out."

" But what if they are stupid and do not suit us? " Levin asked. And again he observed that expression of fear in Sviajsky's eyes.

" Yes, we want to steal a march on Europe! We want to be able to say that we have found what she is looking for! Excuse me, but do you know what Europe is doing in regard to the labour question? "

" I know very little about it."

" The greatest minds of Europe are now occupied with it. Then there is all that mass of literature on the labour question. There is the Schultze-Delitsch school, the Lassalle school, perhaps the most advanced of them all, and then there is the Mühlhausen experiment, about which you know no doubt."

" I have some vague idea about it."

" You only say that, but probably know as much about it as I do. Of course I am not a professor of political economy, but these things interest me. If they interest you it would be quite worth your while going into them."

" But what do they all lead to? "

" Excuse me . . ."

The two visitors rose and Sviajsky escorted them out. Again he had baffled Levin just as he was about to enter the inner recesses of his mind.

XXVIII

LEVIN was horribly bored with the ladies that evening. He was agitated by the thought that his dissatisfaction with farming was not his own exclusive state, but one that the whole of Russia was suffering from. It was brought home to him that they must endeavour to arrive at that relation between farmer and labourer he had witnessed at the peasant's on the way. It was not merely a vain illusion, but a problem that must be solved. It could be solved and some attempts ought to be made to do so. He said good-night to the ladies, after promising to stay over to-morrow in order to go for a ride with them in the state forest to inspect an interesting landslide, and before retiring went into Sviajsky's study for some books on the labour question he had recommended him to read. The study was an enormous room lined with bookshelves. There was a large writing-table in the middle and a round one at the side covered with newspapers and periodicals in various languages. Near the writing-table was a stand, the drawers of which were labelled with gilt lettering.

Sviajsky took out the books and seated himself in the rocking-chair.

" What are you looking at? " he asked Levin, who was turning over the leaves of a periodical at the round table. " Oh, yes, there's a very interesting article in there," he added as he noticed the review that Levin held in his hand. "It appears," he continued gaily, "that it was not Frederick who was the chief cause of the division of Poland. It seems . . ."

And with his characteristic clearness he gave a brief account of these new important discoveries. Although Levin was engrossed in his farm matters he listened attentively. "What is there in him? Why is he interested in the division of Poland?" he kept on asking himself in wonder. "What does it lead to?" But it seemed to lead to nothing and Sviajsky did not even take the trouble to explain why he was interested in it.

"I was very much taken with that cross old landowner," Levin remarked with a sigh. "He's a most sensible man and a good deal of what he says is quite true."

"Really! A confirmed believer in serfdom, like the rest of them!" Sviajsky replied.

"With you as their marshal . . ."

"Oh, but I want to marshal them in the other direction," Sviajsky retorted with a laugh.

"He seemed to me right when he said that rational farming with us is doomed to failure and that only the money-lending farmer, like the quiet man with him, or farming by the most primitive methods, can possibly succeed. Who is to blame for it I should like to know?"

"We ourselves, of course. But it is not exactly true that it does not succeed—Vassilkov makes a success of it."

"He has a factory."

"Besides it is hardly surprising. The people are in such a low state of development, both material and moral, that naturally they resist anything that is foreign to them. In Europe rational farming succeeds because the masses are educated. It is time we began to educate ours."

"But how can you educate them?"

"To educate the people you want schools, schools, and schools."

"I cannot see how schools can help them if they are in such a low state of material development, as you seem to infer."

"You put me in mind of that story about the sick man. One person advised him to try a purgative! He did so and grew worse. Another advised leeches; he tried that and grew worse. A third advised him to pray to God; he did that and grew worse. So it is with you. When I talk of political economy, you say worse; socialism, still worse; education, worse than ever."

" But how can schools help them? " Levin persisted.

" They will create other needs."

" I have never been able to understand," Levin began vehemently, " how schools and education can possibly ameliorate the material conditions of our people. You have just said that education will create new needs. In that case they will be even worse off than before, since they will not be able to satisfy them. For the life of me I cannot see how a knowledge of addition and subtraction nor the catechism can help them to better themselves materially. Three days ago I met a peasant woman carrying a baby, and on asking her where she was going she informed me that she had just been to the midwife to get her baby cured, who was suffering from fits of screaming. ' How can the midwife cure that? ' I asked her. ' She puts the baby on the hen-roost and says some charms.' . . ."

" Exactly! To teach her better than put her baby on the hen-roost it is necessary . . ." Sviajsky began with a smile.

" Not at all! " Levin interrupted him. " That method of curing babies is very much like trying to cure the ills our peasantry are suffering from by schools. The people are miserably poor and ignorant—we see that as plainly as the peasant woman saw that her baby was ill, because it was crying. But how your schools are going to cure their poverty and ignorance any more than the hen-roost the baby, I fail to see. You must remedy the cause of the misery."

" Well, in that at least you agree with Spencer, whom you dislike so much. He says that education is more the result of increased well-being, comfort in life and cleanliness, than learning to read and write."

" Well, I am glad, or perhaps I should say sorry, to agree with Spencer, but I have known that for a long time. Schools cannot help. What we want is an economic change that will make the peasant richer and then schools will spring up of their own accord."

" But schools are now obligatory all over Europe."

" And how is it you agree with Spencer in this? " Levin asked.

A look of fear came into Sviajsky's eyes. " Really, your story of the woman and the baby was too good! Did you actually hear it yourself."

Levin gave up all hope of finding the connection between this man's life and thoughts. It was a matter of utter indifference to him where his reasoning led him, all that interested him was the process of reasoning itself, and whenever that brought him to a blind alley he grew annoyed and changed the subject for something more pleasant.

All the impressions of that day, beginning with the sensations he had carried away from the peasant's house, that served as a basis for all the others, as it were, had a very agitating effect upon Levin. Sviajsky and his ideas that were merely brought out for social use, who had some mysterious basis of life Levin could not fathom, and who, together with others, guided public opinion with arguments that were foreign to him; the cross old landowner, who was perfectly right in his conclusions, yet wrong in his condemnation of a whole class, perhaps the best in Russia; the dissatisfaction he felt in his activity and a vague hope that he might find a remedy for these things—all blended together into a feeling of alarm and expectation of a near solution.

Levin retired to his room and lay down on the springy mattress of his bed, that threw his arms and legs about at the least movement he made. For a long time he could not go to sleep. His conversation with Sviajsky, though many smart things had been said, did not interest him particularly, but the old landowner's arguments demanded consideration. Levin involuntarily thought of all his words, and in his imagination tried to improve upon the objections he had made to them.

"Yes, I ought to have replied to him, 'You say that farming does not succeed with us because the peasant despises all improvements and must be driven by force. Now if it were really a fact that farming could not be carried on without these improvements you would be right, but it can be carried on with the greatest success, in conformity with the peasant's own habits, as was proved by the old man with whom I stopped on the way. Our common dissatisfaction with farming merely shows that either we ourselves are to blame or else the labourers who work for us. We have for a long time been aping Europe without stopping to consider the properties of our working power. Let us once and for all recognise our working power for what it is, the Russian peasant with his peculiarities, and not treat it as a working power in the abstract; then and only then may we hope to organise our agriculture on sensible lines. Imagine,' I ought to have told him, 'that your farm is conducted as that old man conducts his; that you have discovered a method of interesting your labourers in the success of the work and have hit upon the kind of improvements that they are willing to recognise. Supposing as a result of it that you get three times as much out of your land without in any way exhausting it, and you give one part to the working power. You would still be receiving more than you do now, and your workers would be richer too. In order to accomplish this you must lower the level of farming and interest the labourer in the success of the work. But how is that to be done? That is a question of detail, but without doubt it is possible to do it.' "

These thoughts agitated Levin very much. He lay awake half the night reflecting on the details needed to carry out this idea. He had not intended to go home the next day, but now decided to leave early in the morning. Besides, the memory of the young lady with the low-cut dress produced a feeling of shame in him as though he had committed some disgraceful deed. He was anxious to be gone at once in order to lose no time in starting upon his new project before the autumn sowing. He decided to abandon all his former ideas on farming.

XXIX

The carrying out of Levin's plan presented many difficulties, but he persevered, and though he did not attain all the results he desired, still those he did attain seemed to him quite worth the trouble he had taken. One of the principal obstacles was the fact that his farm was in full operation and could not be stopped to start afresh. The machine had to be mended whilst in motion.

When he reached home in the evening and informed his bailiff of his new plan, the bailiff listened to him with pleasure, particularly when he condemned everything that had been done before as utterly useless nonsense. Upon the latter the bailiff agreed with him, saying that he had frequently thought so himself, but that no one would ever listen to him. When, however, it came to the proposition that he and the labourers should become shareholders in the farm, he became quite dejected, offered no definite opinion, and immediately began talking of the necessity of taking in the last of the rye, so that the men could go down and plough the fields. Levin could see that this was not a propitious moment.

In talking about the same thing with the peasants and offering them the land on new conditions he again ran up against the old difficulty. They were so busy and engrossed in the work of the day that they had no time to deliberate upon the advantages or disadvantages of the proposition.

One naive peasant—Ivan, who looked after the cattle—seemed to thoroughly understand Levin's proposition, that is, that he and his family were to share the profits derived from the cattle. He grew quite sad that he could not stay and listen to Levin's glowing descriptions of the advantages that would accrue to him. Unfortunately he had to hasten away to attend to some work that could not be left, such as clearing the hay from the stalls, filling the troughs, or sweeping up the dung.

Another obstacle lay in the insurmountable distrust of the peasants. They could not believe that the master could have any other aim in view than getting as much out of them as possible. They were so firmly convinced of this that though they talked a great deal, they could never be brought to express their real objection. Levin came to the conclusion that the irascible old landowner was right. The first and indispensable condition the peasants insisted on in any new arrangement was that they should not be compelled to adopt any new methods of farming or to use any new implements. They were prepared to admit that the new-fashioned plough worked better, but they invented a thousand excuses against using it. Whatever regret Levin felt at giving up improvements, the advantages of which were manifest to him, he let them have their own way, and by the autumn the new arrangement was in working order, or at any rate, so it seemed to him.

At first Levin had thought of taking the bailiff, the peasants, and labourers into partnership as the farm stood, but was soon convinced that this was impossible, and decided to divide the estate into various parts. The cattle-yard, the orchard, the vegetable garden, the hay and corn, were to form separate lots. Ivan, who looked after the cattle, and who had grasped his idea better than the rest, as Levin thought, got together a company of his own, consisting mainly of members of his own family, who all became shareholders in the cattle-yard. A distant field, that had been lying fallow for eight years, was taken over by six families of peasants, under the leadership of Fiodor, the carpenter, and the peasant Shuraev took over the kitchen-gardens, all under the new conditions. The rest of the estate was managed on the old lines. These three lots were to be the beginning of the new order, and occupied all Levin's attention.

It is true that in the cattle-yard things did not go any better than before, and that Ivan was opposed to the cows being put in warm houses and to the butter being made of fresh cream. He maintained that a cow needed less food in the cold, and that butter was better made out of sour cream. And he would demand his wages as before, not taking any interest in the fact that what he was receiving was not wages in the old sense, but an advance on the profits. It is true that Fiodor's company did not plough their land twice before the sowing, as had been agreed upon, giving as an excuse that the time was too short. It is true that the peasants of this company did not look upon the land as common, though they had accepted the new arrangement, and that even Fiodor himself thought that it would be better if Levin took his rent for it, so as to leave them more free. It is true that the men found all sorts of excuses against building a new cattle-yard and granary that had been agreed upon, and did their best to put it off for the winter. It is true also that Shuraev wanted to allot each peasant a part of the kitchen-gardens under his charge, completely misunderstanding the conditions on which they were handed over to him.

It is true that, while talking to the peasants about the advantages of the new arrangement, Levin felt all the time that they were firmly convinced he wanted to cheat them. He felt this keenly with the most intelligent of the peasants, Fiodor. He noticed a certain twinkle in his eye whenever he had occasion to talk to him, as though he were laughing at him and assuring him that if any one was to be cheated it would not be he.

But in spite of it all Levin was hopeful, and thought that by keeping a strict account and insisting on his orders being carried out, they would be able to see in the future the immense advantages of such an arrangement, and that then things would go of themselves.

These matters, together with the remainder of the estate still on his hands and the book he was writing, occupied Levin so much during the rest of the summer that he had scarcely any time to go out shooting. About the end of August a man brought back the saddle he had lent Kitty and informed him that the Oblonskys had all gone back to Moscow. He felt that by his extreme incivility in not answering Darya Alexandrovna's letter—a thing he could not recall without shame—he had burnt his ships, so to speak, and would never again be able to go and see them. A similar thing had happened in regard to the Sviajskys, whom he had left without a word of farewell. He should never be able to go to them either. But he was quite indifferent about it. The new arrangements on his farm interested him more than anything else he had ever done in his life. He read all the books he had taken away with him from Sviajsky's, as well as a good many others he had sent for on political economy and socialism, subjects dealing with the matter he was interested in, but, as he had foreseen, he found nothing in them of the slightest use to him. In the works on political economy, in Mill, for example, whom he read first with great enthusiasm, expecting to find in him some solution to the questions that puzzled him, he found only certain laws deduced from the condition of European agriculture, but completely inapplicable to the conditions in Russia. It was the same with works on socialism. They were either beautiful, wholly unpractical fancies, such as used to appeal to him in the days when he was a student, or else they were improvements on the state of things prevalent in Europe with which Russian agriculture had nothing in common. Political economy maintained that the laws by which Europe developed her wealth were unquestionable and universal, whereas socialism asserted that those very laws were leading to ruin. At any rate neither the one nor the other offered the smallest enlightenment as to what he, Levin, and all other landowners and peasants should do with their millions of hands and acres to make them more productive for the general welfare.

Having once taken the matter in hand, he conscientiously read everything referring to the subject, and even intended to make a journey abroad in the autumn in order to study things on the spot. He wanted to be prepared against a thing that had frequently happened to him whenever he was expounding his own views. "And Kauffman and Johns and Dubois and Miceli? Have you read them?" he was always being asked. "They have already solved these questions."

He now saw clearly that Kauffman and Miceli had nothing to tell him. He knew what he wanted. He could see that Russia had excellent land and splendid workmen, and that in certain cases, as with the peasant at whose house he had stopped on his way to Sviajsky's, the men and the land produced well, but in others, where capital was applied in the European fashion, scarcely anything was produced. He could see that the labourer wanted to work and worked well in his own peculiar manner, and that his resistance to any other manner was not merely accidental, but a rooted principle that came out of the spirit of the nation. He now saw clearly that the Russian people, whose destiny it was to cultivate enormous stretches of uninhabited land, consciously stuck to the methods best suited for that purpose, and that these methods were not at all as bad as was generally supposed. He wanted to prove this theoretically in his book and practically on his farm.

XXX

TOWARDS the end of September the timber was brought up for the building of barns on the lands taken over in partnership, the butter was sold and the profits divided. In practice the farm was running excellently; at any rate so it seemed to Levin. In order to elucidate his theories and to finish his work, which he hoped would not only create a complete revolution in political economy, but would even abolish the whole science and lay the foundation for a new one, he had to go abroad to find out exactly what had been done in that direction, and bring back convincing proofs that they were working on wrong lines. He was merely waiting for the wheat to be sold, so that he could get the money before taking his departure. But the rainy season set in before the potatoes were got up and the grain harvested. The work was brought to a standstill. The roads were so muddy that you could not cross them, two mills were carried off by a flood, and the weather was getting steadily worse.

On the morning of the 30th the sun appeared, and thinking that good weather had come at last Levin began making preparations for the journey. He gave orders for the wheat to be brought in, sent his bailiff to the merchant who was going to buy it, and went out on a final tour of inspection on the farm in order to make all necessary arrangements before his departure. Having finished all his business Levin was returning home in the evening in the most excellent spirits, though the water was trickling down the back of his neck and into his boots. The weather had grown worse since the morning. The hail struck so painfully against the drenched horse, which was shaking its head and ears, that it was obliged to walk sideways. Levin felt quite happy under his cloak and cowl. He gazed around him at the turbid streams that ran down the deep ruts, at the bare, dripping branches of the trees, at the white hail on the wooden bridge, at the mass of leaves, not yet withered, that surrounded a huge elm. Despite the gloomy aspect of nature he felt extraordinarily light-hearted. His conversation with the peasants in the distant village he had just been to showed him that they were beginning to understand his new project. An old innkeeper to whom he had gone to dry himself had evidently approved of his plan and had offered to go into partnership with him over the buying of some cattle.

" I only need to keep my aim steadily before me and I shall get what I want," Levin thought. " At least there is something to work and strive for. It is not merely my own personal affair; it concerns the general welfare. There must be a complete change in agriculture and the position of the people. In the place of poverty there will be prosperity, contentment: instead of enmity there will be harmony and joint interests. In a word there will be a complete revolution without bloodshed, beginning in our own district, then the county, then Russia, then throughout the whole world. A just idea cannot help bearing fruit. Yes, it is worth while working for such an aim. And because it is I, Konstantin Levin, the same fellow who went to a dance in a black necktie and was refused by Kitty Shcherbatsky, a most insignificant, miserable fellow—that does not prove anything. I am sure Franklin had just as little faith in himself and thought himself just as insignificant. It does not mean anything. He too, no doubt, had his Agafia Mihailovna to whom he confided all his secrets."

It was with such thoughts that Levin reached the house in the dark.

The bailiff who had been to the merchant's had already returned with part of the money for the wheat. An agreement was come to with the innkeeper, and the bailiff learnt on his way home that the grain was still in the fields; thus Levin's one hundred and sixty cocks would be worth nothing in comparison with what the others had received.

After dinner Levin sat down in an arm-chair with a book as usual, and while reading continued his thoughts about his proposed journey abroad in connection with the work he was writing. That day he saw the whole thing quite clearly. Whole periods arranged themselves naturally in his mind, expressing the essence of his central idea. " I must write that down," he would say to himself every now and again. " That will make a short introduction, though I had wanted to dispense with that." He rose to go to his writing-table, and Lasca, who had been lying at his feet, stretched herself, also got up, and looked up at him as though asking where he wished her to go. But there was no time to make notes, the foreman arrived for the next day's orders, and Levin went out to talk to him in the hall.

When he had finished with him, and also with the various other peasants who had called on business, Levin went into his study and sat down to work. Lasca lay down under the table and Agafia Mihailovna seated herself in a corner with a stocking.

After writing for a while a vivid picture of Kitty suddenly rose before Levin's mind, bringing back the memory of her refusal and their last meeting. He got up and began pacing the room.

" There is no reason why you should feel so lonely," Agafia Mihailovna observed. " You stay at home too much. Why don't you go abroad and take the waters? "

" I am going the day after to-morrow, Agafia Mihailovna. I must finish my business first."

" What business? Haven't you given those peasants enough? As it is they are saying that their master expects some reward from the tsar. I can't understand why you trouble yourself so much about the peasants."

" I am not troubling myself about them, I am working on my own account."

Agafia Mihailovna knew every detail of Levin's plans. He had frequently expounded his ideas to her and had even entered into disputes with her when she would not agree with him. This time she completely misunderstood him.

" Of course one must think of one's soul as much as possible," she said with a sigh. " There was Parfen Denisitch, though he could not read and write; God grant that others may die like him. He took the last sacrament and received extreme unction." She was referring to an old manorial servant.

" I did not mean that," Levin said. " I meant that I am working for my own advantage. It is more advantageous to me when the peasants work well."

" No matter what you do, if a man is lazy it won't make any difference to him, and if he has a conscience he will work in any case."

" But you said yourself that Ivan looked after the cattle better than he used to."

" All I have to say," Agafia Mihailovna replied, in a tone as though she had long been considering the point, " is that you ought to get married."

Agafia Mihailovna's reference to the thing he had himself been thinking a moment ago grieved and wounded Levin. He frowned and without replying sat down to his work again. He tried to reinforce himself by going over in his mind all his former thoughts about the significance of it. Every now and again the clicking of Agafia Mihailovna's knitting-needles would break in upon him in the stillness and he recalled the thing he did not wish to think about and scowled again.

At about nine o'clock there was a ring at the front door bell, and the sound of a carriage rumbling on the muddy road.

" Here comes a visitor, so you won't be dull any more," Agafia Mihailovna said, as she rose and walked towards the door. But Levin ran out ahead of her. His work was not progressing well, and he was glad of a visitor whoever it might be.

XXXI

As Levin ran down the stairs he was arrested by the sound of a familiar cough. He did not hear it quite distinctly on account of the noise of his own footsteps, so that he hoped he might be mistaken. In a second or two, however, he caught sight of a tall, bony figure, so well known to him, and though there was no further room for doubt, still he went on hoping that the man removing his coat in the hall was not his brother Nikolai.

Levin loved his brother, but it was painful for him to be with him. Just now, under the influence of the thought that had come to him, and of Agafia Mihailovna's advice, he was in a confused, uncertain state, so that the meeting with his brother seemed to him particularly difficult. Instead of a healthy, happy visitor, some stranger, who would have taken him out of himself, there was his brother, who knew him through and through, who could read his innermost thoughts and would get him to tell him everything. And he did not wish to do this.

Annoyed with himself for such mean thoughts, Levin hastened down into the hall. When he drew near his brother, the feeling of disappointment instantly gave way to one of pity. Nikolai was thinner and more emaciated than ever. He looked nothing more than a skeleton.

He was standing in the hall, trying to unwind a scarf from his thin, long neck, and smiling in a strange pitiful manner. When Levin saw that humble, submissive smile a lump arose in his throat.

" Here I am come to see you," Nikolai began in a hoarse voice, without removing his eyes from his brother's face for a second. "I have long wanted to come, but my health prevented me. Now I am much better," he added, wiping his beard with his large, thin hands.

"That's right!" Levin replied. And he felt more terrible still when touching his brother's shrivelled cheek with his lips he saw the gleam of his enormous, unnaturally brilliant eyes.

A few weeks ago Levin had written to his brother telling him that a small piece of undivided property had been sold and that there were about two thousand roubles for his share. Nikolai announced that he had come partly for the money, but chiefly because he wanted to see the old nest again, to plant his foot on the soil, in order to renew his strength for the battle, like the heroes of ancient times. Notwithstanding his tall stooping form and his frightful emaciation, his movements were just as quick and impetuous as ever. Levin took him to his room.

Nikolai changed his clothes, taking more care than usual over his toilet, brushed his straight, thin hair, and went upstairs smiling.

He was in a most gay and happy mood, such as Levin had known him in his childhood. He even mentioned Sergei Ivanovitch with kindliness. He chaffed Agafia Mihailovna when she came in and questioned her about the old servants. When he heard of the death of Parfen Denisitch, a look of fear came over his face, but he soon regained his composure.

"He was quite old though," he said, and instantly changed the subject. "I shall stay a month or two with you and then I'm going to Moscow. You know Miakov has offered me a place when I get back. I shall arrange my life quite differently now," he continued. "You know I've got rid of that woman, don't you?"

"Marya Nikolaevna? Why? What for?"

"Oh, she was an awful woman and caused me no end of trouble." But he did not say what the trouble had been. He could not tell his brother that he had driven her away because she made his tea too weak and insisted on looking after him like an invalid.

"Besides, I now want to change my life entirely. Of course like everybody else I have been wasting my property, but that is nothing; I do not regret it. If only my health were good . . . but that is better now, thank God."

Levin listened and tried to find something to say, but in vain. Nikolai no doubt noticed it, for he began questioning his brother about his own affairs. Levin was glad to talk about himself, because he could do so without feigning. He told him all about his plans and activities.

Nikolai listened, but was evidently not interested.

There was such a close bond of sympathy between these two men, and they knew each other so well, that the slightest gesture, the merest change in the tone of the voice, spoke to them more than words.

Just now they were both thinking of the same thing—Nikolai's illness and approaching death, and this oppressive thought drowned every other. But neither of them dared speak of it, and so there was a touch of falsehood about everything they said. Levin had never before been so glad for an evening to come to an end and to retire to bed. Never, either with a stranger or on a formal visit, had he felt so constrained and unnatural as he had done during the last few hours. And the consciousness of this, together with the regret he felt, made him more unnatural still. He wanted to cry over his beloved brother who was dying, and he had to listen to and sustain a conversation about how he was going to live.

As the house was damp and Levin's own room the only one that was heated, he got his brother to come and share it with him.

Nikolai went to bed and Levin could hear through the partition that divided them how he kept tossing from side to side. "O Lord!" he would exclaim every now and again when he found it difficult to breathe, or "Damn! Devil take it!" when he could not clear his throat. For a long time Levin could not fall asleep. His thoughts were varied, but they always returned to the one theme—death.

Death, the inevitable end of all, for the first time appeared to him with irresistible force. And death was here with this beloved brother of his, who groaned in his sleep and from force of habit invoked both God and the devil at the same time. Yes, death was not so far off as he had been in the habit of thinking. He felt it in himself too. If not to-day, then to-morrow; if not to-morrow, then in thirty years. It was all the same. But what this inevitable death was he not only did not know and did not think about, but he could not and dared not think about it.

"Here am I working, wanting to accomplish something, and completely forgetting that everything must come to an end, that there is such a thing as death."

He sat up in bed in the dark embracing his knees and holding his breath. He was thinking intensely. But the more he thought the clearer it became to him that in his conception of life he had omitted one little circumstance, and that was that death would come and put an end to everything. It was hardly worth while beginning anything; it was terrible, but there was no help for it, the fact remained.

" But I am still alive. What am I to do now? What am I to do? " he said to himself in despair. He lighted a candle, got out of bed carefully, walked quietly up to the mirror, and began examining his face. There were a few grey hairs on his temples. He opened his mouth. His back teeth were beginning to decay. He bared his muscular arms. Yes, he was still strong. But Nikolinka who was breathing there so painfully with what remained of his lungs, he too had been strong once. And suddenly he recalled how they used to go to bed when they were children and wait for Fiodor Bogdanitch to leave the room so that they could begin a pillow fight. He remembered how they used to laugh and laugh till not even the fear of Fiodor Bogdanitch could drown their mirth and joy in life. " And now that sunken, hollow chest . . . and I not knowing why or wherefore, nor what will become of me. . . ."

" Oh damn! " his brother exclaimed groaning. " What are you doing there? Why aren't you sleeping? " he called to him.

" I can't sleep; I don't know why."

" And I've slept well and hardly perspired at all. Look, my night-shirt is quite dry."

Levin went over and felt his night-shirt, then blew out the candle and returned to bed. It was a long time before he could get to sleep. Just as he was beginning to solve the problem of life he was confronted by the new insoluble problem of death.

" Yes, he is dying; he will be dead by the spring. How can I help him? What can I say to him? What do I know about it? I had even forgotten that such a thing existed."

XXXII

Levin had frequently noticed that when people suddenly become excessively yielding and humble to the point of making others uncomfortable, they are just as quickly turned the other way about and become intolerable in their exactions and quarrelsomeness. He feared that this would happen with his brother. And indeed Nikolai's meekness was of short duration. The very next morning he grew frightfully irritable and began attacking Levin on his most sensitive spots.

Levin felt himself guilty in some way, but could not mend matters. He knew that if they had been frank with one another he would have said to Nikolai, "You are going to die, you are going to die!" while Nikolai would have answered, "I know I am, but I am afraid, afraid, afraid." That is what they would have said to each other, had they spoken what was in their minds. But as this was impossible Levin tried to do what he had frequently failed in before, a thing that it seemed to him others could do without any effort and so well. He talked of indifferent things, but felt all the time there was a falseness about it, and that his brother could see through him and was irritated.

On the third day after his arrival Nikolai began to discuss his brother's new plans, and out of a spirit of contradiction accused him of being a communist.

"You have taken some one else's idea, distorted it, and want to apply it to something to which it is inapplicable."

"But I tell you this is not communism. Communists deny the right to private property, capital, or inheritance, and I do not. I look upon them as the main *stimuli*. . . ." (Levin hated foreign words, but since he had become interested in his work he seemed to use them involuntarily.) "All I want to do is to regulate labour."

"Precisely! You take another's idea, deprive it of all its worth, and then want to pass it off as something new," Nikolai said, with an angry tug at his necktie.

"But I tell you my idea has nothing in common . . . "

"Communism at any rate," Nikolai interrupted him, "has one good feature—geometrical, so to speak. It is perfectly clear and unmistakable. It may be utopia, but admitting that a *tabula rasa* can be made of the whole past—you will have no property, no family, and labour can organise itself. But with you there is nothing . . ."

"Why will you persist in mixing things up? I have never been a communist."

"But I have, and I find that, though it is too premature, it is sensible and has a future before it, like Christianity in the early centuries."

"I merely propose to consider the working power from the

scientific point of view, that is, to study it, to discover all its properties. . . ."

"But that is useless. This force moves of itself and assumes its different forms according to the degree of enlightenment. There have been slaves everywhere, then *métayers*. Even here we have our labourers, those who lease land, and others who work on shares. What more do you want?"

Levin flared up at these words, because in the bottom of his heart he felt that his brother was right. He wanted to balance himself between communism and the existing state of things, and was beginning to fear that it was not possible.

"I am trying to find a means to work productively for myself and for the labourer. I want to build up . . ." he began vehemently.

"You don't want to do anything of the kind. You simply want to appear original, as you've been doing all your life. You want to make believe that you are not exploiting the peasant, but working for a principle."

"If that is what you think, we had better not discuss it further," Levin replied, as he felt a twitching in the muscles of his left cheek.

"You have never had any convictions, nor ever likely to have. You merely want to satisfy your vanity."

"All right, leave me alone."

"So I will. I ought to have gone long ago. I'm sorry I ever came!"

Later Levin tried in vain to calm him, but Nikolai would not listen to him and persisted in saying that they had better part. Konstantin could see that life had grown unbearable to him.

Nikolai had already packed his things when Konstantin again came to him, and asked his forgiveness in a shamefaced sort of way if he had in any way offended him.

"What magnanimity!" Nikolai said with a smile. "If you want to feel yourself in the right, I can give you that pleasure. You were right, but I am going all the same."

Just as he was leaving, Nikolai kissed his brother and gazed into his face with a strange, serious expression.

"Don't think ill of me, Kostia, will you?" he said, and his voice trembled.

These were the only sincere words that had been uttered between them. Levin understood them to the full. "You know what a bad way I am in; we may never see each other again." That is how he interpreted his brother's words, and the tears came into his eyes. He kissed him once more, but could not say anything.

Two days after his brother left, Levin went abroad. At the railway station he ran across Shcherbatsky, Kitty's cousin, who was horrified at his depressed, gloomy aspect.

"What is the matter?" Shcherbatsky asked.

"Oh, nothing; there is little happiness on this earth."

"Why? You had better come to Paris with me instead of going to Mühlhausen. You will see how jolly it can be!"

"No, thanks, my time is over. I am ready to die."

"Really! What a joke!" Shcherbatsky said with a smile. "And my time is just beginning."

"I thought so myself a short time ago, but now I know that I have not long to live."

Levin said what he honestly felt at the time. In everything he could see only death or a preparation for death. But his work interested him more than ever. It was necessary to live his days somehow until death should come. Everything seemed to be enveloped in darkness, and the only guiding light left to him in the dense gloom was his new undertaking, to which he clung with all his might.

PART IV

I

Karenin and his wife continued to live in the same house, meeting every day, yet remaining complete strangers to one another. Alexei Alexandrovitch made a point of seeing Anna every day so as to give the servants no cause for suspicion, but avoided dining at home whenever he could. Vronsky never came to the house, but Alexei Alexandrovitch knew that Anna saw him elsewhere.

The position was tormenting alike to all three, and not one of them would have been able to endure it had they not looked upon it as a temporary, impossible complication that would soon pass over. Alexei Alexandrovitch hoped that Anna's passion would come to an end, as everything else in this world, that people would forget all about it, and that his name would be freed from dishonour. Anna, the cause of the whole situation, and on whom it weighed most heavily, bore it because she was firmly convinced that it could not last, and that something was bound to happen to disentangle the whole difficulty. She had not the remotest idea what that something would be, but waited for it nevertheless. And Vronsky, too, who involuntarily surrendered himself to her, came to believe as she did, and was also expecting that unknown something.

In the middle of the winter Vronsky passed a most tiresome week. He was attached to a foreign prince visiting St. Petersburg, and had to show him the sights of the city. He had been chosen for this duty for his fine presence, his dignified bearing, and also because he was accustomed to meeting such people. Vronsky found the duty a very irksome one. The prince was anxious not to miss seeing anything about which he might be questioned at home, and at the same time wanted to enjoy Russian pleasures as much as possible. Vronsky had to act as his guide in both these capacities. In the morning they drove out to see the sights, in the evening they attended national entertainments. The prince enjoyed exceptionally good health, even for a prince. By the aid of gymnastics and proper attention to his body, he had acquired such great physical strength that in spite of the excesses he frequently indulged in, he was always as fresh as a large, green, Dutch cucumber. He was a great traveller, and found that one of the best advantages of easy communication between one country and another was that it afforded opportunities for participating in the various national pleasures. He had been to Spain and had serenaded a lady who played on the guitar. In Switzerland he had killed a chamois. In England he had raced over hedges in a red coat and shot two hundred pheasants for a wager. In Turkey he had been in a harem. In India he had ridden on an elephant, and now he was eager to taste all the Russian pleasures.

Vronsky as master of the ceremonies, so to speak, had quite a lot of work in arranging for the various amusements that had been recommended to the prince by all sorts of people. There were races and pan-cakes and bear-hunts and troikas and gypsies and carousals, ending with the usual smashing of dishes. The prince soon entered into the spirit of these Russian sports, broke his glasses with the rest, took a gypsy girl on his knees, while his eyes seemed to be asking, " And the next thing, or does the Russian national spirit consist only in this? "

As a matter of fact the prince took far more pleasure in French actresses, ballet-dancers, and champagne with a white seal than in any Russian entertainment. Vronsky was used to princes, but either because he himself had changed of late, or because he had had too much of this one, at any rate the week proved a very tiresome one to him. He felt rather like a man placed in charge of a raving lunatic, who while dreading his patient, feared for his own reason. He had to keep himself well within the bounds of formal politeness not to be insulting. The prince's manner towards people who, much to Vronsky's surprise, would do anything to afford him pleasure was, to say the least of it, contemptible. His remarks about Russian women whom he wished to study, more than once caused Vronsky to blush with indignation. But the real reason why he disliked the prince so much was because he instinctively saw himself in him, and what he saw was not at all flattering to his vanity. The prince was a very stupid, self-confident, clean, healthy man, and nothing more. He was a gentleman, it is true, and Vronsky could not deny it. He was dignified with his superiors, simple and natural with his equals, and treated his inferiors with good-natured condescension. Vronsky conducted himself in the very same manner and was proud of it, but in relation to the prince, he was an inferior, and the latter's condescension annoyed him.

"A stupid ox! Is it possible that I am like him?" he thought.

When he bade him good-bye on the seventh day, before the prince's departure for Moscow, and received his thanks, he felt happy to be delivered from such a disagreeable position, and delighted to be removed from such an unflattering mirror. He took leave of him at the station after their return from a bear hunt, where for a whole night they had given an exhibition of Russian daring.

II

When he reached home Vronsky found a note from Anna. "I am ill and unhappy," she wrote; "I cannot go out and cannot live longer without seeing you. Come this evening. Alexei Alexandrovitch will be at the council from seven to ten." He was surprised at the invitation, considering that her husband had forbidden him the house, but he decided to go.

At the beginning of the winter Vronsky had been promoted to the rank of colonel, and had consequently left his regiment and lived alone. After breakfast he stretched himself on the couch and began dozing. The various sights and incidents of the last few days became curiously mixed in his mind with Anna and a peasant bear-baiter who had played an important part in the hunt. In about five minutes Vronsky fell fast asleep. He woke up with a start when it was quite dark and hurried to light a candle. "What was it? What? What was that terrible thing I saw in my dream? Oh, yes; that dirty little peasant, the bear-baiter with the unkempt beard, was bending down while doing something and muttering some strange words in French. There was nothing else in the dream. I wonder why it seemed so terrible?" he asked himself. Again a vivid recollection of the peasant and the incomprehensible words he had muttered came back to him, and he shuddered from head to foot.

"What nonsense!" he thought as he glanced at his watch. It was already half-past eight. He rang for his valet, dressed hastily, and went out. He completely forgot his dream in the thought that he was late. It was ten minutes to nine when he reached the Karenins' house. A tall narrow carriage drawn by two grey horses stood at the door. He recognised it as

Anna's. "She is coming to me," he thought; "so much the better. I hate going into this house. However, I can't hide myself." And with the manner of a man who has nothing to be ashamed of, a manner he had acquired in his boyhood, he got out of his sleigh and went up to the door. A footman with a rug over his arm opened it and called for the carriage. Vronsky, who was never in the habit of noticing details, could not however help seeing the look of surprise with which the man greeted him. In the doorway he almost ran against Alexei Alexandrovitch. The gas lamp threw its full light on his pale face under his black hat, on his white tie that shone out from under the beaver collar of his coat. Karenin's steady, weary eyes fixed themselves on Vronsky's face. Vronsky bowed and Alexei Alexandrovitch, pressing his lips together, raised his hat and passed out. Vronsky saw him get into the carriage, take his rug and opera glasses through the window, and without once looking round he disappeared from view. Vronsky entered the hall. He was frowning, and there was a proud, angry light in his eyes.

"What a position!" he thought. "If he fought to defend his honour, I could act, express myself, but this is either cowardice or baseness. . . . He puts me in the position of a deceiver, when I have never wanted to be that."

Since his explanation with Anna in Madame Vrede's garden, Vronsky had changed. Involuntarily submitting to the weakness of Anna, who surrendered herself to him completely and looked to him for the solution of her fate, he had long given up thinking that their relations would come to an end as he had then expected. His ambitions again receded to the background, and freed from the round of activities that had occupied him formerly, he completely abandoned himself to his feelings, and they drew him closer and closer towards Anna.

In the hall he caught the sound of her footsteps. He knew she was waiting for him and listening at the door. She was no doubt returning to the drawing-room.

"No, things cannot go on like this!" she greeted him as soon as he appeared, and at the sound of her own voice the tears appeared in her eyes. "If they do it will come much sooner, much sooner!"

"What, my dear?"

"What? I have been waiting in torture for the last two hours . . . No, I won't, I won't quarrel with you. I suppose you couldn't help it. No, I won't . . ."

She laid her hands on his shoulders and gave him a long searching look, her eyes full of love. She was trying to detect any change in his face since she had last seen him. At every meeting she compared him as he really was with her imagination of him.

III

" Did you meet him? " she asked as they sat down near a table with a lamp on it. " It was a sort of punishment for you for being late."

" But why was he here? I thought he was to have been at the council."

" He had returned from the council and has gone off again somewhere. But it doesn't matter. Don't let us talk of him. Where have you been? With the prince all the time? "

She knew every detail of his life. He wanted to tell her that after being up all night he had lain down and fallen asleep, but the sight of her happy, excited face made him feel conscience-stricken. He told her that he had had to present a report after the prince's departure.

" Is it all over now? Has he really gone? "

" Yes, thank the Lord. You can't think how utterly intolerable it was."

" But why? You young men are accustomed to that kind of life," she observed with a frown as she took hold of a piece of crochet on the table and began pulling out the crochet-hook.

" I have long given up that kind of life," he said, wondering at the change in the expression of her face and trying to discover its meaning. " I confess," he added with a smile, showing his fine, even teeth, " it was not at all pleasant to see the old life again in a mirror as it were."

She held the work and crochet-hook, but did not use it. She gazed at him with a strange, unfriendly light in her eyes.

" Liza came to see me this morning—they are not yet afraid of calling, in spite of the Countess Lydia Ivanovna," she added; " she told me all about your Athenian evening. I thought it disgusting! "

" I was about to say that . . ."

But she would not allow him to finish.

" And that Thérèse whom you used to know, was she there too? "

" I wanted to tell you . . ."

" How disgusting you men are! You don't seem to understand that a woman cannot forget it," she went on, becoming more and more heated, and thus revealing the cause of her irritation. " Especially a woman who can know nothing of your life. What do I know? What did I know? Nothing more than you tell me. And how can I be sure that you tell me the truth? "

" Anna, you are insulting me! Don't you believe me? Have I not told you again and again that I have not a single thought I would not share with you? "

" Yes, yes," she replied, evidently trying to dispel her jealous thoughts. " But if you only knew how I suffer! I believe in you, believe in you implicitly. Now tell me what you were going to say."

But he had forgotten what it was. These attacks of jealousy that of late came over her more and more frequently frightened him. Though he knew they were the result of her love for him, yet they produced a chilling effect in him which he was always trying to hide. How many times had he not assured himself that her love was the greatest happiness that life could bestow, but now that she loved him, as only a woman loves for whom love outweighs everything else in the world, he was farther away from happiness than he had been on the day when he followed her from Moscow. At that time he had thought himself unhappy, but had happiness lain before him, he now felt that the greatest happiness lay behind. She was no longer the woman he remembered in those early days. She had changed for the worse both morally and physically. She had grown stouter, and when she mentioned the actress, her face had assumed a distorted, spiteful expression. He looked at her as a man looks at some withered flower, in which he tries to discover the beauty that had once made him pluck it and ruin it. Yet he felt that when his love was strongest, he could sooner have torn it out of his heart than now when it was not so strong. He knew that the bond between them would never be broken.

" Well, what were you going to tell me about the prince? " she asked again. " I have chased away the demon," she added, meaning her jealousy. " What was the matter with him? Why did you find it so unbearable to be with him? "

" It was awful! " he said, trying to gather up the thread of his broken thought. " He does not improve on acquaintance, I assure you. He is nothing more than a well-fed animal, of the kind that take first prizes at cattle-shows," he added with a shade of annoyance that attracted her attention.

"What makes you think so?" she asked. "After all, he is a cultured man and has seen a great deal."

"Their culture is very different, though. The only use he makes of his is to scorn everything except animal pleasures."

"But don't you like these animal pleasures yourself?" she asked, and again he noticed her frown as she looked at him.

"Why are you so anxious to defend him?" he asked with a smile.

"I am not defending him—it is all the same to me. Only I was thinking that if you yourself did not like these pleasures, you could easily have got out of accompanying him. But you enjoy seeing Thérèse in the costume of Eve . . ."

"The demon again," Vronsky said as he took the hand she had placed on the table and kissed it.

"I know, but I can't help it! You don't know what torture it has been waiting for you. It seems to me that I am not jealous. And I am not when you are with me. I have the fullest faith in you, but when you are away from me, doing all sorts of things I know nothing about . . ."

She moved away from him and began plying her crochet-hook nervously, the white wool shining in the lamp-light as it moved between her fingers.

"Well? Did you see Alexei Alexandrovitch?" she asked in an unnatural tone of voice.

"We ran against each other at the door."

"And did he bow to you like this?"

She pulled a long face, half closed her eyes, and folded her hands. In an instant her handsome face had assumed the same expression with which Alexei Alexandrovitch had greeted Vronsky. He smiled and she laughed with her merry, ringing laugh, that constituted one of her principal charms.

"I simply can't understand him," Vronsky observed. "Had he left you after what you told him, or challenged me, I could have understood, but this is beyond me. How can he endure such a position? It is easy to see that he suffers."

"He?" she asked scornfully. "I assure you he is perfectly satisfied."

"Why do we all go on tormenting ourselves when everything could be arranged so well?"

"He does not torment himself. He is saturated with falsehood through and through. If he had any feeling, could he possibly live with me as he does? He understands nothing, feels nothing. Could a man with feelings live in the same house with a wife whom he knows to be unfaithful? Could he speak to her? address her as *thou?*" And again she began imitating the way in which he spoke to her. "He is not a man, not a human being, he is a puppet. Nobody knows it but I. Had I been in his place I should long ago have killed or torn to pieces that wife—such a woman as I am; I should not be calling her *ma chère* Anna! He is not a man, he is nothing but a ministerial machine. He does not understand that I am your wife, that he is a stranger . . . in our way. . . . But don't let us talk of him!"

"You are unjust, my dear," Vronsky said, trying to calm her. "But we won't talk about him. Tell me what you've been doing? What is the matter with you? What is this illness of yours? What does the doctor say?"

She looked at him with a mischievous light in her eyes. She had evidently thought of another amusing trait in her husband's character and waited for an opportunity to turn him into ridicule. But he continued.

"I suppose it is not an illness though, but your condition. Tell me when it's to be."

The mischievous light in her eyes died out and a sad smile, incomprehensible to him, spread over her face.

"Quite soon. You say that our situation is painful and that we ought to put an end to it. Oh, if you only knew how hard it is for me! What would I not give to be able to love you freely and openly. I would not torture myself, nor torment you with my jealousy then. It will soon be over though, but not in the way you think."

And at the thought of how it would happen, tears of self-pity appeared in her eyes and she was unable to proceed. She laid her lovely white hand on his sleeve, her rings flashing in the lamp-light.

"It will not be as we think. I did not mean to tell you, but you made me. Soon, soon all will be over; we shall all be at peace and not torment ourselves any more."

"I don't understand," he said, though he understood perfectly.

"You asked me when . . . It will be soon, and I shall not live through it. Don't interrupt me!" she said and continued hastily. "I know it, I know it for certain. I shall die and am glad of it. I shall set you both free and myself as well."

The tears rolled down her cheeks. He bent over her hand

and began kissing it, trying to hide his agitation, but he did not succeed.

"That's right; that's better," she said, pressing his hand passionately. "That is all there is left to us."

He collected himself and raised his head.

"What an idea! What utter nonsense you talk!"

"No, it is true."

"What is true?"

"That I am going to die. I had a dream about it."

"A dream?" Vronsky repeated, recollecting the peasant of his own dream.

"Yes, a dream," she said. "I have had it many times. It seemed to me that I ran into my bedroom to get something or to see something—you know how things happen in your sleep," she added, her eyes wide open with terror, "and as I looked I saw something standing in the corner . . ."

"What nonsense! How can you believe . . ."

But she would not allow him to interrupt her. The thing she was telling him was far too serious for her.

"And this something turned round and I saw that it was a horrible little peasant with an unkempt beard. I wanted to run away, but he bent over and began rummaging in a bag . . ."

With her hands she showed him how the peasant had rummaged in the bag. There was an expression of terror on her face. And as Vronsky recalled his own dream, the same terror filled his heart.

"And while he was rummaging, he muttered very quickly in French with a guttural pronunciation, '*Il faut battre le fer, le broyer, le pétrir*. . .' I was so frightened that I tried to wake up, and it seemed to me that I did so, but it was still part of the dream. 'What does it mean?' I began asking myself, and I suddenly heard Korney saying to me, 'You will die in childbirth, you will die in childbirth, in childbirth . . .' and then I woke up."

"How absurd! What nonsense!" Vronsky said, but he felt that his words did not sound convincing.

"Don't let us talk of it. Ring the bell, dear, and I'll order tea. But wait a moment. I have not long now. . . ."

Suddenly she stopped and the expression of her face changed. Her terror and agitation gave way to an expression of gentle sweetness, calm and serious. He could not understand the meaning of this sudden change. She had felt the quickening of a new life within her.

IV

After his meeting with Vronsky, Alexei Alexandrovitch went to the Italian opera as he had originally intended. He stayed there through two acts and saw everybody whom he had wished to see. On reaching home he glanced towards the coat and hat stand, and not seeing a military overcoat on it, proceeded to his own room. Contrary to his habit, he did not go to bed, but paced up and down his study until three o'clock in the morning. A feeling of anger against his wife for not having observed the proprieties and for having broken the only condition he had imposed on her—that of not receiving her lover in her own house—gave him no rest. She had not fulfilled his conditions, therefore he must punish her. He must carry out his threat—bring an action of divorce against her and take away the boy. He knew all the difficulties that attended such a course, but he had threatened to do it and must keep to his word. The Countess Lydia Ivanovna had hinted that it would be the best way out of the situation, and as legal formalities had of late become much simpler, Alexei Alexandrovitch began seeing possibilities of bringing it about.

Misfortunes never come alone. Besides this, his case about the condition of alien tribes and the irrigation of fields in the government of Zarai had given him a good deal of trouble in his official capacity. Lately he had been in an extremely irritable state.

He did not sleep the whole night, and his anger grew and grew until it had reached its utmost limits in the morning. He dressed hastily, his cup of anger full to the brim, so to speak, and fearing lest he should expend too much energy before the explanation with his wife, he went to her as soon as he heard that she was up.

Anna, who had always imagined she knew her husband thoroughly, was amazed at his expression when he entered. His brow was dark, his eyes looked severely before him, trying to avoid her glance; his lips were firmly pressed together with a shade of contempt about them. Firmness and decision were expressed in his walk, in his movements, in the very sound of his voice. Anna had never seen him like that before. He walked in without greeting her, went straight up to her writing-table, and taking her keys unlocked the drawer.

" What do you want? " she cried.

" Your lover's letters," he replied.

" They are not here," she said, shutting the drawer, but he understood by her action that he had guessed correctly. He pushed her hand aside roughly and took out a portfolio, where he knew she kept all her important papers. She wanted to tear it from him, but he pushed her aside.

" Sit down; I have something to say to you," he said, putting the portfolio under his arm and pressing his elbow so firmly against it as to raise his shoulder.

She looked at him timidly, in wonder and amazement.

" I told you that I did not wish you to receive your lover in my house. . . ."

" I had to see him in order to . . ."

She stopped at a loss for an excuse.

" I do not wish to enter into the particulars as to why a woman wants to see her lover."

" I wanted . . . I only . . ." She blushed. But his rudeness provoked her and gave her courage. " It is easy enough for you to insult me," she said.

" You can only insult an honest man or an honest woman, but to tell a thief that he is a thief is only *la constatation d'un fait.*"

" I did not know you could be so cruel."

" You call it cruelty when a man gives his wife full liberty and the protection of his honourable name, and demands nothing more in return than that she should observe the proprieties? Is that cruelty? "

" It is worse than cruelty, it is baseness, if you want to know! " Anna cried angrily as she got up and turned to go out.

" No! " he cried in his squeaky voice that had risen a note higher than usual, and seizing her by the wrist forced her into her place again. He had clutched her so firmly that the bracelet left a red mark on her skin.

" Baseness! If you want to use such a word, then it is better applied to a woman who forsakes her husband and child for her lover, yet continues to eat her husband's bread! "

She bent her head. She could not have told him what she had said the evening before, that though he was her husband, he was a superfluous individual; she did not even think it at this moment. She felt the full justice of his words.

" You cannot paint my position worse than I see it myself," she said softly. " But why are you saying all this? "

" Why? Why? " he continued angrily. " In order to inform you that as you did not obey my commands, I am compelled to take the necessary measures to put an end to this situation."

" Soon, soon it will end of itself," she said, and again tears of self-pity came into her eyes as she thought of her approaching death, now so much desired.

" It will end sooner than you and your lover think! All you want is the gratification of your animal lust. . . ."

" Alexei Alexandrovitch! It is not generous, it is not decent to strike a person who is down."

" Yes, you only think of yourself! The suffering of a man who was your husband does not interest you. It is all the same to you that his life has been ruined, that he has su . . . su . . . suff . . ."

Alexei Alexandrovitch spoke so rapidly that he began to stammer and could not pronounce the word. His stammering struck Anna as ridiculous, but she instantly felt ashamed that anything could appear ridiculous to her at such a moment. For the first time she felt sorry for him and tried to put herself in his place. But what could she do or say? She merely hung her head and was silent. He too was silent for a while, and when he spoke again his voice was less squeaky and more cold. He gave special emphasis to the words he chose, as they had no special importance in themselves.

" I have come to tell you . . . " he began.

She glanced up at him. " No, it was only my imagination," she thought, as she tried to recall the expression of his face when he had stammered over the word " suffered." " Can a man so self-satisfied, with eyes like those, feel anything? "

" I cannot change anything," she whispered.

" I came to tell you that I am going to Moscow and will not return to this house again. My lawyer, to whom I am entrusting the divorce case, will let you know of my decision. Serioja must go to my sister's," Alexei Alexandrovitch added, trying to recall what he had intended to say about the boy.

" You only want Serioja in order to spite me," she said, looking at him from under her eyebrows. " You don't love him. . . . Leave him with me! "

" Yes, I have even lost my love for the boy in my loathing for you. But I will take him all the same. Good-bye."

He was about to go to the door, but she held him back.

" Alexei Alexandrovitch! Leave me Serioja! " she implored in a whisper. " At any rate until my . . . my confinement."

Alexei Alexandrovitch blushed and tearing himself away from her, walked out of the room without a word.

V

THE waiting-room of the famous St. Petersburg lawyer was full when Alexei Alexandrovitch entered it. Three ladies, an old woman, a young one, and a merchant's wife and three men, a German banker with a ring on his finger, a merchant with a beard, and an angry civil servant with a cross round his neck, had evidently been waiting for a long time. Two clerks were writing at a table. The writing materials, of which Alexei Alexandrovitch was a good judge, were unusually fine. He could not help noticing it. One of the clerks turned to him without rising.

" What do you want? " he asked angrily.

" I have come to see the advocate."

" He is engaged," the clerk replied severely. He pointed to the other people in the room with his pen and continued writing.

" Can't he find time to see me? " Alexei Alexandrovitch asked.

" No, he is much too busy, but perhaps you can wait."

" Will you please take him my card," Alexei Alexandrovitch said, seeing it was absolutely essential to disclose his identity.

The clerk took the card, gazed at it with disapproval, and walked towards the door.

In principle, Alexei Alexandrovitch approved of public courts, but permitted himself to criticise their workings from high official considerations, as much as he would ever permit himself to criticise anything instituted by order of the sovereign. Having passed his whole life in administration, his disapproval of anything was always slightly modified by the knowledge that it was difficult to avoid mistakes, and also that any institution was open to improvement. He had always looked with disapproval on the power given to lawyers under the new regulations, but as he had never had recourse to the law, his objections were purely of a theoretical nature. Now, however, these objections were greatly strengthened by the bad impression he had received in the lawyer's waiting-room.

" He will see you in a moment," the clerk said to him as he

returned. And, indeed, two minutes had scarcely passed when the lawyer appeared, accompanied by the tall figure of an old jurist, who had been consulting him.

The lawyer was a small, thick-set man with a bald head, a darkish red beard, long light eyebrows, and an overhanging forehead. He was dressed like a bridegroom, from his necktie and double chain to his patent leather boots. He had a common though intelligent face, and his clothes were foppish and in bad taste.

"Will you come this way, please," he said to Alexei Alexandrovitch, and standing aside solemnly to let him pass, he shut the door.

"Won't you sit down?" he said, pointing to a chair by his writing-table which was piled up with papers. He sat down too, leaning his head a little to one side and rubbing his little hands together, the fingers of which were overgrown with tiny white hairs. Just then a moth flew across the room and the lawyer, with a rapidity one would not have expected of him, caught it between his hands and instantly assumed his former pose.

"Before disclosing my business," Alexei Alexandrovitch began, "I should like to observe that I want the matter to remain strictly secret."

A scarcely perceptible smile appeared on the lawyer's lips, slightly moving his reddish moustache.

"I should not be a lawyer if I could not keep the secrets entrusted to me. But if you would like to feel quite certain . . ."

Alexei Alexandrovitch looked at him and saw a smile lurking in his shrewd grey eyes, as though he understood everything.

"Do you know my name?" Alexei Alexandrovitch asked.

"I know you and like everybody else am aware of the valuable services you have rendered to the state," the lawyer replied, catching another moth and inclining his head.

Alexei Alexandrovitch heaved a sigh to gain courage. But having once decided on his course, he lost all timidity and continued in his squeaky voice, laying special stress on certain words.

"I am unfortunate enough to be a deceived husband," he began. "I want to divorce my wife, only in such a way as to give me the custody of our child."

The lawyer did his best to hide his joy, but Alexei Alexandrovitch could see a look of triumph about him such as he had noticed in Anna.

" So you want my legal help to obtain a divorce? "

" Yes, but I must warn you that I may be wasting your time uselessly. I have merely come to consult you about the preliminary stages. Unless a divorce can be obtained under conditions such as I would approve of, I shall have to abandon the idea."

" That is always the case," the lawyer remarked. " It will remain in your power to proceed or not as you wish."

The lawyer dropped his eyes on Alexei Alexandrovitch's boots, fearing to offend his client by the joy his face was unable to conceal. A moth flew past his nose. He put out his hand to catch it, but refrained out of a feeling of respect for Alexei Alexandrovitch's position.

" As I have only a vague knowledge of the law in these matters," Alexei Alexandrovitch continued, " I should like to know the general forms that have to be gone through."

" Do I understand you to say," the lawyer asked, not raising his eyes and following up his client's tone with a sense of pleasure, " that you want me to explain the conditions under which divorce is granted? "

In response to Alexei Alexandrovitch's affirmative nod, he continued, every now and again casting a look at his client's flushed face.

" According to our laws," he said with a shade of disapproval in the words " our laws," " divorce is possible, as you know, under the following circumstances. . . . Tell them to wait," he said to the clerk who had put his head in at the door. He got up however, exchanged a few words with him, and came back to his seat again. " To begin with, divorce is possible when there is a physical defect in either party, or in case of desertion of either party for a period of five years." He enumerated the instances on his short hairy fingers. " Then there is adultery." He pronounced the word with evident satisfaction. " There you have the theoretical side. But I presume that you have done me the honour of coming to consult me on the practical. I find from experience that all divorce cases reduce themselves to . . . There is no question of physical defect or desertion, I suppose? "

Alexei Alexandrovitch replied by a motion of the head.

" As I was saying, nearly all divorce cases reduce themselves to the following: either the guilty party is acknowledged guilty by mutual consent, or else the guilty party has to be proved guilty. I must say, however, that the latter is very rarely met with in practice," he added with a look at Alexei Alexandrovitch

He seemed like a dealer in pistols, who having described the advantages of this weapon and that, is waiting for his customer to make his choice. As Alexei Alexandrovitch was silent, he continued: " Of course the most customary and sensible is adultery by mutual consent; it is the easiest form of all. I should not take the liberty of expressing myself in this manner if I were speaking to an inexperienced person, and I hope you follow me."

Alexei Alexandrovitch was so upset, however, that he could not quite grasp the meaning of adultery by mutual consent. The lawyer noticed his perplexity and instantly came to his help.

" Suppose that a man and wife can no longer live together, if both consent to a divorce, the details and formalities are a matter of indifference. That is the simplest and surest way."

Alexei Alexandrovitch comprehended now, but his religious scruples were opposed to such a course.

" In the present case this is out of the question," he said. " Could not proofs, such as correspondence, establish her guilt in an indirect way? I have letters in my possession."

At the mention of letters the lawyer pressed his lips together and gave a contemptuous snort.

" You must not forget," he said, " that affairs of this sort are in the province of the upper clergy, and they love to investigate every detail." He gave a sympathetic smile. " Letters are only partial proofs, you will need witnesses. If you do me the honour to entrust your case to me, you must leave me the choice of the measures to be pursued. He who wants results must not be too shy of the means."

" In that case . . ." Alexei Alexandrovitch began, turning pale . . . But at this moment the lawyer got up again and walked towards the door to his clerk who had just come in.

" Tell her we are not cheapjacks! " he said to him, as he turned back to Alexei Alexandrovitch. He caught another moth unobserved. " My reps will be ruined this summer! " he thought with a frown.

" You were just saying . . ." he began.

" I shall let you know my decision by letter," Alexei Alexandrovitch said, as he got up and held on to the table. " From what you say, then, I gather that a divorce is possible," he added after a pause. " I should be obliged if you would let me know your terms."

" Everything is possible if you give me full liberty of action," the lawyer said, paying no attention to Alexei Alexandrovitch's remark. "When may I expect to hear from you?" he asked, accompanying his client to the door, his eyes as shiny as his patent boots.

"In about a week. You will then be so kind as to let me know if you will take the case and on what terms."

"Very good."

The lawyer bowed respectfully as he let his client pass out, and when left alone abandoned himself to his joyful sensation. He was in such a good humour that, quite contrary to his rule, he lowered his fee to the haggling lady and left off catching moths, having decided that next winter he would have his furniture re-upholstered in plush, like the Sigonins'.

VI

THE brilliant victory won by Alexei Alexandrovitch at the assembly of the 17th of August proved to be his undoing. The new commission for investigating into the condition of alien tribes was formed and despatched to the spot with an amazing rapidity, thanks to the untiring efforts of Alexei Alexandrovitch. A report was promptly produced in three months. It dealt with the political, administrative, economic, ethnographic, material, and religious aspects relating to these tribes. Every question was followed by an admirably concise reply, which left no room for doubt, it being not the product of human thought, always liable to mistakes, but the work of an infallible bureaucracy. The whole report was full of official data, based on the reports of governors and bishops, who got their information from county chiefs and priors, the latter having in their turn based their information on the reports of town councils and parish priests. Consequently there was no room for doubt anywhere. Such questions, for instance, as to why there was a constant failure of crops, or why the inhabitants adhered to their peculiar faiths, and so on, questions practically insoluble were, by the aid of the official machine, settled in a most convincing and lucid manner, in conformity with Alexei Alexandrovitch's opinions.

Stremov, who had been touched to the quick at the assembly in question, resorted to tactics that Alexei Alexandrovitch had not foreseen. On the receipt of the report he went over to the latter's side, bringing several other members of the commission along with him. He was not only enthusiastic in his support of the measures proposed by Karenin, but suggested others along the same lines, even more radical still. His suggestions were adopted, and then only did Alexei Alexandrovitch understand the meaning of his sudden change. Carried to extremes these measures proved so ridiculous that the government, brilliant society ladies, the press, and the public in general came down in a torrent of indignation and abuse against them and their originator—Alexei Alexandrovitch. Stremov withdrew modestly to the background, making it appear that he had merely followed Karenin's lead, and was himself amazed at the consequences. This proved fatal to Alexei Alexandrovitch. But in spite of his failing health and domestic troubles he did not give in. A split took place in the commission. Some of the members, with Stremov at their head, tried to justify their mistake by asserting that they had believed implicitly in the report of Alexei Alexandrovitch's revisionary commission, and that it was not their fault that the report was absurd and proved merely a scribbling on paper with no real observation behind it. Alexei Alexandrovitch with another party of men, seeing the danger of such a revolutionary attitude towards documents, continued to uphold the findings of the said revisionary commission.

As a result of this, society as well as the public at large became so confused over the issues, that though the greatest interest was shown in this matter, no one could make out whether the alien tribes in question were in a bad condition or in a flourishing one. This did not add to Alexei Alexandrovitch's reputation, and coupled with the contempt thrown upon him through his wife's relations with Vronsky, his position became somewhat precarious. But Alexei Alexandrovitch made an important move. Much to the surprise of the other commissioners he announced his intention of applying for leave to go and investigate the conditions personally, and when this was granted him he departed to the distant provinces. His departure created a great sensation, particularly as he had refused the money allowed him officially for expenses, including a sum sufficient to cover the cost of twelve horses.

" I think it very noble of him," the Princess Betsy observed, while discussing him with the Princess Mahky. " Why pay for stage-horses when there are railways everywhere? "

But the Princess Mahky did not agree with her and was even a little irritated by her remark.

"It is all very well for you when you possess I don't know how many millions, but as for me, I like my husband to go on his tours of inspection in the summer. It is good for his health and he enjoys himself exceedingly. Besides, were it not for this money we could not afford to keep a carriage."

Alexei Alexandrovitch broke the journey at Moscow, where he stayed for three days.

On the day after his arrival he set out on a visit to the governor-general. At the crossing near Gazette Lane, where it is always crowded with vehicles, Alexei Alexandrovitch suddenly heard his name called in such a loud, merry voice that he could not help turning round. Stepan Arkadyevitch, in a smart coat and fashionable hat, was standing at the side of the pavement calling to him and making signs for the coachman to stop. He looked just as gay and beaming as ever. With one hand he was holding on to the window of a carriage that had stopped at the corner of the street, while with the other he beckoned to his brother-in-law. A lady in a black velvet hat thrust her head out of the window and two little children could be seen inside. The lady, too, was waving to Alexei Alexandrovitch. It was Dolly and her children.

Alexei Alexandrovitch did not wish to see any one in Moscow, least of all his wife's brother. He raised his hat and wanted to drive on, but Stepan Arkadyevitch ordered the coachman to stop and ran across to him over the snow.

"What a shame not to let us know you were coming!" Stepan Arkadyevitch said, putting his head in at the window. "Have you been here long? I was at Dusseaux's last night and saw 'Karenin' among the list of arrivals, but it never occurred to me it was you, or I should have gone in to see you. What a shame not to let us know!" he repeated, knocking his feet together to shake off the snow.

"I had no time; I was very busy," Alexei Alexandrovitch replied coldly.

"Come over to my wife; she would like to see you."

Alexei Alexandrovitch unwound the rug from his chilly legs, got out of the carriage, and walked across the snow to Darya Alexandrovna.

"Why, what has happened, Alexei Alexandrovitch, that you avoid us in this way?" Dolly asked him with a smile.

"I was very busy. I am delighted to see you," he added in a tone that plainly denoted the reverse. "How are you all?"

"And how is my dear Anna?" Dolly asked.

Alexei Alexandrovitch muttered some reply and was about to turn away, but Stepan Arkadyevitch detained him.

"I say, you mustn't go like this! Dolly, invite him to dinner! We'll get Kosnishev and Pestsov to come as well to give him a sample of our Moscow intellectuals."

"You'll come, won't you? We shall expect you at five, or at six if you like. Well, how is my dear Anna? It is so long . . ."

"She is very well, thank you," Alexei Alexandrovitch muttered with a frown. "Glad to have met you," he added, as he walked away to his carriage.

"You'll come?" Dolly called after him.

Alexei Alexandrovitch made some reply, but Dolly could not hear it above the roar of the traffic.

"I shall look in to see you to-morrow," Stepan Arkadyevitch shouted after him.

Alexei Alexandrovitch got into his carriage and leaned far back so that no one could see him.

"What a strange person he is!" Stepan Arkadyevitch said to his wife. He looked at his watch, made a hasty motion of farewell to her and the children, and walked quickly down the pavement.

"Stiva! Stiva!" Dolly called after him, blushing.

He turned back.

"You must give me some money; I have to get some clothes for Grisha and Tania."

"Oh, tell them to send in the bill!"

He nodded his head gaily to a passing acquaintance and disappeared from view.

VII

The following day was Sunday. Stepan Arkadyevitch drove to the Grand Theatre to attend a ballet rehearsal and to take a coral necklace to Masha Chibisov, a pretty dancer, who had entered the theatre under his protection—a gift he had promised her the day before. In the dim light of the green-room he planted a kiss on her pretty face that shone with pleasure as she received her present. He had also come to alter an appointment he had made with her, explaining that he would not be able to come to the theatre that evening until the last act, and that he would take her out to supper after the performance. From there Stepan Arkadyevitch drove to the market where he chose a large fish and some asparagus for dinner, and at twelve o'clock he called at Dusseaux's hotel, where, as luck would have it, all the three people he wished to see happened to be staying. They were his chief, who had just been promoted and was on a tour of inspection in Moscow, Levin who had just returned from abroad, and his brother-in-law Karenin, whom he intended to bring back to dinner at all costs.

Stepan Arkadyevitch was fond of a good dinner and was never more happy than when he was giving one at home, in his own house, to a select circle of friends. He was most particular about the choice of wines and viands. The menu for this evening's dinner satisfied him completely. There would be perch, asparagus, and *la pièce de résistance,* excellent roast beef, and various wines. The guests, too, satisfied him no less. There would be Kitty and Levin, and to make it less pointed he had also asked a girl cousin of his and young Shcherbatsky. *La pièce de résistance* of the guests was to be Sergei Kosnishev and Alexei Alexandrovitch. The first a Moscow philosopher, the second a St. Petersburg man of affairs. To set them off, as it were, there would be the eccentric enthusiast Pestsov, musician, historian, great talker, and liberal—a most charming youth of fifty.

Stepan Arkadyevitch had received the second instalment of money for the wood he had sold, and this fortunately was not yet all spent; Dolly had been very nice to him of late, so that the thought of the dinner was in every respect pleasing. He was in the happiest of moods. There were only two circumstances that were somewhat annoying, but even these were forgotten in his general good-humour. The first was that Karenin had been very cold at their meeting yesterday, and coupling this with the fact that he had not been to see them, and the various rumours he had heard about Anna and Vronsky, he was led to think that something was wrong between husband and wife. The second disagreeable incident was the fact that his new chief was reputed to be a terrible man who got up at six o'clock in the morning, worked all day like a horse, and expected his subordinates to do the same. Besides which he was said to be a perfect bear in his manners and was openly opposed to his predecessor's liberal tendencies which Stepan Arkadyevitch had always shared.

Yesterday Stepan Arkadyevitch had appeared at the office in

his uniform and the new chief had been very amiable and treated him as an acquaintance. That is why he considered it his duty to call on him to-day in civilian clothes, though he was rather doubtful about the sort of reception that awaited him. But Stepan Arkadyevitch had hopes that everything would turn out for the best. " We are all sinners alike, so why should we quarrel? " he thought as he entered the hotel.

" Halloa, Vassily! " he greeted the porter as he walked down the corridor, his hat poised jauntily on his head. " Why have you shaved your whiskers? Is Levin in number seven, eh? Show me the way, please. And find out if Count Anitchkin is in." This was his new chief.

" Right, sir," Vassily replied with a smile. " It is long since you've been here."

" I was here yesterday, but I came in at the other door. Is this number seven? "

When Stepan Arkadyevitch entered, Levin was standing in the middle of the room with a peasant, measuring a bear-skin with a yard-measure.

" I say, did you kill it? " Stepan Arkadyevitch cried. " What a fine specimen! A she-bear, I suppose. How are you, Arhip? "

He shook hands with the peasant and sat down without removing his hat or coat.

" Why don't you take your things off? " Levin asked, taking his hat off for him.

" I mustn't really; no time. I've only looked in for a moment," Stepan Arkadyevitch replied. He unbuttoned his coat, but took it off in the end and stayed for a whole hour, talking to Levin about hunting and all sorts of intimate subjects.

" Now tell me what you've done abroad and about all the places you've been to," he began as soon as the peasant had left them alone.

" I've been to Germany, Prussia, France, and England, but I stayed in all the manufacturing towns, not in the capitals. I am very glad I went."

" Of course I know your views on the labour question."

" There is no labour question in Russia. With us there is only a question of the relation of the labourer to the soil. They have it there too, but it is an artificial affair, while here . . ."

Stepan Arkadyevitch listened attentively.

" Yes," he said, " perhaps you're right, but I'm delighted to find you in such excellent spirits. I see you go in for bear-hunting and are generally enthusiastic. From what young

Shcherbatsky told me a while ago, I was afraid you were depressed. He said you talked of nothing but death."

"Well, I have not left off thinking about it," Levin replied. "You can't get away from the fact that we all have to die and that everything is vanity. I love my work, but when I think that this world of ours is nothing but a little mildew covering the surface of the smallest of the planets—when I think of the vastness of the universe, all our thoughts and ideas seem to me as insignificant as tiny grains of sand."

"What you say is as old as the hills."

"That may be, but when once you realise it, everything loses its importance. When you think that either to-day or to-morrow you may be dead, what does anything matter? I used to look upon my ideas as important, but even if they were accomplished they would have no more significance in the vast scheme of things than the act of walking round this bear-skin. It is to keep away thoughts of death that we hunt and work and try to divert ourselves."

Stepan Arkadyevitch smiled affectionately as he listened to him.

"So you have come over to my way of thinking at last. Do you remember how you used to attack me for seeking pleasure in life? Be not so severe, O moralist!"

"There is a certain amount of good in life, though that . . ." Levin became confused. "I really don't know; the only certain thing is that we shall die soon."

"But why soon?"

"Of course life is not so pleasant when you think of death, but it is much more peaceful."

"On the contrary I think it is much more fun. However, I must go," he added, rising for the tenth time.

"What's the hurry? Stay a little longer," Levin said, trying to detain him. "I may not see you again, I am going away to-morrow."

"Dear me! I had nearly forgotten, and I came on purpose to ask you. Be sure to come to dinner to-day. Your brother is coming and my brother-in-law Karenin."

"Is he in Moscow?" Levin asked. He would have liked to hear news of Kitty who at the beginning of the winter had gone to stay with her sister, the diplomat's wife, at St. Petersburg, and he did not know if she had returned or not, but he could not summon up enough courage to ask.

"I don't care; I'll go in any case," he thought.

" You'll come, won't you? "

" Of course I will."

" Come at five. No dress clothes."

Stepan Arkadyevitch rose and went downstairs to his new chief. Instinct had not deceived him. The terrible man turned out to be very nice. Stepan Arkadyevitch stayed to lunch with him and sat talking so long that it was nearly four o'clock by the time he got t Alexei Alexandrovitch.

VIII

Alexei Alexandrovitch went to hear mass, after which he returned home and remained there for the rest of the morning. He had two important things to accomplish that day. In the first place he had to receive a deputation of aliens who were now in Moscow on their way to St. Petersburg, and in the second he had to write the promised letter to the lawyer. The deputation, for which Alexei Alexandrovitch was largely responsible, turned out to be very unsatisfactory, so that he was very glad to have met them before they got to headquarters. The men composing it had not the remotest ideas of what their duties consisted in. They merely thought that all they had to do was to explain their wants and the government would help them. They could not be got to understand that some of their demands supported the hostile party, and that if they persisted in them they would ruin the whole cause. Alexei Alexandrovitch had a good deal of trouble with them. He made out a programme for them from which they were not to deviate and despatched several letters to St. Petersburg, apprising various people of their coming. He looked to the Countess Lydia Ivanovna to be his principal help in the matter. She had had a good deal of experience in deputations, and no one was more capable than she of giving the right tone to one. Having disposed of this business, he wrote a letter to the lawyer, giving him full freedom to act as he thought best, and enclosing three notes of Vronsky's to Anna that he had found in the portfolio he had taken from her.

Ever since Alexei Alexandrovitch had gone out of his house with the fixed intention of never returning to his family again and had been to the lawyer's, thus communicating his intention to another person, and especially since he had put the case on paper, he had grown more and more accustomed to the thought of a divorce, and began feeling hopeful about the possibilities of obtaining one.

He was just sealing the letter when he heard the sound of Stepan Arkadyevitch's voice. Stepan Arkadyevitch was insisting that Alexei Alexandrovitch's servant should announce him.

"What does it matter?" Alexei Alexandrovitch thought. "I may as well see him and tell him everything, then he will understand why I cannot come to dinner."

"Come in!" he called as he began clearing up his papers and putting them into his blotting case.

"So he is at home; I knew you were lying," Stepan Arkadyevitch was heard saying to the servant, who had refused to admit him. He took off his overcoat as he walked along and entered the room.

"I'm so glad to find you in! Now I hope . . ." he began gaily.

"I am sorry; I cannot come," Alexei Alexandrovitch said coldly. He was standing and did not ask his guest to sit down. He had resolved to be distant in his manner towards Stepan Arkadyevitch as seemed fitting in view of the circumstances, but he had not counted on that sea of good-nature that flowed through the latter's heart.

Stepan Arkadyevitch opened his bright eyes very wide.

"Why not? What is the matter?" he asked in French, full of amazement. "You promised to come and we've been counting on you."

"I cannot come to your house because the relations that have existed between us are about to be severed."

"How? What do you mean? Why?" Stepan Arkadyevitch asked with a smile.

"Because I am going to take divorce proceedings against your sister, my wife. I was compelled . . ."

Alexei Alexandrovitch had hardly finished what he was about to say when Stepan Arkadyevitch dropped into a chair with a cry of alarm.

"Alexei Alexandrovitch, you can't mean it!" he cried, his face full of pain.

Stepan Arkadyevitch had not expected him to take it like that.

"I do, unfortunately," he replied.

"Excuse me, but I can't, I can't believe it. . . ."

Alexei Alexandrovitch sat down. He felt that his words

had not had the effect he had expected and that he would have to explain; but he knew at the same time that no matter what the explanation might be, his relations to his brother-in-law would remain unchanged.

"Yes, I am placed under the painful necessity of taking divorce proceedings," he said.

"I will say this much, Alexei Alexandrovitch; I know you as an excellent, just man, and Anna—excuse me, but I cannot change my opinion about her—as a good, splendid woman. That is why I cannot believe what you say. There must be some misunderstanding. . . ."

"I only wish there were a misunderstanding!"

"Of course, I quite see . . ." Stepan Arkadyevitch interrupted him; "but really . . . I should like to ask you one thing. You must not do things in a hurry; you really mustn't."

"I am not hurrying," Alexei Alexandrovitch replied coldly. "But unfortunately one can't take advice in these matters. I have definitely decided upon it."

"It is terrible!" Stepan Arkadyevitch said, heaving a deep sigh. "There is one thing I want you to do, Alexei Alexandrovitch, and I implore you to do it. Since the action has not yet begun, go and see my wife and talk things over with her. She loves Anna like a sister and you too. And she's a wonderful woman. For Heaven's sake go and talk it over with her! Grant me this one favour, I beg of you!"

Alexei Alexandrovitch stood considering, while Stepan Arkadyevitch looked at him compassionately.

"You will go and see her, won't you?"

"I really don't know. I did not call at your house because I supposed that our relations must change."

"But why should they? I can't see it. I may presume to think that apart from our relationship you entertain at least part of the friendly feelings for me that I have always had for you. I've always had the greatest respect . . ." Stepan Arkadyevitch pressed his hand. "Even if your worst suspicions were true I should refrain from taking either one side or the other. I really see no reason why our relations should change. You will come and see my wife, won't you? Do come, please!"

"What would be the good? We look at things differently," Alexei Alexandrovitch said coldly. "However, we had better not talk of it further."

"But why not come, if only to dinner to-night? My wife is

expecting you. Do come. Talk things over with her. She's a wonderful woman. For God's sake; I implore you on my knees!"

"If you want me to so much, I will come," Alexei Alexandrovitch said with a sigh.

To change the subject he began talking about a thing of common interest to them both—that is about Stepan Arkadyevitch's new chief. Alexei Alexandrovitch wondered that so young a man should get such a high appointment. He had never liked Count Anitchkin and had always differed from him in opinion. Now he could hardly conceal his hatred, natural to an official who had suffered disappointment, to one who had won success.

"Have you seen him?" he asked with a little smile.

"Oh, yes; he came to the office yesterday. He seems to know his business well and is very active."

"But what does his activity consist in?" Alexei Alexandrovitch asked. "Does he do anything, or merely go about undoing what has already been done? Our country is beridden by a paper administration of which he is a worthy representative."

"Really, I know nothing about it. I am not aware of his political views, but as far as I can judge he seems a very nice man," Stepan Arkadyevitch replied. "I've just been to see him and he was most amiable. I had lunch with him and showed him how to make that drink, you know, wine mixed with orange juice. A most refreshing drink. I was surprised he did not know it. He liked it very much. He seems a jolly good fellow."

Stepan Arkadyevitch glanced at his watch.

"Dear me! It's five o'clock and I have to go to Dolgovshin's yet! So you'll come to dinner? You can't think how hurt we should be otherwise."

Alexei Alexandrovitch parted from his brother-in-law in a manner different from that in which he had received him.

"I shall keep my promise," he said dejectedly.

"I can't tell you how grateful I feel, and I promise you you shall not regret it," Stepan Arkadyevitch said with a smile.

He put on his overcoat as he walked along, laid his hand on the servant's head with a laugh, and went out.

"At five o'clock, please. No dress clothes," he called out once more, returning to the door.

IX

It was nearly six o'clock, and some of the guests were already waiting when the host himself arrived home. He came in together with Kosnishev and Pestsov, who had both met at the door. Oblonsky looked upon them as the chief representatives of the Moscow intellectuals. They were generally respected both for their high characters as well as their wit. They respected each other too, but never agreed upon anything; not because they belonged to opposite camps, but for the very reason that they belonged to the same. There were subtle differences in this camp that an outsider failed to observe; and as there is nothing less conducive to agreement than differences over small things, they had long given up discussing seriously and merely made fun of each other's little errors. They were talking about the weather when Stepan Arkadyevitch came upon them.

Prince Alexander Dmitrievitch Shcherbatsky, Turovtsin, Karenin, Kitty, and young Shcherbatsky were already sitting in the drawing-room when they entered.

Stepan Arkadyevitch could see at a glance that things were not going well. Dolly in a grey silk dress, worrying over the children who had to dine alone in the nursery and also over the fact that her husband had not yet come, did not seem to know how to bring this company together. They all sat straight and prim, " like a clergyman's daughters out calling " as the old prince expressed it, evidently wondering why they had come, and forcing themselves to speak in order to avoid a still more awkward silence. Good-natured Turovtsin seemed out of his element, and when he caught sight of Stepan Arkadyevitch, his thick lips broke out into a smile, as much as to say, " Why did you bring me among all these clever people? A bottle of wine in the Château des Fleurs is more in my line! " The old prince sat in silence, casting a sidelong look at Karenin every now and again with a twinkle in his eye. Stepan Arkadyevitch could see that he had already hit upon some witticism to describe this statesman, whom they had all been invited to meet. Kitty was looking towards the door and hoping that she would not blush when Levin entered. Young Shcherbatsky, who had not been introduced to Karenin, was trying to show that this circumstance did not in the least embarrass him. Karenin himself, according to his St. Petersburg habit, was in dress clothes. Stepan Arkadyevitch could tell by the expression of his face that he had merely come to keep his word. He looked as though he were performing some painful duty. It was he who had frozen the other guests before Stepan Arkadyevitch's arrival.

Stepan Arkadyevitch excused himself for being late, explaining that he had been detained by a certain prince, who was largely responsible for all his delays and absences. He introduced every one all round, and bringing Alexei Alexandrovitch and Sergei Kosnishev together, he launched them on a discussion on the Russianising of Poland, into which Pestsov was also drawn. Then he left them, and clapping Turovtsin on the shoulder he whispered some joke into his ear and joined his wife and the old prince, not forgetting to tell Kitty how pretty she looked. In one minute he had kneaded the social dough to such a consistency that the company began enjoying themselves and the voices rang out merrily. Only Levin had not yet arrived. But this turned out to be very fortunate, for Stepan Arkadyevitch, walking into the dining-room to see how things were progressing, saw to his great horror that the port and sherry had been bought at Dedré's instead of Levé's as he had ordered. He despatched the coachman to change it as quickly as possible, and was about to return to the drawing-room when he came upon Levin.

" Am I late? " the latter asked.

" You're always late! " Stepan Arkadyevitch replied, taking his arm.

" Are there many people? Who is here? " Levin asked with a blush as he shook off the snow from his cap with his gloves.

" All our own people; Kitty too. Come, I'll introduce you to Karenin."

In spite of his liberalism, Stepan Arkadyevitch was proud of a connection such as Karenin, and was eager to show him off to all his best friends. Levin, however, was hardly in the mood for appreciating the value of such an acquaintanceship. He had not seen Kitty since the evening she had refused him, without counting the glimpse he had had of her in the carriage on the road. His heart had told him that he would meet her to-day, but he had been trying not to listen to it. Now that he knew for certain, such joy and terror seized him that he caught his breath and was unable to say what he wanted to.

" I wonder what she is like? The same as before, or as she

appeared in the carriage? Supposing what Darya Alexandrovna said should be true! Why should it not be?" he thought to himself.

"Very well; introduce me to Karenin," he said with difficulty. He entered the drawing-room with a desperately determined step and immediately caught sight of her.

She was not the same as he had known her before, nor as he had seen her in the carriage; she was quite different. She seemed shy and frightened, but on that account all the more charming. She saw him the very moment he entered the room. She had been waiting for him. She was overjoyed and ashamed of her joy. Levin went up to the hostess, and it seemed to both of them as they glanced at Kitty that she was on the verge of tears. She was trembling all over and grew from pale to red as she waited for him to approach her.

He came to her at last, bowed silently, and extended his hand. Her smile was almost calm, though her lips trembled and a moist film came over her eyes as she took it desperately in her own.

"What a long time it is since we've met!" she said.

"But I have seen you though you did not see me," Levin said, with a smile of happiness. "I saw you coming from the station on your way to Yergushov."

"When?" she asked in surprise.

"When you went to stay with Darya Alexandrovna," Levin replied, almost overcome by the joy that flowed through his heart. "How could I have thought anything evil of this beautiful creature? Darya Alexandrovna must have been right," he thought to himself.

At this moment Stepan Arkadyevitch came up, took him by the arm, and led him over to Karenin.

"Allow me to introduce you . . ."

"Glad to meet you again," Karenin said coldly as he shook hands with Levin.

"Have you met already?" Stepan Arkadyevitch asked in surprise.

"We spent three hours together in a railway carriage," Levin said with a smile; "and came away interested as from a masquerade—at any rate I did."

"Really! Now will you come to dinner, please," he said with a gesture in the direction of the dining-room.

The men went into the dining-room and walked up to a little table on which various appetisers were standing. There were several kinds of brandies and as many kinds of cheese, some with forks, others without. There were several varieties of caviar and pickled herrings, preserves, and plates of French bread.

The discussion on the Russianising of Poland carried on between Kosnishev, Karenin, and Pestsov began to die down in the expectation of dinner. Sergei Kosnishev availed himself of his peculiar knack of bringing a conversation to a close in the most piquant way. Alexei Alexandrovitch was maintaining that the Poles could only be Russianised by the government's adopting higher principles in their administration, while Pestsov insisted that one nation could only absorb another when it had a larger population. Kosnishev to a certain extent agreed with the one and the other. In order to wind up the discussion, he said with a smile as they were leaving the drawing-room—

"There seems to be only one means of absorbing the aliens, and that is to have as many children as possible. My brother and I have not done our duty in that direction. But you married men, especially Stepan Arkadyevitch, are acting in a most patriotic manner. How many have you?" he asked, turning to the host and handing him a small glass of brandy.

Every one burst out laughing, Stepan Arkadyevitch the loudest of all.

"That is certainly the best way," he said, munching a piece of cheese and drinking his brandy. And the conversation ended with that joke.

"Won't you try this cheese? It's not at all bad," Stepan Arkadyevitch said encouragingly.

"Have you gone in for gymnastics again?" he asked as he turned to Levin and felt the muscles of his arm with his left hand.

Levin smiled and tightened his muscles under Stepan Arkadyevitch's fingers.

"What biceps! A perfect Samson!"

"I suppose you need great physical strength for bear-hunting?" Alexei Alexandrovitch asked, whose notions about hunting were of the vaguest. He was spreading some cheese on a thin slice of bread.

Levin smiled.

"Not at all," he said; "on the contrary, a child could kill a bear." He bowed slightly and made way for the ladies, who, headed by the hostess, were approaching the table.

"Did you really kill a bear?" Kitty asked as she tried to stick her fork into a slippery mushroom that resisted her attempts. Levin could see her white arm through her lace sleeve. " I did not know you had bears in your part of the world," she added as she turned her beautiful head towards him with a smile.

There was nothing particular in what she said, but what inexplicable meaning there was for him in the very sound of her voice, the motion of her lips, eyes, hands! She seemed to entreat his forgiveness, was so tender, caressing, and confident! He could see that she loved him and was filled with a wild hope. His happiness was beyond bounds.

" No, we went down to Tver, and on my way back I met your brother-in-law, or rather I should say your brother-in-law's brother-in-law. It was a funny meeting."

And in a very amusing manner he proceeded to relate how, in a short fur coat and dishevelled after a sleepless night, he had broken into Alexei Alexandrovitch's compartment.

" The conductor, judging me by my clothes, wanted to turn me out, but I assumed a high and mighty air. And you too," he said, turning to Karenin (he had forgotten his name), " were suspicious of my short coat and wanted to do likewise, but I must say you interceded for me in the end, for which I was very grateful."

" The rights of passengers in the choice of seats are altogether too indefinite," Alexei Alexandrovitch said, wiping the tips of his fingers with his pocket-handkerchief.

" I could see that you still felt suspicious of me, though," Levin continued with a good-natured smile, " so I hastened to open a brilliant conversation to atone for my short fur coat."

Sergei Ivanovitch was talking to the hostess and at the same time listening to his brother. " What is the matter with him to-day? He looks like a conqueror," he thought. He did not know that Levin felt as though he had suddenly grown wings. He knew that Kitty heard his words, and that it gave her pleasure to listen to him. This was the only thing that interested him. He was alone with her, not only in that room, but in the whole world, and looked down from those dizzy heights at these excellent people—Oblonskys, Karenins, and the rest of humanity.

Stepan Arkadyevitch with his usual tact placed Kitty and Levin beside each other.

" You might as well sit here," he said to Levin as though there was no other place available.

The dinner was excellent and well served. The Marie-Louise

soup was delicious, and so were the little patties that almost melted in one's mouth. Two footmen with the help of Matvey in a white tie moved about noiselessly as they waited at table. In short, the dinner was a great success. The conversation, too, was unusually lively. Now private, now general, it never lagged, and when the men rose from the table even Alexei Alexandrovitch had completely thawed.

X

PESTSOV liked to bring an argument to a logical conclusion and felt displeased with Kosnishev's words, the more so as he was somewhat dissatisfied with the opinion he had expressed.

"I did not mean," he said during soup, turning to Alexei Alexandrovitch, "that we should set about absorbing other nations on principle, but that it would come about naturally if our population were larger."

"That amounts to the same thing," Alexei Alexandrovitch replied in a drawling tone. "In my opinion only a nation with a superior culture can hope to influence another. A culture that . . ."

"That is precisely the question!" Pestsov interrupted him in his bass voice. He was always in a hurry to speak, and seemed to put his whole soul into what he was saying. "To whom do you accord the preference? Which nation is to take the lead? Which will enforce its nationality on the others? The Rhine has become French, yet the Germans do not stand on a lower level. There must be another law at work!" He had grown heated and raised his voice.

"The advantage is always on the side of true culture," Alexei Alexandrovitch observed, raising his eyebrows slightly.

"But what are the signs of this true culture?" Pestsov asked.

"I should have thought they were well known to everybody," Alexei Alexandrovitch replied.

"But are they known?" Sergei Ivanovitch asked with a faint smile. "It is now accepted that true culture can only be classic. We hear violent arguments on both sides, and it cannot be denied that the opposition has some very strong points in its favour."

"But you are a classicist, Sergei Ivanovitch," Stepan Arkadyevitch remarked. "Would you like some red wine?"

" I am not expressing an opinion about this or that culture," Sergei Ivanovitch said with a condescending smile, as though he were talking to a child; " all I say is that there are strong arguments on both sides." He turned to Alexei Alexandrovitch. " I am a classicist by education, but in this discussion I cannot exactly place myself. I see no clear reason why the classics should be placed above the natural sciences."

" The natural sciences have just as great an educational value," Pestsov put in. " Take astronomy, botany, or zoology with its system of common laws . . ."

" I am afraid I cannot agree with you there," Alexei Alexandrovitch said. " It seems to me that the very process of studying the forms of a language has a favourable influence on mental development. And besides, it cannot be denied that the influence of classic writers has been moral in the highest degree, whereas the study of the natural sciences has been confused with those false, dangerous doctrines that are the worst signs of our times."

Sergei Ivanovitch was about to say something, when Pestsov interrupted him in his heavy bass. He grew hot in his condemnation of such a view, while Sergei Ivanovitch waited patiently for him to finish, having evidently prepared some crushing retort.

" We cannot help admitting," Sergei Ivanovitch began, turning to Karenin with a smile, " that it is extremely difficult to weigh the merits or demerits of any particular science. It would have taken long to decide in favour of the one or the other had not classic education the moral—*disons le mot*—anti-nihilist influence on its side."

" Exactly."

" Were it not for this we should probably have felt inclined to give both influences a chance, but as it is we offer our classic education in the form of pills as a cure against nihilism. And are we so very sure of the healing properties of these pills? " Sergei Ivanovitch asked.

At the mention of pills every one laughed, especially Turovtsin, who had been waiting patiently for the conversation to take a funny turn.

Stepan Arkadyevitch had done well to invite Pestsov. With him there, the conversation would not lag for a moment. Sergei Ivanovitch had no sooner concluded than Pestsov started again.

" You can hardly say that the government has this aim in view," he said. " It is obviously guided by general considerations and is perfectly indifferent to the influences that the measures taken may produce. According to what you say it ought to consider the education of women harmful, yet we find it opening courses and universities for women everywhere."

The conversation immediately went over to the question of women's education.

Alexei Alexandrovitch was of opinion that women's education was too much confused with questions of emancipation, and that on that account alone it was harmful.

" I believe on the contrary that these two questions are inseparable," Pestsov observed. " It is like a vicious circle. Woman is deprived of her rights because of her lack of education, and her lack of education is due to the deprivation of her rights. We must not overlook the fact that the bondage of woman is so great and so old that we frequently fail to understand the abyss that separates her from us."

" When you spoke of rights," Sergei Ivanovitch began as soon as Pestsov had finished, " did you mean the right to perform duties on a jury, a county council, as presidents of law-courts, or members of parliament? "

" Precisely."

" If you think that women can fulfil these functions, would it not be more correct to speak of them as ' duties ' and not as ' rights? ' You will all agree that in sitting on a jury or town council, or doing the work of a telegraph operator, we are performing duties. Thus it would turn out that women are seeking duties, and quite legitimately so. We cannot but sympathise with their desire to aid men in their labours."

" Quite so," Alexei Alexandrovitch remarked. " But it seems to me that the question resolves itself into this: are women fitted for these duties? "

" Without doubt they will be when education becomes general among them," Stepan Arkadyevitch put in. " We see . . ."

" And the proverb? " the old prince asked, who had been listening to the conversation with a twinkle in his eye. " I may repeat it in the presence of my daughters. Woman has long hair, but . . ."

" We thought the same of the negroes before their liberation! " Pestsov interrupted him, angrily.

" It seems strange to me that women should be looking for new duties while we men are trying to escape from them," Sergei Ivanovitch observed.

" Duties are accompanied by rights, power, money, honour; that is what women are after," Pestsov remarked.

" It seems to me to be the same as though I demanded the right to be a wet nurse and felt injured because it was not granted me, while women were being paid for it," the old prince put in.

Turovtsin burst out laughing, and Sergei Ivanovitch felt a touch of envy that he had not made the remark. Even Alexei Alexandrovitch smiled.

" But a man cannot nurse," Pestsov remonstrated, " while a woman . . ."

" Why not? I knew of an Englishman who brought up his child on a ship," the old prince said. He permitted himself a little freedom in his speech in the presence of his daughters.

" There are about as many women fitted to be officials as there are Englishmen of that kind," Sergei Ivanovitch hastened to add.

" Yes, but what is a girl to do who has no family? " Stepan Arkadyevitch asked. He had Masha Chibisov in his mind and supported Pestsov on her account.

" If you investigate the history of such a girl you will probably find that she abandoned her family, either her own or her sister's, where she could have performed the duties becoming to a woman," Darya Alexandrovitch remarked with a certain amount of irritation, evidently guessing what kind of a girl Stepan Arkadyevitch had in view.

" But we stand for a principle, for an ideal! " Pestsov thundered. " Woman claims the right to be independent and educated; she is oppressed and crushed by the consciousness that this is impossible."

" Just as I am oppressed and crushed because I won't be received as wet nurse in a foundling hospital," the old prince said, much to the delight of Turovtsin, who laughed so much that he dropped the thick end of a piece of asparagus into the sauce.

XI

ALL took part in the conversation except Kitty and Levin. At first, when they were discussing the influence of one nation over another, it flashed through Levin's mind that he had something to say upon the subject, but he really could not trouble to recall what it was. He felt himself in a dream and all his former thoughts and ideas had not the slightest interest for him. It even appeared absurd to him that they should all be bothering themselves about something that was of no use to any one. Kitty, too, ought to have been interested in the discussion on woman's rights and education, for not only had she often considered the question in relation to her friend Varenka's dependent position, but also on her own account, in the event of her not marrying. How often had she not quarrelled with her sister on the subject! But she paid little heed to it now! She carried on a private conversation with Levin. It was not exactly a conversation, but some mysterious communion that bound them closely together and produced in them both a sensation of fear and joy at the unknown into which they were entering.

Kitty asked him how he could have seen her in the carriage last year, and Levin explained how it had happened.

"It was very early in the morning; you had evidently just awakened. Your mother was still asleep in the corner. It was a beautiful morning, I remember. I was walking along and wondering who could be coming in that beautiful carriage with bells. As it passed I glanced in at the window and there you were, sitting like this and holding the ribbons of your bonnet in both hands. You seemed wrapped in thought," he added with a smile. "How I should like to know what you were thinking of then! Was it about something very important?"

"I wonder if I was untidy?" she thought, but noticing Levin's smile as he was describing these details, she was convinced that the impression she produced must have been a good one.

"I really can't remember," she said with a smile and a blush.

"What a jolly laugh Turovtsin has!" Levin said, as he gazed at him in admiration.

"Have you known him long?" Kitty asked.

"Who does not know him?"

"You don't think him a good man, do you?"

"He is not bad, he is merely insignificant."

"You are quite mistaken and had better change your opinion at once!" Kitty said. "I too had that idea of him once, but he is a dear, wonderfully good man. He has a heart of gold."

"How did you get to know his heart?"

"He and I are great friends, so I know him very well. Last

winter, soon after . . . after you were at our house," she added with a guilty, yet confident smile, " Dolly's children all fell ill with scarlet fever. He happened to call about something and, would you believe it? " she said in a whisper, " he felt so sorry for her that he stayed and helped her nurse them. Yes, for three weeks he remained in the house and looked after them like a real nurse. I am telling Konstantin Dmitritch about Turovtsin and the scarlet fever," she said bending over to her sister.

" Yes, it was wonderful! " Dolly said with a glance at Turovtsin, who could tell by her smile that they were talking of him. Levin looked at him again and was surprised that he had never been able to appreciate the charm of the man until now.

" I am sorry; I shall never think ill of people again! " he said gaily, giving full expression to what he was feeling.

XII

In the discussion on women's emancipation the question of the inequality of the rights of women in marriage was touched upon —a very delicate subject in the presence of the ladies. Pestsov attacked it several times during dinner, but Sergei Ivanovitch and Stepan Arkadyevitch warded it off carefully. But when they rose from the table and the ladies left the room, Pestsov turned to Alexei Alexandrovitch and began explaining where the principal inequality lay. In his opinion the inequality consisted in the fact that the infidelity of a wife was more severely condemned both by law and public opinion than that of a husband.

Stepan Arkadyevitch hastened to offer Alexei Alexandrovitch a cigarette.

" No, thanks, I don't smoke," the latter replied coldly, and wishing to show that he was not afraid of the subject, he turned to Pestsov with a faint smile.

" The reasons why this is so are to be found at the very root of things," he said, and was about to go into the drawing-room when Turovtsin suddenly turned to him.

" Have you heard about Pratchkinov? " he asked, a little excited by the champagne he had drunk and eager for a chance of breaking his oppressive silence. " You know Vasia Pratchkinov!" he added with a good-natured smile on his moist red lips, addressing himself to the chief guest of the evening, Alexei Alexandrovitch. "I heard this morning that he fought a duel in Tver with Kvitsky, and killed him."

It seemed to Stepan Arkadyevitch that the conversation was fated to touch upon Alexei Alexandrovitch's one sore spot. He tried to lead him away, but Alexei Alexandrovitch would not go.

"Why did Pratchkinov fight?" he asked with a touch of curiosity.

"On account of his wife. He behaved like a hero! Challenged the man and killed him!"

"Really?" Alexei Alexandrovitch asked indifferently with a slight motion of the eyebrows as he turned to go into the drawing-room.

"I'm so glad you've come," Dolly said with a half-scared smile as she met him in the ante-room. "I should like a talk with you. Let us sit down here."

Alexei Alexandrovitch sat down beside Dolly with a forced smile. He wore the same indifferent expression as when Turovtsin had told him about the duel.

"I shall be delighted too, because I was about to ask you to excuse me for leaving early. I am going away to-morrow."

Dolly was convinced of Anna's innocence and felt furious with this cold unfeeling man who was about to ruin her innocent friend.

"Alexei Alexandrovitch," she began, looking into his eyes with desperate determination, "I asked you how Anna was, but you did not tell me; how is she?"

"She seems quite well, Darya Alexandrovna," Alexei Alexandrovitch replied, avoiding her gaze.

"Alexei Alexandrovitch, excuse me; I know I have no right . . . but I love and respect Anna as my own sister . . . I beg of you, implore you, tell me what there is between you. What do you accuse her of?"

Alexei Alexandrovitch frowned, half shut his eyes, and lowered his head.

"I suppose your husband has told you why I consider it necessary to change my former relations to Anna Arkadyevna," he said still avoiding her glance and casting a look of apprehension, at Schherbatsky who was coming through the drawing-room.

"I don't believe it, I can't believe it!" Dolly said, as she pressed her thin, bony hands together. She rose quickly and put her hand on Alexei Alexandrovitch's sleeve. "We shall be disturbed here; come this way, please."

Dolly's agitation communicated itself to Alexei Alexandrovitch. He rose and followed her submissively into the nursery. They sat down by the table, which was covered by a piece of American cloth that had been cut all over with a pen-knife.

"I can't, I can't believe it!" Dolly repeated, trying to catch his glance that was avoiding hers.

"You can't help believing facts, Darya Alexandrovna," he said, laying special stress on the word "facts."

"But what has she done?" Dolly asked. "What has she done?"

"She has treated her duties with contempt and deceived her husband. That is what she has done," he replied.

"But it's impossible, impossible! I can't believe it! You must be mistaken!" Dolly exclaimed, as she clutched her head in both her hands and covered her eyes.

Alexei Alexandrovitch gave a forced smile, desiring to show her the firmness of his conviction; but her warm defence of Anna, though it did not shake him, opened his wound afresh.

"It is difficult to be mistaken when your wife tells you herself that eight years of married life and her boy count for nothing, and that she wants to begin life all over again," he said bitterly.

"Anna and sin—I cannot connect the two, I cannot believe it!"

"Darya Alexandrovna!" he said, now looking straight into her kind agitated face, and feeling for the first time that he could speak freely, "I would have given much if doubt had still been possible. So long as I doubted, it was hard for me, but less hard than now. Until I was sure, there was hope, but now there is no hope. I am suspicious of everything. I cannot bear to see my son, and I sometimes doubt too if he is my son. I am very unhappy."

There was no need for him to say that, for Dolly could see it written plainly on his face. She grew sorry for him, and her faith in her friend's innocence was shaken.

"This is terrible, terrible! But have you really decided on a divorce?"

"That is the only course open to me. There is nothing else to be done."

"Nothing else to be done, nothing else to be done . . ." Dolly repeated with tears in her eyes. "But there must be something else!"

"The most dreadful part about a misfortune like this is, that you cannot go on bearing the cross as in the case of a loss or death; it becomes necessary to act," he said as divining her thought. "You must get yourself out of the humiliating position; three people can't go on living together."

"I know, I know," Dolly said as she lowered her head. She grew silent as she thought of her own sorrow, but suddenly she raised her head again and held up her hands entreatingly. "Alexei Alexandrovitch! You are a Christian! Think of her! What will become of her if you cast her off?"

"I have thought of it many times," he replied. His face was covered with patches of red and his weary eyes looked straight into hers. Darya Alexandrovna now pitied him from the bottom of her heart. "When she first told me of her disgrace I did what I could. I left everything as of old. I had hopes of saving her. I gave her an opportunity to mend, but nothing came of it. She would not even fulfil the smallest of my requests to observe the proprieties. You can only save a person who wants to be saved. But if a woman's nature is so corrupt that ruin appears as salvation to her, what can you do?"

"Anything except a divorce!" Dolly said.

"But what do you propose?"

"It is terrible to think about. She will be nobody's wife . . . she will be lost!"

"But what can I do?" Alexei Alexandrovitch asked with a shrug of the shoulders. The memory of his wife's last transgression hardened him. He grew as cold as he had been at the beginning of their conversation.

"I thank you very much for your sympathy, but it is time for me to go," he said, rising.

"No, wait a moment! You must take pity on her. Just think of what happened to me. My husband deceived me and in my jealousy and anger I wanted to throw up everything, I wanted to . . . But it was Anna who brought me to my senses and saved me. And you see, here I am still living. The children are growing up, my husband is returning to his family and is beginning to realise that he has done wrong and is getting better and purer. . . . I have forgiven and you too must forgive!"

Alexei Alexandrovitch listened, but her words no longer affected him. All the hatred he had felt on the day he had decided on the divorce rose up in his heart. He shook himself and began in a loud piercing voice—

"I cannot forgive; I do not want to forgive; I consider it unjust to forgive. I have done everything I could for this woman, but she has trampled everything in the mire. It is just like her. I am not a bad man; I have never hated anybody in my life, but now I hate her with my whole soul for all the wrong she has done me!" Tears of anger stood in his eyes.

"Love them that hate you," Dolly murmured timidly.

Alexei Alexandrovitch gave a bitter smile. He had known that long ago, but it did not apply to his case.

"We can love those who hate us, but we can't love those whom we hate. I am sorry I have upset you. We each have our own sorrows." He regained his self-control, bade her good-bye calmly, and departed.

XIII

WHEN they had all risen from table, Levin wanted to follow Kitty into the drawing-room, but was afraid she might be offended by his rather marked attention. He remained with the men, taking part in the general conversation, yet conscious of Kitty all the time. It seemed to him that he could feel her glance, her movements, and knew the very spot she happened to be standing on in the drawing-room.

He had not the smallest difficulty in carrying out the promise he had given her to try and love all men. The conversation had turned on the Russian village commune. Pestsov looked upon it as a grand institution, destined to serve as an example to the rest of the world. Levin did not agree either with Pestsov or with his brother, who recognised, yet at the same time denied, the value of this institution, but he tried to pacify them both and toned down their rather severe expressions. He was not in the least interested in what he was saying and still less in what they were saying, but he was anxious for every one to be happy and contented. He now knew the one important thing. And that one thing was walking about in the drawing-room, and began coming closer, and stopped at the door. He could feel her glance and smile directed to him and instantly turned round. She was standing at the door with Shcherbatsky and looking at him.

"I thought you were going to the piano," he said, walking over to her. "The only thing I miss in the country is music."

" No, we were merely coming to find you," she said, rewarding him with a smile. " Thank you for having come. There is no sense in arguing; you can never convince anybody."

" That is true," Levin said. " You mostly argue for no other reason than because you can't understand what your adversary is driving at."

Levin had often noticed that in discussions between people of even superior intellect, after an enormous struggle and an expenditure of fine logical arguments, the disputants generally arrived at the consciousness of the fact that they were in reality agreed upon the thing in question, but did not like to confess as much, because they preferred to differ. Levin had felt it again and again.

Kitty wrinkled her forehead, trying to understand what he meant, but as soon as he began explaining, she comprehended at once.

" I see, you have to know what your adversary wants, what he stands for, then it is possible . . ."

She had fully caught his badly expressed idea. Levin gave a smile of pleasure. He was struck by the difference in the lengthy complex dispute with Pestsov and his brother, to this clear, simple expression of a subtle thought.

Shcherbatsky left them, and Kitty, going up to a card table near by, sat down, took a piece of chalk, and began drawing circles on the green cloth.

They renewed the discussion started at dinner on women's rights and duties. Levin agreed with Dolly that a girl who did not marry could always find some feminine occupation in a family. He confirmed this by the statement that no family could get along without a woman's help, that every family, whether rich or poor, had to have nurses, be they hired or otherwise.

" No," Kitty said with a blush, as she looked at him boldly with her frank eyes, " a girl may be so situated that it is humiliating for her to enter a family. Take myself . . ."

He instantly understood her.

" Oh, yes, you are right! " he said.

He now saw clearly what Pestsov had been driving at at dinner. He could see that Kitty feared maidenhood and humiliation, and loving her he could not help feeling with her. He at once renounced his former conclusions.

A silence ensued. Kitty continued scribbling on the table with the chalk. Her eyes shone with a soft light. Surrendering himself to her mood he felt an ever increasing sense of happiness throughout his whole being.

"Oh dear! I have scribbled all over the table!" Kitty exclaimed as she put down the chalk and was about to rise.

"What shall I do without her?" Levin thought in horror as he took the piece of chalk.

"Don't go yet," he said, sitting down. "I have long wanted to ask you something." He looked into her caressing though somewhat frightened eyes.

"What is it?"

"Here it is," he said, writing down the first letters of the words he intended to say: w, y, s, i, c, b, d, y, m, t, o, n? They signified: "When you said it cannot be, did you mean then or never?" It was hardly probable that she would be able to decipher this complicated sentence, yet he looked at her as though his whole life depended upon it.

She gazed up at him with a serious expression, then rested her head on her arm and knit her brows as she began to read. Now and then she would look at him as though asking, "Have I guessed right?"

"I have made it out," she said with a blush.

"What is this word?" he asked, pointing to the last letter "n."

"That means 'never,'" she replied, "but it is not true."

He rubbed out the letters hastily, gave her the chalk and stood up. She wrote down: I, c, n, a, d, t.

Dolly felt consoled for the grief Alexei Alexandrovitch had caused her when she saw these two together. Kitty was sitting with the chalk in her hand, gazing up at Levin with a timid, happy smile, while Levin's handsome figure was bending over her and looking eagerly now at her, now at the table. His face suddenly brightened He had understood. The letters meant: "I could not answer differently then."

He gave her a timid searching look.

"Only then?"

"Yes," her smile replied.

"And n . . . And now?" he asked.

"Well, read this. I will tell you what I should like very, very much." She wrote down: I, w, y, t, f, a, f, meaning: "I want you to forget and forgive."

He seized the chalk feverishly and wrote down the first letters of the following sentence: "I have nothing to forgive and forget; I have never ceased loving you."

She looked at him with a smile.

" I know what it means," she murmured.

He sat down and wrote a long sentence. She understood it all, and without asking any questions she took the chalk and wrote down the answer.

For a long time he could not make out what it was and kept gazing into her eyes. His happiness nearly blinded him. He could not see what she had written, but the light in her eyes told him what it was more plainly than words. He took up the chalk and began writing, but he had barely finished when she took it from him and wrote down the word " yes."

" Are you playing *secrétaire?* " the old prince asked, approaching them. " We ought to go if you want to be in time for the theatre."

Levin rose and accompanied Kitty to the door.

In their curious conversation everything had been explained. Kitty had confessed that she loved him, and said that she would tell her father and mother. It was arranged that he should go and see them in the morning.

XIV

WHEN Kitty had gone and Levin was left alone, he began feeling so restless and uneasy that he grew terrified at the prospect of spending fourteen whole hours without her, and longed for the morning to come, when he should see her again. He wanted to be united to her for ever. He was burning with a desire to talk to some one so as to kill time and avoid being alone. He would have liked talking to Stepan Arkadyevitch, but the latter announced that he was going to a reception. (He was in reality going to the ballet.) Levin had just time to tell him how happy he was, how he loved him and how he would never forget what he had done for him. Stepan Arkadyevitch's glance showed Levin that he fully appreciated this feeling.

" Well, do you still think it's time to die? " Stepan Arkadyevitch asked, pressing Levin's hand with a certain amount of emotion.

" N . . . no! " Levin replied.

Dolly, too, seemed to offer her congratulations when she said to him at parting, " I am so glad you and Kitty have made it up again. We must value old friends." These words seemed to jar on Levin. She could not understand what he was feeling; it was far beyond her, and she should not have alluded to it. Levin took leave of them and tacked himself on to his brother.

"Where are you going?"

"To a meeting."

"Can I come with you?"

"Yes, if you like," Sergei Ivanovitch replied with a smile. "What has come over you to-day?"

"Me? Happiness!" Levin said, as he let down the window of the carriage. "You don't mind, do you? It's so close in here. I am so happy! Why did you never marry?"

Sergei Ivanovitch smiled.

"I am very glad. She seems a very nice gi . . ." he began.

"Don't speak of it, don't speak of it!" Levin cried, as he seized the collar of his brother's coat and wrapped it round him. "She seems a very nice girl" were such commonplace words compared to what he was feeling.

Sergei Ivanovitch burst into a merry laugh, a thing that rarely happened with him.

"You'll let me congratulate you at any rate."

"To-morrow you can, but not now. You mustn't say anything now; you must keep complete silence!" Levin said, and again wrapping his collar round him, he added, "I love you very much! Well, may I come to the meeting?"

"Of course you may."

"What is the meeting about?" Levin asked, still smiling.

They arrived at the meeting. The secretary was reading the minutes, evidently not understanding what they were all about; but Levin could see by his face and from the way he stumbled and hesitated over the reading that he was a kind sensitive man. When he finished, the speeches began. They were discussing the disposal of certain sums of money and the laying of certain drains. Sergei Ivanovitch made an eloquent speech, completely crushing two other members of the council. Another member, after making a few notes, began replying to him, at first timidly, then very sarcastically. Sviajsky, who happened to be there, got up next and made a grand high-flown speech. Levin listened to them, feeling that the money to be expended, the sewer-pipes and the rest, were of no serious importance and that all these dear, excellent people were not really quarrelling, but were enjoying themselves immensely. What surprised Levin so much was that he seemed to be able to see through them. And they were all such dear good men and appeared to like him so. Even strangers came up and talked to him!

"Well, how do you like it?" Sergei Ivanovitch asked.

"Very much. I had no idea it would be so interesting!"

Sviajsky came up next and invited him to tea. Levin could not understand why he had been displeased with Sviajsky, or what he had expected of him. He seemed such an excellent intelligent man.

"Thank you," he said accepting the invitation, and began questioning him about his wife and sister-in-law. By a strange association of ideas, he was glad of an opportunity to see them. Sviajsky's sister-in-law had always connected the idea of marriage in his mind, so he imagined that no one would be more glad to hear of his happiness than they.

Sviajsky asked him about his agricultural ventures, expressing his old opinion that nothing could be discovered in that direction that had not already been tried in Europe. But Levin did not mind this in the least now. On the contrary, he felt that Sviajsky was right and that all his former schemes were of no importance. He also could not help admiring Sviajsky's delicacy and modesty when he admitted it. The Sviajsky ladies were particularly charming. It seemed to Levin that they knew all and sympathised with him, but refrained from mentioning the subject out of a sense of delicacy. He stayed with them for three whole hours, talking about all sorts of things, while thinking only of one, and did not notice that he was tiring them to death and that it was long past their time for retiring. Sviajsky accompanied him to the door, yawning and wondering what had come over his friend. It was two o'clock. Levin returned to his hotel and was again terrified at the idea of spending ten whole hours alone. A waiter lighted his candles and was about to go out when Levin stopped him. This man, Yegor, whom he had not noticed before, now seemed to him wonderfully kind and intelligent.

"Well, Yegor! is it very hard to do without sleep?"

"What can you do, sir? Such is our business. The work is not so hard in the houses of private gentlemen, but we make more money here."

Levin learnt that Yegor had a family of three sons, and a daughter whom he wished to marry to a clerk in a harness shop.

Upon this Levin began explaining to Yegor that love was the chief thing in marriage, that with love you could always be happy, because happiness was in yourself.

Yegor listened attentively as though he had fully grasped his meaning, but in reply he brought out the irrelevant remark that when he had lived in the houses of good gentlemen he had always been satisfied, and that now he was quite satisfied with his master, though he was a Frenchman.

"What a fine fellow he is!" Levin thought.

"Well, and you, Yegor, were you in love with your wife when you married?"

"Of course I was!" Yegor replied.

Levin saw that Yegor, too, was in an ecstatic state and wanted to give expression to his innermost feelings.

"My life, too, has been remarkable. In my childhood . . ." he began, his eyes beaming, evidently infected byLevin's mood, just as people are infected by a yawn.

But just then a bell was heard. Yegor had to go and Levin was left alone. He had eaten scarcely anything at dinner, had refused tea and supper at the Sviajskys', but could not think of eating. He had not slept the previous night, yet could not think of sleep. It was cold in the room, but he felt oppressively hot. He opened both windows and sat down by a table near them. Beyond the snow-covered roofs the tall spire of a church with a carved cross and chains could be seen, and above that were the constellations of the Charioteer and the bright Capella. He gazed now at the cross, now at a star, drew in deep draughts of the keen frosty air that flowed freely into the room, and as in a dream, one picture after another rose up in his mind. At about four o'clock he heard steps in the corridor, opened the door, and looked out. It was Miaskin, a gambler, coming home from his club. He was coughing as he walked along and his face wore a dark, gloomy expression. "Poor man!" Levin thought, as tears of pity came into his eyes. He wanted to talk to him, to comfort him, but recollecting that he was in his shirt, he changed his mind and went back to the window again to bathe in the fresh, cold air and look at that weird, silent cross, so full of meaning for him, and at the glorious yellow star. At seven o'clock the sound of the floor-polishers at work brought him to himself. He could hear the sound of church bells, calling people to early mass, and realising that he was nearly frozen, he shut the windows, dressed hastily, and went out.

XV

The streets were still empty. Levin went straight to the Shcherbatskys' house. The front door was still closed and all were asleep. He went back to his hotel again and ordered coffee. A day waiter, not Yegor, brought it up to him. Levin wanted to enter into conversation with him, but a bell rang and he had to go. Levin tried to drink his coffee and eat his rolls, but could not. He put on his coat and went out again. It was nearly ten o'clock when for the second time he approached the Shcherbatskys' house. The inmates were just beginning to stir and the cook was going to market. He must make up his mind to wait at least another two hours.

The whole of the night and morning Levin had spent in an unconscious state, quite indifferent to the material conditions of existence. He had not eaten for a whole day, had not slept for two nights, had been exposed to the cold for several hours with scarcely any clothes on, and felt not only fresher and sounder than ever, but completely independent of his body. He seemed to move without an effort of his muscles, and felt that he could do anything, from flying to moving a house, if necessary. He passed the rest of the time walking about in the streets, consulting his watch every minute or two, and looking around him.

He never saw again what he saw that morning. The children on their way to school, the silvery grey pigeons that flew from the roofs to the pavement, the little loaves of bread that some invisible hand had put out, all seemed to him divine. Two little boys ran towards a pigeon and looked smilingly at Levin; the pigeon fluttered its wings and flew off, glistening in the sun, through the quivering snow-dust in the air; from a window came the odour of freshly-baked bread, as a few little rolls were laid on the sill. It was all so touching that Levin laughed and wept for joy. He made a large circle round by Gazette Lane and Kislovka Street, got back to his hotel, and sat down to wait until twelve with his watch before him. In the adjoining room some one was talking of machines and swindlers, and the sound of a cough could be heard. He was too dazed to see that the hands were pointing to twelve. They passed it. Levin went out again. The cabmen evidently knew everything. Their happy faces surrounded him, jostling each other in their efforts to offer him their services. Levin chose one, and promising the others that he would engage them some other time, he set off for the Shcherbatskys'. The driver looked splendid in his white shirt, the collar of which projected above his coat and covered his powerful red neck. The sleigh was high and comfortable, such as Levin had never ridden in before. The horse looked good and tried its best to run, but did not seem to move from the spot. The driver knew the Shcherbatskys' house and drew up at the steps respectfully. The Shcherbatskys' porter, too, knew all, as was evident from the smile with which he greeted him.

" It is long since you were here, Konstantin Dmitritch! " he said.

It seemed to Levin that the porter not only knew, but rejoiced over it, and was making an effort to conceal his joy. As he looked into the dear old man's eyes, all his happiness struck Levin anew.

" Are they up? "

" This way, sir! Leave it here, please," he said with a smile, as he noticed that Levin had taken up his hat.

" To whom shall I announce you, sir? " a footman asked.

This footman belonged to the newer generation and was a dandy, but he seemed to Levin a nice young man who understood everything.

" To the princess, the prince, and the young princess," Levin replied.

The first person he met was Mlle Linon. She was crossing the large drawing-room and her face and curls were radiant. He had barely exchanged a few words with her when suddenly the rustle of a dress was heard from the other side of the door. Mlle Linon disappeared, and his heart nearly stood still at the thought of the happiness that awaited him. Light, rapid steps resounded over the polished floor as his happiness, his life, he himself—the better part of himself, that for which he had been longing and waiting—came quickly towards him. She did not seem to walk, but was borne along by some invisible force.

He could see her bright, trusting eyes that were frightened by the same joy that filled his own heart. They drew nearer and nearer, blinding him with their light of love. She came close to him and placed her hands on his shoulders. She yielded herself to him joyfully and timidly. He embraced her and pressed his lips to hers.

She too had passed a sleepless night and had been waiting

for him all the morning. Her parents had given their consent and were happy in her happiness. She had wanted to be the first to tell him. She had been preparing herself to meet him alone, and was overjoyed and ashamed at the thought. When she heard his voice she did not know what to do. She waited behind the door till Mlle Linon had gone, and without stopping to think she rushed up to him.

"Let us go to mamma!" she said after a moment, taking his arm.

He could not speak for a long time, not so much because he was afraid of desecrating his feelings by words, but that he was prevented by the tears of joy that rose to his eyes. He took her hand and kissed it.

"Is it really true?" he said at last in a husky voice. "I cannot believe that you love me, dear!"

She smiled at the word "dear," and at the timidity with which he looked at her.

"Yes," she said softly, "I am so happy!"

Without letting go his arm she led him into the smaller drawing-room. On seeing them together the princess began to laugh and cry at the same time, and running up to Levin with an energetic step he would not have expected of her, she took his head in both her hands and kissed him, bedewing his face with her tears.

"Then it's all settled! I am so glad. Love her, won't you? I am so happy, Kitty!"

"They've arranged things quickly!" the old prince said, trying to appear indifferent. But Levin could see that his eyes were full of tears as he turned to him.

"I have always hoped for this," he said, as he took Levin by the arm and drew him to himself; "even when this frivolous child thought of . . ."

"Papa!" Kitty cried reproachfully, as she put her hand over his mouth.

"All right, I won't!" he said. "I am very, very . . . gl . . . How stupid I am!"

He embraced Kitty, kissed her face and hands, and made the sign of the cross over her.

Levin was suddenly seized with a strange affection for this old man as he saw Kitty showering kisses on his round, fat hand.

XVI

THE princess was sitting in an arm-chair with a smile on her face; the prince sat down near her. Kitty stood by her father's chair, still holding his hand. All were silent.

The princess was the first to speak. She liked to call things by their proper names and to bring all feelings into the domain of every-day life. When she spoke, the others could not help feeling jarred.

"Well, when is it to be?" she asked. "We must tell every one of the engagement. When shall we fix the wedding, Alexander?"

"There is the hero; let him decide," the old prince replied with a gesture in the direction of Levin.

"When?" Levin asked with a blush. "If you ask me, then I should say announce the engagement to-day and the wedding to-morrow."

"What nonsense, *mon cher!*"

"Well, in a week."

"He's absolutely mad."

"Not at all."

"But, my dear!" the mother said, smiling at his impatience; "you've forgotten the dowry."

"Will there be a dowry and all that?" Levin thought in terror. "But I don't care! Can a dowry or anything spoil my happiness? Nothing can spoil it!" He glanced at Kitty and saw that she was not in the least offended at the idea of a dowry. "Perhaps it is necessary," he thought.

"I know nothing about it; I have merely expressed my desire," he said, excusing himself.

"Then we shall decide. The announcement, at any rate, we can make now."

The princess approached her husband, kissed him, and was about to turn away, but he detained her. He put his arms about her and kissed her many times, tenderly, like a young lover. The old people were evidently confused for the moment; they could not quite tell whether it was they who were in love or their daughter. When they both left the room Levin approached Kitty and took her hand. He felt master of himself now and had a great deal to tell her. But he spoke of something quite other than he had intended to.

"I knew it would come!" he said. "Though it sometimes seemed to me hopeless, yet in the bottom of my heart I was always sure of it. I believe we were predestined . . ."

"I, too," she said, "even when . . ." She stopped and looked at him resolutely with those frank eyes of hers; "even when I turned away from my happiness," she went on. "I always loved you alone, even when I was attracted . . . Can you ever forget it?"

"Perhaps it was for the best. You will have so much to forgive me. I must tell you . . ."

He had made up his mind to tell her two things. The first was that he was not as pure as she; the second that he was an unbeliever. It was painful, but he considered it essential that she should know.

"But no, I won't tell you now!" he said, "Later on will do."

"Very well," she said. "But you must tell me everything; I am not afraid. All that is over now."

"But you will have me, such as I am? You won't take back your word, will you?"

"Oh, no!"

They were interrupted by Mlle Linon, who with a tender smile came to congratulate her favourite pupil. She had scarcely gone when the servants came with their congratulations and after them came relatives and friends, and there began that ridiculous hubbub from which Levin did not escape until the day after his marriage. He was horribly uncomfortable all the time, but his happiness kept on increasing. A great deal was demanded of him about which he knew nothing, and he did what every one told him to do. He had thought that his engagement would have nothing in common with other engagements, but it ended in his doing exactly what everybody else did, and his happiness, far from being marred as a result of it, grew greater day by day.

"Now we shall have all the chocolates we want!" Mlle Linon happened to say, and Levin ran to the confectioner's.

"Delighted!" Sviajsky said when he heard the news. "I should advise you to get some flowers at Fomin's."

"Is it necessary?" And off he went to Fomin's.

His brother advised him to borrow some money, as there would be a great many expenses in the way of presents, etc.

"Are presents necessary?" And he instantly departed for Fulde's.

At the confectioner's, at Fomin's, and at Flude's it seemed

to him that they were all expecting him and that every one rejoiced in his happiness as he himself had done for the last few days. Everybody seemed to love him and treat him with special consideration, even people who had formerly been indifferent to him. They all shared his belief that he was the happiest of men and that Kitty was the pink of perfection. And Kitty, too, felt just as he did. When the Countess Nordston permitted herself to hint that she had hoped for a better match, Kitty grew quite angry and declared that there was not a better man in the world than Levin, and that the Countess Nordston ought to have realised it. Since then the Countess Nordston never failed to greet Levin with a most enthusiastic smile in Kitty's presence.

The confession he had promised was the one oppressing incident of that time. After consulting with the old prince, Levin gave Kitty his diary, wherein were written those events that tormented him so. He had kept the diary on purpose for his future wife. The confession of his unbelief passed by unnoticed. She was religious, had never doubted her faith, yet his external unbelief did not even touch her. She knew his soul through and through and was quite satisfied with it. His second confession, however, caused her to shed bitter tears.

Levin had not given her the diary without an inner struggle, but he had decided that there should be no secrets between them. He could not have foreseen the effect the knowledge would have upon her. It was only when he called to take her to the theatre that evening and on entering her little boudoir saw her pitiful, sweet face bathed in tears, that he realised the sorrow he had caused her and what an immeasurable abyss divided his past from her virgin purity. He grew horrified at what he had done.

"Take those horrid papers away!" she said pushing his diary towards him. "Why did you give them to me? Perhaps it is better that you did though," she added, softened by the look of despair on his face. "But it's terrible, terrible!"

He hung his head and was silent.

"I suppose you will never forgive me," he murmured at last.

"I have forgiven you; but it's terrible!"

His happiness was so great that even this confession could not mar it. Another drop was added to his cup of joy. She had forgiven him. But from that time he considered himself still less worthy of her and valued his undeserved happiness more than ever.

XVII

On his way back to the hotel, Alexei Alexandrovitch began involuntarily reviewing the impressions of the conversation at dinner and after. Darya Alexandrovna's words about forgiveness had merely annoyed and irritated him. The application or non-application of the Christian rule in his case was too serious a matter to be talked of lightly. Besides, he had long ago decided it in the negative. Of all that had been said that evening, the remark of the good-natured fool Turovtsin had most impressed his mind. "He acted like a hero. He challenged his rival and killed him." They had all agreed with it, though they had refrained from saying so out of sheer politeness.

"However, the thing is all settled; it's no use thinking about it," Alexei Alexandrovitch said to himself, and turned his mind to his forthcoming journey and the business of inspection. When he got to the hotel he asked the porter if he had seen his valet, and having learnt that he was out, Alexei Alexandrovitch went up to his own room. He ordered tea, and taking Frum, he sat down by the table and began planning the route of his journey.

"Two telegrams," his valet announced, entering the room. "Excuse me, your excellency, I had only run out for a moment."

Alexei Alexandrovitch took the telegrams and tore them open. The first contained the news that Stremov had received the very appointment that he himself had desired. He threw the telegram on the floor and began walking up and down the room, growing red in the face. "*Quos vult perdere dementat,*" he said to himself; by *quos* meaning the people who had been responsible for the appointment. He was not so much annoyed because he had been overlooked as by the fact that they should have given that wind-bag Stremov the place, who was less capable than any one of filling it. They had ruined their prestige by the appointment!

"Another pleasant piece of news of the same kind, no doubt," he thought, as he picked up the second telegram. This was from his wife. The signature "Anna," written in blue pencil, was the first thing that caught his eye. "I am dying. I beg you, I implore you, come to me. I shall die easier if I have your forgiveness," he read. He gave a disdainful smile as he threw it down. He had not the remotest doubt that it was a ruse on her part.

" There is no deception she would not stoop to," he thought. " It is getting near her confinement. She may be ill as a result of it. But what is their purpose? To make the child legitimate; to compromise me, and prevent the divorce. But she said she was dying . . ." He re-read the telegram and was suddenly struck by the full meaning of what it said. " Supposing it should be true? " he said to himself. " If she is really repenting at the approach of death, it would be cruel of me not to go. Every one would condemn me for it, and besides, it would be extremely foolish on my part."

" Peter, order the carriage; I am going to St. Petersburg," he said to his valet.

Alexei Alexandrovitch decided to go to St. Petersburg to see his wife. If she was not ill he could leave directly; if she really was ill and at the point of death, he would forgive her, if he arrived in time, or do his last duty by her if too late. On the journey he no longer thought of what he should do.

The next morning, with a feeling of fatigue and uncleanliness, produced by a night in a railway carriage, Alexei Alexandrovitch drove down the deserted Nevska in the early mist, looking straight before him and trying not to think of what awaited him. He could not bring himself to think of it, because he could not rid himself of the idea that her death would at once solve the whole difficulty of the situation. Bakers, closed shops, cabs, night-watchmen sweeping the pavements, flashed before his eyes. He gazed at them all, trying to drown the thought of what he desired. He drove up to his house. As he walked up the steps, a decision seemed to come out of the deep recesses of his brain, which was something like this: " If she's deceived me, I'll go away calmly. If not, I will do what is necessary."

The porter, in an old coat and bedroom slippers and without a tie, opened the door before Alexei Alexandrovitch rang the bell.

" How is your mistress? "

" She had a satisfactory delivery yesterday."

Alexei Alexandrovitch turned pale and stopped. He now realised how much he had desired her death.

" How is she? "

Korney, in a morning apron, rushed down the stairs.

" Very bad," he replied. " There was a consultation yesterday, and the doctor is here now."

"Take my things," Alexei Alexandrovitch said, and with a slight feeling of relief that there were still some hope of her dying, he entered the hall.

A military overcoat hanging on a peg caught his eye.

"Who is here?" he asked.

"The doctor, the nurse, and Count Vronsky."

Alexei Alexandrovitch went into the drawing-room, but it was empty. At the sound of his footsteps a nurse in a white cap with lilac ribbons came out of Anna's boudoir. She approached Alexei Alexandrovitch and with a familiarity possible only in the presence of death she took his arm and led him towards the bedroom.

"Thank God you have come! She talks of nothing but you," she said.

"Some ice, quickly!" the doctor's commanding voice was heard from the bedroom.

Alexei Alexandrovitch entered Anna's boudoir. Vronsky was sitting at her writing-table on a low chair. His face was covered with his hands and he was crying bitterly. He jumped up when he heard the doctor's voice, and as his hands dropped from his face he caught sight of Alexei Alexandrovitch. He grew so confused that he sat down again as though wishing for the earth to open and swallow him up, but making a supreme effort to control himself he stood up again.

"She is dying," he said. "The doctor says there is no hope. I am entirely in your power, but permit me to stay here. . . . However, I am in your power, I . . ."

On seeing Vronsky's tears, Alexei Alexandrovitch was seized by a feeling of pity that the sight of suffering in others always produced in him. He turned towards the door without waiting to hear the end of his words. Anna could be heard talking in the bedroom. Her voice was wonderfully gay, animated, and clear. Alexei Alexandrovitch entered the room and approached the bed. She was lying with her flushed face turned towards him. Her eyes sparkled, her small white hands, protruding from the cuffs of her dressing-jacket, were playing with the edge of the counterpane. She seemed not only sound and well, but in the best of spirits. She was talking very quickly and her voice had a clear, ringing sound.

"Because Alexei . . . I mean Alexei Alexandrovitch (isn't it strange that they should both be Alexei?), Alexei would not have refused me. I should have forgotten and he would have forgiven. . . . Why doesn't he come? He is so good; he does not know himself how good he is. Oh Heavens, what torture! Give me some water quickly! But no, it will be bad for my little girl! All right, you can give her to a wet-nurse. I quite agree; it will be much better. He is coming. He won't like to see her. Give her away then . . ."

"Anna Arkadyevna, your husband has come. Here he is," the nurse said, trying to attract her attention to Alexei Alexandrovitch.

"What nonsense!" Anna continued, not seeing her husband. "Give me my little one, give her to me! He has not come yet. You think he won't forgive me because you don't know him. Nobody knows him but me; that is why I got tired. His eyes, you know . . . Serioja's eyes are exactly like them, that is why I can't bear to see them. Has Serioja had his dinner? I know they will all forget him. He would not have forgotten. Serioja must be moved to the corner room, and Mariette should be asked to sleep with him."

She suddenly stopped and shrank back. In terror she raised her hands to her face, as though warding off a blow. She had recognised her husband.

"No, no, no!" she cried. "I am not afraid of him; I am afraid of death! Come here, Alexei, I am in a hurry; I have no time . . . I have not much longer to live. My delirium will come on again; soon I shall know nothing. Now I see and understand everything."

Alexei Alexandrovitch's face was distorted with pain. He took her hand and wanted to say something, but could not utter a word. His lower lip trembled as he struggled with his agitation and looked at her. Every time his eyes caught hers he was struck by their look of tenderness and submission. He had never seen them like that before.

"Wait a moment; you don't know. . . . Wait, wait. . . ." She stopped, as if trying to collect her thoughts. "Oh yes," she began; "I wanted to say . . . don't be surprised at me. I am just the same as I used to be, but there is another woman in me, and I am afraid of her. It was she who fell in love with him. I wanted to hate you, but could not forget myself as I was before. I am not that one. I am my real self now. I am dying, I know I am; you ask him. My hands and feet are as heavy as lead, and my fingers—look at them; they are enormous! But it will soon be over. . . . I only want you to forgive me, forgive me completely! I am wicked, but nurse told me that holy saint . . . what was her name?—she was worse. I, too, will go to Rome; there is a desert there and I won't be in anybody's way. I will only take Serioja and my little girl with me. . . . No, you can't forgive! I know you can't! No, no, no! go away! You are too good." With one hand she held him while with the other she tried to push him away.

Alexei Alexandrovitch could struggle with himself no longer. What he had thought a state of spiritual confusion was really a blissful state of the soul that suddenly gave him a strange, new sense of peace such as he had never experienced before. He had not believed that the Christian law he had been trying to follow all his life enjoined him to love and forgive his enemies, yet now his soul was filled with love and forgiveness. He knelt down by the bed, and placing his head on the bend of her arm, that burned him through her sleeve, he burst out sobbing like a child.

She moved closer towards him, embraced his bald head, and raised her eyes proudly.

"Do you see him? I knew it! Now good-bye, everybody, good-bye! Why have they come in? What do they want? Why don't they go away? Take these furs off me!"

The doctor took her hands, laid her back on the pillow, and covered her shoulders. She lay submissively on her back and looked before her with a strange light in her eyes.

"You must remember that I only wanted forgiveness and nothing else. . . . Why does *he* not come?" she asked, turning towards the door where Vronsky was standing. "Come, come here! Give him your hand!"

Vronsky approached the foot of the bed, and as he caught sight of Anna he buried his face in his hands again.

"Uncover your face and look at him. He is a saint! Uncover it! uncover it!" she cried angrily. "Alexei Alexandrovitch, uncover his face! I want to see him."

Alexei Alexandrovitch removed Vronsky's hands from his face. It was terrible to look at for the expression of shame and suffering that was there.

"Give him your hand. Forgive him."

Alexei Alexandrovitch gave him his hand without restraining the tears that ran down his cheeks.

"Thank God, thank God!" she said; "now I am ready. I will just stretch myself. That's better. How ugly these flowers are; they are not at all like violets," she said, pointing to the wall-paper. "O God, O God! when will it end?

Give me some morphia. Doctor! give me some morphia! Oh God, oh God!"

And she began tossing about on the bed.

The doctors declared that she was suffering from puerperal fever, and that there was only one chance in a hundred that she would recover. She passed the day delirious and unconscious. Towards midnight her pulse became very low and the end was expected any moment.

Vronsky went home, but returned early in the morning to find out how she was. "You had better stay; she may ask for you," Alexei Alexandrovitch said to him as he met him in the hall, and proceeded to his wife's bedroom. Her restlessness and delirium began again and ended in unconsciousness towards the evening. The same thing was repeated on the third day, and the doctors began to hold out hopes. On that day Alexei Alexandrovitch went into his wife's boudoir where Vronsky was sitting, and closing the door he sat down opposite him.

"Alexei Alexandrovitch," Vronsky began, feeling that the moment of explanation had come, "I cannot speak, I cannot understand. Spare me! However hard it may be for you, believe me, it is still harder for me."

He was about to rise, but Alexei Alexandrovitch took his hand and made him sit down again.

"I want you to listen to what I have to say; it is very important. I am forced to explain to you the feelings that guide me and will continue to guide me, so that you should not be mistaken in me. As you know, I had decided on a divorce and have even begun proceedings. I must confess that when I began the action I was undecided, and I suffered. I will not conceal from you that I was pursued by a desire to avenge myself on you and her. When I received her telegram, I came back with the same sentiments, and what is more, I desired her death. But . . ." He stopped, hesitating whether to disclose his feelings to him or not. "But I have seen her and forgiven her. And the joy of forgiveness has revealed to me what my duty is. I have forgiven her completely. I want to offer my other cheek; I want to give away my cloak when my coat is taken from me. I only pray to God that he may not take away from me the joy of forgiving!"

The tears stood in his eyes, and Vronsky was struck by their calm, clear light.

"Such is my position. You can drag me through the mire, make me ridiculous in the eyes of the world, but I shall not forsake her, nor ever speak a word of reproach to you," Alexei Alexandrovitch continued. "My duty is clear before me. I must be with her, and I will do it. Should she want to see you, I will let you know, but now I think you had better go."

He rose. Sobs choked his voice. Vronsky rose too, and stood humbly looking at him. He could not understand Alexei Alexandrovitch's feelings, but he felt it was something far beyond him, something outside his conceptions of life.

XVIII

WHEN Vronsky left the Karenins' house after this interview he stopped on the steps to ask himself where he was and what he had to do. He felt guilty, ashamed, and humiliated, yet deprived of the means of throwing off his humiliation. He was completely thrown out of the rut in which he had walked so proudly and light-heartedly until now. All his seemingly firm rules and habits of life suddenly appeared false and impractical. The injured husband, whom he had been accustomed to look upon as a pitiful object, an accidental and somewhat ridiculous obstacle to his happiness, had suddenly been called back by Anna and raised to such a height as to inspire the greatest respect. And what is more, on that height he was not vindictive, false, and ridiculous, but kind, gentle, and dignified. Vronsky could not help feeling that the tables had suddenly been turned. It was he who was humiliated and base, while Alexei Alexandrovitch was great in his magnanimity. He felt that the husband was generous in his sorrow, while he was mean and little in his deception. But the consciousness of his meanness before the man whom he had unjustly despised formed only a small part of his grief. He was immeasurably unhappy at the thought of losing Anna. His passion, which had grown cool for a time, now flamed with double force. He had seen her during her illness as she really was; her soul was bared before him, and it seemed to him that he had never loved her until now. And now that he had discovered her, had come to love her as she should be loved, she was lost to him for ever, with nothing but a shameful recollection of him in her heart. He had been humiliated before her! It was terrible to think how ridiculous he must have looked when Alexei Alexandrovitch removed his hands from his face.

He stood by the Karenins' door like one lost, not knowing what to do with himself.

" Would you like a cab, sir? " the porter asked.

" Yes, please."

When he reached home he lay down on the couch, fully dressed, folded his hands and placed his head upon them. He had not slept for three nights. His head felt as heavy as lead. The strangest impressions and pictures floated before his mind with an extraordinary rapidity and clearness. Now he was pouring out the medicine for the patient and spilling it over the spoon, now he could see the white hands of the nurse, now Alexei Alexandrovitch on the floor beside the bed.

" I will go to sleep and forget! " he said to himself, with the calm confidence of a healthy man who knows that if he is tired he will fall asleep at once. In a few moments his ideas became confused, and he felt himself sinking into oblivion. Suddenly an electric shock seemed to shoot through him. He shuddered violently and jumped up on his knees in terror. His eyes were wide open as though he had never been asleep. The heaviness in his head and the weary feeling in his limbs had completely disappeared. " You may drag me through the mire." He could hear Alexei Alexandrovitch's words and saw him standing before him. And there was Anna's flushed, feverish face and sparkling eyes, looking with love and tenderness, not at him, but at her husband. Again he saw his own ridiculous figure as Alexei Alexandrovitch removed his hands from his face.

He stretched out his legs, threw himself on the couch in his old posture, and closed his eyes.

" To sleep! to sleep! " he said to himself. The image of Anna as he had seen her on the memorable evening before the races rose more distinctly before his mind.

" That is over now; she wants to efface it from her memory. But I cannot live without it! How are we to make it up? How are we to make it up? " he said aloud, unconsciously repeating the words again and again. This repetition held back new recollections and impressions that began crowding into his brain. But he could not keep them back for long. Again recollections of his former happiness and his recent humiliation began rising with an amazing rapidity.

" Uncover your face! " Anna's voice could be heard. He

took away his hands and felt the shame-faced, ridiculous expression on it.

He lay still, trying to go to sleep, though he knew there was not the slightest hope of it, and continued repeating some stray word or other in a whisper in order to keep back the influx of new thoughts. "You did not appreciate her, you did not value her; you did not appreciate her, you did not value her," he heard his own voice saying again and again.

"Am I going mad?" he asked himself. "Perhaps I am. Why do people lose their reason? Why do they shoot themselves?" He opened his eyes and was surprised to see near his head a cushion embroidered by Varia, his brother's wife. He began playing with the fringe, and tried to recall Varia as he had last seen her. But it was painful for him to think of indifferent things. "This won't do; I must go to sleep!" He pulled the cushion towards him, pressed his head against it, and made an effort to close his eyes. But suddenly he jumped up. "This is ended for me," he said to himself; "I must make up my mind what to do. What is there left?" His imagination vividly pictured what life would be like without Anna.

"Ambition? Serpuhovsky? Society? The court?" He could not fix his mind on anything. All those things had lost their meaning for him now. He got up, took off his coat, loosened his belt, bared his chest in order to breathe more freely, and began walking up and down the room. "This is how people go mad," he said to himself. "This is how they shoot themselves . . . to avoid shame," he added slowly.

He closed the door, and with clenched teeth and a look of determination he walked up to the table, seized a revolver, examined it, turned the loaded weapon upon himself, then stopped to consider. For about two minutes he stood motionless with bent head and the revolver in his hand, thinking deeply. "Of course," he said to himself, as though a clear, logical march of arguments had brought him to an unquestionable conclusion. But in reality he was continually revolving round the same circle of impressions that he had gone over for the hundredth time in the last hour. There was the same consciousness of a happiness lost for ever, the same sense of meaninglessness in life, the same unbearable humiliation. Nothing had changed.

"Of course," he repeated, as his thoughts went over the same ground again. He placed the revolver to his breast and giving a powerful jerk with his hand as though clenching his fist, he pulled the trigger. He did not hear the report, for a violent blow knocked him off his feet. He tried to catch hold of the table to steady himself, but the revolver fell out of his hand, he tottered and sat down on the floor, bewildered, looking around him. He did not recognise his room as he looked up from below at the curved legs of the table, the waste-paper basket, and tiger-skin. The quick steps of his valet hurrying through the drawing-room brought him to himself. He tried to think, and seeing that he was on the floor with blood on his hands and on the rug he realised what he had done.

"Stupid! I did not aim right!" he thought, fumbling for the revolver. It lay touching him, but his hand was stretched out beyond. He leaned over on the other side in his efforts to find it, and unable to retain his balance, he fell, bathed in his own blood.

His smart valet with elegant whiskers, who had frequently complained to his friends about the weak condition of his nerves, was so terrified when he saw his master lying on the floor that he immediately rushed out for help without doing anything to stop the flow of blood.

In about an hour, Varia, his brother's wife, aided by three doctors who had been sent for in all directions and appeared simultaneously, placed the wounded man on his bed and remained to look after him.

XIX

Two months after his return from Moscow, Alexei Alexandrovitch was brought face to face with the fact that he had made a mistake in not considering the possibility of Anna's recovery when he had resolved to forgive her. Such a possibility had occurred to him, but it was not until the meeting with his dying wife that he realised what was in his own heart. At her bedside he had given way for the first time in his life to that feeling of compassion for the suffering of others that he had always considered a shameful weakness in himself. His unbounded pity for her and remorse at having desired her death, and, above all, the joy of forgiveness, changed his former suffering to a spiritual peace such as he had never experienced before. He suddenly felt that what had been the source of his sufferings had become the source of his spiritual joy; what before had appeared insoluble, when he had condemned, reproached, and hated, had become simple and clear when he loved and forgave.

He had forgiven his wife and pitied her for her suffering and repentance. He had forgiven Vronsky, and since he had heard about his desperate attempt, pitied him too. He pitied his son more than ever, and reproached himself for having neglected him. The new-born baby-girl, however, inspired him with a feeling not of compassion only, but of tenderness. At first he only pitied the poor little thing, who was neglected during her mother's illness and would have died had he not looked after her, but later he grew to love her. He would come into the nursery several times a day, much to the discomfort of the nurses, though they soon grew accustomed to him. He would sometimes stay for half an hour, gazing at the red, wrinkled, downy face of the child, who was not his own, following her movements as she screwed up her face and rubbed her eyes and nose with her chubby little clenched fist. At such moments Alexei Alexandrovitch felt calm and at peace with himself, and saw nothing in his situation that need be changed.

But as time went on, he saw more and more clearly that no matter how natural his position might seem to him, he would not be allowed to remain in it. He felt that besides the spiritual force that guided his soul, there was another force, brutal, all-powerful, that directed his life in spite of himself, and gave him no peace. He felt that every one regarded him with curiosity as though expecting him to do something, and that there was an unnaturalness and constraint in his relations with his wife.

When the tenderness caused by the expectation of her death had passed off, Alexei Alexandrovitch began to notice that Anna feared him, grew tired of his presence, and dared not look him in the face. It seemed as though she was always on the point of telling him something, but could not make up her mind to do so. She, too, had a feeling that their relations could not last, and expected him to take some action.

Towards the end of February, the little girl, who had been named after her mother, fell ill. Alexei Alexandrovitch had gone into the nursery in the morning, and after having despatched some one for a doctor he departed for the ministry. It was about four o'clock when he finished all his business and returned home. A handsome footman in a silver-embroidered livery and a bear-skin cape was standing in the hall with a magnificent white fur cloak over his arm.

" Who is here? " Alexei Alexandrovitch asked.

" The Princess Elisaveta Fiodorovna Tversky," the footman replied, and it seemed to Alexei Alexandrovitch that he smiled.

All through this painful period, Alexei Alexandrovitch had noticed that all his society acquaintances, especially the women, took a keen interest both in himself and his wife. They beamed with a suppressed joy whenever they saw him, just as the lawyer had done. They seemed as delighted as though they were getting some one married, and would ask after Anna's health with the greatest sense of enjoyment.

The presence of the Princess Tversky was particularly disagreeable to Alexei Alexandrovitch, partly because he disliked her personally, and partly because of certain associations connected with her. He walked straight into the nursery. In the first room Serioja was lying flat on the table with his feet dangling on a chair, drawing something and talking merrily. An English governess, who had taken the place of the French one since Anna's illness, was sitting by him with some delicate crochet. She got up hurriedly when she saw Alexei Alexandrovitch, then sat down again and began tugging at Serioja.

Alexei Alexandrovitch patted the boy's head, replied to the governess's questions about his wife's health, and asked her how baby was.

" The doctor said there was nothing serious and ordered baths, sir."

" But she seems in pain," Alexei Alexandrovitch said as he heard the child crying in the next room.

" I don't think the nurse is any good, sir," the governess replied resolutely.

" What makes you think so? " he stopped to ask.

" It was just the same at the Countess Pol's. They tried to cure the child with all sorts of things, but it turned out that it was simply not getting enough to eat. The nurse had insufficient milk."

Alexei Alexandrovitch thought for a moment, then went into the next room. The child was wriggling in the arms of the wet-nurse, refusing to take the breast offered her and screaming as hard as she could in spite of the double efforts of the nurse and wet-nurse, who were trying to soothe her.

" Is she no better? " Alexei Alexandrovitch asked.

" She is very restless, sir," the old nurse replied in a whisper.

" Miss Edward thinks that the nurse has no milk," he said.

" It occurred so to me, Alexei Alexandrovitch."

" Then why did you not mention it? "

" Whom was I to tell? Anna Arkadyevna is still ill," the old nurse replied discontentedly.

She was an old servant of the house. And in these simple words of hers Alexei Alexandrovitch suspected a hint at his situation.

The child screamed louder than ever and rolled from side to side. The old nurse, with a gesture of despair, took her from the other one and began walking up and down the room with her.

The neat, robust little woman who acted as wet-nurse grew alarmed at the prospect of losing her place. She muttered something to herself as she covered her large breast and gave a disdainful smile at the idea that she had insufficient milk. Even in this smile Alexei Alexandrovitch saw a reference to his situation.

" Poor little one! " the nurse said, rocking the child and trying to soothe it.

Alexei Alexandrovitch sat down and gazed at the nurse walking up and down the room with a look of pain and sadness on his face.

The child grew quiet at last. The nurse put her in a deep crib, adjusted the pillow, and went away. Alexei Alexandrovitch got up and walked over on tiptoe to look at her. For a moment he stood silent, gazing down at the child with the same sad expression on his face. Suddenly a smile spread over it, and he walked quietly out of the room.

When he got to the dining-room, he rang the bell and ordered the servant answering it to send for the doctor again. He was annoyed with Anna for not paying more attention to the child and did not like to go and see her in such a mood. Besides, he had no wish to meet the Princess Betsy. However, fearing that Anna would be surprised at his not coming, he made a great effort to command himself and turned to go into her bedroom. As he walked over the soft carpet he unintentionally overheard the conversation within.

" Had he not been going away, I could have understood your refusal, and his too. But your husband ought to be above it," Betsy was saying.

" It is not because of my husband, but for my own sake that I don't wish it. Don't talk to me about it! " Anna replied in an agitated voice.

" But you can't help wanting to say good-bye to a man who shot himself on your account. . . ."

"That is the very reason that I do not want to."

Alexei Alexandrovitch stopped with a frightened guilty expression and wanted to turn back unnoticed, but thinking that this would be undignified, he gave a cough and walked on further. The voices ceased as he entered the room.

Anna, in a grey dressing-gown, with her closely cropped curly hair standing out like a brush round her shapely head, was sitting on a couch. As usual, at sight of her husband her animation instantly vanished; she lowered her head and looked restlessly at Betsy. Betsy, dressed in the latest fashion, with a hat like a lamp-shade soaring somewhere above her head, and a dove-coloured gown with severe, slanting stripes running one way on the bodice and the other on the skirt, was sitting beside Anna, holding herself very erect. She nodded her head and greeted Alexei Alexandrovitch with a sarcastic smile.

"Ah!" she said, as though surprised to see him. "I am very glad you are at home. I have not seen you since Anna's illness; you never show yourself anywhere now. I have heard all about you though. You are indeed a remarkable husband by the way you look after your wife!" She gave him a significant, kindly glance, as though rewarding him for his magnanimous behaviour.

Alexei Alexandrovitch bowed to her coldly, and kissing his wife's hand he asked her how she was.

"I am better, thank you," she said, trying to avoid his glance.

"But your face looks flushed and feverish," he said, laying special stress on the word "feverish."

"We must have talked too much," Betsy said. "It was very thoughtless of me; I had better go."

She rose, but Anna, suddenly flushing red, seized her hand.

"Don't go yet; I have something to say to you. . . . No, to you . . ." She turned to Alexei Alexandrovitch, the flush spreading over her neck and forehead. "I cannot, nor do I wish to have any secrets from you," she said.

Alexei Alexandrovitch cracked his fingers and hung his head.

"Betsy tells me that Count Vronsky wants to come and say good-bye before leaving for Tashkent." She spoke rapidly, not looking at her husband, as though anxious to get through with it. "I said that I could not receive him."

"No, my dear, you said it would depend on Alexei Alexandrovitch," Betsy corrected her.

"No, I cannot receive him; it won't lead to . . ." She

stopped suddenly and looked beseechingly at her husband. He was watching her. " In short, I don't want . . ."

Alexei Alexandrovitch drew closer to her and wanted to take her hand. Her first impulse was to shrink from the clammy hand with the swollen veins held out to her, but mastering herself by a supreme effort she pressed it.

" Thank you for your confidence," he said, " but . . ." He stopped in confusion.

In the presence of the Princess Betsy he could not say what he wished to. She seemed to him the very incarnation of that brutal force that governed his worldly life and prevented him from abandoning himself to his feelings of love and forgiveness.

" Well, good-bye, my dear! " Betsy said, rising. She kissed Anna and went out. Alexei Alexandrovitch accompanied her.

" Alexei Alexandrovitch! " Betsy said, stopping in the small drawing-room and pressing his hand a second time; " I know you can be generous. I am an outsider, but I love her and respect you so much that I take the liberty of giving you advice. Let him come. Alexei Vronsky is the soul of honour, and he is going to Tashkent."

" I thank you for your advice and sympathy, princess. As to whether my wife can receive him or not, she will decide that herself."

He said this in a proud, dignified manner from force of habit, raising his eyebrows in surprise, but he instantly realised that no matter what his words might be, there could be no dignity in his position. He saw it in the malicious, mocking smile with which Betsy regarded him when he had finished.

XX

Alexei Alexandrovitch took leave of Betsy in the hall and returned to his wife. She was reclining on the couch, but on hearing his footsteps she sat up hastily in her former position and looked at him nervously. He could see that she had been crying.

" Thank you for your confidence," he said gently, in Russian, repeating the phrase he had used before Betsy in French. He sat down beside her. His tender tone irritated Anna. " I must also thank you for your decision. I quite agree with you that there is no necessity for Count Vronsky to call here since he is going away. However . . ."

" I have said it already, so why repeat it! " Anna interrupted him irritably. " There is no necessity," she thought, " for a man to come and bid good-bye to a woman he loves and has ruined himself for; a woman who cannot live without him. No necessity whatever! " She pressed her lips together and dropped her bright eyes. They fell on his hands as he rubbed them together slowly, and she noticed their swollen veins.

" Don't let us ever speak of it," she said more calmly.

" I left you to decide this question, and I am very glad to see . . . " Alexei Alexandrovitch began.

" That my wishes accord with yours." Anna finished the sentence for him. She was irritated to hear him speak so slowly, when she knew in advance what he was going to say.

" Yes," he said. " It is rather tactless for the Princess Betsy to meddle in these difficult family matters; particularly as she . . . "

" I don't believe anything they say of her," Anna interrupted him hastily; " and I know that she loves me sincerely."

Alexei Alexandrovitch gave a sigh and was silent. She was playing with the tassels of her dressing-gown nervously, and as she gazed at him she felt a sense of physical repulsion for him that she could not possibly overcome, no matter how much she blamed herself for it. She desired only one thing—to be relieved of his loathsome presence.

" I have just sent for the doctor," he said.

" Why? I am quite well."

" It was for baby. She keeps on crying, and they say the nurse has not enough milk."

" Why did you not allow me to nurse her myself when I begged you to? All the same . . ." (Alexei Alexandrovitch understood what she meant by " all the same.") " She is such a tiny little thing; they will kill her." She rang the bell and asked for the child to be brought to her. " I begged to be allowed to nurse her, but no one would let me, and now I am blamed for it."

" I was not blaming . . . "

" Oh, yes, you were! O God, why did I not die! " she burst out sobbing. " I'm sorry I'm so unjust; I'm so irritable," she said, controlling herself; " but go now . . . "

" No, things cannot remain as they are," Alexei Alexandrovitch said to himself resolutely as he left his wife's room.

Never before had his impossible position and his wife's hatred struck him so forcibly as they did now. Never before had that brutal mysterious power that ran counter to his spiritual state so strongly asserted itself and demanded a change in the situation at all costs. He saw clearly that Anna and the whole world were waiting for him to do something, but what it was precisely he could not make out. A feeling of resentment and anger rose up in his soul, disturbing his well-earned peace. Though he considered that it would be better for Anna to break her relations with Vronsky, he was nevertheless prepared to let them go on seeing each other if they could not do otherwise; only so that the children should not be disgraced, so that he should not lose them, so that the position should remain unchanged. However bad that might be, it would be better than a complete break, that would disgrace her for ever and deprive him of everything he loved. But he felt himself powerless; he knew beforehand that every one was against him, that he would not be allowed to do what seemed to him good and natural, but would be compelled to do something bad, because it seemed to them necessary.

XXI

As Betsy was about to leave the hall she almost ran into the arms of Stepan Arkadyevitch, who had just come from Yelisaev, where there was a plentiful supply of fresh oysters.

"Ah, princess! What a lucky meeting!" he greeted her. "I have just been to your house."

"Unfortunately, I am just going," Betsy said with a smile, as she drew on her glove.

"Don't put your glove on, princess; I want to kiss your lovely hand. It is one of the few old fashions that I'm grateful for." He kissed her hand. "When shall I see you?"

"You don't deserve to," Betsy said with a smile.

"Oh, yes, I do; I've become a most serious person. I not only arrange my own domestic affairs nowadays, but look after other people's as well," he said with a significant expression.

"Really! I am glad to hear it." She instantly understood that he was referring to Anna. They moved up to a corner of the hall. "He is killing her," she said in a whisper. "It's impossible, impossible!"

"I am glad to hear you say so," Stepan Arkadyevitch said, shaking his head with a solemn, sympathetic expression on his face. "I have come to St. Petersburg for that very reason."

" The whole town is talking of it," she said. " The situation is impossible. She is simply fading away. He does not understand that she is a woman who cannot make light of her feelings. One thing or the other—either he must take her away and act decidedly, or else give her a divorce. But this is wearing her out."

" Precisely," Alexei Alexandrovitch said with a sigh. " That is why I have come; but no, it was not entirely for that. They have made me a chamberlain, so I had to put in an appearance to express my thanks. However, this was the chief matter . . ."

" Well, may God help you! " Betsy said.

He conducted her to the door, kissed her hand once more above her glove, where the pulse was beating, paid her a few naughty compliments, at which she knew not whether to laugh or be angry, and left her to go in search of his sister. He found her in tears. In spite of his extreme gaiety, Stepan Arkadyevitch passed very easily into that tender, sympathetic tone becoming to his sister's frame of mind. He asked how she was and how she had spent the morning.

" Very badly," she replied. " Both the morning and the day, and all past days and all future days."

" You mustn't give way too much to your depression. You must take yourself in hand a little and look life straight in the face. I know it is hard, but . . . "

" I have heard it said that women can love men even for their vices," she began suddenly, " but I hate him for his virtues. I cannot live with him. The very sight of him drives me nearly mad. I cannot, I cannot live with him! What am I to do? I was unhappy before. I used to imagine that I could not be more unhappy, but this surpasses anything I could have dreamed of. I know he is good and generous; I know that I'm not worth his little finger, but I can't help hating him. I hate him for his very goodness and generosity. There is nothing else for me to do, but . . . "

She wanted to say " to die," but Stepan Arkadyevitch would not allow her to finish.

" You are ill, and your nerves are out of order," he said. " Believe me, there is nothing so very terrible in it. You exaggerate too much."

Stepan Arkadyevitch smiled. No one but he could have smiled at such a moment without appearing coarse and brutal, but there was so much sympathy and good-nature in that smile of his that Anna was soothed by it.

" No, Stiva," she said; " I am lost, lost! Worse than lost; for I cannot say that all is over; I feel that much remains yet. I am like a string that has been over-strained and is bound to break. It is not over yet, but it will end terribly."

" Not at all; you can loosen the string by degrees. There is no situation without an issue."

" I have thought and thought; there is only one thing . . . "

Again he could see by the look of terror on her face that she was referring to death, and would not allow her to finish.

" My dear," he said, " you cannot see your position as I can. Let me tell you my opinion frankly." Again he smiled his soothing smile. " I will begin from the beginning. You married a man twenty years older than yourself; married him without love, or rather not knowing what love was. Let us admit that it was a mistake . . ."

" A terrible mistake! " Anna said.

" But it is a fact that cannot be altered. Later, you had the misfortune to fall in love with another man; that is also an accomplished fact. Your husband got to know of it and has forgiven you." He stopped after every sentence, to see if she had any objection to make, but she said nothing. " That is how matters stand. The question is—can you continue to live with your husband? Do you wish it? Does he wish it? "

" I don't know, I don't know anything."

" But you've just said that you could not bear him."

" No, I did not. I take it back. I know nothing, I understand nothing."

" Yes, but permit me . . . "

" You can't understand. I feel that I am falling headlong into an abyss, but that I mustn't save myself. Besides, I can't."

" Never mind; we will do it for you. I understand you; I know that you shrink from expressing your wishes, your feelings.

" I want nothing, nothing—only that it should all end."

" But he sees and knows it. Do you think it is less difficult for him? You suffer, he suffers, and what is to come of it all? A divorce would solve everything," Stepan Arkadyevitch got out at last, with an effort, looking at her significantly.

She made no reply, but only shook her closely-cropped head. From the expression of her face, that lighted up with its former beauty, he could see that her only objection was that she considered it an impossible happiness, too good to be true.

"I feel so sorry for you both, and should feel so happy if I could arrange things for you," he said, smiling a little more boldly. "Don't speak! Don't say a word! If God will only let me say what I feel! I will go to him."

Anna looked at him with a pensive look in her beautiful eyes, but did not utter a word.

XXII

STEPAN ARKADYEVITCH walked into his brother-in-law's study with the same expression of solemnity with which he seated himself in the president's chair at the council. Alexei Alexandrovitch, with his hands behind his back, was walking up and down the room, thinking of the very thing that Stepan Arkadyevitch had been discussing with Anna.

"I am not hindering you?" Stepan Arkadyevitch asked. An unexpected feeling of confusion suddenly came over him at sight of his brother-in-law. To conceal it he drew out a new cigarette case, with a new patent clasp, and sniffing at the leather, he opened it and took out a cigarette.

"No; did you want anything?" Alexei Alexandrovitch replied, unwillingly.

Stepan Arkadyevitch did not realise that his confusion was nothing more than his conscience telling him that what he intended doing was bad. He made an effort over himself to conquer it.

"I hope you believe in my love for Anna and in my sincere attachment and respect for you," he said, blushing.

Alexei Alexandrovitch stopped, but made no reply. His face struck Stepan Arkadyevitch by its expression of humility and submission.

"I intended to . . . I wanted to speak to you about my sister and the general position," Stepan Arkadyevitch said, still struggling against his timidity.

Alexei Alexandrovitch gave a bitter smile as he looked at his brother-in-law, and without replying he walked over to the table, took up a letter he had just begun, and handed it to him.

"I am constantly thinking of the same thing. Here is a letter I have begun. I thought I could write things better than say them; besides, my presence irritates her."

Stepan Arkadyevitch took the letter, and looked in surprise

and wonder at the weary eyes that were fixed on him. He began to read.

"I can see that my presence oppresses you. It has been painful for me to realise it, but I know that it is so, and cannot be otherwise. I do not blame you, and God is my witness that when I saw you during your illness I decided to forget everything there had been between us and begin life anew. I do not regret, nor shall I ever regret, what I have done; I had only one thing in view, and that was your welfare and the welfare of your soul; but I see that I have not accomplished it. Tell me plainly what will give you peace and happiness; I surrender myself entirely to your will and to your sense of justice."

Stepan Arkadyevitch returned the letter and continued looking at his brother-in-law in wonder, not knowing what to say. The silence grew oppressive to them both. Stepan Arkadyevitch's lips began twitching nervously.

"That is what I wished to tell her," Alexei Alexandrovitch said, turning his face away.

Stepan Arkadyevitch could not reply. A lump rose in his throat, and the tears came into his eyes.

"Yes, yes. . . . I quite understand you," he got out at last.

"I should like to know what she wants," Alexei Alexandrovitch said.

"I am afraid she does not understand her own position," Stepan Arkadyevitch ventured. "She is hardly fit to judge. She is so crushed—crushed by your very generosity. If she reads this letter she will not have the strength to say anything; she will only drop her head the lower."

"Yes, but what am I to do? How can I explain. . . . How can I get to know what she desires?"

"If I may state my opinion—I think it depends entirely on you. It would be better if you told her plainly what measures you intended to take in order to put an end to the situation."

"So you think an end should be put it to?" Alexei Alexandrovitch asked. "What would you suggest?" he added with a nervous gesture of the hands. "I see no possible issue."

"There is an issue from every situation," Stepan Arkadyevitch said with more animation, as he stood up. "There was a time when you wanted to break . . . Since you are now convinced that you cannot make one another happy . . ."

"There are many conceptions of happiness. Let us suppose, then, that I agree to everything, that I want nothing; what issue is there from our situation?"

"If you want to know my opinion," Stepan Arkadyevitch began, with the same soothing smile with which he had been talking to Anna. Alexei Alexandrovitch, feeling his own weakness, involuntarily abandoned himself to the influence of that smile, and was prepared to believe anything that Stepan Arkadyevitch might have to say to him. "There is only one thing she can desire," Stepan Arkadyevitch continued, "but she will never be brought to say it—and that is—a complete break in your relations that will take her away from all memories connected with them. That can only be brought about by absolute freedom on both sides."

"In other words a divorce," Alexei Alexandrovitch added, in horror.

"Yes, I think a divorce would be best. A divorce," Stepan Arkadyevitch repeated, flushing red, "is by far the most sensible solution for a husband and wife who find themselves in the position that you are in. What else can they do if they find life unbearable together? It is a thing that is constantly happening."

Alexei Alexandrovitch heaved a deep sigh and closed his eyes.

"One thing should be taken into consideration, and that is —does one or the other party wish to marry again? If not, the case is very simple," Stepan Arkadyevitch said, by degrees losing his embarrassment.

Alexei Alexandrovitch frowned. He grew so agitated that he muttered something to himself, but made no reply. The thing that seemed so simple to Stepan Arkadyevitch he had considered a thousand times. Divorce, with all its proceedings that were known to him now, appeared utterly impossible. His personal dignity, his respect for religion, would not allow him to accuse his wife publicly of adultery. He could not bring himself to convict and disgrace Anna, whom he had forgiven and loved. Besides, there were other still more important reasons that made a divorce impossible.

In the event of a divorce what would become of his son? To leave him with his mother would be impossible. She would soon have a new family of her own in which the position of the child would be wretched, without taking into consideration the fact that the moral influence would be bad for him. Should he keep him? That would be cruel on his part, and he did not wish to be cruel. But the real reason that made divorce out of the question was that he would be handing Anna over to ruin. Darya Alexandrovna's words in Moscow had made a deep impression on him. She had said that in deciding on a divorce he was thinking only of himself, and not caring for the fact that Anna would be lost for ever. Since he had forgiven her and become attached to the children, these words of Dolly's had come to have a special meaning for him. To consent to a divorce would mean giving up his last hold on life—the children whom he loved—and to take away from her the last hope of salvation—to hand her over to destruction. If she were divorced she would marry Vronsky, and such a union would be sinful and illegitimate, because according to the law of the Church a woman could not marry again so long as her husband was alive. " She will marry him, and in a year or two he will either desert her or she will enter into a new liaison," Alexei Alexandrovitch thought. " And I, having consented to a divorce, will be the cause of her ruin." Hundreds of times had he gone over this, and was convinced that a divorce was not only far from simple, as his brother-in-law supposed, but completely impossible. He did not agree with a single word Stepan Arkadyevitch had said, and had a thousand objections to make, but he listened to him, feeling that he was the expression of that brutal force that governed his life, to which he would have to surrender in the end.

" The question is, on what conditions are you prepared to consent to a divorce? She does not want anything, and would not dare ask you. . . . She leaves everything to your generosity."

" O God, O God! What for? " Alexei Alexandrovitch thought in agony, as he recalled the details of a divorce in which the husband had taken the guilt upon himself. And he covered his face in shame, just as Vronsky had done.

" You are agitated . . . I can quite understand. But if you consider . . . "

" If a man smite thee on thy right cheek, turn to him thy left also, and if a man take away thy coat offer him thy cloak also," Alexei Alexandrovitch thought.

" Yes, yes," he began in a thin voice; " I will take the disgrace upon myself and give her my son too. . . . But is it not better to leave things as they are? However, do as you please."

He sat down by the window and turned his face away from his brother-in-law. He felt bitter and ashamed, but together with his sorrow and his shame he experienced a sense of joy at his own meekness and humility.

Stepan Arkadyevitch was touched. For a few moments he was silent.

" Alexei Alexandrovitch, believe me, she will appreciate your generosity," he said. " It is the will of God," he added, but instantly felt that this was stupid, and tried to repress a smile at his own stupidity.

Alexei Alexandrovitch wanted to make some reply, but the tears choked him.

" It is a fatal misfortune and must be treated as such. I look upon it as a fact that cannot be altered, and am therefore doing my best to help you both," Stepan Arkadyevitch said.

Stepan Arkadyevitch was touched when he left his brother-in-law, but this did not prevent his feeling satisfied at having achieved what he had set out to do. He was fully convinced that Alexei Alexandrovitch would not take back his word. To this pleasure was added the thought that when the whole thing was over and done with he would be able to put the following riddle to his wife and intimate friends: " What is the difference between me and a field-marshal? A field-marshal only controls divisions, while I make them. Or, what is the difference between me and a field-marshal when . . . However, I can think out a better one," he said to himself with a smile.

XXIII

VRONSKY's wound was dangerous, even though it had missed the heart. For several days he lay between life and death. When he was able to speak for the first time, he was alone in his room with Varia, his brother's wife.

" Varia! " he said, gazing at her solemnly, " I discharged the pistol by accident. Tell everybody so, and never speak of it to me. It is altogether too silly! "

Without replying to his words, Varia bent over him and looked into his face with a glad smile. His eyes were bright, but not feverish, and there was an expression of severity in them.

" Well, thank God! " she said. " Have you any pain? "

" A little here." He pointed to his chest.

" Let me dress it for you again."

He clenched his teeth and looked at her silently as she changed his bandage.

" I am not delirious; I really do want you to prevent people saying that I shot myself on purpose."

" Nobody says that, in any case. But I hope you won't make a practice of shooting yourself by accident," she said, looking at him with a smile.

" I suppose I won't, but it would have been better . . ." He smiled sadly.

In spite of these words and the smile that had so frightened Varia, as soon as the inflammation passed and he began to mend, Vronsky felt that he had freed himself of at least one part of his grief. With this deed he had wiped out the shame and humiliation that he had experienced formerly. He could now think of Alexei Alexandrovitch with a certain amount of equanimity. He recognised his extreme generosity, but no longer felt himself brought to the dust. Again he fell into the old rut. Once more he could look people straight in the face and be guided by his former rules and habits. One thing alone he could not tear out of his heart, no matter how hard he tried to do so, and that was his regret and despair at having lost Anna for ever. Now that he had atoned for the wrong he had done her husband, he took the firm resolve never to come between them again. But do what he would, he could not forget the memory of her love and the moments of happiness they had spent together. He had valued them so little then, but now they pursued him with all their charm, and gave him no peace.

Serpuhovsky had secured him an appointment in Tashkent, and he had accepted it without the slightest hesitation. But the nearer the time for his departure came, the more difficult did the sacrifice appear to him.

His wound had quite healed and he was able to go out and make preparations for his journey.

" To see her once more and then disappear and die," he thought, and when, making a farewell call, he expressed this thought to Betsy, Betsy took his message to Anna and brought him back her reply in the negative.

" So much the better," Vronsky thought. " It was a weakness on my part and would have deprived me of any remaining strength."

The next morning Betsy herself came to see him and told him that she had received positive information through Oblonsky that Alexei Alexandrovitch had consented to a divorce, and that he could see Anna.

Without troubling himself to see Betsy off, completely forgetting all his resolutions, without stopping to ask himself whether he could do so, or where the husband was, Vronsky drove straight to the Karenins' house. He bounded up the stairs, taking no notice of anything or anybody, rushed into her room, and without thinking or looking round to see who was there, he took her in his arms and began showering kisses upon her face, neck, and hands.

Anna had been preparing herself for this meeting. She had a great deal to tell him, but she could not utter a word; his passion overwhelmed her. She wanted to calm him and calm herself, but it was too late. His feeling had communicated itself to her. Her lips trembled so that she could say nothing.

"Yes, I am yours, I am yours," she murmured at last, pressing his hands to her breast.

"This had to be!" he said. "So long as we live it will always be so! Now I know it!"

"Yes!" she said, growing paler and paler, as she clasped his head. "But there is something terrible in this, after all that has happened."

"It will all pass — everything will pass, and we shall be so happy! If our love could possibly grow stronger, it would do so because of that terrible something about it," he said, raising his head and smiling in his happiness.

She could not help replying with a smile—not to his words, but to the fond, loving look in his eyes. She took his hand and passed it over her cool cheeks and short hair.

"I hardly know you with your hair like that. You look so nice; just like a boy. But how pale you are!"

"Yes, I am still weak," she said, with a smile, and again her lips trembled.

"We shall go to Italy; you will soon get well there," he said.

"Is it really possible that we two shall be like husband and wife, alone together, with our own family?" she asked in wonder, looking closely into his eyes.

"I am only surprised that it has not always been so."

"Stiva says that *he* consents to everything, but I cannot accept his generosity," she said, gazing pensively into Vronsky's face. "I don't mind if we never get a divorce; it is all the same to me now. I am only worried as to what he is going to do about Serioja."

He could not understand how she could think of a divorce, or even her boy, at such a moment. Was it not all the same to them whatever happened?

" Don't talk about that, don't think about it," he said, turning her hand round and round in both his, and trying to attract her attention to himself; but she kept her gaze averted from him.

" Oh, why did I not die! it would have been better!" she said, and the tears flowed down her cheeks. She tried to smile so as not to grieve him.

A while ago he would have thought it disgraceful as well as impossible to refuse the flattering and dangerous appointment in Tashkent, but now he did not hesitate for a moment, and observing a certain shade of disapproval in high quarters at his having declined it he immediately asked for his discharge.

A month later, Alexei Alexandrovitch was left alone in his house with his boy, and Vronsky and Anna went abroad. Anna had not been divorced and positively refused to be divorced.

He could not understand how she could think of a divorce even for herself at such a moment. Was it not all the same to them whatever happened?

"Don't talk about that, don't think about it," he said, turning her hand round and round in both his and trying to attract her attention to himself; but she kept her eyes away from him.

"Oh, why did I not die! it would have been better," she said, and the tears flowed down both cheeks; but she tried to smile so as not to grieve him.

A while ago it would have been thought disgraceful as well as impossible to refuse the flattering and dangerous appointment in Tashkend, but now he did not hesitate for a moment, and observing a certain shade of disapproval in high quarters at his having declined it he immediately asked for his discharge.

A month later Alexey Alexandrovitch was left alone in his house with the boy, and Vronsky and Anna went abroad. Anna had not been divorced and positively refused to be divorced.

This book, designed by
William B. Taylor
is a production of
Edito-Service S.A., Geneva

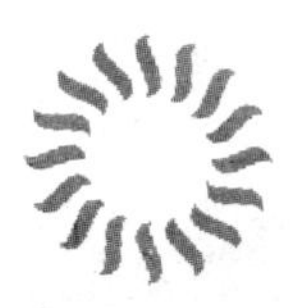

Printed in Switzerland

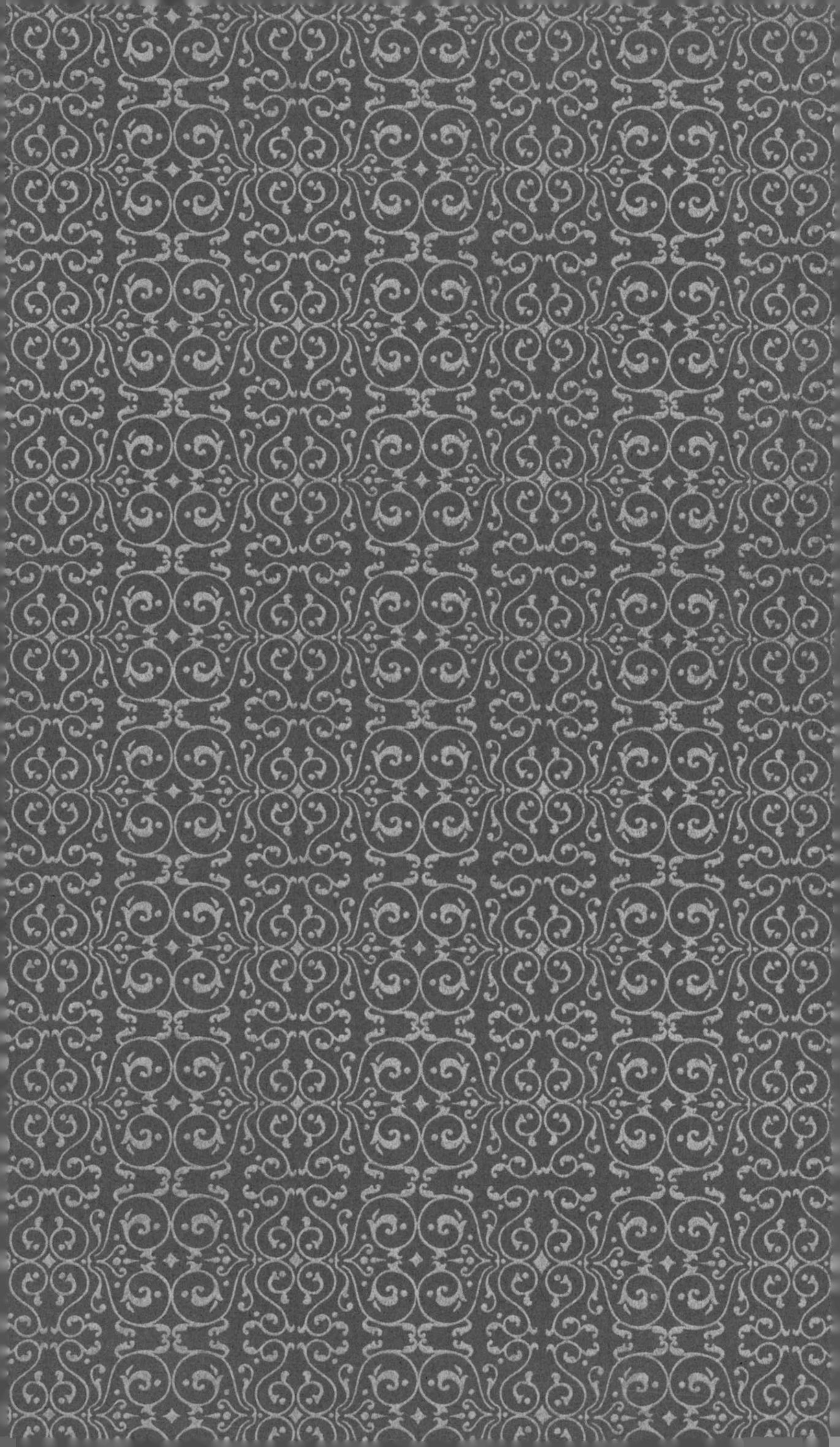